THE JUNKYARD DOG

THE JUNKYARD DOG

Harlan Wygant

Writers Club Press

San Jose New York Lincoln Shanghai

The Junkyard Dog

Writers Club Press
an imprint of iUniverse, Inc.

For information address:
iUniverse, Inc.
5220 S. 16th St., Suite 200
Lincoln, NE 68512
www.iuniverse.com

ISBN: 0-595-21098-8

Printed in the United States of America

Contents

CHAPTER 1

"Dammit it, Sam, what the hell's going on here?"

Brad's words sounded harsher than he intended. The frustration of the past four months had stretched his patience. Neither he nor Sam had ever investigated a bombing before this spring. Now, they were getting on-the-job training and it frustrated them.

"Four bombings since April. Why now? Why here? We never have a bombing in Langston, at least not in my twenty years on the force. If this is a sample of big city life, I vote for hick towns." Brad vented his anger. "At this rate, we'll need more than two bomb techs. I doubt Randy and his partner can keep up with it…and we sure aren't much help."

Brad Logan and his partner Sam Hardy sat in their unmarked car, comparing notes of their investigation into this most recent blast. The pungent smell of fireworks saturated the area, stinging their nostrils even through the closed windows. Shards of glass cluttered the street in both directions. A long, shiny ribbon of yellow police tape fluttered from pole to pole, embracing the mangled building as a mother protects her injured child.

Both men grew up in Langston, in the high desert area of Southern California, where their home town began blossoming in the late 1970s. The last census report indicated Langston was no longer a small town. The population now exceeded 100,000. Additional traffic flowed constantly through the area because the town was on the main freeway between Los Angeles and Las Vegas.

Sam Hardy glanced toward Brad. "One thing's for sure, Partner, we've got a new element to deal with. Either some slime from outside moved in on us or some of our locals are importing technology. The guys at ATF figure someone who knows his business pulled off these jobs."

Sergeant Brad Logan stared off into the distance.

"Sam, we've been lucky so far. No one's been hurt. That's no accident. The location and timing of the blasts sounds like a warning—not necessarily to kill anyone. 'Course that can change at any minute. You got everything you need from here?"

Sam just nodded, then started the car and the two officers drove back to their office, where Sam went directly to the large city map on the wall. He placed a red marker at the spot of the most recent bombing. Three other markers appeared in the same part of the city. It was an older part of Langston, now populated mostly by various ethnic groups.

"I need some caffeine, Sam. How 'bout you?"

"No thanks. Had a couple gallons already, okay? These early morning calls get tougher the older I get. Sure could use some sleep. Damn stomach's killing me."

Brad grinned as he headed for the coffee room. He'd heard the same complaint from Sam Hardy for the past ten years. The man was nearly 60; looked like a walking broomstick; popped antacids and bitched about his acid stomach constantly. But he worked harder, knew more about police work, and had more pure guts than anyone Brad knew.

If he was reading, Sam perched his ridiculous little tortoise shell glasses on the end of his nose, peering over them to look about. When not in use, he let them dangle from his neck on a yellow cord. This image caused his fellow officers to call him "Fish", after the old

Barney Miller cop show, but not to his face. Sam was an icon to the younger officers, who never hesitated to ask his advice. He always gave it freely.

At their desks, the partners settled into the dreary routine of crime investigation. That meant digging out all the pieces to the puzzle and pushing them around until they fit together, making a picture. Hours of daily drudgery and large doses of good luck were the stuff of success.

"Did you get anything helpful from the Fire Marshall?" Sam asked.

"No, they know it was a pipe bomb made of black powder available at any sporting goods store in town. Detonated by a remote control—maybe a garage door opener—ignited by a couple of dry cells. They're working with ATF and FBI bomb people. Did you know the Feds have every known bombing in the U.S. stored in a computer base?"

"Yeah, I heard that. Look, Brad, you and me been in Langston our whole life, okay? Used to know everybody by sight, but not any more, man. Seems like there's a hell of a lot of strange faces in our neighborhood in the last four—five—years. You hear what I'm sayin'?"

"Yeah, I know what you mean. It's called progress, Sam. This place suddenly grew up around us. We've been too busy to notice. Now we got us a big city and the good guys are gettin' outnumbered. Chief says he's working to get some more bodies out on the street but City Council says they got no money. You can bet one thing…as soon as someone gets his ass blown off in a bombing, they'll be screaming for our necks."

"You got that right. Look, maybe there's no connection, but seems like most of the growth came along after we got Kurasawa Electronics, okay? I know it's been good for our economy, but the down side is that it attracted undesirables to our area. You know?"

"Yeah, you may be right, Sam, but don't let anybody down at City Hall hear you say that. It's time we got Mooch working out on the street. He knows people out there and no one will think he's a snitch. The guy's so squirrelly he shouldn't attract suspicion."

Sam looked up, letting his glasses drop down onto the dangling cord. "Partner, you sure that old punch drunk can handle this kinda job? Always acts like he hears voices no one else can hear. He scares the hell outta me, you know?"

"He's not as dumb as he acts, Sam. Besides, he needs some extra dollars to keep him in beer. I know it's a risk, but we need some eyes and ears out there. I'll take the heat if he screws it up. I'm gonna get him settled in tonight."

"How you gonna do it? Hope you don't try anything too elaborate with him. You sure can't afford another failure out there. We just lost a snitch, remember?"

"How could I forget?"

Brad noticed a uniformed cop several desks away looking in their direction. He got up from Sam's desk and returned to his own. His frown told Sam to change the subject.

"Let's get back to this bombing thing. What's the motive? Why does somebody use a bomb? Revenge? A warning? Intimidation? Showing off?"

"My gut tells me it ain't showing off, Brad. Those pipes weren't toys. They're real enough to kill. If we don't stop them, they probably will kill. Every one of these bombs blew up near a business owned by an Oriental, right? The victims swear they know nothing. Don't know anyone who wants to hurt them. We got a pattern here, partner. Just need to put a label on it. That make any sense?"

"I copy that, Sam. This stuff 's new to Langston. Either we're dealing with outside elements, or some locals getting big city ideas. You don't suppose we've overlooked the arrival of some new gang, do you?"

"Bound to be some here, Brad. We're no different from other growing towns in California."

The partners agreed that Langston had all the necessary elements. Fast growth, high unemployment , local punks copying big city crime. Jerks with too much time on their hands. Just like on TV.

"Yeah, and don't forget your old buddy, Judd Worley," Sam reminded. "He's up to his neck in something illegal. Just can't seem to hang anything on him. He'd sure get my vote for our most undesirable citizen."

"I don't know, Sam. Judd and I go back a long way. Got into our first fight in grammar school, I think. Judd was always an outlaw, even in high school. But I don't think he has the personality to be in a gang—he was a loner. But Hell, anything's possible. Maybe we need a gang unit in the department. You think?"

"Yeah, maybe. Meantime, you and me—*we're* the gang unit and it's our call—near as I can tell. Any ideas?"

"Yeah, Sam, and it starts with getting Mooch on the street."

Brad looked around to be sure no one was listening. "Gonna do it tonight. Kathleen and I are taking in a concert tonight. On the way home, we're dropping in at the new bar out on Fourth. Conner's Bar. You know the place?"

Sam Hardy shook his head in disbelief and frowned at his partner. "You're gonna take your beautiful redhead to that dive? Good God, Brad, you got less sense than I gave you credit for. Why in hell do you wanna expose her to those losers?"

Brad shrugged his shoulders. He didn't like to be second-guessed. "Sam, she's been in worse places than that. This place is Judd's new hangout. Give me a little credit. I won't put her in any real danger. I need her to get Judd Worley's attention. He's had the hots for her since we were all in high school. If I know him, he'll break his ass getting close enough to sniff her before I stop him."

The look Sam gave his partner would have wilted any other man. "You're crazy, man. I'd never put a woman in that kinda spot. Sure hope you know what you're doing. Not sure I wanna hear what comes next"

"That's the easy part. Worley's gonna pick a fight with me. It always happens. When he does, I'll take him down. Then Mooch comes to Worley's defense. Hopefully, the jerks in the bar will think he's on their side and they'll make Mooch their hero. Crude plan, but Christ, we're not dealing with Einsteins here. These people are low lifes."

Sam shook his head. "...And you're gonna take them both on? With Kathleen right there? No wonder they call you 'Junk Yard Dog'. That's the dumbest thing I ever heard. Jesus, Brad—"

Brad waved his partner off. "Don't worry, Sam. She'll be mad and scared, but she'll be fine. Mooch knows he's playing a part; he did it for years. He was always the bad guy in the ring. He'll pull his punches."

Sam shook his head. "Yeah, right. But just remember, I think the plan sucks. Too chancey. You gonna do this all by yourself without backup?"

"I can't tell anyone. But I've got a black and white working the area so they'll be close. Don't worry, Sam. I can handle Worley. By the way, if something does go wrong, Mooch knows he's to stick with Kate so nobody bothers her. Anything else?"

Sam just shrugged.

"And, Sam, I'm going to kick Mooch's ass to make it look real."

"You kidding? You're out of your head. Mooch can squash you like a bug."

"Not a chance, Sam. He's soft. Besides, I haven't been in a good brawl for a long time. Mooch will pull his punches. Did it in the ring for years."

❦   ❦   ❦

Brad and Kathleen pulled into Conners' parking lot at 10:45. It wasn't the most elegant place they might have picked for a nightcap.

"Brad Logan," Kathleen wailed, "you're not taking me in *this* place. This dress cost over three hundred dollars. That's more than they paid for that stupid bubbling neon sign. Just forget it."

"The dress is beautiful, Kate, and so are you. I just want to check this place out to see who hangs out here. It just opened. We'll just stay for one drink, I promise. It's not your kind of place, but I'll make it up to you. Please."

Five more minutes of wheedling and Brad helped Kathleen out of the car. The knotty pine interior of Conner's reeked from cigarette smoke and too hot kitchen grease. Pieces of tacky wallpaper hung from the walls. Cigarette burns gave a tweedy look to the hardwood floor. Overhead fluorescents cast a sickly yellow glow over the entire room. The jukebox blared "Boot Skootin' Boogie".

They found a small table in a corner, where Kathleen reluctantly sat on the creaky wooden chair. Brad knew she was skittish, being in a bar on the seamy side of town, but she put on her best face.

He hated deceiving her. He wasn't very good at it. He knew their evening at the theater brought her great pleasure but now her evening was about to be destroyed. Judd Worley slouched on a bar stool less than twenty feet away!

They sat quietly enjoying their drinks for ten minutes before Judd Worley suddenly caught sight of them in the mirror as he lifted his glass. Brad checked his watch at that moment. It was 11:15. The patrol car should be in the area.

The scruffily dressed man almost fell off his bar stool getting to his feet. He swaggered to their table, a dirty Dodger baseball cap crammed on his head. A grungy, almost-yellow ponytail was pulled through the strap at the back of his head. The rolled up sleeves of his T-shirt revealed a horde of tattoos covering his arms. Most prominent of the skin murals was the one on his right forearm, a fist raised with middle finger extended. It accurately described the attitude of this man and shouted his motto: 'Screw You'. Dirty Levis hugged his legs and barely contained his expanding waistline.

The cigarette in Judd's lips danced as he spoke. An inch-long ash fell onto their table. He casually brushed it to the floor, leaving a streak of dust on the black table top.

"Well, look at this. It's my ass-hole buddy, Brad Logan, and his foxy wife. You're lookin' good, Kathleen…real good."

Judd's mouth flashed into a lecherous leer as he ogled smooth breasts overflowing Kathleen's sleeveless cocktail dress. Her hand rushed defensively to cover herself as her face reddened. She made no effort to hide her contempt, turning her body as far away from him as possible. Her green eyes reflected her disgust as she looked to Brad for help.

Brad glared into Judd's bloodshot, bleary eyes and growled his greeting. "What's up, Judd? Hoped you wouldn't see us."

He wrinkled his nose as if there was an unpleasant odor. Instinctively, Brad pulled his feet back underneath his body, making it easier to rise quickly. A charge of electricity crackled between them. It always did when they met. Ever since high school, their hate was notoriously volcanic. Judd's voice dripped with contempt.

"Listen, you bullheaded piece of crap. Don't give me your snotty airs. Big ass hero cop. You ain't no better'n me. Hated your guts in school and nothing's changed. You two slummin'? Why ain't you at the Country Club with the other snobs?"

Judd leaned forward to get into Brad's face. The move made Brad flinch.

"Judd, you piss me off. Back off and get outta my face or I'll bust you for being a public nuisance."

Judd stepped back and raised up, glaring down at Brad. "Oh, I get it. Show your honey what a big hero you are, then go home and she gives you a little reward. You ain't no different since you growed up. You always figured your shit don't stink."

Worley leered at Kathleen and rubbed his crotch. "Honey, you don't know what you missed in high school when you snubbed me. I was screwing Patty Clark when this guy here was still floggin' his donkey. I'll show you a good time, Darlin'. I got the moves."

The volcano in Brad's head erupted when he saw Judd undress Kate with drunken eyes——eyes that constantly shifted from one person to another. "If you think you're man enough to take me in, let's get it on, Big Shot."

"That does it, creep. You're going down. *Now back up.*"

When Brad pointed a finger at Judd, it was as if he pulled a trigger. Judd Worley lunged across the table and swung his right fist. Brad's instincts took over. He moved his head enough so the blow glanced off his cheek. It stung, but barely fazed him. At the same time, he grabbed Judd's wrist and tugged the man toward him, kicking Judd's leg just below the knee. He took Judd's wrist in both hands and bent the fingers upward. The stunned man was already in Brad's control. It took ten seconds.

Kathleen screamed as the table tipped over. Brad lunged to his feet, never releasing the firm grip on Judd's wrist. In a maneuver he had practiced daily for years, he twisted the arm until Judd turned his back. Brad put his entire body strength behind a shove, knocking Judd to the floor. Before he recovered, Brad sat astride him, forcing his arm higher between his shoulder blades. His anger forced more violence into the move than he planned. Judd's shoulder dislocated with a loud snap. He roared in pain.

"You lousy, son of a bitch, Logan! You're breaking my arm. I'm gonna turn your face to mush." Judd let out a string of blue language. By now a large part of the barroom crowd had gathered to witness the one-sided confrontation.

The owner, Harry Conner, pushed his way to the front of the crowd. "What the hell's going on here? Jesus Christ, I don't need this kind of crap in my bar. Get off that man and get the hell out of here!"

He pointed a finger at Brad then bent over to set the table upright.

At that moment, Brad heard Kathleen scream just as something hit him from behind, breaking his hold on Judd's arm. When Brad turned to face this new menace, he caught the full force of a well-placed kick. It caught him high on his forehead and propelled him backwards off of Judd, where he landed awkwardly on his butt. The sudden attack caught him by surprise because of the intensity. The foot in his face was not friendly fire.

He quickly shook the swarm of bees from his head and looked up to see which wall had fallen on him. Looming over him was an incredible sight. Was it Paul Bunyan? Huge shaved head, blue-black beard hiding a red, blotchy face; eyes of an angry bull, and arms resembling a normal man's thigh. Coarse, black hair oozed from under the shirt. This was some fierce looking animal!

A wolf-like snarl erupted from the giant's lips as he crouched with arms outstretched. A rush of excitement washed over Brad as he anticipated his next move. The thrill of the anticipated confrontation was heady stuff.

He got warily to his feet, knowing he must be swift and decisive to avoid getting hurt. Without a word, he whirled around, letting his right leg swing free in an arc. His size twelve snakeskin boot found its mark in the pit of the man's stomach. The behemoth's breath escaped in a loud whoosh as he staggered backwards. Brad closed in quickly before the man could recover, driving his fist into the man's throat. It was very deliberate—designed to immobilize.

Mooch went down in a huge heap, gasping for air. Brad brought out his badge, holding it high over his head for the crowd to see. Reverting to his most commanding, authoritative voice he shouted so there was no mistaking his words: "*I'm Sergeant Logan of the Langston Police Dept. These men are my prisoners. Now back off and get back to your own business or I'll close this place down.*"

He turned to Kathleen. He could see pure terror on her face. "You all right, Katie?"

"Get me out of here, Brad. *Now*! I mean it." Her face was ashen and he could see her hands shaking. He realized she had never been this close to him during a physical confrontation. What he considered an exciting part of his dangerous job, his wife viewed with great distaste and terror. He put both arms around her and allowed her to vent against his chest. When she calmed down a little, he sat her down and handed her a glass of water offered by the waitress. He never took his eyes off his two assailants.

Reaching into his side pocket, Brad pulled out his flip phone, dialed his precinct number and asked that a backup car be sent. When his request was confirmed, he turned to the owner of the bar. "Mister Conner, I'm going to tell you this one time. If you allow scum like this to intimidate your patrons, you won't stay in business long. My wife and I came in here to enjoy a quiet after-dinner drink and this man insulted my wife and tried to assault me. You can bet your ass this place will be under scrutiny by my department from now on." Brad jabbed a finger into the man's chest.

It was obvious, Conners wanted exoneration from this policeman. "Listen, Sergeant, I don't need no trouble with the cops. These guys ain't welcome here no more, but get 'em the hell out of here, will you?" The tavern owner gestured to the rest of the crowd. "Okay folks, the excitement's over. Order up. This round's on me."

Brad confirmed that his two assailants were no longer warriors. Judd Worley was back on his feet, cradling his useless arm next to his chest. There was no fight left in him. He was obviously in great pain. "Logan, you son of a bitch, you'll pay for this! You broke my arm, you bastard. I'm going to make sure you never forget it."

He turned to the crowd. "Hey, you seen this pig attack me. It was police brutality. Look what he done to this guy." He pointed at the plaid-shirted hulk who was just now able to catch his breath and sit up.

Brad glared at Judd and drew back a fist. "Put a lid on it, Judd. You're both through for the night. Now get your ass out of here! There's a squad car waiting. Come on, Kate, let's go."

When they reached the front door, two uniformed cops were just entering. When they caught sight of Brad, they asked what he wanted done. He pushed Judd toward them. "Thanks for getting here so quick, guys. This slime may have a broken arm, so call him an ambulance. The other one will make it, once he catches his breath. Make a note in your log to keep this bar under surveillance. Too many unsavory characters hanging out. The owner's gotta learn which patrons he can do without."

Brad pulled one of the patrol cops a little to the side, out of ear-shot of the others. "Listen, Brian, take care of Mooch Kaiser in there. He's the one that looks like Paul Bunyan. I hit him pretty hard, but he's tough, he can take it. Give him a good lecture, then turn him out. He's okay."

After verifying he was no longer needed, Brad took Kathleen's hand and led her out of the bar and helped her into their car. She was calmer, but he could tell she was furious at him. She didn't say a word as she buckled her seatbelt.

Brad climbed behind the wheel and started the car. He reached across the seat to pat his wife's hand. "I'm sorry, Hon. I had no idea it would get so far out of hand. Judd just can't stop trying to make up for high school. You gonna be all right?"

"Brad Logan…that's the *worst* thing you've ever put me through! And you, you bastard, you enjoyed it! I never realized you enjoyed violence so much. My God, Brad, if you knew how scared I was…I…I…thought they were going to kill you."

"I'm fine, dear. Just upset that it happened with you there. That damn Judd Worley. Ever since high school, he's been trying to get the best of me." The lie nearly choked him.

Kate was far from finished. "There's more to it than that, Brad. I know you two always hated each other. How many fights did you guys have? I remember at least five. You always beat him up, but he'd never give in. He's never been scared of you."

Brad looked at her reflection in the windshield. Tears coursed down her face, drawing little black lines of mascara along her cheeks.

He reached across the seat to take her hand, but she pulled *hers* back and turned her face toward the car window.

It dawned on him; Kate was *really* pissed!

CHAPTER 2

Captain Owens' voice raised to another level as he faced the man across his desk. "Now listen to what I'm saying, Glen, I don't care how many calls you get from Judd Worley's attorney, I won't be bull-dogged into any hasty action over this thing."

The two men were in Owens' office with the door closed. Papers covered the top of his desk; personnel files relating to Sergeant Brad Logan.

"I hear what you're saying, Captain, but from where I sit, he looks like a loose cannon. That temper of his will lead to serious trouble for the department one of these days. Look what he did this time, for God's sake. He dislocated the man's arm."

"That wasn't his fault, man. According to my sources, an old high school acquaintance provoked him. This Worley character is a minor hoodlum who carries a perpetual hard-on for Brad Logan. He goes out of his way to pick fights with him. It's been going on since the two were in grammar school, dammit. You can't fault Logan for every scrape he gets into."

"Captain, he's probably a good cop, but we just can't ignore his mean streak Don't forget, it's happened before. Isn't that why they call him Junkyard Dog?"

Captain Owens chuckled as he answered. "Not to his face they don't. You run Internal Affairs, Glen; you know most lawsuits are phony. We're sitting ducks for every kook out there who challenges our authority. How much dough is Worley suing for?"

The I.A. man referred to his notes. "There's no mention of money yet, but they'll get around to it. The fact remains, a complaint was filed. That means I investigate. Now let's go over his file so I don't run into any surprises down the road."

"Put this piece of information in your files, Glen: Sergeant Logan has *never* fired his weapon at a suspect. There are not too many others in this department who can say that."

Lieutenant Nichols did a double-take. "You kidding? You mean he's still a virgin after twelve years on the force? You sure of that?"

"Positive. We keep precise statistics on the use of firearms. He won't pull his weapon unless he feels his own life or another officer's life is threatened. But, despite that, he has more arrests than any other officer except Sam Hardy—and Sam's been around five years longer. That says something about Sergeant Logan's ability."

"Yeah, it does, Captain; I'm impressed. All right, let's go over his service record. He's a local man, right?"

For the next half hour, the two men reviewed Brad Logan's history. He attended local schools; was an All-star football player who earned a full scholarship to Midwestern College; majored in Criminology. Starred as quarterback on the varsity football team until a knee injury ended his career in the third game of his Senior year. That was the end of a promising career in Pro Football. It took several major operations to repair the knee. Graduated at age 24 and married his high school sweetheart, Kathleen Spencer. Returned to Langston and was hired by the police department.

"He began at the bottom in the 'kiddy car patrol', writing traffic tickets. Rode his Honda motorcycle around town for two years. Then asked for something more exciting and was put on foot patrol. Let me tell you, he created excitement. Made more collars in his first year than anyone before him. How much more of this do you want?"

Nichols looked up from the notes he was taking. "Need it all, Captain. I want to be totally prepared when I start my investigation. Didn't Logan go to the FBI academy?"

Captain Owens fumbled with the service file. "Yep. In '82 and got his promotion to Senior Detective when he finished. That's when we assigned him as Sam Hardy's partner in Homicide. Great team. Their record of cases solved is outstanding."

"Right. I'm familiar with their record. Then two years ago, he got his promotion to Sergeant?"

Owens confirmed that. "Right."

"Does he talk to our shrink every year?"

"Oh yeah, the regular sessions, but the doc says Brad doesn't open up much. Just goes in as often as we require it. Nothing changes. Doctor Fisher says he never voices any complaints. Just says that he hopes to be Chief some day. Wouldn't surprise me if he makes it."

Nichols chuckled. "I can just see it—'Chief Junkyard Dog'. His nameplate would be a riot. Okay, let's hear the list of complaints. Read me any disciplinary actions against him and give me specifics."

Captain Owens fumbled through the file until he located the record of complaints against Brad. Small file cards were held in a separate envelope. Each card summarized the details of any perceived misconduct. As Captain Owens' voice droned on, Glen Nichols made notes on the legal pad in front of him. Every once in a while, he would ask for more details about an incident.

"Okay, we have—let's see—one Unlawful Arrest and three for Excessive Force and here's one for Improper Search. In two incidents, the City paid small out-of-court settlements for injuries. About par for a foot soldier. It's a cinch he's not afraid to get his hands dirty. You're right, nothing out of line for his time on the job. That sure makes it easier to defend him."

Captain Owens began replacing the paperwork into the folder. "I'll tell you what, Glen, I wish I had several dozen more cops like Logan. He may be a little rough around the edges, but he gets a thankless job done efficiently and without putting any of the other officers in danger. As far as I'm concerned he's a credit to his badge."

"You aware of any problem with booze?"

"Not to my knowledge."

"Does he belong to any clubs or organizations I should know about?"

Captain Owens referred to the records, then shook his head. A look of relief crossed his face when he saw Lieutenant Nichols gather his yellow sheets of notes, straighten his tie and slowly get to his feet.

Nichols extended his hand. "Captain, I really appreciate your input. I think we have good grounds to defend the charges, but my investigation is just starting. Think I'll get him out of town for a couple days so he doesn't get in the way of my guys. Thanks for the coffee."

The two men shook hands and Nichols left the office. He walked directly down the hall to his own office, checked in with his secretary, then entered and closed the door behind him. Within minutes, the phone was in his hand. The conversation lasted almost an hour.

❧   ❧   ❧

At three o'clock that afternoon, Sergeant Brad Logan sat across the desk from Lieutenant Glen Nichols, well aware he was being sized up while the Lieutenant spoke on the phone.

Moments later, Lieutenant Nichols hung up the phone and turned his attention to the man across the desk. "Good to see you, Sergeant. I'll get right to the point. Your little set-to at Conners' the other night led to a complaint being filed. You've been through it before, so you know the drill. You're on suspension from your regular duties for a week, but I have another job for you so you won't get bored."

The suspension was no surprise to Brad. News of the complaint spread around the department as soon as the attorney called. The action upset him, but was expected. So far, only the Chief and Sam Hardy were aware of the real reason he went to the bar. He hoped to keep the information quiet as long as possible. Mooch's safety was at stake. Not even Kathleen knew about the staged fight. "I don't like it, Lieutenant, but hell, I know there's no choice. You want my badge?"

"No, just stay out of here for a week. I'm sending you out of town for a couple days so no one can serve papers on you before I finish my investigation. Here's the deal: the FBI office in Seattle has discovered a new criminal underground on the west coast. They're holding a special seminar in Seattle over the next couple days. You're going as the rep for Langston PD. Any questions?"

It all happened so fast, Brad couldn't quite comprehend everything. The words just buzzed around in his head, looking for explanations. He couldn't get a good read on Nichols. The two of them didn't travel in the same circles. The head of Internal Affairs came across as a stiff, no-nonsense type of officer. Probably had never been on foot patrol. He wore his hair in a military burr cut. Steely gray eyes peered out through wire-framed glasses. Brad decided Nichols was the reincarnation of GI Joe.

"This is a first for me. Never been to a special crime seminar before. I'm in the Homicide Division, not Intelligence Division." A slight smile crossed his face.

"Yeah, it's a little out of your line, but just indulge me, okay? By the way, where do you buy your boots? You always wear the greatest looking boots. Are those lizard?"

The quick change of direction caught Brad by surprise. "Well, as a matter of fact, they're not lizard, they're snakeskin. My cousin down in Texas makes them for me. If you want a pair, I can arrange it for you."

Nichols waved his hand. "I'll talk to you about it when you get back. You always wear boots of some kind. It's kind of your trademark, right?"

"Yeah, I've worn them since college. The habit kinda grew on me. I changed the rest of the wardrobe on account of the boots. It began with this silver buckle. It was my dad's. I started wearing it after he died. It didn't seem to go with regular suits and sport coats so I grad-ually switched to western clothes. Guess that's why a lot of folks call me a cowboy. Do you object?"

"No, not really. It's a cinch it makes you stand out in a crowd. Kind of reminds me of Wyatt Earp, you know, that big, bushy mus-tache and mangled nose. All you need is to wear your holster tied down at your hip to really look the part."

Nichols started laughing at the portrait he had painted, but Brad wasn't amused. "Sir, are you putting me on? If you have some objec-tions to my appearance, just spit it out. No need to pussy foot around with me."

Brad's well-known short trigger was spring-loaded, and it came undone. He figured the I.A. man was testing him and he resented it. Nichols held his hands up as if to surrender. "No offense meant. Just interested for strictly personal reasons. Frankly, I admire the way you dress as you want. Most of us fall into the trap of conformity. Any-way, let's get back to reality. Any questions about the Seattle detail?"

Again that quick change of direction by Nichols. Brad's anger faded. "Not really. I assume you've arranged for a hotel and every-thing?"

"Yes. Everything's in the packet." Lieutenant Nichols shoved a manila envelope across the desk.

Brad picked it up and briefly scanned the contents. "I guess that's all I need, sir. Sorry to cause another investigation. My history with this Worley guy goes back a long way—all of it bad. He *does* push my buttons." Brad pushed his chair back and got to his feet.

Nichols rose and leveled his gaze into Brad's eyes. "I'm aware of your history with him, Sergeant. We'll keep in touch. Maybe we can head him off at the pass. Enjoy your R and R in Seattle."

Brad shook the extended hand and exited the office. He was cer-tain Nichols was not being entirely truthful. Somehow this little trip didn't make a lot of sense. It seemed too convenient at this particular time. But, what the hell. Walking back to the Homicide Division, he casually thumbed through the sheaf of papers in the envelope. There were no details about the seminar in Seattle.

"So tell me, Brad, did you get your ass chewed again for getting into another fight? I won't tell you I told you so." Sam Hardy looked up from his desk as Brad walked by. The tiny pair of glasses sat on the lower portion of his nose.

Brad resisted the urge to say, 'Hi, Fish.' He just nodded.

The glasses came off the nose and swung from their cord on Sam's neck. "So did that scum Worley really sue? Man, he's got more stinkin' gall. You get suspended? Did you tell Nichols the real reason you went to that bar?"

"No, I didn't, Sam, because it never came up. Just keep it quiet as long as we can. Got to make sure Mooch gets established out there. It's only been a week. Listen, Nichols gave me a special detail to handle, so I'll be gone for a couple days. I know how much you'll miss me, but try to bear up, will you?"

"Well, of course, I'll miss your ugly butt, but I'll probably get more done without you under foot, okay? What's the skinny on the new assignment?"

"I'm going to an FBI seminar about some new gang activity on the West Coast. Maybe it'll tie in with what we were talking about. Hope I find out something that'll help us with these bombings."

Sam shuffled through the papers on his desk, looking for nothing in particular. "Hot damn, wish they'd ask me to go to Seattle. Ever tell you about the piece of fluff I knew up there? That used to be quite a swinging town for Navy boys." Sam chuckled and returned to his reading.

Brad reached over and kissed the shiny bald spot on the top of his partner's head. "Geez, old man, all you gotta do is get suspended. If you do, maybe next time they'll send you. I've got it down to a science. Now, since I'm leaving early in the morning, I'm going home to break the news to Kate. Imagine she'll get all pissed at me again."

Brad hadn't told his partner how Kathleen reacted to the fight at Conner's Bar. He knew Sam would give him that knowing look he was famous for. The smart ass was always right.

"Will you keep an eye on her when I'm gone? It would be just like that slime Worley to make her uncomfortable if he knew Kate was alone."

"I'll make sure the black and whites go by your house every couple hours, buddy."

Brad waved his arm and, after checking out with dispatch, left the building.

❦   ❦   ❦

"You're going *where* tomorrow?" Kathleen's voice became shrill as she responded to his announcement when he entered the house.

"Seattle, Kate. They want to get me out of town for a week, so I'm going to an FBI seminar. I'm on suspension this week. Hope that doesn't bother you."

Brad took off his holster and 9MM automatic as he spoke. It was a regular ritual with him whenever he came into the house. He would take off his weapon, remove the clip and lock the piece in the gun safe over the kitchen sink. Brad was paranoid about gun safety. He never took a chance, especially around Kathleen.

"You're on suspension again? It's about that fight with Judd, isn't it? Did you tell them what that bastard said to me?"

Brad nodded as he opened the refrigerator door and removed a bottle of Cordoba beer, flicked the top off and squeezed a precut piece of lime into the thin neck of the bottle. Kathleen kept a small dish of fresh lime pieces near his stash of beer so he could indulge himself his preferred libation.

"Yeah, for all the good it did. Guess Judd went to a Civil Rights attorney. Those guys just love attacking the cops. It'll all blow over. Don't worry, Hon."

"I'm sorry, dammit, but it's just not fair. He insults me and threatens you, but you end up getting suspended. I hope you broke that bastard's arm." Brad knew his wife wore her heart on her sleeve and could never hide her feelings. She took a long sip from the glass of wine on the counter, letting her anger dwindle away. "You can tell me about it over dinner. Why don't you go on in and watch the news while I finish here?"

She turned to stir the skillet contents.

Brad hung his coat in the closet, jacked his boots off, then padded in his stocking feet into the den. He plopped into his form-fitting leather recliner and flicked the television on. Taking a long swallow on his beer, he reached for the newspaper. Within minutes, he was totally absorbed in world events.

Kathleen's sudden scream from the kitchen brought Brad out of his chair at a dead run! She stood white-faced with a hand to her mouth, pointing toward the back door. In two strides, Brad reached the door and yanked it open.

The form standing there in the dimly lit patio resembled a mountain except for the bald head gleaming in the moonlight. There was no mistaking the man's huge bulk. Brad's last recollection of the form was looking down at it in Conner's Bar a week ago. Without a word, Brad stepped out into the patio, closing the door behind him. He could hear Kathleen calling his name, but he ignored her.

"What in hell are you doing in my back yard, Mooch?"

"You gonna kick me again? You know, for a puny little thing, you kick like a mule. Not quite as good as some I took in the ring, but sure glad you wasn't mad at me."

The mountain moved towards Brad, palms thrust upward. Brad slapped the huge mitts. This giant had at least a three inch height advantage over Brad. It didn't happen very often since Brad was 6'2". He turned and headed for the corner of the garage, motioning for Mooch to follow him.

"You took an awful chance, man. What if someone saw you? This better be really important."

"Sorry, man, but I couldn't reach Sam, and this can't wait. Our clash at Conners' last week musta been too good. Worley and me both been banned from the bar. Besides, he's been out of circulation, you know, with his busted arm. Haven't seen him since that night, so I didn't know what to do."

"Damn it. Hate to think that whole tussle was for nothing. You gotta find him, Mooch. We can't leave him out there doing his thing without us knowing. Listen, Worley used to hang out at the bar in the Flamingo Motel on Sixth. When he finds a place he likes, he sticks with it until someone throws him out."

Brad's fingers subconsciously went to the welt on the side of his head, it was still tender to the touch. "Incidentally, you big horse, you damn near knocked my head off with that kick! Your timing's off since you stopped wrestling last year. Need to get back in the gym and practice."

"Hey listen, little fella, that boot you planted in my gut wasn't no dud. Damn near made me puke at first. Maybe some day you an' me can get in the ring for real, pal." When he grinned, Mooch displayed a few gaps in his smile. He called the missing teeth 'tools of the trade'.

"Any time, Fats. Now, let's do this…since I'll be gone to Seattle for two days, you just cool it at the Flamingo and see if Judd shows up. Just be sure you stay sober. If he shows up, act surprised to see him. Don't let him know you been looking for him. Got that?"

Brad pulled out his wallet and handed fifty dollars to his huge colleague. "Keep your nose clean, pal. Sam knows all about you, but don't talk to anyone else at the police department."

"Sure, I can do that, no problem. If you wanna reach me later this week, leave a message with my ole lady. Sorry to scare your wife. She don't know, huh?"

"I'll have to tell her now, man. But she's cool. Once she knows you won't hurt her, she'll want you as a friend. She's also brings home stray dogs. See you, Mooch."

The two men banged fists together and Big Foot merged into the darkness. Brad shook his head and went back into the kitchen. It was the last time he saw Mooch.

Kathleen's green eyes hurled daggers as he entered the room. "Damn you to hell, Brad Logan…that's the goon who kicked the crap out of you at Conners'. Too bad he didn't kick harder. I should've known your fight was phony. You were enjoying yourself too much. You scared me out of my wits. How can you do that to me, you son of a bitch? I hate you." She turned her back and returned to the stove and her chores. Brad knew he couldn't smooth things over yet. Kathleen was just too angry. It wasn't like her to be this upset with him, but he hoped by leaving her alone she would calm down.

After slamming around the kitchen for fifteen minutes, Kathleen finally announced he could come to the table. Brad walked up behind his wife and put his arms around her. He held her tightly without saying a word, resting his head on the back of her neck.

At first, she ignored him, just standing with the casserole dish in her hands. Finally, Kathleen put the casserole with his dinner on the table, then turned into his embrace and wrapped her arms around his neck. "You smart-assed cop, you're not out of the doghouse yet. Don't you *ever* do that to me again. I'm serious."

Brad kissed her with great feeling, but Kathleen's response didn't match his enthusiasm. He held the chair for her as she sat. How would he make it up to her?

He knew it was just the first serving of crow he'd be eating for awhile.

CHAPTER 3

$\mathcal{B}$rad's flight to Seattle landed at 9:45 the next morning, about thirty minutes behind schedule. Severe turbulence and rain over much of Oregon and Southern Washington bounced the 707 off course. The pilot finally made a wide detour around the worst of the disturbances, but the seat belt sign remained lit most of the flight.

The skies cleared as they began their final approach, much to Brad's relief. He did not relish flying, preferring ground transportation, where he felt more in control of his fate. His favorite part of any flight was the screech of tires as the plane touched down on the runway. The breath he exhaled at that moment helped release his tension. Today it was especially true, his stiff forearms reflecting his firm grip on the armrests.

As he debarked, carrying his one-suiter bag, he mentally reviewed the memo he carried in his suitcase. He would check into the Airport Hotel, drop off his bag, then call the local FBI office. They would arrange his meeting.

"Sergeant Logan?"

A deep, confident voice startled him. He looked around for the owner. A middle-aged man in a dark blue suit walked toward him with hand extended. His well-tailored suit spelled corporate CEO. The face was vaguely familiar, but Brad couldn't put a name to it. The grip was strong, the smile real.

"Agent Garrett of the local FBI office. Decided I'd meet your plane and get you checked in to save time. Do you remember me?"

"Yes, I think so. Don't you teach anti-terrorism at Quantico?"

"Right. At least, I did until two years ago when I took a special assignment. How was your flight?"

"Kinda bumpy, but okay, I guess. I'm not exactly fond of airplanes."

"I'm with you. Don't like roller coasters either. Let's take this exit, it'll take us right to the hotel lobby. I've already checked you, in so you can just drop off your bag and we can get to work. That okay?"

Ten minutes later, in Garrett's plain, blue sedan, they shared the morning traffic with hordes of local citizens. Ribbons of cars filled every roadway in every direction. At the Federal Building, they left the car in an underground garage and elevatored to the third floor offices shared by Garrett and numerous other agents.

The office was typical of other Federal offices in Brad's memory: Boring off- white vinyl tile covered the floor; plain, dull white-painted walls displayed enlarged photographs of several FBI dignitaries including J. Edgar; and banks of fluorescent lights bathed the office in a soft, shadowless light. At one end, a large window overlooked the edge of SeaTac harbor. The main office contained gray metallic desks, but it was a different story when they entered Garrett's own private digs; the walls were paneled and his desk was a large walnut number.

Agent Garrett motioned Brad to a dark brown leather chair facing his desk. "Make yourself comfortable, Sergeant; we'll be here a while."

"When are you going to tell me why I'm *really* here, Garrett?"

A steaming pot of coffee sat on the desk between them. The FBI man poured out two cups before he answered. He pushed a cup towards Brad, along with a creamer. "You're certainly direct, Sergeant. I remember, you were the impatient one in my class. You never let me wander far from the subject at hand. We'll get into the briefing right now, so just relax."

Garrett loosened his tie before he continued. "I'm sorry for the hush-hush crap, but you'll understand after you hear the briefing. For your information, I picked you for this job because I remember you from the Academy. I need a cop from the Langston Police Department—right now. You were my only choice. To be honest, you were the only person in Langston P.D. I can share this with."

Brad sipped his coffee and eyed the speaker without expression. The occasional raising of his eyebrows was the only indication he was even listening.

"Now, before we go on, let me tell you that this information is for *your* knowledge only. No one—I *repeat*—no one else in your department knows anything and that's the way it must stay. You cannot trust anyone, not even—"

"I get the picture, Garrett. I have to keep my mouth shut. You're assuming, of course, that I decide I'll do this…this…whatever job."

"Listen, Brad, let's stop being so formal. Call me Kelly. That all right with you?"

"Sure, Kelly. Now that you've got my curiosity aroused, how about dropping the other shoe?"

Brad's brusque manner often was taken as surliness, but he just figured life was too short to waste it on pleasantries.

"You got it. Stop me any time you need some input or clarification. I don't want any misunderstandings. Total clarification is essential in every detail. You follow?"

Brad just nodded. He drummed his pencil on the yellow legal pad in front of him. Now he was certain his intuition was correct; this meeting was more than he'd been told.

"I'm sure you're familiar with a company in Langston called Kurasawa Electronics? They've been in your town almost ten years now and currently employ over two hundred persons. They manufacture different kinds of electronics for computers—circuit boards, chips, and they recently began producing soft-wear programs for retail markets. You know, games, business software and the like."

Garrett ran fingers through his graying hair. From the folder in front of him, he picked up a color brochure, then passed it across the desk to Brad. "This is a sample of their sales brochure. You can see, they've got a first-class marketing department. The whole company appears to be first class."

Brad shrugged. "Yeah, but so far nothing looks too sinister."

"It gets better, believe me. Do you have any idea how many Japanese people now live in your town? Are you aware of the increase since, say, ten years ago?"

"I'm aware there's been an increase, but not familiar with the numbers. Is it very significant?"

"Depends on how you look at it. Since the plant was built, we tracked the increased population of Japanese people and found it has gone up dramatically every year since the plant opened. Like, *drastic*. Over ten thousand, according to last census figures. These people don't all work at Kurusawa—-something other than the plant is attracting them to Langston."

"Wait a minute, Kelly…maybe they like living in the desert. A lot of them work in the hot houses, growing flowers. Besides, we're a growing town between L.A. and Vegas. There's been increased hiring at the Naval Weapons Station. There could be all kinds of logical reasons. Our overall population is triple what it was twenty years ago. So what? I can't see how that affects Langston P.D."

"Jesus, you're an impatient bastard. Just relax! Sorry if it's boring. I'm going to fill in the background, whether you like it or not. Just be patient; the dicey part is coming up."

Agent Garrett leaned back in his chair and stared at Brad. His face took on a look of grim determination. His words were clipped and his manner tense. He pressed the fingertips of each hand together in front of his chest. "You ever hear of the *Yakuza*?"

"Doesn't sound familiar to me. Should I know it?"

"Believe me, you're going to know more about it than you want before this is all over. It's one of the oldest social orders in the world. Maybe as old as the Chinese *Tongs*. Nobody knows, for sure—at least three hundred years old. Older than anything in the U.S. Older than the Mafia. You get the idea?"

Brad's interest level jumped.

"This underworld culture goes back to the 17th century. *Yakuza* is organized into so-called family and sub-family groups, called *Gumis*. Each group is loyal to a boss-man known as *Oyabun*. Their loyalty to their leaders is legendary. The so-called soldiers of each *Gumi* often have tattoos all over their body. It's been rumored some of the younger members will cut off a finger to show their loyalty and be accepted into the clan. Getting more interesting?"

Brad found himself leaning forward over the desk, taking in every word. The chattering pencil now lay forgotten on the desktop.

"The West Coast is now home base to a number of *Yakuza* cells. Started in Hawaii about twenty years ago. Then moved into the mainland on the West Coast. They've grown quite a bit since then, but stayed pretty quiet—until now. They're mostly into prostitution, drugs, smuggling, gun running and pornography; you know, the dirtiest crimes against the public. They don't get a lot of publicity because their victims are usually from the Japanese community. These victims tend to keep it quiet. In the old country, the *Yakuza* were pretty much accepted by the citizens. Kind of like Robin Hood's Merry Men."

Brad held up his hand. "Wait a minute, man. I think I see where this is going. You're telling me this is going on in my town, aren't you?"

"Yes, but that isn't even the bad part, Brad. I'm just building up to it. You need to know the background so you can see why we're concerned." Garrett turned over another paper in his folder. "We know they're working in your town, as they are in several cities with large populations of Asians. They use extortion against their own people.

Many Japanese in the U.S. have close family ties to Japan. Japanese people working for large Japanese firms are threatened by the *Yakuza*. They're told their families back in Japan will suffer violence or even death unless protection money is paid every month. Old racket with new players."

Garrett stopped talking and looked at his watch. "Jeez, it's after one o'clock, Brad. Let's go down to the commissary for some lunch. Had no idea I'd talked so long. Your bladder bustin', too?" He rose to his feet and reached up to straighten his tie. At the same time, he whisked the papers on his desk into the top drawer, which he then locked.

Brad was ready for the break. He was so engrossed in the conversation he didn't realize his stomach was complaining and he needed to stretch his legs. "I finally understand why you're so deep into this, but can't understand all the secrecy between the Bureau and Langston PD. I assume you'll clear that up?"

Garrett just nodded as he led the way from his office.

During the lunch break, their conversation avoided the topic of the day. They talked about the Academy and the class Garrett instructed there for many years. Brad filled his host in on events in police work over the past few years. He talked about the recent bombings in his town and wondered if they were related to this new threat. The cop from Langston was quite impressed by the energy of this man. Despite thirty years as a Federal Agent, Garrett was still enthusiastic about his job and gave Brad the feeling he still looked forward to each day's challenge.

By 2:00 they were back in Garrett's office. Brad felt refreshed and looked forward to more details about this growing crime threat to his community.

"I think it's time you learned why this gig requires so much secrecy. I first became involved a couple years ago. The Bureau knew about my knowledge of various terrorist groups. They asked me to get a handle on the *Yakuza*. I head up the investigation on the entire

West Coast. I operate out of Seattle because we have a large contingent of them right here. In the last four years, four of our people infiltrated the group at one time or another. They've all been murdered. You don't realize it, but two of those persons were right there in Langston in the last year." Kelly Garrett paused, silently scanning the contents of the open file.

"We kept a lid on it, but we know that someone connected with local police or Bureau, or both, fingered our inside people. It had to be that way. Our inside people couldn't be uncovered accidentally. Someone in Langston's law enforcement is on the payroll of *Yakuza*, sure as you're sitting there."

Brad let his breath out with a loud whistle. "Jesus. You're saying there's a snake in the egg basket, is that right?"

"Yeah and that snake caused my people to *die*. That's the Cardinal Rule in our profession, as far as I'm concerned. We don't betray fellow officers. Brad, I've got to say it again: *No one*—I mean, *no one*—can be trusted. I can't stress that enough. Your life won't be worth a spit in the holler if anyone realizes you're in this operation."

Brad realized he was concentrating so hard he was forgetting to breathe once in awhile, so he forced himself to take deeper breaths. "I know what you're saying, Kelly. There's nothing I hate worse than a dirty cop. Do you have any hints who it could be?"

"Not a clue, but the information about these informants wasn't known to many people in Langston P.D. or the local Bureau office. *You* weren't even aware, were you?"

Brad shook his head and withstood the steady gaze from Garrett's gray eyes.

"Only someone within the top echelons had access to the information—unless someone had a loose mouth. You know how these clandestine things go. You try to keep a lid on it, but someone tells his wife, or girlfriend or grandson, whatever. The fact remains, someone burned our guys and, as a result, they got sliced up. Real nasty. I won't bore you with the details other than to say we're para-noid about this."

"Hell, I can understand that. But tell me…how do you know the bad apple's not in your local office down there?"

"He may be, Brad. That's why *you're* here and not someone from the Bureau. Now, let's go on. You haven't heard the good stuff yet."

"Christ, I can hardly wait."

"About two years ago, something odd happened. We have a pretty large group of Skinheads in our area. They're a pain in the ass, but normally don't commit much major crime—you know, just penny ante stuff. They stand around in their leather boots and jackets and shaved heads and try to act tough. They're mostly a racial hate group, prejudiced against non-whites. That's bad enough, but not high on our priority list of criminal activity."

Garrett waved his hand dramatically. "At any rate, one of these Skins was found in an alley without his head. It probably wouldn't have interested me, but the police found the murder weapon the next day—-a *Samurai* sword."

Brad couldn't stop the cold chill racing along his spine.

"Someone made the Skin kneel with his head on a box. With one stroke, his head was rolling on the ground. Now that's not your nor-mal method of killing someone who perhaps insulted you, right?

"Thank God, it isn't. Guns are about all we run into in Langston. Maybe a few petty-assed knifings. But no, never a *Samurai* sword. Jesus."

"When the Seattle P.D. made the information public, we suddenly took a great deal of interest. We discovered the Skins were muscling in on the *Yakuza's* territory. They threatened people in the Japanese community with violence. You know…the protection racket. It's as old as Sin. Well, you can guess what comes next. The *Yakuza* caught one of these lightweight hoods and decided to make a big spectacle of murdering him. A brutal message to the Skins—stay out of our territory."

Brad realized he was holding his breath again. The details of Garrett's briefing shocked him. The Langston Police Department was not familiar with such levels of brutality. He needed to break the tension. "Jeez, this is getting heavy as hell. Listen, Kelly, I need a walk and a whiz. Can we take a break?"

Both men stood to stretch, then headed down the hallway. When they returned to the office, it surprised Brad to see that it was almost 4:00 and he knew the story was far from over. He removed his coat and threw it over a chair.

"I know I'm cramming a lot of stuff in your head, Brad. I knew this was a two-day ordeal. That's why I made up the story about wanting someone for a seminar. I couldn't just come out and tell your people why I really needed you to come here. The information may have reached the wrong ears. As it is, someone may figure it out anyway."

"Well, I was going to say, let's hope it fooled other people better than it fooled me. I was suspicious right away when Nichols told me I was coming."

"I know the story's pretty hokey, but it was the best I could come up with. When I talked to Nichols, I found out he suspended you because of the thing in the bar. He mentioned he wanted you out of town. It was a break for me. I could just ask for you outright. He didn't seem to notice how eager I was."

"Well maybe, but Nichols is a crafty dude. You know, he's in I.A. and those guys are suspicious of everyone."

Then Garrett tossed out another thunderbolt. A real trumpet blare.

"Are you aware that Chief Preston has a Japanese wife?"

Brad's level of interest climbed another notch. "*Preston's* wife? I had no idea. Never met her. Wouldn't it be ironic if *she* was involved with the *Yakuza* group? How'd you find out about her?"

"We have files at NCIC on every law enforcement officer in the country. I even saw copies of your wedding license. How does that strike you?"

"Your ass. My wedding license? What the hell for?"

"I have no idea why they have it. Don't ask why Big Brother does the things he does. Paranoia I guess. Anyway—-"

Without warning, Brad's temper erupted, spilling out and venting in a violent outburst. "What the hell's going on in this freaking government? Whatever happened to the concept of personal privacy? This really pisses me!" The words exploded from his mouth as his fist slammed down on the desk. The violent nature of his outburst even caught Brad by surprise. Kelly Garrett's demeanor was etched in stone. Only his eyes narrowed as he observed Brad's tirade. It was over in seconds and the red disappeared from Brad's face. His hands returned to rest in his lap.

Kelly Garrett's steady voice was a sharp contrast. "I think maybe you've O.D.'d on information, Brad. Look, it's after 5:30, and I figured it would take two days to cover, so let's knock it off. That approved? I'll take you back to your hotel and pick you up about 9:00 in the A.M. That'll give you time to get some breakfast without having to rush."

Brad realized his outburst had shattered Kelly Garrett's concentration, so he rushed to repair the damage. "Listen, Kelly, I'm sorry for the outburst, but I get awfully sensitive about my personal life. I don't even talk to the departmental shrink about it. We can go on if you like, and I'll try not to get so emotional."

"No, I mean it, Logan; this session's over. We'll have plenty of time tomorrow and you'll be fresher then. Go get yourself some dinner and a bottle of Schnapps, or whatever. We both need a break." Garrett stood up. The session was over.

CHAPTER 4

*K*athleen Logan sat at the breakfast counter with her coffee. A ray of sunlight splashed onto her hair, producing a glowing frame of tousled copper around her face. The sunbeam spotlighted her face, creating a patchwork of light and dark as it filtered through the slats of the window shutter. She was deep in thought.

She pulled her robe tighter across her chest as a sudden chill washed over her body. Last night's argument with Brad troubled her. It was so unlike her, losing her cool at him. She remembered telling her husband she hated him. It wasn't true. She was every bit as much in love now as when they met in high school.

"God, how long ago was it? I'm thirty-seven…well, thirty-eight actually…but who's counting? I was only sixteen when we started dating. Guess what, kids, that was twenty-two years ago. Good Lord, it can't be possible."

Kathleen looked around, making sure she really was alone. She giggled.

"I can't remember ever being so angry with him. Am I losing it? Granted, he's a bonafide insensitive bastard for keeping that stuff from me. But, dammit, his job is eating on him a lot lately. Dealing with such rotten people all the time must be treacherous. Maybe I shouldn't have climbed his butt over it. I know he didn't mean to make me crazy." She shook her head and snorted. "Dammit, Kathleen, your temper is almost as bad as his."

When the phone suddenly sprang to life, it startled her so, she nearly fell off the stool. It was Brad's sister, Joan, checking to be sure she would be all right. She volunteered to come over, while Brad was out of town. Kathleen assured her she was safe. The alarm system was active. A cop patrol went by the house every hour. She hoped her voice sounded confident. She wouldn't hurt Joan's feelings, for all the world, but having to entertain her for two days wasn't on Kathleen's agenda. "Thank you, Joan; I appreciate you thinking about me."

After she hung up the phone, Kathleen felt alone and vulnerable. Since high school, she and Brad were seldom apart, except while he was in college and at the FBI Academy. For twenty-two years he was always nearby—close enough to catch her if she fell. Close enough to protect her and keep her safe.

"Kathleen, you're a big girl now. The boogieman won't get you just because Brad's out of town. You've got things to do, so get off your dead butt and shake a leg."

She unplugged the coffee pot and put her cup in the sink as she left the kitchen and headed up the stairs to the bedroom. She made the bed hours before, but still stooped to brush out one last wrinkle before dropping her robe onto the bedside chair.

She bent at her dresser and removed clean lingerie from the drawer. A cold chill swept across her body again. She instantly straightened and looked around her room.

"Dammit, Kathleen Spencer Logan, you're too old to be getting the heebies. Don't give that macho husband of yours the satisfaction of needing him. Never."

She carried the clothing into the bathroom and laid it on the counter as she continued her self-criticism. She shook her head from side to side.

"Now that's the dumbest thing you've ever said, lady. Of course you need him. Just like he needs you. Isn't that the way it's supposed to be?"

Standing in front of the mirror in her nothingness, she examined herself from head to toe. It was a daily ritual, a type of reaffirmation.

"Not too bad for a middle-aged broad. Body's still firm. Maybe the butt's a little flabby, because I sit too much. Need to get back to walking. Face still passable, isn't it? Almost the same person he always found exciting. So why the big worry?"

She moved closer to the mirror and ran hands over her face, exploring, pinching. She knew it was a pretty face, even without makeup. Still, she worried at herself in the mirror when she noticed the slight drooping under her chin. She patted it with the back of her hand, turning her head one way, then the next.

"Brad always told me my green eyes attracted him first. Grandpa Spencer used to say in his best Irish brogue, 'She's me lass wi' tha emerald eyes.'"

Her eyes traveled down her body.

"Of course, the boobs attracted him, too. He was such a hormonal pimple factory. I remember he told me he loved to see me run the track because my—what did he call them?—*jugs* bounced so great. He never realized I didn't wear a bra under my sweats just so they *would* jiggle. Hell, if you got it flaunt it. Shameless hussy. Worked, didn't it? The poor guy never caught on."

Kathleen giggled, then held her breasts, as if to weigh them. The movement transformed her nipples into hard, pink buttons. With effort, she turned away.

In the shower, as warm water washed over her body, she allowed herself to give in to the luxurious, pulsating water, and relaxed. The feeling lasted until she turned off the water. But, as she toweled off, her mind returned to anxieties about Brad's recent attitude.

By the time she finished dressing in the powder blue pant suit, she had made up her mind. She would call Dr. Fisher and talk to her.

Brad would have a fit when he found out she went to a shrink. But she needed some relief from worry—the worry of their wonderful love affair sinking slowly into the toilet.

To her amazement, Dr. Fisher was in the office and could see Kathleen at 2:00 that afternoon. As soon as she confirmed the appointment and hung up the phone, she regretted it. She would call back and cancel the appointment. Her hand was on the phone when she convinced herself the decision to call was correct.

At 1:45 she sat in the waiting room, fighting off the urge to get out before it was too late. Before she gave in to those thoughts, the receptionist ushered her into the inner sanctum. It was too late now!

"Kathleen, what a pleasure to see you again. Come in and sit. What a stunning pant suit. You have such marvelous taste in clothes. How are you, dear?"

Marilyn Fisher, the on-call psychiatrist for the Langston Police Department, possessed a most glorious smile. It lit up her entire face and gave her a glow of cheerfulness hard to resist. This day, she wore a fashionable two-piece pink suit; a pearl choker circled her pale, white neck. Her shoulder length black hair was generously sprinkled with flecks of gray. The doctor exuded confidence.

Kathleen's anxieties received instant relief. She always experienced the same tranquility in this office. There was something about the ambiance—something made her fears melt just as soon as she was inside. She was back in her mother's womb.

"I'm just fine, Doctor, and probably shouldn't even bother you. But they always say, police wives should express their fears to you at any time. My fears for Brad make me crazy. Last night, I blew up at him because he deceived me. I had no right to bug him about it because it was police business, but I just couldn't hold it in any longer."

The doctor's smile slowly massaged Kathleen's tenseness.

"Of course you had a right to bug him, Kathleen. Even policemen's wives have a right to expect their men to trust them. Tell me what brought this on."

Dr. Fisher leaned back in her chair. Holding a pencil between well-manicured fingers, she gently tapped the eraser against the side of her neck. Her frameless glasses sat on top of her head, pinning the front locks of hair. The smile gradually faded as she listened intently.

Eagerly, Kathleen recounted the events of the past two nights. The fight at Conners' Bar; how Brad relished the confrontation; how he ignored the fright she felt as the episode progressed. Then finding out the fight was a phony.

"Yes. I see, I see. Tell me, dear, is this the first time you've witnessed Brad in an act of physical violence?"

"I guess so. At least while he's been a cop. When we were in high school, he must have gotten into quite a few fights. I witnessed a couple of them. Well, I suppose it was more than a couple. He was on the football team—I guess he loved the physical contact. I remember one game…he was in the clear and could have run right past the last man who could stop him. Instead, he ran right at the guy and knocked him over. I never thought about it before, but that's part of the same thing, isn't it?"

The doctor nodded and dropped her pencil onto the desk. "Yes, it would seem to be part of his particular psyche. That's not the least bit unusual for policemen, my dear. They couldn't do the job very well if they feared physical violence. His type makes a good policeman. They're not fearful of physical pain. The problem with some of them is they enjoy it too much. That's one of the reasons the Police Department hires me. Many other police wives express the same concerns."

Doctor Fisher looked into Kathleen's eyes with a reassuring smile. "Can you tell me anything else about your fears?"

Kathleen recited the incident of the past evening. Brad went outside to talk with a stranger she recognized as one of the men from the bar fight. There was something about the meeting her husband wasn't telling her. It made her believe he didn't trust her. To her knowledge, they never kept secrets from each other. Was that a sign his love was fading?

"My goodness, Kathleen, I don't know any policeman who doesn't have secret contacts in the criminal population. That's part of the secret of good detective work. They all want someone who keeps them in touch with talk on the street. You can't let this kind of thing torture you into thinking you're losing him. I'm surprised it even crossed your mind. In the few times I talked to Brad, it impressed me how much he loves you and relies on you to keep him healthy and happy. You should be very confident in your relationship. I remember how he grieved when you lost your babies. He was crushed."

"Yes, I know. We both were. There's one other thing, Doctor…the same dream keeps coming back to Brad. It's been going on for more than five years. He tells me about it, but then he turns right around and says it means nothing. Did he ever tell you about it?"

Doctor Fisher pulled her glasses down onto her nose. She picked up the folder and thumbed through the documents it contained. "There's no mention in my files. Tell me what you remember about it."

"I have it almost memorized. He's told it so many times. In the dream, he sees himself in an old western town. He's dressed like a cowboy and he's wearing a badge. Some loud mouth cowboy challenges him. Brad walks into the street and moves toward the other guy, just like in the movies. He can't see the guy's face because of the wide brim on his hat. Suddenly, the guy pulls his gun. Brad reaches for his holster and discovers he has no gun! That's where he always wakes up, covered with sweat and sitting bolt upright. It's so scary to see him like that. Do you think Brad has a death wish?" Kathleen's words caught in her throat. She watched the psychiatrist shuffle the papers on her desk, mulling over this new revelation. The face was expressionless, revealing nothing of her inner thoughts.

"That's really quite a movie scene, Kathleen. You say he has this same dream over and over? How often do you suppose it's happened?"

"Gosh, I don't know, Doctor Fisher. It seems quite often as I look back on it, but I can't give you a number. I guess, three or four times in the past year. Maybe more, but I don't know for sure. What does it mean?"

"Kathleen, the interpretation of dreams isn't an exact science, no matter what anyone tells you. If you're worried it's a hidden death wish on Brad's part, I wouldn't give it much credence. Such serious mental turmoil is very hard to diagnose. I think your husband is one of the most stable officers in this department. I've always greatly admired his abilities. I'm sure his dreams have a much subtler meaning. They may be a result of a movie which really impressed him."

She swiveled her chair and gazed out the window. A slight frown crossed her face. "Don't start reading your own fears into Brad's actions. It's not at all unusual for a policeman's wife to have these fears and frustrations. The pressure on you ladies is tremendous. It amazes me the way you all cope. I'm not sure I could handle it nearly as well."

"Wish I felt as confident about it. It helped me just to talk to you about it, Doctor. If you think there's nothing to worry about, I'll accept that. It'll be hard, but I know I can do it. Do you think I should tell him I came here?"

"I'm a firm believer in honesty and trust, Kathleen. You can tell him you came because of your own fears. You needn't tell him your concerns were about him. This conversation is now part of Brad's file, so I can talk to him about it the next time he is scheduled in. That will be in just about a month. Is there anything else you want to talk about?"

Doctor Fisher looked at her watch and made a note of the time on her pad. When she sensed her patient was through talking, she rose and held out her hand. "Kathleen, you must relax as best you can and trust your husband. I'm sure he loves you as strongly as ever. He's kind of a cowboy, you know. Maybe he can't tell you as often as you'd like. Tell you what, when he comes home from Seattle, why not fix a special dinner with candles and the whole shot? Put on something sexy, then seduce him, right there on the living room floor. I promise it'll take him by surprise and should get both your juices perking. Good luck, Dear, and call me any time you need help."

Kathleen felt better as she walked through the huge walnut door and padded across the richness of wool carpet leading out of the lobby. She was certain some of the baggage fell from her shoulders during the hour.

She met her friend Paula at the Outlet shopping mall and spent the next few hours wandering about the shops. Neither bought a thing until they were in a negligee store where they each found something slinky to purchase. They swore they'd model them for their husbands before the week was over. Kathleen vowed to be the first.

After grabbing a quick sandwich at Fosters, the ladies said their good-byes. As she got into her car, Kathleen looked at her watch. It was 6:30.

As she pulled into the garage and pushed the button to close the door, the darkness surrounded her, bringing instant panic. Nervous fingers found the light switch next to the back door and flooded the garage with stress relieving light. Fumbling with the disarming code for the alarm, she successfully managed the combination after two tries.

Inside, the house was well-lit because of the timers Brad had installed on the lights. The brightness of the house eased her tension even more. The panic attack subsided.

Inside the front door, Kathleen picked up the assortment of envelopes and junk mail scattered about the floor. Sorting through the stack as she made her way into the kitchen, she put a kettle of water on. She craved a cup of cappuccino.

She opened the envelopes, finding her water bill, phone bill and a statement from a credit card company.

The next envelope in her hand sent a chill down her spine. The lettering on the front looked like a child had written it with a crayon. The way it was addressed created the chill:

'To Foxy Logan'

There was no address and it lacked postage. The sender must have pushed it through the slot. Kathleen dropped it on the table as if it were on fire. Only one person ever called her that. My God—he was on her front porch some time this very day!

A sense of panic washed over her in waves. There was no escape from the feeling of terror invading her soul. She'd never felt more alone.

Kathleen was so overwhelmed, she didn't hear the whistling of the tea kettle announcing her water was ready. Slumped on the stool, she waited for her hands to stop shaking. Her stomach was an elevator on its way the top floor.

"Oh, Brad, I *need* you…why are you in Seattle? Oh, God."

She wanted to throw the envelope into the trash, but thought better of it. Finally, the screeching tea kettle caught her attention, giving her momentary relief from her fright. She poured hot water into her cup and stirred the powder into a thick, brown liquid, never taking her eyes off the envelope.

Returning to the counter, she sat on a stool and sipped her cappuccino. She picked up the offensive piece of mail and turned it over and over in her hand. It kept getting heavier and heavier, taking on a life of its own.

In a final frenzy, she ripped the 'beast' open. An old-fashioned valentine fell onto the counter top. There was no name signed. Just a big red heart and the printed words, 'Be Mine'. At any other time, those two words would not be so menacing to her. This time, the words tore at her with gnarled fingers, clutching her very heart.

Sipping the hot liquid helped restore a refreshing sense of calmness and replaced her anxiety, but in a sudden flash, her safety net abruptly collapsed. *The burglar alarm rudely pierced the silence with its shrieking horn, tearing an involuntary scream from her mouth!*

CHAPTER 5

$\mathcal{A}$s Brad entered the hotel lobby, his mind raced over the events of the day. There was so much information to sort out. His emotions surged as he reflected on the harsh nature of crimes committed by *Yakuza*. Crimes of violence and acts degrading other humans always produced a violent response in him. Many times, a thirst for revenge was his sole motivation for hunting down criminals with such passion.

Since it was after 7:00 o'clock, he went right into the dining room before going to his room. He ordered a Cordova beer with lime, and eyeballed the other diners as the cool beer infiltrated his body.

Throughout dinner, he agonized for letting his temper get away from him again. During the ride to the hotel, Agent Garrett made no mention of Brad's tantrum, but Brad was sure the man was upset over the outburst. It was common knowledge—his bad temper had caused several glitches in his career path. This case could have international significance. He didn't want to screw up again. His career goal was to become Chief by his 50th birthday.

It was past 8:30 when he finally made his way into the elevator and rode to the third floor. His room was halfway down the hall. He smelled the faint odor of fly spray in the air. This must be fly-hatching season in Seattle.

Once inside, he threw his coat onto the bed, struggled out of his boots, then turned on the television. Propped up by pillows, he stretched out and surfed the channels looking for some news. He found CNN and settled down onto the bed, letting himself relax and unwind from the day's activities.

He shut his eyes for a moment and must have been dozing when the shrillness of the telephone jolted him awake His fumbling fingers found the instrument in the semi darkness. When he answered, a panic-filled voice caught his immediate attention.

"Brad, it's Joan!"

Both feet hit the floor with a thud as he snapped to attention. What the hell was his sister doing on the phone? He looked at his watch. It was 9:30. "Joan, for God's sake, what's going on? Are you all right? Is Kate all right?"

"Brad. Don't get excited. We're both all right. I came over to give Kate a tranquilizer. She got quite a scare. Believe me, she's not hurt or anything, just had the crap scared out of her when your burglar alarm went off. The police were here within minutes and found nothing. If someone was outside, he got scared off. The police called me and I came over to help calm her down. She's sleeping now, poor thing. She'll be mad 'cause I called you, but I figured you should know."

The trip hammer in his chest slowly returned to normal. "Never mind that, Joan. When did this happen?"

"About an hour ago, I guess. Dammit, Brad, I can tell by your voice you're upset. Please believe me, everything's calmed down now and no one's hurt. I'll stay here until you get home. Probably just a malfunction in your alarm system. Don't worry."

"Sis, it's hard not to worry, but if you promise me she's all right, I'll take your word for it. How are you doing, by the way?"

"I'm fine. Just the usual complaints, but you know them all. Lord knows, I tell you often enough. I'll make sure Kathleen gets some rest, Dear. We'll call you in the morning. Don't worry."

"Thanks, Sis, and I'm sure glad you were there for her. Good night." He hung up then lay on the bed until his adrenaline rush subsided. Finally, he got out of his clothes and in half an hour was sleeping soundly. He could sleep without worry because of his trust in his sister. She would never lie to him about Kathleen's safety.

His day began on a bright note. Kathleen called him and sounded none the worse for wear. She reaffirmed that Joan wouldn't go home until he returned. The alarm company was checking on the possibility of a malfunction.

On the ride to Garrett's office, Brad apologized for the previous day's outburst and was assured no hard feelings existed. Garrett seemed quite interested in Brad's athletic career. Their casual conversation continued until they were back in Garrett's office with coffee in hand. " Tell me something, Brad. Did you prefer offense or defense?"

"That's easy—offense. It took a lot more planning to be successful. There's a big thrill in launching a long pass to your wideout as he streaks toward the end zone. But, I have to admit, I also got a lot of satisfaction from banging into a running back when I played defense. I never got tired of the competition. If I hadn't hurt my knee, my career as a cop might never have happened. There were big dreams of playing pro. Did you play?"

Garrett took a sip of coffee. "Oh yeah. Not nearly as well as you, but still enjoyed it. I was always a D-back and know what you mean about crushing a running back. But, you know, I'm sure I got more kicks out of defending against a long pass. It's one-on-one, just like in basketball. Lots of thrills."

"Thrills? Man, you must have a lot of them with the Agency. This kind of job can never get boring. At least not to me." Brad was aware of Garrett's reputation.

"Yeah, I sure can agree with that. Guess we're just a couple of hardcases, right? Okay, that's enough of the glory days. Let's get back to reality here. Next phase of this briefing deals with the White Knights. Ever heard of them?"

"Only by reputation. I suppose you're gonna tell me I've got *them* in my neighborhood, too, aren't you? Are you making this up, or is it all for real?"

"I'm afraid it's for deadly real, Brad. Not only are they in your area, but they're becoming a serious threat. The competition between them is heating up in your town. My sources tell me the Knights spend a lot of time and energy in the Japanese community. They're intimidating those people into dealing with *them* instead of *Yakuza*."

Brad poured himself another cup of coffee and passed the pot to Garrett who poured another cup as he continued his briefing. "Mostly they're into extortion, protection—anything that takes muscle and no brain. Near as we can tell, they aren't into the drug trade or running girls. Anyway, it's turning into a deadly turf war. Crooks against crooks. Too bad we can't just let them kill each other."

"Kelly, something really bugs me about all this. Why isn't it widespread knowledge, you know, like other gang warfare? I mean, here I'm in the business of fighting crime and I don't have a clue this crap is going on right under my nose. Is it a military secret?"

Kelly Garrett shook his head. "Not at all. The Bureau isn't hiding anything, but both groups are very secretive. They avoid publicity. They keep to themselves, stay in their own territory and take care of their own. They have strict codes of behavior within their ranks."

Agent Garrett looked pensive as he continued his narrative. "It's the violence between the groups that's becoming a great concern. As far as your own P.D. is concerned, I know for a fact your brass knows about it. I send them bulletins all the time. I guess they don't think it's important enough. That's a mystery, too."

"Okay, Kelly, are you saying there's a cover-up in Langston PD?"

"I'd bet a bundle on it. We're certain the Langston Police Department, and probably our own office, harbors a group of hard core White Knights in its ranks. They may even be the gang leaders. They don't want the gravy train to end, so they keep it quiet. Maybe some of the other cops just sympathize with the Knights' racist views. At any rate, our top priority now is smoking out those dirty badges. Nobody's safe 'till we do."

"That's a big assignment, Kelly. Why me? What makes you think I can do it?"

"Your reputation as the 'Junkyard Dog' sets you apart from a lot of the others. We checked you out as best we can, but I'm still taking a great chance on trusting you. Right now, I want you to stand up and take off your shirt."

Brad didn't know whether to laugh or blow his stack. "*Say what?* You yanking my chain? You really *serious*?"

"If you're clean, you've got nothing to worry about, Brad. Just take your shirt off and turn around. Don't give me any trouble about this, or our conversation is over."

Kelly Garrett's eyes turned to flint. Brad realized this man was not to be denied, so he did as he was ordered. He stood up and grudgingly unbuttoned his shirt, pulled the tails from his pants and lowered the shirt into his chair, then turned his back to the agent.

"That's a relief, Sergeant. There's no tattoo on your shoulder. I'm sorry to make you do it, but, for everyone's safety, I had to be sure. That's the only way you can tell if a man is in the White Knights. He'll have a tattoo of a white chess piece—-you know, the knight—on the back side of his right shoulder. It's part of the initiation into the club. Keep that in mind as you deal with them. That's it, Brad, you can get dressed again."

Brad stood as he rebuttoned his shirt and tucked it into his pants. He knew Garrett had no choice. He'd have done the same thing, if the roles were reversed. Probably not so delicately.

"Brad, I hate to keep beating the same horse, but I can't warn you enough how much danger you'll be in if you take on this job for us. You won't be able to trust any of your fellow cops and that's a lonely feeling, I can tell you. Pretty soon, you'll be suspicious of everyone around you. You'll look over your shoulder every time you work with another cop. How do you get along with your partner, Sam Hardy?"

"Trust him with my life. He's the best cop I know. Of all the people on the force, Sam's the least likely to be dirty. Don't worry, I'm not in bed with anyone on the force."

"I have no reason to suspect Hardy, but just remember what I told you. Don't trust *anyone*. Your *life* will depend on it. You ready for some lunch?"

Brad nodded. "Yeah, for sure. Think I could eat half of Seattle's crab population."

"Oh, you're a crab eater? Sorry they don't serve it here in the commissary. Wish we could accommodate you. You settle for tuna salad?"

The two men took the elevator to the commissary. The food was ample in quantity, but reminded Brad of hospital fare. One word described Brad's meatloaf plate: 'bland'.

Their conversation focused on items of a personal nature. Brad discovered that Agent Garrett had started with the Bureau while Brad was still in school. His wife, June, was a pari-legal in a large legal firm in Seattle. Their two boys were in college. Their daughter, Cheryl, was a senior in high school. Brad couldn't help thinking how disgustingly normal and well adjusted the whole family sounded. He found himself a great admirer of the man's calm, determined and self-confident persona.

On the ride back up to the office, Brad made a mental note to add the name of Kelly Garrett to his annual Christmas card list. After two days of meetings with this man, Brad finally recognized Garrett as someone he trusted, but it still bugged him that the FBI man was holding something back. What was the real reason he was called to Seattle?

As soon as they returned to the office, Garrett spoke into his intercom. "*Tanaka-san. Dozo o-hairi kudasai.*"

The FBI man grinned as he saw the stunned look on Brad's face. "There's someone I want you to meet. It's part of this 'seminar'. We recruited Tanaka-san right out of the University of Washington. I picked up a little of the language during the training sessions over the last six months."

Garrett stood up as the door opened. Brad jumped to his feet when he caught sight of the new arrival. She didn't walk, she floated into the room. He mentally transported her to Tahiti, complete with sarong and gyrating hips. It was an exotic fantasy.

The Oriental woman's face was exquisite. Almond eyes, light brown skin and lush red lips framed a delightful smile. A smile of coy shyness. Perhaps her most striking feature was a cascade of lustrous, jet-black hair tumbling past her shoulders, almost to her waist. The top of her head barely reached Brad's chin.

Awkwardly, Brad held out his hand. Expecting one of those namby-pamby-little-girl-squishy hand shakes, he was surprised by the strength of the red tipped fingers which disappeared into his palm. It was sensual, and lingered much longer than he expected. The hand embrace accompanied a bold and direct gaze. It occurred to Brad his mouth was hanging open. He wondered if he was drooling.

"It is great pleasure to make your acquaintance, Logan-san." Her voice was melodic and child-like. Brad struggled to regain his composure.

"Likewise, Mrs. Tanaka. I—I—I was not expecting a—-"

"Please, my name Sumiko, or Sumi. And is not Mrs."

Why did he find that such a relief?

Agent Garrett pulled another chair up to the desk and held it while Sumiko gracefully sat, smoothing her knee length skirt as she settled into the chair. The light coral silk scarf at her neck enriched the rust color of her expensive looking dress. She wore no jewelry. Brad tried not to stare.

The FBI man smiled as he saw Brad's uncertainty. "Sorry, Brad. Didn't realize you expected a man. You've got to admit, she's a lot kinder on the eyes than any guy."

"'Surprise' doesn't quite express it. Guess that serves me right for jumping to conclusions. You told me you recruited someone from college. I just assumed…"

"I'll tell you something, Brad. We recruited this young lady at the University. She has an MBA in International Marketing. She's fluent in four languages. She was born in Osaka, but came to this country when she was in high school. Go ahead, Brad. Sit down and relax, I don't think she bites."

"Sorry. Didn't realize I was still afoot. Jeez, I can't remember getting so flustered meeting someone. I'm embarrassed."

"Sorry if I embarrass you, Logan-san. I am surprised. You think your wife maybe get jealous?" Brown eyes flashed as a full-face grin took over the room.

At that point, Brad looked to Kelly Garrett to rescue him from his own social ineptness. He knew he was drowning in his embarrassment and needed a lifesaver.

"Okay, you two, let's get this meeting back on track. There is much to do and time's running out. When does your plane leave tomorrow?" He looked at Brad.

"It leaves at ten, but I should be there an hour before. Are you meeting me at the plane?"

"*We* are meeting you at the plane. *Sumiko's returning to Langston with you.* She has obtained a high level job in the Marketing Department for the Kurasawa Electronics Corp. in Langston. She obtained the job by legitimate application. The Bureau pulled no strings, so her job should create no suspicions to anyone who may be watching.

You're going to be her contact. We don't trust anyone else to work with her. Think you can handle that?"

Brad bristled. "Wait a minute, Kelly. Number one; you're assuming I'll agree to do this job. Number two; how can you put this little girl who's no bigger than a penny, into such a dangerous job?"

The 'penny-sized little girl' roared to life. "Pardon me, Logan-san, you think 'cause you big shot policeman you can speak for me? I train long time for this job. I can do it better than anyone. You be careful—maybe I knock you on your butt. I can take care of Sumiko. You better believe." Her voice sounded serious, but her eyes twinkled with the devil's delight.

Brad got his second surprise of the afternoon. This tiny little bit of fluff showed the heart of an Amazon. His Neanderthal attitude had tripped him up again. His afternoon was not going well. "Hey, no offense meant, Miss Tanaka. The FBI is putting you in lots of danger; are you aware of that? Kelly, how come you keep getting me in trouble?"

"Hey, man, you do a terrific job of that by yourself. Don't blame me for your own shortcomings. Stop being such a chauvinist. Now, you have ten seconds to give me a yes or no about your part in this. I won't discuss our strategy until I know you're coming aboard. What's it gonna be?"

"Man, you don't give me much wiggling room do you? Okay, suppose I agree to be your fall guy. What's the game plan and where do I fit in? Why me instead of a Fed? Where does this young lady fit in and is she going to have backup, in case she gets worked into a corner?"

"Wow! So many questions from one who just came aboard. We don't trust everyone in the local office, so can't take a chance. We have a mole buried so deep into the White Knights we'll probably never get him out. Now we have a good chance of getting a mole into the *Yakuza*. That's where we begin. You and Sumiko will work together without benefit of local backup. It's dangerous, but necessary for security purposes. The local office will think she's in the Federal witness program. That's all they'll know about her."

Brad focused on the words of Kelly Garrett. It took his mind off his embarrassment.

"Your job is to find out which of your cops is dirty and keep them from burning any more of our people. You'll also be Sumi's watchdog. She'll report directly to you. You'll have to find a way of explaining your relationship. Can you work that around without your wife kicking you out?"

Brad just sat there without saying a word. He and Kathleen's relationship never suffered from jealousy on either side. He was sure it would be a workable situation. "I have no idea, Kelly. It's never been a problem before, but if Kathleen gets the idea I'm fooling around, she's likely to take my head off. She has red hair and an Irish temper. No telling how she'll react…but, I'm sure it won't create big problems."

Sumiko broke in, "No need to worry, Logan-san. I'm no *pan-pan* girl. I don't give your lady any worry. Besides, I maybe don't like you anyway, okay?"

That broke up the two men. Kelly actually got tears in his eyes. As he used his handkerchief to blot his eyes, he looked at Brad and began to laugh again. It took him several minutes to regain his composure.

"She puts it all right out front, doesn't she, Brad? Just the way you like it. Right? Now, let's get serious and see what kind of a system of controls we can work out."

For the rest of the afternoon and until the sun settled into the Pacific Ocean, the three of them discussed the dangers, the need for secrecy, emergency contingencies, a safe withdrawal plan and what fall-back procedures would be installed.

Sumiko was very helpful in talking about the cultural relationship between the *Yakuza* and the citizens of Japan. For centuries, the citizens accepted the gangs as part of their society. She made no bones about that. "Maybe like Robin Hood in England. You know?"

She explained how the group made no attempt to hide from the public in Japan. They even opened offices in all major towns and advertised openly. Part of the *gumi* was involved heavily in gambling, the others were described as merchants. They would set up roadside stands to sell their wares, usually inferior quality with unreasonable prices. Their stands would be quite noticeable during local carnivals and fairs. They paid *Yakuza* for prime location. In turn, the *Yakuza* gave them protection.

In recent years, a new, more dangerous, brand of gangster was emerging in the *Yakuza*. A group of young street toughs, known as *bosozuki*. They patterned themselves after American biker gangs. They became the enforcers. The strong arms.

"The *bosozuki* are very dangerous. They're not disciplined like older *Yakuza* and they don't respect the elders. They must be feared."

"Is there anything about the gang members to make them identifiable?" Brad asked Kelly.

"Most of the older members have body tattoos, but newer ones may just have a band of color around their arms. It used to be a custom to cut off the end of a finger to show how dedicated you were. That is no longer common. But here's the kicker—these gang members usually wear a lapel pin, showing what group they're in. Kinda like the Lions or the Rotary Clubs. Isn't that arrogant?"

"Are these groups all tied together under one umbrella?"

"Not really. You know, like the various Mafia families, you have many *gumis* who work separately. They don't work each other's territory. They do have strict codes."

Finally, at 7:30, Kelly dropped Brad off at his hotel. They would meet at the airport at 9:00 in the morning. It was a tired trio who said their 'good nights'.

Brad grabbed a quick dinner and was in his room by 9:00. As promised, he put in a call to Kathleen. There was no answer at his home. He tried again in ten minutes and then tried to call his sister's home. There was no answer. "Damn it, Kate, where in the hell are you?"

Twice more, his effort to reach his home number met with frustration. Just as he reached for the phone to call the Langston PD, it jangled to life. Relief drained his whole body as he heard Kathleen's voice.

"My God, Kate. What's going on? Are you all right? Where've you been? Talk to me, Honey."

He could tell she was upset. Her voice was quivering, her breathing tortured.

"Darling. We're all right, but...but we've been through a scary time. I won't bore you with all the particulars, but the police evacuated us. They just now allowed us back into the house. I know you've been worried, but we couldn't call."

"Kate, what are you talking about? Why were you evacuated?"

"Honey, they found a dead body in our back yard."

CHAPTER 6

They met in the airport lobby at 9:00 the next morning, and, to Brad's great relief, the sky above was brilliant blue. There was no sign of storm clouds in any direction. The twinge of anxiety he felt before a plane trip was diminished for some reason. It was a good sign. Garrett and Sumiko entered the terminal looking every inch like a couple heading out on a safari. The F.B.I. man struggled under the burden of numerous bags. His excuse was that all the porters were busy when they drove up. Brad accused him of trying to impress Sumiko.

Brad's soon-to-be traveling companion looked fresh and excited. She wore a tailored red pantsuit and spike-heeled black boots. Her hair was fashioned into a single thick braid that swirled down her back between her shoulder blades. Her obvious poise turned heads as she made her way to the ticket counter. A pair of exotic sunglasses, shoved back onto her forehead, gave the impression she might be a Hollywood personality.

After checking in with the airlines, the trio went to the coffee shop and made small talk as they scoped out their fellow travelers. Their surveillance included anyone who came within shouting distance of Sumi, or even looked her way.

Brad told them about Kathleen's frightening experience during his absence. When he had talked directly to Sam, he received a brutal shock. Sam told him the dead man found in the Logan's back yard was Mooch Kaiser! Brad's plan for an undercover man on the street had evaporated before it began. It made him furious.

When Kelly Garrett heard what happened in Langston, he told Brad they must assume the killing was a warning. This meant even tighter security and more caution—for all of them. As they said their good-byes, Kelly warned them to be especially careful during the flight and at the Langston airport. He ordered Brad to send Sumiko back to Seattle immediately if he sensed any threat to her.

Flight 89 left Seattle right on time. They taxied down the runway at 10:20. As the plane began to move, Brad made up his mind there would be no white knuckle approach to the takeoff on this day. He let Sumi sit at the window seat, both as a protective measure, but also because he didn't care to look down during the flight.

As their plane pierced the clear, turquoise sky, the blue stretched to the horizon with hardly a cloud in sight. Brad's mind turned cartwheels. 'Hey, maybe this would be a smooth flight for a change'.

Once the seat belt sign was turned off, he unbuckled and moved the back of his seat to a more comfortable position. The 'Out West' magazine he brought aboard was rolled and tucked into the seat beside him. He made a cursory eyeball scan of the cabin to see if anyone was watching them. To his relief, no one caught his eye. He didn't relish the thought of doing battle aboard a highflying airplane. He had told the flight attendant as he boarded that he was a policeman and was armed. It was the law.

"Hey, Logan-san, look down here. You wanna see Puget Sound? It looks beautiful from here. Maybe you wanna look?"

Sumi motioned out her window and leaned back so Brad could stretch across her to look downward. The sight of shimmering blue water against the contrasting landmasses was truly breathtaking. He picked out the Seattle-Tacoma waterfront and the lines of major freeways running south. The few wispy clouds below them created a 3D image he couldn't remember from previous flights. He seldom looked down from an airline window, having some problem with vertigo. This time, he suffered no such ill effects.

The subtle fragrance of Sumiko's perfume suddenly filled his senses. He couldn't pull away from her magnetism. His body temperature climbed several degrees as he brushed against her arm. When their bare skin made contact, it sent a charge racing up his arm. It startled him, but he didn't draw back. He continued staring out the window, seeing nothing, but knowing he didn't dare look at her.

When the incendiary moment passed, they eased the tension during the remaining flight with small talk. The electricity wasn't totally removed until the pilot announced the start of their final descent. It was both a welcomed relief and a disappointment to know their first adventure was coming to an end.

During the flight, Brad discovered how tenaciously Sumiko clung to the culture and tradition of her family. Her parents came to America while she was in high school. Her father was a successful merchant in Japan. Now he owned several stores in Seattle. She told him her family spoke Japanese exclusively at home, even though both her parents spoke English. In the work place, she always spoke English, but purposely allowed Japanese phrases and pidgin English to creep into her conversation to be true to her heritage. It was clear to Brad; honor was the foremost ingredient of Sumi's character.

"When I go to University, I learn to speak four Asian languages to help my career in International Marketing. I want to work for large company with ties to Japan. Maybe then I can go visit sometimes. I have cousins in Japan. When F.B.I. contact me, they promise I get job where I can use my education. They train me for this job for a year. Pretty soon, I work for Kurasawa Electronics. Then maybe I stop *Yakuza* from hurting my people. You think so, Logan-san?" Her voice took on a decided hard edge as she spoke about her ambitions.

Brad assured her she could do anything she set her mind to, but she must work with him and not be careless about the danger she was in. He made her promise to be watchful.

They grew silent as the ground rose to meet them. Finally, the screech of rubber on tarmac told Brad he was home. It was a relief to be 'grounded' again. Right now, embracing his wife was foremost on his mind. Kathleen needed his assurance she was safe.

He spotted her right away, waiting at the gate with a hand shielding her eyes. Kathleen always attracted attention in a crowd. The fiery crown of hair fluttered gently in the air currents. Brad never tired of the visual pleasure she brought and his pride when they walked together in public. Now, she wore a flowery brown dress which whipped around her legs in the airport breeze. She caught sight of him and waved enthusiastically.

Brad forgot about Sumiko as he hurried to meet his wife. He dropped his bag and opened his arms to her. Kathleen launched herself into his arms. All the tension of the past two days escaped as she cried against his chest.

As Brad stroked his wife's hair, he remembered Sumiko, standing silently beside them, looking uncomfortable. He managed to pry Kathleen off him and stepped back.

"Kate, this is Sumiko Tanaka. Sumi, this is my wife Kate."

"Sumiko? Is that right? I'm embarrassed I'm so emotional in public. It's just been a rotten two days. So glad to meet you. Brad told me you were coming with him, but didn't tell me you were so pretty."

Kathleen held out her hand. The look aimed at Brad was full of questions. Sumiko made a slight bow before she took Kathleen's hand.

"Is very nice to meet you, Kathleen-san. Logan-san tell me all about wife with red hair. You're so beautiful. You must be good person to have such good husband. He keep me safe."

Brad grinned at his wife and put his arm around the waist of both women.

"Katie. You gonna let me keep her?"

"I don't know, Brad. Is she house broken?"

The brief exchange between them sailed right over Sumiko's head. She made no sign that she understood. For the Logans, it relieved the tension of introductions. They both had a good laugh. Brad picked up his suitcase and headed to the terminal.

"Come on, Sumi, let's get your bags. Katie, where did you park?"

"Right at the curb. Probably got a ticket by now, but no sweat...I know someone who fixes tickets."

Kathleen led the way into the terminal and up to the baggage rack, where they waited for Sumiko's luggage. It took fifteen minutes for the bags to arrive. During that time, Brad noticed Kate and Sumiko chattering constantly. His wife was succumbing to the wide-eyed naiveté of the young lady from Japan. He wondered how Kate would react if she knew Sumi was a Federal agent about to take on a very dangerous assignment.

"Sumi, do you have hotel reservations yet? We can help you find one if you want. The town is really growing, so we have some good choices."

"Thank you, but my room is reserved. You can take me to hotel called Commodore? Maybe you have lunch with me before you go home? I don't feel so lonesome then. Okay?"

"Sure, Sumiko, we can do that. There's a nice dining room right in your hotel."

During their lunch, Brad was amazed at the bonding taking place between the two women. He could hardly squeeze in a word the entire time. He could see this young woman fascinated Kathleen and it was obvious Sumiko enjoyed visiting with "Logan-san's red haired lady." The diversion also acted as a relief for some of the trauma Kathleen had experienced in the past two days. Brad was delighted to see her relaxing.

Brad observed Sumi's incredible self-confidence. She never gave the slightest indication she was concerned about the danger she was in. The two women laughed and made jokes about Brad being a cowboy. Sumi said he was like a *Samurai*, except he didn't have a braided pony tail. Kathleen told Sumiko she couldn't imagine seeing Brad in a kimono. Not with his hairy legs. An embarrassed smile crossed Sumi's face at the mention of something so intimate. Brad wondered if she was picturing him in a kimono.

"Maybe I have *Mama-san* make you both nice kimono. She make them all the time for my family. Would you like that?"

"That's very thoughtful of you, Sumi, but, my gosh, you don't have to do that for us. Your mama probably has lots of other things to do."

"I want to do it. You are nice new friends. *Mama-san* she like you."

"If you think she wants to, we would be very pleased to accept a kimono."

"You make me very happy. We can be *ichi-ban tomodachi*. Okay?"

"What's that, Sumiko?" Kate wanted to be sure she understood the reference.

"That means 'best friends'. That would make me happy."

"Of course, Sumi. I like that idea. Is that okay with you, Brad?"

Brad nodded. "Sure. I like it, too. But how do you say it? *To-mo-da*—what?"

"*To-mo-da-chi*," she stressed each syllable. "Logan-san. Maybe I teach you some Japanese, you think?"

"Yeah, that's great, Sumiko, but not right now. I'm afraid we need to go home and get our act together. Now, listen, you have our phone number and, as long as you're in town, you're always welcome in our house. You call me anytime you want to talk—and take care of yourself, will you promise us that?"

"I promise, and I call you when I can."

As they said good-bye, Sumiko surprised Brad when she stood on her tip toes and kissed him on the cheek. Then she hugged Kathleen, turned her back and walked to the hotel desk without a glance back.

Suddenly, Brad felt he was losing a member of his family. This tiny young woman from a different culture had made a profound impression on him. He fought off the feelings of pending danger as he watched her walk away. She was now a valuable asset.

Kathleen stared after their new friend. "She's such a little doll, Darling. Why didn't you tell me you were going to bring a woman back with you? Especially one so gorgeous. From what you told me on the phone, I expected a doddering old man with chin whiskers. You say she's in the Federal witness program? I think I'm jealous. She really likes you."

"I was afraid to describe her to you last night. Figured you might be waiting for me with a shotgun. No reason for you to be jealous, since she told me she doesn't even like me. Now, tell me about your adventures while I was gone. I was really scared when Joan first called me."

Kathleen wasn't too anxious to recall the details of her last two days, but, once she began, the words kept flowing out as if the dam had burst. "Brad, I'm really ashamed I didn't handle it better. It's just—God—I haven't been alone very often since we got married. Everything got worse as time went on. I must've had a panic attack when that alarm went off. Finally, when they found the body in the back yard, I just lost it. I had no idea I was so unstable. I know I scared you and I'm sorry."

Brad let her unload as he drove home. It was the first time she told him the part about getting the valentine. He knew right away Judd Worley was getting even. He also knew he owed Judd Worley a suitable response.

"I'm going to stop this guy, Kate, I promise. If I have to blow his head off, he's going to pay for your panic. No one's ever pissed me off like he does. *Nobody*. Trouble is, he knows he can stir me up and gets great delight from it. Soon as I get back on duty I'm gonna see if there are any warrants out for him. I'll find some way to make his life miserable."

"Brad, dammit, don't you see what's going on? He's pulling your chain just to get you upset. Neither one of you is willing to bury the past. Someone's gonna really get hurt if you don't call off your feud. Please, honey, stop it. The man scares the crap out of me and I hope to never hear his name mentioned again. Please?"

As they pulled into the driveway, Brad noticed a patrol car parked across the street from his house. He waved at the officer behind the wheel. It was Gorman Reed, one of the new rookies. The man didn't acknowledge Brad's wave.

When he got out of the car, Brad noticed that the black and white car was no longer parked out front. That surprised him.

As soon as they were inside the house, Kathleen asked if he wanted a cup of cappuccino. When he told her it sounded great, she filled the tea kettle with water and set it on the stove.

"You know, Sweetheart, I was frightened so badly the other night, I decided you could never leave me alone again. Now I'm not afraid any more. Thank you for that."

Kathleen stepped into Brad's arms and crushed herself against him, burying her head against his chest. Once again, the tears streamed, soaking the front of his shirt in seconds. Her body convulsed as each sob overwhelmed her. He held her tightly, sensing she was near panic as the trauma revisited her. When she raised her tear-stained face to look into his eyes, he saw a little girl terrified of the dark. Her smudged mascara turned her face into a clown's mask. A frightened clown. Suddenly, Brad couldn't resist kissing those quivering red lips.

Brad's tender intentions triggered a wholly unexpected response from Kathleen. With a moan, she crushed his mouth with her own eager lips, knocking him back against the counter. Their teeth clicked together as he responded to the fire bursting from her body. Her darting tongue sought his as she ground her body into him, breast to breast, thigh to thigh.

"God, Katie, what brought this on? Do you want to go upstairs?"

"Just shut up, Brad, I want you right here and right now. Only having you inside me will give me back my courage. Don't deny me this, Darling. Don't spoil it by asking questions. Just enjoy me. Make me happy. Please, Darling, I love you."

He had never made love to Kathleen on the kitchen floor. Now they gave in to the heat of the moment. With fingers made useless by their urgency, they pulled aside any clothing which hindered them. The aroused passion and excitement rushed them to levels not experienced during their recent love-making. In a spontaneous explosion of feeling, two loving people merged into one body. Not even the cold, unyielding floor could hinder them.

They were so intent on cresting the final wave, they were oblivious to the shrill whistle of the tea kettle as it impatiently announced it was ready. Somehow, its impatient voice seemed insignificant. They lay in each others arms, basking in the receding wave of feelings.

"Oh, Brad, Darling, *thank* you. I needed that. In just that way. I can't remember ever letting go like that before. I can only tell you it was glorious. I love you so much. Oh, God, look at the mess you made on the floor, you horny old toad. Can you reach the towel?"

"*Me,* horny? Why you uninhibited tart. Do you think you can waggle your sweet little behind at me and get me on the floor any time you want? Well, I've got news for you, lady. I have my scruples. I'm not just some cheap thrill, you know. You—you—mmmmm, you'd better be careful. Moving like that will get you in trouble…Kate…why you devil. Wait…first, you better tend to that kettle before it goes dry. I'd hate to have the fire department find us like this. They might spray us to get us apart."

"Wouldn't that be a hoot? Now, hand me that towel so I can go turn the kettle off. Sure hope the neighbors don't take this moment to look in the window."

Kathleen kissed him gently as she released him. Gingerly, she got to her feet, feeling the results of the hard floor now as she moved to the stove. Brad had to fight back his laughter at the sight of his half-dressed wife standing at the stove. She was still wearing one shoe, but her panty hose were draped around her ankles, creating a set of nylon leg shackles.

"I wish I had a video camera. You're a sight!"

"You've got a lot of nerve, laying there with your pants down around your knees. Just don't make fun of me. You still want some cappuccino?"

"I'm still so warm I think I'll settle for the cold beer, if it's all the same to you. You know, maybe I should go out of town more often. That was one dynamite welcome home, Katie."

"Thank you, kind sir. Leave the money on the counter. Honey, you know, we can have that same experience any time. Sometimes you just forget how it can be. Maybe now you'll remember. Here's your beer. You planning to stay there on the floor or what?"

Brad got to his feet and straightened his clothes. He was still stunned by the ardor with which Kathleen responded to his kiss. He only meant to console her. Brad made a note to remember this technique for future reference. Maybe they could restore their sexual pleasure to the quality of past years.

"Did you check to see if there was any mail?"

"No, I didn't have a chance. Something important came up. Why don't you check it while I go upstairs and change my clothes?"

Kathleen kissed him on her way to the stairs. He watched her disappear down the hallway carrying her shoes, her panty hose draped across her shoulder.

A pile of assorted envelopes and pieces of obvious junk mail cluttered the floor beneath the mail slot. He stooped to retrieve it, carried it back into the kitchen and dumped it on the counter.

One envelope stood out from the rest as he sorted through them. The words 'Foxy Logan' written in a childlike script with a red crayon, leaped out at him. He felt instant fury. "Goddam you, Judd Worley! That does it. You're going down, you bastard."

CHAPTER 7

*B*rad drummed his fingers on the counter top as he waited for Sam Hardy to answer his phone. It was a cinch Sam wouldn't help him if he came right out and asked. Sam Hardy was no dummy. This would take finesse. Brad strategized as he waited.

"Hey, partner, what's up? Hope you didn't discover you can do without me."

"Well, well, if it's not my used-to-be partner. You have a good trip?"

"Glad it's over. Might have been a waste of time, but it's not up to me, is it? Clue you in about it later. Listen, man, I appreciate what you did for Kate and Joan. They were both near hysterics before the evening was over. Has anything happened I should know about?"

"Tell you what…this whole station is jumpin' since that night. As for Mooch, the poor slob never had a chance. He caught one round behind his left ear at point blank range. The 9MM blew the side off his head. It sure didn't happen at your place, okay? There was no mess around him. They dumped him in your back alley. Musta been damn sturdy guys. Mooch weighed over three hundred pounds."

"Closer to four hundred, I think. Had to be at least three sturdy guys."

"Mooch's knuckles were raw and there were contusions to the head. Musta put up a helluva fight. Whoever did it will have marks on him, know what I'm sayin'? My guess is, two or three persons cornered him; probably cold-cocked him so they could blow a hole in his head. Poor guy was dead several hours before they dumped him. Not much blood at the scene, but there's gotta be a spot someplace in town covered with blood and brains. Lab's still doing the post mort."

Brad heard Sam turn pages in the leather bound note pad he worked from. "Anything else show up at the scene?"

"Neighbors heard nothing. The guy on the south side—what's his name?—Harris, says his dog barked for a few minutes, but it shut up when he yelled at it. I make that about 10:15. He looks out the window and sees a body lying in the alleyway. Sees nothin' else, okay? Dials 9-1-1 and two cars are on scene inside of two minutes. They secure the scene soon as they see the body and confirm the guy's dead. We have guys crawling all over the area most of the night. The place is damn near sterile, okay? Not even a stray hair. But—oh yeah—we found a matchbook cover lying under the body. Do you know if Mooch smoked?"

" No, Mooch didn't smoke. The matchbook have a name on it?"

"Yeah. Lemme see…you know the Frontier Grill?"

The name brought instant identification to Brad. It was a small restaurant on Second Street. The Frontier was a favorite hangout for members of the Langston Police Department and other law enforcement agencies.

"You know if Mooch hung out there?"

"I doubt it, Sam; the guy had no buddies on the force—that's why I picked him."

"Christ, partner. That leaves just one answer. Someone knew Mooch was a plant. They dropped the poor guy on your doorstep for one reason…"

"Yeah, someone's sending me a message. Sam, did you tell anyone about Mooch?"

"Just Nichols from I.A. When he asked me about your fight with Worley, I told him the real reason you went to Conner's. I'm sorry, pal, but you shouldn't get a bad rap for this, okay? You don't think Nichols told someone, do you?"

"Dammit, Sam, I hoped we could protect Mooch as long as possible. Somebody found out—someone set Mooch up for a hit. Sam, you've got to be careful who you talk to. Someone's got a big mouth—besides you, I mean."

"Hey, don't lay that crap on me. I saved your ass. Nichols was hot on your trail. Do you think someone fingered Mooch on purpose?"

Like a lightning flash, the information from Kelly Garrett emerged into clear focus. All the bizarre events of the past two days screamed of conspiracy. Someone was dealing a lethal deck of cards, and so far, he and Sam were getting all the bad cards. "Listen, Sam, we can't take any chances. Keep the matchbook to yourself. Don't let anyone know about it. One of the shooters must've dropped it. Hand-carry it over to Mark Goddard in Forensics. Tell him no one else gets any information about this. He's to report results to you or me, no one else."

"You got it, partner. When you comin' back to work?"

"Got no idea, man. You heard anything?"

"It's pretty hush-hush. Guess the Chief talked to Judd's attorney. The guy admits he doesn't have much of a case against you, but says his client is demanding he file suit. Guess Nichols talked to people in the bar and his boys are still nosing around."

"That reminds me, Sam…when we pulled up to the house today, there was a black and white patrol car out front. Gorman Reed was at the wheel. As soon as I pulled into the drive, he took off. Didn't even wave at us. Is he working for Nichols now?"

"Reed? Hell no, man, he's just a rookie, okay? Don't have the slightest idea why he'd be at your house. It's not on his beat, far as I know. That's weird. Want me to check around? Sounds like something's got you disturbed."

An overwhelming sense of foreboding gnawed at Brad's stomach when he heard Sam's response. What the hell was *that* cop doing on *his* street?

"Yeah, check around, Sam, but keep it quiet. Something's got my hackles up, that's for sure. Just can't put a handle on it. Listen, I need a big favor, old buddy. Kathleen got a couple scary pieces of mail the last two days."

"I heard about it. Know who sent them?"

"Sure, I can guess who sent them, and I'm gonna nail him. Look, I need to get into Worley's apartment. I'd like you to run a computer check on him. I bet good ole Judd has tickets outstanding—much as he drives his cab around. If he's even been cited for spitting on the street I want him yanked in."

"You kidding?"

"No, damn it. I'm altogether serious. When you locate him, call me so I can get over to his place. It'll take me about a half hour to get there. You've gotta keep him under wraps long enough for me to look around. I'm sure he's the one harassing Kate because he thinks I'm closing in on him. God, I just wish I was. At any rate, I wanna get into his place to see what I can see. You with me?"

"Wait a minute, Brad, you're on suspension already, okay? You're just asking for more trouble if you break into his place without a warrant. It's too risky, pal."

"I don't need to break in, partner. The landlord owes me some favors. If he lets me in and stands there and watches me, it'll be safe. Besides, Kate's gonna go crazy if I don't put a bag on that weasel. It wouldn't surprise me if he set off the burglar alarm the other night. The envelope was delivered in person. That means the guy was at our house sometime while I was gone. Now, don't squirrel out of this, Sam, I need your help."

He heard Sam let out a big breath before he answered. "Listen, numb nuts, I want to nail Worley as much as you. But you're gonna get your ass in a sling if you're not careful, you know? Tell you what…I'll run 'Wants and Warrants' tomorrow. If we get lucky, I'll get some uniforms out there to locate him. If there's enough cause, we'll run him in. That should hold him a couple hours, okay? I'll call you either way. But you be careful, pal, I'm too old to break in another new partner."

"I owe you big time, Sam. Talk to you tomorrow. And listen, we've got to be very careful from now on. Watch who you talk to. There's a damn snitch in the department. Oh yeah, and if anyone turns up at work with a face full of fist marks—probably be great, big ones—make a note of it. Bye."

Brad hung up the phone. He didn't realize Kathleen was standing behind him. Her expression told him she overheard at least some of his conversation.

"What are you doing, Brad? Dammit, you promised this feud was over. Why must you keep rubbing more crap in his face?"

Brad said nothing; he just picked up the valentine from the mail and handed it to Kathleen without a word. She wouldn't even touch it. She just looked at him with a pained expression.

"This was in today's mail, Kate. Someone dropped it into the mail slot. I called Sam. I asked him to see if Judd has any warrants outstanding—anything we can use to make his life miserable. I'm looking for a legal way to stop him. If I can't, he's going to pay with pain. This isn't just a feud; I'm concerned for your safety."

"Oh God, Brad. What does he want from us?"

"Honey, try not to get too upset. I don't think Judd has the guts to hurt you. He knows I'd kill him. Let's not think about it any more. What do you say I fix up a blender of Margaritas?"

"Sounds terrific. I have an urge to get a little stinko. Just promise me you won't let Judd get you in any more trouble. I couldn't handle it. Promise?"

Brad nodded, but mentally crossed his fingers. He stood up and put his arms around his wife. She was trembling. Kathleen now wore the ankle-length, Kelly green caftan he gave her for Christmas. It hung in a soft drape from the tips of her breasts.

When she pressed her body into him, he could feel all the softness, warmth and sensuality he loved about her. He let his hands run across her back and pulled her close. There were no restraints under her caftan. Body heat brought instant memories of their last passionate encounter on the floor. Kathleen purred and looked into his eyes. Her expression told volumes. She was a wily cat about to pounce on her prey. Brad gently pushed her away.

"Kathleen Logan, you witch, you're making it hard for me. I mean that literally. You been taking some kind of hot pills?"

"Are you complaining, Slick? You seemed to enjoy thrashing around the floor this afternoon. As I remember, you were panting a bit yourself."

"You don't hear me complaining…no way. Just wondered what brought on this new found lust. If you'll stop rubbing against me, I'll get into the kitchen and make those drinks."

"You wimp. Just thought I'd perk up your love life. Besides, you been thinking too much about the Geisha girl you brought home. Sumi's not the sweet little innocent schoolgirl she appears. Take my word for it. Women know these things."

Brad tried to look puritan. "I never said she was sweet and innocent—well, she *is* sweet—but she's a full-blown woman. Even I know that. Does she threaten you, or something?"

"I'll scratch her little sloe eyes out if she looks at you."

"I thought you liked her. What happened?"

"I'm just kidding, Sweetheart. I think Sumiko's a sweet, thoughtful young lady who will make someone a good wife some day. But not you. Now go fix those drinks."

A pitcher of Margaritas later, the Logans sat at the table, feeling mellow as they devoured the platter of tacos and burritos Kathleen had prepared.

"Brad, I have a confession. I went to see Doctor Fisher a couple days ago."

"Doctor Fisher, the shrink? Why in hell did you go see her?"

"God, I don't know. It seemed like a good idea at the time. You were gone, and I felt sorry for myself. Guess I had some doubts about myself and about our relationship. She was a big help. You know, just talking things out. You P.O.'d at me?"

"Hell no, Kate. Kinda surprised is all. Why don't you just tell me when you have those worries? I'm trained to listen to people and solve problems. I'm surprised you had worries about our relationship. I would think the little demonstration I just gave you on the floor should make you worry less."

Kathleen stuck her tongue out at him. "You're right, I should never doubt your manliness. But you don't demonstrate it often enough. I've decided we'll do the moany-sweaty-licky-face thing in every room of this house until I decide where you do your best work. That a deal?"

"Jeez, Kate, you embarrass me. What would the neighbors think? Is this all part of Doctor Fisher's therapy?"

"I ain't saying, you just better enjoy it. You want some more food?"

"Christ no. You got me so hot again, food doesn't interest me at all. You decided where we get it on tonight?"

"Who says *you* get it tonight, Malcolm? Right now, I need to clean up this kitchen. You go in and finish your margarita in the den. When I'm finished out here, I'll see how I feel about further entertainment."

Kathleen got to her feet, stooped to kiss him, ducked out of a potential caress with practiced agility, and began clearing the table. Brad remembered, in years gone by, his wife was coquettish, but never quite this obvious. He loved it. He never tired of 'Kathleen the Seductress'.

With drink in hand, Brad plopped down in his leather chair and pushed back until his feet were supported. Television held no appeal. He had too much on his mind. What brought this wonderful new sexuality to Kathleen? How could they be sure it remained in their life? Could he keep up with her new energy?

A short breath later, his thoughts turned to darker things. Who killed Mooch? Who in the department fingered the giant for death? Were the bombings tied in with everything? How involved was Judd Worley? Where does the *Yakuza* fit into all of this?

He drained the last of his drink and set his chair upright to put his glass down. As he turned, Kathleen entered the room, brushing the wall to flick off the light.

Her robe lay at her feet. Was her negligee made of cellophane? The light from the hallway embraced her, exaggerating every curve and angle of the body Brad knew so well. Without moving, every part of her beckoned him. He imagined he could see waves of heat pouring from her body. Her arms reached out as the tip of her tongue circled her lips. Brad's breath caught in his throat as his eyes devoured every inch of her. Pangs of pure lust growled in his body. Kathleen's voice cooed in her throat.

"Stand and deliver, Pilgrim. Be out of your clothes in ten seconds or I start ripping. My hormones are raging."

"My God, Katie, you take my breath away. You—you're—sizzling. Have I ever seen that—that—whatever it is you're almost wearing?"

Kate rushed to him, put her hand over his mouth and pulled at his clothes. He needed no encouragement, pulling her into his arms and covering her face with kisses. With uncommon hunger, his kisses strayed from her mouth, moved to her neck, her ears and soon covered her entire body. Her hands guided his mouth until every inch of her flesh received its reward. No spot was overlooked.

With undeniable urgency, Brad lured her to the floor. The heat was overwhelming. As they sank to the carpet, she moaned against his mouth.

"Please, take it slow this time, Lover. That all right? Make it last."
He didn't answer.

It was after ten the next morning and Sam Hardy still hadn't called. Brad relaxed by polishing several pairs of boots. The action of bringing a luster to the leather gave him a certain amount of satisfaction, but it didn't keep him from wishing the phone would ring.

He had abandoned their bed soon after five, his mind too busy to sleep. He remembered standing at the bedside for a moment, his eyes savoring Kathleen's sleeping body. She had been sprawled across the center of the bed. He fought the urge to renew their reunion. After one last visual caress, he had tucked the covers under her chin.

During his shower, with great reluctance, he forced all memory of Kathleen's new-found sexuality from his mind. He concentrated on sorting fact from fiction, hard fact from rumor. The puzzle was daunting.

Starting with what he knew as fact, Judd Worley kept rising to the top of the priority list. Judd was up to his ponytail in something dirty. In some way, his hands were mixed up in this whole mess. His harassment of Kathleen was done as a distraction to keep Brad from finding evidence. Judd was behind everything. But how could he prove it?

Brad was positive something incriminating would turn up soon. He had to get into the bastard's apartment. He didn't know what the evidence was, but it would just jump out and bite him in the ass. He'd settle for anything—anything. An old valentine. Maybe hate literature. A recipe for making a bomb. A Nazi flag or swastika. If Judd was involved with a gang, there would be some evidence of it.

The phone rang, jarring Brad out of his musings. It was Sam.

"Brad, we hit pay dirt." Sam didn't waste time with formalities.

"Lay it on me, man. Tell me he scratched his balls in public."

"Nothing quite so obscene, but there are seven outstanding traffic warrants, okay? This guy ignores authority of any kind. It's time he learned a little respect. Don't you think?"

"You got that right, pal. How long before you'll find him?"

"That's simple. He's on his morning break. A harness bull located him in a coffee shop on Main Street. They'll wait 'til I talk to you before they haul him in. I'm hoping it'll take him a couple hours to post bail, so you'd better get on your horse if you want to get in and out of his place before he comes home. Can you move right now?"

"Sam, I'm steaming out the door right now. Soon as you stop gabbin' and hang up. You're a prince. Be sure they get a good set of his prints. They may come in handy later. Thanks, partner."

Brad yelled up the stairs to tell Kathleen he was running an errand and would return in a couple of hours. He didn't wait for a response, then grabbed his jacket and was out the door.

He reached the Kings Way Apartments in less than ten minutes. The large complex was a two-story structure built around a central courtyard with swimming pool, children's play area and barbecue stands. Brad was very familiar with it. It harbored many of the town's less desirable citizens. In Brad's mind, it was a perfect place for Judd to live.

A sign on the door of the manager's office directed interested parties to unit #210. That's where Brad found a man on his hands and knees, replacing the kitchen linoleum.

"Hey, Tyrone, long time no see. Someone steal your linoleum again?"

The huge, well-muscled man looked up from his labor. Droplets of sweat bathed the moon-shaped face. A grin replaced the scowl on his face as he recognized Brad.

"Hey there, Sergeant, what's happenin'? I ain't seen you roun' here in a while. Maybe that's a good sign. Hope you ain't here to run off no more'a my tenants."

Tyrone wiped his hands on a dirty pant leg, then extended half of a ham for Brad to shake. He and the police department enjoyed a great deal of mutual respect. When he found bad elements moving into his apartments, he called the police for a quick computer check. In return, the police, and Brad in particular, made sure a patrol car made regular visits to the area. It was a good arrangement.

"Tyrone, I'm not here officially, but I'm investigating your tenant, Judd Worley. I need you to let me into his apartment for just a few minutes. You can stand and watch to be sure I don't steal anything. By the way, how's Ty Junior?"

Years before, when Tyrone's young son was on the verge of turning into a street punk, Brad physically dragged the youth to the police gym. He bought him a membership in the Police Athletic League and spent many personal hours in the boxing ring with the kid. It worked. The young man was now enrolled in college. Tyrone senior thought Brad was 'Top Gun'.

"You wanna look in Worley's place? Watch out for that dude. He's poison. Some of your people was asking about him the other day. He done somethin' I should know about?"

"Don't know yet, Tyrone, just hoping I can uncover something right now. You gonna let me in?"

"Yeah, but sho hope he don't come back too soon. He's bad ass dude when he gets mad. Let's go. He's in one-five-four."

Brad followed the shuffling feet of this good-hearted man. It almost made Brad's feet hurt, watching the man walk, with his awkward limp. His body reflected years of abuse. Tyrone Hayes had worked the cotton fields around Langston for most of his lifetime until he no longer could tolerate the pain of stoop labor.

"Here you go, Sergeant. Don't mess the place up or he come lookin' for me with a stick. I'll wait out here and fix this doorbell."

He stepped aside as the door swung open and Brad slipped inside.

Judd's living quarters reflected the very essence of the man. Dirty clothes and assorted debris were strewn throughout the apartment, covering chairs, the bed, counter tops and even the floor. The smell of dirty clothing and dirty bodies was overpowering.

Without knowing what he was looking for, Brad found himself improvising. He decided the drawers in the bedroom would be a good place to start. With practiced care, he opened a drawer at a time, expecting a cockroach to come scurrying out at any moment. Expert powers of observation made the routine a simple matter. He barely moved anything as he searched.

Ten minutes of rooting around in the snake pit created nothing but more frustration. He found no valentines. He found no suspicious literature. There was no bomb-making formula. No diary. It was unreasonable to believe a man this sloppy never left some evidence of his private life lying around.

About to quit in disgust, Brad opened a kitchen drawer jammed with papers. Bills, past due notices, several speeding tickets. A treasure house of mementos of Judd's total antagonism toward authority. At the bottom of the drawer was a small, brown passbook issued by the Langston National Bank. Curious fingers pulled the book into the light.

"Pay dirt, folks. Let's see what kind of financial dealings old Judd is making."

He opened the small book to the most recent entry. Just the previous day there was a deposit of $5,000.00. Leafing back through the book, Brad found many entries for large amounts, dating back several years.

"Looks like our Judd is a wealthy man. Bless his heart. Christ, looks like I'm in the wrong business. I should drive a hack. That's where the big money's at. Well, at least this wasn't a total dry run."

With extreme caution, Brad returned the passbook to the drawer, taking pains to leave the pile of papers as they were before he started. Judd must know exactly where, in all this mess, he kept every little thing. No sense letting him know his turf had been invaded.

A sudden rap on the door, and Tyrone's deep voice brought a sense of urgency to his departure. He could see them from the front window—two policemen, walking toward the apartment where he stood.

Brad froze with his hand on the doorknob.

CHAPTER 8

❀

Kathleen hummed while she finished making the bed. The bedroom windows were open, letting fresh air and sunshine launder the stale air in the upstairs. The sun sparkled in the sky, birds chirped in the pines, and she walked again with the joy of fulfillment in her stride. Her skin still remembered the heat of his kisses. Her body tingled with reminders of his ardor. Even her lips felt a little swollen. Kathleen's fingers wandered to the love bite on her neck. It was her first hickey since high school. Life was good!

She was so immersed in reliving the previous night's rapture, Kathleen almost overlooked the ringing telephone. When she did become aware of it, she dashed to the bedside and grabbed the phone. It was Sam Hardy, in a state of agitation.

"Kathleen, it's Sam Hardy. Let me talk to Brad, it's urgent."

"Morning, Sam. Isn't it a beautiful morning? I think Brad left about five minutes ago. He must've been in a hurry 'cause he just yelled up the stairs and took off. Is there a problem? Can I give him a message?"

She could hear the urgency in Sam's voice.

"No, no. Just hoped I'd catch him before he left. Have him call me as soon as he gets back, okay?"

"Sam, why don't you call him on his cell phone? I'm sure he's carrying it. He always does. I know you have the number."

"I tried that, Kate, but he must have turned it off. Anyway, I'll catch up with him later. Just tell him I called, okay? Bye."

The phone clicked and was silent. Kathleen let the receiver dangle in her hand as she pondered Sam's call. "Boy, that's strange. Brad's home on suspension and they can't leave him alone. Serves them right. They should know they can't get along without him. Just like me."

Kathleen puttered around in the upstairs bedroom for several more minutes, then made her way down to the kitchen. As she filled the tea kettle with fresh water, the phone rang again. She picked it up and tucked it under her chin as she continued filling the pot. The sound from the other end froze her in terror. It was just a whisper, but the sound was so ominous it screamed at her.

"Morning, you fox. Watched you and Junkyard last night. Great performance. The hot little number on the floor got my total attention. But it's pretty tame compared with what I'll do to you. It's time for my turn. Be ready. Bye, Foxy. Tell the A-hole I called."

The phone went dead. The teakettle lay in the sink where she dropped it. Water splattered over everything, including the floor, until she reacted and turned it off. She groped her way to a stool and sat down, fighting for breath. The jackhammer in her chest threatened to break through her ribs.

"Oh, my God! Oh, my God! Brad, Brad, I need you now! Please come home. Oh, dear God. I can't handle any more of this."

She staggered back to the sink and drew a glass of water, spilling most of it down the front of her sweater. Her shaking hands wouldn't function in a normal way. When her brain stopped whirling about in her head, she ran to the front door. Overcoming her temporary affliction, she attached the night chain and activated the alarm.

By invoking sheer willpower, she worked the combination to Brad's gun safe, and removed the .38 snub nose. Then, despite dropping several cartridges, she got it loaded. For years, Brad had drilled her on the proper handling of his weapons. She was quite proficient on the firing range. Facing a human with a loaded weapon was another matter.

Taking a deep breath to calm herself, she sank onto the kitchen floor with her back pressed against the cupboard, holding the gun in both hands as she waited. One thing was sure, anyone breaking into *this* house was in for a surprise.

Brad strained to identify the uniformed cops walking toward his hiding place. The slats of the venetian blinds were tilted in such a way it was impossible to see anything but the uniforms. He took his hand off the door and plastered himself against the wall. He could hear the words coming through the closed door.

"Hello, officers. Help you with somethin'?"

"Yeah, boy…this Judd Worley's pad?"

The voice of the cop didn't register with Brad, but the rude tone grated on him.

"Mister Worley, he ain't home. He don't come home 'til late at night."

"Tell you what, old man, you just forget we were here. We'll catch up with him sometime. Have a nice day."

Brad let out his breath as he regained control of his tense body. He saw the backs of the cops retreating down the sidewalk. He waited until he got the all-clear signal from Tyrone.

"Come on, Sergeant, get outta there. Those cops they scare me. They ain't pleased with people with skin like mine. You gotta go, quick."

Brad pulled the door open and peered after the retreating cops. There was no sign of them, so he pulled the door closed behind him. To kill some time, he spent five minutes calming an agitated Tyrone Hayes before returning to his car. He didn't let his breathing return to normal until he was several blocks away.

It was then he reached for his cell phone and dialed headquarters. It took him a few minutes to get through to Sam Hardy.

"Jesus, Sam, where the hell you been?"

"Man, am I glad to hear your voice. Been calling your number for half hour. Don't go to Worley's place. It ain't safe. Where are you?"

"Already been there and done that. Piece of cake, except for the two uniforms who surprised me. What the hell was that all about?"

"That's why I was calling. Lieutenant Nichols in I.A. sent two of his guys out to Worley's place, I guess to question him, okay? Nichols didn't know Worley was in our custody. I could just see his jakes walking in there with you going through Worley's stuff. Glad you didn't get caught. Your suspension might have become permanent. You find anything?"

"Nothing earth shattering. Is Judd still in custody?"

"He got bailed about half hour ago. Was not a happy camper when he left. Vowed we'd hear from his attorney. So what else is new? You say your search was a waste of time?"

"Mixed results, Sam. Listen, do we have enough on Worley to get a subpoena for his bank records?"

"I doubt that. You did find something, didn't you?"

"Yeah…but I don't wanna tell you on the phone. Trust me, it means something. Only thing is, we need to get it under authority. Talk to Captain Owens about a subpoena, will you?"

"I'll talk to him, partner. Why don't I call you at home when I can get to a public phone? I'm anxious to hear your story, okay? Look, I gotta go. Good luck."

Brad disconnected and dialed his home number. He let it ring over a dozen times, but Kathleen didn't answer. That concerned him and inspired him to cover the last half-mile in record time.

As he pulled onto his street, he just glimpsed the back end of a black and white patrol car rounding the next corner. Instant rage boiled up. He fought the impulse of chasing the car down. His first concern was Kate's welfare.

Brad left the car in the driveway and sprinted up the porch steps. With nervous fingers, he disarmed the alarm system and unlocked the door. When the night chain reached its limit the door bounced back into his face, with a bang. He shouted through the small opening.

"Katie…are you in there? It's me, Babe. You all right?"

When he received no answer, he braced himself against the door frame and kicked the door with every ounce of strength he could muster. It flew back into his face and slammed shut. It took three more tries before the wooden framing around the door splintered and the door slammed open.

Brad had no weapon, but his own safety was of no concern. He rushed into the house, shouting her name at the top of his lungs.

At the doorway to the kitchen, he pulled up short when he spotted his wife's legs, sprawled out on the floor. He dove into the kitchen and found her sitting on the floor. A vacant, but terrified look transfixed her face—a face devoid of color and wet with tears. In her lap lay his .38 revolver. The hammer was back and her finger was inside the trigger guard.

Brad fell to his knees. With great care, he took the pistol from her hand, disarming it and emptying the cylinders. He set the gun on the floor and took his wife in his arms.

"Katie, what is it? What's happening here? Talk to me, Sweetheart."

He patted her cheeks as he crooned his concern. Several anxious minutes passed, before Kathleen showed any sign of response. Brad picked her up and carried her to the sofa in the den. He tossed a blanket over her, then rushed to close the front door.

Brad retrieved his gun from the floor and reloaded. With the cold steel tucked into his waist band, he began an inspection tour. Once satisfied the house was empty, he returned to his wife. Kathleen was awake. Her head moved from side to side in slow motion, as if shedding a bad memory. Brad poured a small glass of brandy, then sat on the edge of the sofa.

"Kate, come on, Hon, take a sip of this. It'll clear your head."

He propped her head up and held the glass to her lips. With his urging, Kathleen took a large gulp of the brown liquid and responded with a fit of coughing. Brad forced another gulp past her trembling lips. This time, it went down with no problems. The color began returning to her face.

As she became more familiar with her surroundings, she screamed and turned her face into Brad's chest. "Oh, God, Brad. Who's doing this to me? What did I do to him?"

"Kate. Tell me what happened here. Did someone come to the house? Talk to me. I can't help you until you tell me what's wrong."

Despite numerous stops and starts, Brad extracted the details of Kathleen's traumatic phone call. The more he heard, the more enraged he became. Seeing his wife in such terrible fear drove him into a wild-eyed rage. It was at that precise moment the front door bell rang.

Brad left his wife on the sofa and raced to the front door. Whoever stood outside was in for the shock of a lifetime.

He flung the door open with such force, it bounced against its stopper and almost closed again. Brad's voice roared out into the neighborhood. "What the hell do you want?"

A startled Sam Hardy stood on the front porch, holding his arms over his face as if to ward off a potential attack. In his blind rage, Brad didn't recognize his partner right away. He stuck the .38 into Sam's face. Sam pushed the barrel aside with great care.

"Whoa, whoa, whoa, Brad...I'm one of the good guys, okay? Calm down before you kill someone."

With sudden clarity, Brad realized he held the gun. It dazed him because he didn't remember pulling it from his waist band. As soon as he realized there was no danger, he put the gun away and motioned Sam into the house.

As they passed the front doorway, Brad noticed Sam inspecting the splinters of wood on the floor—remnants of Brad's attack on the door. Sam said nothing as he followed Brad to the den. Brad was sure the sight of Kathleen lying on the sofa would help Sam put several more pieces into the puzzle. Brad's loud tirade added another. "Sam, I'm going to kill that son of a bitch! He can't get away with what he's doing to Kate. You may as well arrest me now. His day's coming soon."

"Partner, if you keep raving and waving that piece around under my nose, I'll run you in; I mean it. Now calm the hell down and tell me what's going on here. Who broke in your door? Did someone hurt Kathleen?"

"I kicked in the Goddam door! I kicked it in because Kate was so frightened she locked herself in and was holding this .38 in her lap when I found her. She was so terrified she was in shock."

"But what brought it on, Brad? Did she get another valentine?"

"No, this time it was a phone call. The worst kind of phone call. A raunchy, filthy, up close and personal kind of call. I'm telling you, he's going to pay for this. Worley's dead meat, man."

Each time Brad repeated the name, his voice turned into a snarl. The hate boiling out of him startled even the unflappable Sam Hardy. This was the most rage he had ever witnessed in his partner. He eyed the open brandy bottle on the counter.

"Hey, if you don't calm down, I'm getting the SWAT team. You'll hurt someone or yourself. Now start taking some deep breaths. Let me get some of that brandy for you, okay? Come on, man, sit down and give me your piece. I'll go lock it up, okay?"

Sam held out his hand. Brad pulled the weapon from his belt and handed it over. The soothing affect of Sam's words pierced the red curtain of rage. He went over and sat beside his wife, took her hand in his, then leaned over to kiss her. She gave no response. Her gaze remained stony and unfocused.

Sam returned to the room with the brandy bottle and a glass. He handed the glass to Brad, then poured a stiff belt which Brad downed in one toss. Two more quick shots produced a softer, calmer disposition, which Sam Hardy welcomed with a sigh of relief.

"Thanks, Sam. God, am I glad it was you at the door. Mad as I was, I'm not sure what could have happened. Sorry to greet you like a caveman. It's been a rough morning."

"No sweat, man. You might've made my wife a rich woman. You ready to talk about this, or you wanna wait?"

"I've gotta get Kate squared away first, Sam. Let me take her upstairs. I'll find something to give her and put her to bed. You got time to stick around?"

"Sure, pal, take your time. I'll see if you got anything to eat in the 'frig', okay?"

"Help yourself, Sam. I won't be long. Appreciate your sticking around. I've gotta figure out how I can take care of this without killing someone."

Brad picked Kathleen up and carried her up the stairs and into the bedroom. Gently, he lowered his wife onto the bed. Her head rolled back and forth on the pillow and she clung to his hand as if she were drowning.

"Kate, honey, let me go get something for you. You need to relax and get some sleep. Turn loose of me for a second. I'll be right back."

With some difficulty, Brad extracted his fingers from her death grip. In the medicine cabinet he found the remainder of a prescription tranquilizer she used on occasion, when she couldn't sleep. He shook out two pills and returned to her side with a glass of water.

"Here, Katie, take these. It'll help you forget. Just push this out of your mind. Just shut it out and think of how much I love you."

Brad stroked her head and waited for signs she was asleep. As he sat on the bed, he collected his thoughts. He was becoming more rational. His hatred for Judd Worley could not be denied, but he started viewing it with more composure.

As soon as he knew Kathleen was settled in, he went down to the den. Sam was sitting on the sofa. He was eating a cold leftover burrito, gleaned from the refrigerator. A can of diet soda was on the floor at his feet.

"Jesus, Sam, why don't you let me zap it in the microwave? Cold salsa and beans isn't the greatest thing to put in your poor abused stomach. Here, let me have it."

Sam snatched the burrito away from Brad's grasp. "No way, man. Most of the food I eat is cold. I like cold food. I'm fine. Sit down and let's talk. I'm signed out, so there's no rush. Go get a beer. It's on me."

"Mighty big of you, partner." He walked to the kitchen. "Listen, this thing with Kathleen is getting out of hand. I found her sitting on the floor with my .38 in her hands. It scared the crap out of me. She's about to crack, man. I can't let anything happen to her."

Brad told Sam about the events leading up to the phone call she received that morning. "The bastard is so disgusting, he just strips her of her defenses. She panics and he gets the satisfaction of knowing he's got her terrified. He's gone over the edge this time, Sam. This is a new low, even for Worley. He told her he saw us last night. The asshole must be a peeper. I won't let him do this to her. He—-"

Sam held up his hand. "Hey pal, wait a minute, okay? What time did she get this call?"

"Oh, I don't know…must have been around 10:45 or so, why?"

"You're forgetting, Worley was in custody this morning. We had him under wraps for almost three hours. Doesn't seem to me he could call her, unless he called from our interrogation room."

That revelation stunned Brad. The possibility never occurred to him. "What? That can't be, Sam. I know Worley's behind this. You gotta be wrong."

"No way, pal. He was within my line of sight most of the time. Rethink your theory, okay? It can't be Worley. He can't be in two places at once."

"My God, Sam…someone else must be doing his dirty work for him. I don't even want to think it's someone else. At least, with Judd, I knew what to expect. If it's not him, Kate's in even more danger."

"You're right about that. There's no way we can tell if the threat's real. We can't take a chance either way, okay? No matter how you look at it, her emotional well-being is at risk. She shouldn't be exposed to any more trauma. You know?" Sam wiped his mouth with a napkin.

"That's a given, Sam. As it turns out, it's been a blessing I'm on suspension this week. Don't know what I'd do if she was here alone all day. At least I have some time to make arrangements."

"Not to change the subject, but just what did you find at Worley's place today?"

"God, I'd almost forgotten about that. For sure, I found the dirtiest stink hole I've seen in a long time. You wouldn't believe it. He's a pig. At first, I found nothing, but then, at the last minute, I found a bank deposit record. Our friend Judd is not as poor as he'd like us to believe. I figure he's deposited over seventy-five big ones in the bank over the last year. We know he didn't make that kinda dough drivin' a hack. We've got to get a better look at his records. I'd sure like to get a tap on his phone—I suppose that's out, for sure. How do you read that?"

Sam shrugged. "I'd guess chances are slim on the bank records—more like impossible on the tap. I'll talk to the captain tomorrow. I'll tell him about these phone calls and threats to Kathleen. He doesn't need to know Judd has an alibi. Maybe we can get the bank records anyway. Do we have anything else to go on?"

Brad shared some of the F.B.I. data with his partner. "Old friend Worley belongs to a white supremacist group known as the White Knights. Ever hear of them?"

"White Knights? Yeah, but they're not a racist group. Some of our younger cops are members. It's kind of a fraternal thing, I think. You know…basketball games, golf tournaments…that kinda stuff. Where did you hear about them?"

"Sam, the F.B.I. told me they're a dangerous hate group. How come you knew about them, but I never heard of them?"

"Hey, man, *you're* the Junkyard Dog. *Nobody* wants you to join their club."

CHAPTER 9

❀

*D*uring the next two days, Brad concentrated on getting his wife over her emotional trauma. At his request, Sam put a police monitor on the phone. He bought an answering machine so Kathleen could avoid answering the phone herself. Most of all, he provided 'TLC' in hopes of ridding her of her anxieties.

He knew that catching Kathleen's violator would be a monumental task. Brad never wavered in his belief that Judd Worley was responsible. He meant to stop him, whatever it took.

On Saturday morning, Brad received a call from Captain Owens with the good news: Internal Affairs had cleared him of wrongful action, saying only that he used bad judgment. Langston P.D. accepted responsibility for Worley's medical bills and Worley dropped his suit. Brad could report to work on Monday morning.

For Brad, it didn't sit too well, seeing Worley get away without punishment, but he knew it was the best he could hope for. Worst part of all, with Mooch Kaiser dead, the whole episode was for naught.

On Sunday morning, Kathleen surprised him by rising before him. She insisted on making a big Sunday morning breakfast, and looked to him to be over the worst of her trauma. Brad knew, without a doubt, she was tired of being a victim. Kathleen was not a quitter.

After a brief discussion, they agreed that Kathleen should go back to work at the boutique, at least for a few days. It would keep her busy and she wouldn't be home alone. Kathleen called her former boss. It was all set; she could start on Monday morning. Brad breathed a sigh of relief.

At 11:00, the phone rang. After six rings, the speaker phone was activated. Brad always held his breath during that waiting period. The suspense concluded when they heard a familiar lilting voice: "Logan-san, it's Sumiko. Sorry you're not home. I need to talk to you. Please call me back today."

Brad rushed to pick up the phone so the caller wouldn't hang up.

"Hello, Sumiko, we're *here.* Are you all right?"

"Logan-san, I think you're not home. It's good to hear your voice again. I can ask you for big favor? I wish to buy a car. My new job starts next week. I can't keep riding in cab every day. You will help me find car?"

"Do you know how to drive, Sumi?"

"Of course. Did you forget I graduate college? I have driver license for ten years. Can you help me?"

"Hold on just a minute, Sumi."

Brad put his hand over the phone and called Kathleen, who was cleaning up after their breakfast. "Kate, it's Sumiko. She needs help buying a car. Do you feel like getting out today? Maybe we can help her find something. Might be a good idea to get you out of the house."

Kathleen dried off her hands and came over and took the phone from Brad's hand. "Good morning, Sumiko, how are you?"

"Good morning, Kathleen-san. I am well. *Ikaga desu ka?*"

"If you're asking how I am…fine, I guess. Brad says you need a car. That might be fun. Maybe we should make a day of it. Why don't you come over for dinner when we're through? Would you like that?"

"Dinner? Oh, yes. I don't like hotel food. You sure it is okay for you?"

"We'd love to have you, Sumi. Here, you can talk to Brad about the car."

" Thank you, Kathleen. *Sayonara.*"

Brad took the phone from Kathleen. He was amazed at the change in his wife. The tortured outlook of the past few days had disappeared, as if by magic. It was as though Sumi's cheerful attitude infected her right through the phone. "Sumi, when can you be ready to go? I'll check the morning paper ads."

When Sumiko informed him she was ready to go right now, Brad chuckled and told her it would take them at least an hour to arrive at her hotel. She told him she'd be waiting in the lobby. Brad guessed she would be in the lobby within ten minutes. Her excitement was contagious. He hung up the phone, shaking his head in wonderment.

"Boy, what a buzz saw of energy she is. Are you sure you can handle this, Kate?"

"Of course, Hon, I think a dose of Sumiko is just what I need to get out of this mood. It'll be fun."

Sumiko was indeed sitting, serene as a Buddha, in the hotel lobby when they arrived. She wore form-fitting blue jeans and a clingy red silk blouse. A thick, black braid hung down her back, with a big red bow tied in the middle. Bright red toe nails peeked from the end of her flat sandals. She resembled a twelve-year-old school girl.

When she spotted them walking in, she bounced to her feet and sprinted across the lobby to greet them with enthusiastic hugs and kisses. In her fervor to express her happiness, she reverted to her native tongue, jabbering as if afraid she'd lose her turn to speak. Only after seeing the blank look on their faces did she realize they didn't comprehend a thing she said.

"*Gomen nasai.* I am sorry. I get so excited to see you. You are my only friends here. I feel kind of alone, you know? Thank you for coming."

"You're welcome, Sumi. Let's go find you a car. What kind do you like?"

"*Papa-san* he tell me Toyota is best car for little person. You think so, too?"

Brad swallowed the laughter on the tip of his tongue. He looked at Kathleen to see if she had the same reaction. Her raised eyebrows confirmed it.

They spent the afternoon making the rounds of car dealers. A few hours later, they located a little red coupe which fit Sumi as if made with her in mind. To Brad's surprise, the dealer agreed to repair several things needing attention. Sumi wrote a check for the entire purchase. Her car would be ready in the middle of the week.

Brad couldn't restrain Sumi's childlike enthusiasm over her new toy. She showered the Logans with hugs and kisses. She then embarrassed the middle-aged salesman when she got him in a bear hug and expressed her undying gratitude. The helpless look on his face delighted the Logans. Sumi's enthusiasm for life kindled joyfulness in everyone within viewing distance of her demonstration.

For Brad Logan, Sumi's unabashed joy produced mixed feelings. When he witnessed her twelve-year old school girl exuberance, his feelings were sterile and fatherly. At other times, when the full bodied and sensual creature emerged, he fostered lustier feelings. It was the lustier feelings Brad took great pains to bury.

For the balance of the afternoon, they took Sumi on the grand tour of Langston. Brad made a special point of driving to the Kurasawa Electronics plant, showing Sumi the route she would travel getting to work. Just the sight of the high rise of steel and concrete gave him a feeling of dread, knowing there were unseen dangers waiting inside. He resisted giving her another lecture about being careful. Kathleen might find it unusual.

Kathleen asked Sumi if she knew yet what her job would be.

"They say job is named Assistant Director of Overseas Marketing. They say I will learn how products fit into world markets. It is what I studied in university. Maybe some day I will be boss of department. You think?"

Kathleen assured her she could do anything she set her mind to. Brad agreed, without reservation. He knew this young lady's honesty, determination and enthusiasm would take her to any heights she desired.

Driving back into town Brad took the route which took them through the area known as Little Ginza. It was a twenty-block area of commercial and residential buildings clustered on the eastern outskirts of Langston. Kathleen carried on a running commentary, taking the part of tour guide.

"This is one of the oldest parts of Langston. As you can see, many of the buildings have been restored with great care. Some of them look better than when they were new. In several places, buildings were torn down and later rebuilt with modern architecture. I think they're doing a beautiful job of fixing up this part of town. It's even becoming a kind of a tourist attraction. I've wanted to come and browse, but never get around to it. Maybe you could come with us one day. What do you think of it?"

Brad saw Sumiko's eyes sparkle with delight, seeing the bustling activity which must have resembled, in a small way, her native land. Crowds of people filled the sidewalks on both sides of the street. Most sauntered along casually, but many stood gazing into the store fronts. It was a distinct surprise to the Logans that as many Occidentals as Orientals filled the streets.

Without making a big issue of it, he made a point to drive by the locations of the recent bombings. He knew Sumiko would understand why he showed them to her. He made nothing more than a general comment, but saw her eyes grow serious. He hoped she made a mental note of all the damage. It was important for her to realize that her undercover work was very dangerous.

Kathleen had never seen the blast sites before, and was shocked at the damage. "Was anyone hurt when these places were bombed? It's so awful to see what people do to each other. Does anyone know who did it?"

"No, I'm sorry to say, we're having a very hard time finding out anything. The Japanese people down here won't talk to us. No one will tell us anything."

Sumiko shook her head. "My people too proud. Bringing dishonor to one's family is considered a disgrace. It is foolish, but is very difficult giving up old traditions. It makes me very sad."

Brad saw an opportunity to bring her into his investigation without alarming Kathleen. "Hey, Sumiko, would you come down here with us when we have more time? You can show us around and maybe talk to some of the people here. I feel like I should know more about them. You think you might like that?"

"Oh, yes...that's very nice idea. Then I take you to Japanese restaurant and teach you about Japanese food. You like that, maybe?"

Kathleen was very receptive to the idea. She loved to try new foods. Brad said it would be nice, but told himself he would reserve his enthusiasm until he saw what she was talking about.

If was after five when they pulled into the Logan's driveway. Brad did not say anything to either of them, but he spotted the tail end of a police car as it turned the corner and disappeared just as he pulled onto their street. Was it just a patrol for their safety, or was there a more sinister meaning to the car in his neighborhood?

When Sumiko told Kathleen her favorite food was spaghetti and meat balls, it brought a roar of laughter from Brad, who was fixing them all a drink.

"What'sa matter, Logan-san...you think Japanese girl only eat raw fish and noodle?"

"No, no, no, Sumi, I never thought about it. Please forgive me. I've led a sheltered life. Been in Langston most of my life, except for college. About all I know is about the *Po-lice*. Never studied other cultures much. I should learn more about yours."

"I know you like Japan, Logan-san. Except so full of people they have no room to move around. I will go back some day. You'll see. Some day, maybe I teach you all about my country and my people. What are you making?"

"It's called a Mai-Tai. It comes from Hawaii. I think you'll like it"

"Maybe it makes me drunk, Logan-san. I never drink anything but wine before. If I get goofy, you maybe take me home and put me to bed? Kathleen get mad at you, I think."

As usual, Sumiko's simplistic way of verbalizing things was accompanied with that disarming, childlike smile. Her presumed naiveté kept the Logans captivated. Brad saw his wife giggling under her breath as she set about making spaghetti sauce for their dinner. He saw a mental image of Kathleen shaking a finger at him, reminding him of her threat to scratch out those almond eyes.

At nine, Brad and Kathleen drove her to her hotel. Brad discarded the idea of taking Sumiko home by himself, even though he could have talked to her about her new job. He couldn't leave Kathleen home alone. He knew the trauma she had experienced made her especially vulnerable.

His other concern was just as urgent. He must protect both of these women from the danger posed by having knowledge of his investigation. He took the threats of violence very seriously. Kathleen must not find out he would be seeing a lot of Sumiko in the future. He couldn't put either of them at risk. The less his wife knew of the danger they all were in, the more he liked it. When he walked Sumiko into the lobby, he told her he expected a call from her the next afternoon.

In the car, as they drove home, Kathleen was thoughtful. "Do you know something, Honey? The more I see of her, the more I'm impressed with her. She's an extraordinary human being. I'm so glad we're getting to know her. But, just remember…there's no reason that *you* should know her better than me. You got that?" Kathleen reached across the car seat and rubbed his leg. Her territorial rights were thus established—lest anyone suffer a doubt.

Upstairs, in the relative safety of their bedroom, Brad lay atop the covers and watched as his wife prepared for bed. It was a pastime he never tired of and he could predict each move as if it was being choreographed. She was such a creature of habit.

First, her shoes and hose came off. The shoes went into the rack in the closet, the hose into the hamper in the bathroom. Next, her blouse made the journey over her head. After that, her slacks were dropped to the floor, then picked up and folded neatly over the back of a chair. Next she sat in her panties and bra while she removed her makeup. He never tired of her performance, in particular the Grand Finale—when she removed the last of her clothing. She slipped into something transparent and sat at her dressing table to brush her hair. The rise and fall of her breasts always created a subtle stirring in Brad. He knew it was a staged event, but it made no difference. She repeated the show night after night without a cover charge.

When Kathleen finished brushing her hair, Brad got under the sheet. Kathleen turned out the light and crawled into his arms. He took great pleasure in letting each curve and hollow of her body conform to him. He would hold her and gently stroke her back until she gave him a sign she was ready for more affection or for sleep.

The swirling dust kicked up all around him as he stepped down from the boardwalk. He tugged at his hat, pulling it down to shade his eyes from the afternoon sun. The brilliant glare of light made a stark silhouette of the man in the street. The man shouted at him, but Brad couldn't make out the words.

He tugged at his gun belt and walked with measured steps toward the man. As he approached, he squinted against the sun, trying to make out the man's features. The large brimmed hat he wore was crammed down over his head. It cast a shadow that obscured the man's face.

When the distance between them was no more than six feet, the man suddenly crouched, drawing the gun from his holster. The huge black hole in the gun barrel was obvious; pointing directly at Brad's heart. It resembled a cannon. At any moment, he expected a huge bullet would exit the barrel, heading toward his body.

As if it had a life of its own, his right hand darted to the holster on his hip. It was then he realized the holster was empty! The other man took careful aim and fired.

"Brad, Brad, Darling, wake up, wake up! You're dreaming again."

He felt Kathleen shake him fiercely from side to side and slap his cheeks.

He sat bolt upright. Beads of sweat rolled off him. His tee shirt was soaked through. His heart pounded against his ribs with the fury of a howitzer. He reached for the light switch and crashed his feet to the floor, throwing off the sheet.

"Brad, relax, Dear, it's that damn dream again. Go take an aspirin and you'll be all right. It's much too early to get up. Look, it's only 2:30."

Brad could not yet speak. His tongue glued itself to the roof of his mouth. He went into the bathroom and took two aspirins from the bottle in the cupboard. As he tilted his head back to slide the aspirin and water down his throat, he heard and felt the boom.

It wasn't terribly loud, but it rattled the windows in the house and staggered him for just an instant. There was no mistaking it. Another bomb had just exploded somewhere in Langston. A feeling of helplessness intimidated him.

"My God, Brad, what was that? Was it an earthquake? That's all I need to totally destroy my peace of mind."

"I don't know, Kate. My guess is, there was another bombing. I'll call and see if they need me. You go on back to sleep."

From the dispatcher he learned that a reported bomb blast was the cause of the noise. The fire department was not on scene yet, so they had no other information. He volunteered his services if he was needed, then hung up the phone and returned to bed.

He lay awake for a long time, anticipating the phone call, but none came. At last, he fell asleep, hoping he wouldn't get into another gunfight before morning.

In the morning, the TV news carried a live, on-the-scene report of the latest bombing. It had happened in the same general vicinity as the others. This time, the store contained living quarters on the second story. The fire department still couldn't reach those quarters because of the intense blaze, but they assumed there were fatalities this time since they found none of the residents.

Brad dropped Kathleen off at her new job and drove to the station. He was filled with dread as he anticipated the worst possible scenario. The odds were against another clean blast. They were due for fatalities, sooner or later.

Inside the station, he made his way down the hall to the locker room where he kept personal papers and his favorite coffee cup. To his surprise, the door wasn't locked. He was usually so careful about that. He yanked at the door because it always stuck. It opened abruptly and flopped against the next locker with a bang.

As he reached in for his portfolio, his eye was drawn to something which did not belong in his locker. On the center of the shelf was a small, plastic chess piece. A horse's head.

It was a White Knight!

CHAPTER 10

"I'm telling you right now, Sergeant Logan, this department won't tolerate another lawsuit resulting from your disregard for departmental rules. I know this Worley character's a thorn in your side, but you're supposed to be a professional, so just steer clear of him. If there's a need to confront him on an official basis, send another officer. Is that understood?"

Captain Owens' words only partially filtered through Brad Logan's thoughts. Finding the chess piece in his locker really disturbed him. Was the danger real? Could he protect Kathleen?

There was no mistaking the meaning of the little piece of white plastic. It was a clear warning. The suspicions in his mind bordered on paranoia. Could he trust anyone in the department? Now the captain's words just added to the aggravation, but he finally managed a reply. "I understand that, sir. I'll make every effort to stay out of his way unless it turns out he's involved in any of the cases I'm investigating. Especially those involving my wife."

"Did I hear you right? You think Worley is responsible for the harassment of your wife? What makes you think it was Worley?"

"Not just harassment, sir, my *wife was terrorized*! Worley gets his kicks by intimidating someone he thinks is weak. Matter of fact, I want a tap on his phone. Did Sam Hardy talk to you about getting an order?"

Captain Owens peered at Brad with eyebrows raised. There was no mistaking the look of doubt on his face. "Sergeant, your suspicions don't constitute grounds for a phone tap. Getting his bank records might prove a little easier. I'm working on that one. But you keep your nose clean, Sergeant. We all have a tendency to protect our own. Just don't step over the bounds of good police work. That's an order." It was obvious, Brad needed a lot more to convince Captain Owens.

"Are you aware we think he's involved in Mooch Kaiser's death?"

"Yes, Sam brought me up to speed on that—really flimsy, I'd say. You'll need a lot more detective work before you can point a finger at him. Putting Mooch out there sure blew up in our faces. How'd they spot him so soon? What went wrong?"

Brad shrugged his shoulders. It was obvious there was a turncoat in the Langston Police Department. It could even be the man across the desk from him. The captain was one of the three people who knew Mooch's identity. Was Captain Owens just a plodding old harness bull, or did he have his own agenda?

"That's enough ass chewing, Logan. Is there anything else I should know about? I know you're a week out of the loop. You'll need time to catch up. By the way, the FBI and ATF are taking over the entire bombing investigation because of the deaths last night."

The news was a relief to Brad. He had so many other matters to investigate, this would allow him to spend more time with cases he understood. "That doesn't surprise me, sir. Are we to stay out of it altogether?"

"No, just stay in close touch with them and don't step on any toes. Do you have any ideas, other than Judd Worley?"

"As a matter of fact, something very interesting came to my attention recently. It makes me think we're dealing with some new gang activity in Langston. Have you ever heard of the *Yakusa* or the White Knights?"

"Yes, of course. We get bulletins from other departments all the time. Thank God, we don't have them in our town. They say the Japanese group—-what did you call them—-*Yakuza?*—-is becoming a serious problem on the coast. I understand they're particularly vicious, especially to their own people. As far as the supremacist group is concerned, they're just a group of bigots who think of themselves as patriots. We—-"

Brad interrupted "...and you don't think we have elements of both groups in our town? There's a chance it's happening as we speak. It's happening in other areas of the West Coast. Why should we be different? We'd better assume we're infected, at least to some degree. These bombings may even be part of gang warfare. If that's true, we may need to form a gang unit."

It was not the first time Brad had offered advice to his boss. Captain Owens often relied on Brad's college background in Criminology. Most of the time, Brad was more subtle, but now, he couldn't spare the time. He needed an excuse for exploring gang activity.

"A gang unit? You think it's that big a problem? Christ, I can't even fill department vacancies now. We don't have the manpower. Chief Preston would laugh at me. Tell you what, if there's a gang problem, then go out and get some evidence. I need something we can take to the City Council. If you can make a case for conspiracy, I'll listen. In the meantime, keep your nose clean or we'll promote someone else to sergeant. You follow?"

Brad just nodded his understanding. It was a high wire act with no net. His relationship with Captain Owens was respectful and above board. He couldn't lose that. He needed someone with clout for backup if everything hit the fan.

As he left the office, he hoped the captain would be there when it happened—whatever 'it' was. Sam was at his desk when Brad approached. "Hey, partner, glad to see you're back. You ready to get caught up on things?"

"Yeah, Sam, I'm anxious to get going. But first, look what I found in my locker. You still think these Knights are some kind of fraternal group?"

Brad held out the chess piece. Sam took it and kept turning it over in his hand as he shook his head. Sam's look confirmed the feelings of danger the chess piece brought to Brad.

"This was in your locker? Hey, man, you've got a serious problem. You've been getting an awful lot of warnings the last couple of days. What in the hell are you onto?"

"That's the trouble, Sam. I have no idea whose toes I'm stepping on unless it's Judd Worley's. Owens says I'm to let the butthead alone, but I don't see how I can. Every inch of my intuition screams out that Judd's responsible for everything. I'm also certain he's getting some help from someone in this building. Did you get an answer to your request for subpoenas yet?"

"Owens wasn't too receptive. He doesn't want Worley upset again if we're wrong. You convinced we have some dirty cops?"

"Who else had access to my locker? How about all those patrols going by my house? By the way, did anyone show up at work with facial injuries?"

"Nothing major. A guy in traffic department is still off work. Of course, I haven't checked out the whole department. Don't wanna stir up anything, okay?"

"Have you been to the scene of last night's blast?"

"No, as a matter of fact, the FBI and ATF locked up the whole block. They not too politely invited me to stay out for twenty-four hours. This blast was much worse. From what I can get out of the Bureau guys, an Oriental couple lived upstairs over their food market, okay? When the bomb went off, it collapsed the walls. The upper story just fell in a heap of rubble and started burning."

Brad shook his head as the details became clear.

"By the time the fire trucks got there, the blaze was too hot to handle. Everything went up, including anyone in the building. They evacuated the entire block. A shelter was set up in a church down there. You want to go down and snoop around?"

"Yeah, let's see what we can find out. Someone's doing a number on people down there. Captain Owens wonders if we have a gang problem. Seems like that's the best place to look. Got anything back from the lab on the matchbook yet?"

Sam shook his head. "Mark's trying to keep everything quiet. He works when no one's around. Says he's picked up a couple prints, but hasn't run them through the computer yet. He'll tell me soon as he makes a match. Maybe a couple days."

"Sure hope he can give us some help. You know, it was two days before Kate calmed down. Now I've talked her into going back to her job, so she'll be out of the house. Sunday, we went out looking for a used car for a new friend of ours. When I pulled onto our street, I saw a black and white going around the corner. Are the guys from I.A. still picking through the garbage in my neighborhood?"

"I doubt it, partner. Far as I know, the case is closed. Maybe the patrol guys are just watching your house for you."

"Yeah, maybe."

Brad's telephone rang. The voice at the other end was all too familiar. It sent a tremor through his body. Sam picked up his phone when Brad nodded at him.

"Well, well, the hero cop's back on the job. The whole world's safer now ain't it? You sure Foxy Loxey is safe at home alone? You listen to me, A-hole, I ain't done with you yet. I dropped the case 'cause you're a goddam cop. My lawyer said I had no chance. I've got news, sucker, I'm gonna get my pound of flesh. Don't care if it comes outta your hide or Kathleen's. Don't matter to me. Come to think of it, I kinda prefer her flesh. As I remember, it's a lot more edible."

Brad's fury hit a trip wire. He made sure Sam was listening before he answered.

"Worley, you scum, you're through torturing her! If you so much as look cross-eyed at her, you're a dead man! You got that?"

"What was that, you bastard, another threat? If you want a rematch, I still got one good arm. You're welcome to break that one, too. It won't keep me from getting what I want. See you in church, you horse's *ass!*"

Brad slammed the phone down when he heard the dial tone. Sam Hardy pulled his phone from his ear just in time. He shook his head, a dazed look on his face. "He's got more brass than a Civil War cannon. It's obvious he gets his kicks by giving you a tough time. Doesn't—-?"

"…and I always bite. Sam, I think he puts up a smoke screen so I won't nail him. You know, the old misdirection ploy. I've threatened him so often he'll claim harassment if I try to arrest him. Damn his rotten soul. Let's get out of here so I can cool down."

In fifteen minutes, they pulled their squad car onto the main street running through the heart of the Japanese settlement, Little Ginza.

Brad pointed out some of the things he noticed about the area. The streets were clean. Flower boxes were common at the fronts of many stores. The residential areas were noteworthy for their neatly trimmed lawns and colorful gardens. It was an eye-opener for Brad who got the feeling he was in another world.

"Pull in here, Sam. Let's get out anyplace around here and walk the streets for a couple blocks. See if people will talk to us."

The two men exited their gray car and walked along the well-kept sidewalks looking into shop fronts. Neither of them was familiar with the area. Brad's drive-through, the previous day, was just the second time he remembered being there.

The people on the street provided a kaleidoscope of costuming. The clothing varied from typical Occidental California Casual to the more traditional kimono, obi, wooden geta and colorful parasols. It was a revelation to both men, who, without warning, had been transported into another culture right in their hometown.

"I don't know about you, Sam, but I'm amazed. Also a little embarrassed I haven't bothered coming down here before. I had no idea it was like this. Did you know?"

"I don't come here, but Audrey comes here quite often. She loves the food and this is the only place she can find it. Says she thinks the folks here are really great."

"You don't sound too impressed. You feel brave enough to try some food?"

"Are you kiddin? Not with *my* stomach. I want to know what I'm puttin' in it, okay? Don't relish eating a bunch of seaweed and octopus. Don't tell me you're hungry already?"

"No, not starving. Just figured it would be a good way to meet some of the people without flashing my shield. Maybe I'll have Sumiko bring Kate and me here sometime."

"Sumiko? Isn't she the gal you brought down from Seattle? You getting cozy with her?"

Brad detected a tone of disapproval in Sam's voice.

"Kinda by accident. She's a very nice young gal, Sam. Kathleen thinks she's great and she intrigues me. Her enthusiasm is contagious. Looks like a Tahitian. Very exotic."

"Well, I gotta say I'm surprised. You know, her being a Jap and all."

Brad went slack-jawed. He couldn't believe Sam's comment. He always assumed his partner was without prejudice. Brad had never noticed any indications of racial bias before. "Why would you say something like that, partner? Sumiko's a very bright young lady. We even asked her over for dinner last night. You got some ax to grind?"

"Hey, for your information, my old man was in World War Two and fought the Japs in the Pacific, okay? He was killed at Guadalcanal, so you'll hafta forgive me if I don't think too much of them. They started the war. You're too young to know what terrible things they did, so let's just drop it, okay?"

"Fine. If you're uncomfortable, we can go. I'll come back alone sometime. I need some input from the area about the bombings. Sam, I had no idea how you felt. Sorry about your dad. You never told me about him before."

They fell silent. Sam's apparent hatred for the people was a shock for Brad. Maybe even his own partner concealed a silent agenda. Just another thing confusing the issues.

With a sudden rush, Kelly Garrett's words about feeling alone and suspicious settled over him like a blanket. He took a sidelong look at his longtime partner and saw a totally different person. Was it his imagination or did Sam sprout a set of horns, just overnight?

Brad looked at his watch. It was 11:30. He'd drop Sam off at the station, then go pick up Kathleen for a bite of lunch. He needed some time to think about this new revelation from his partner. Was it significant?

He spent a pleasant lunchtime with Kathleen, and thought she seemed herself again, with no outward signs of fear. Brad hoped it was a sign he could stop worrying about her mental health. He was so protective of her, any crack in her exterior armor caused instant concern. She seemed very upbeat when he dropped her off at the store.

As he drove back to the station, his cell phone rang. It was Sumiko, checking in with him. On a spur of the moment decision, he asked her if she could take a ride with him. When she agreed, he changed directions and headed to her hotel. He desperately needed some inroads to the Japanese community. Waiting was not an option.

When he entered the hotel lobby, Brad anticipated another open display of affection from Sumiko. Instead, she left him slack-jawed with surprise when she deliberately walked up with hand extended. A slight frown crossed her face when he expressed his surprise. He took her hand and was further surprised by the limp nature of her handshake. Her actions left no doubt that something was amiss.

Neither said a word until they were in his car and underway.

"Okay, Sumiko, what's up?"

"Maybe you gonna say I'm crazy, but I think someone following me. I see same guy in lobby every time I go in. He always sits with newspaper, but I know he looks at me. You think FBI looking after me?"

"Garrett said he'd keep an eye on you, but we better be sure. When I take you back, you point him out to me and I'll find out who he is. I'm glad you're being careful, Sumi. Your job is getting even more dangerous."

Brad filled her in on the bombing of the previous night when two persons were killed. The stakes were so much higher now, that his concern for her safety was trebled.

"Sumiko, I drove down to the Japanese settlement this morning. I'm really impressed with how much pride the people have in their neighborhood. I didn't speak to anyone, but hope maybe you can take me down and introduce me around. It's important that I make contact with their leadership. I can't help them unless they trust me."

"*Dai jobu*, Logan-san, I take you there. Japanese people very proud of their community, but don't trust outsiders. It will take some time before they trust you. I will help. You'll see. Maybe teach you about *sashimi* and *sushi*. You gonna like Japanese food."

For the next two hours, Sumiko took him from one shop to another. In each store, she explained the nature of the business. If the merchandise wasn't familiar, she told him what purpose it served. In many cases, she introduced herself to the person behind the counter and then introduced them to Brad. They discovered quite soon, if she mentioned he was a cop, the response was not just cold, it was frigid.

"Just tell them I'm your friend. They shut us out when they find out I'm a cop. Something is all screwed up in this part of town. Don't they know we're supposed to be on their side? We need to do a lot of PR out here."

"Logan-san, these people are afraid. They don't tell me anything. Something's not right here. Maybe I can find out more if you're not with me. Maybe I come back alone."

"That's a good idea, Sumi. But remember…be careful. Don't take any chances. It's possible they're afraid of *Yakusa*, not cops."

"Logan-san, you worry too much about me. Why you do that?"

"It's part of my job, Sumi. Agent Garrett told me to watch out for you, remember?"

"Yeah, I guess. Sometimes you sound like *Papa-san*. Sometimes *Papa-san* say I can't trust American. He says I gotta be careful or I get hurt. His *Papa-san* died in war when America dropped big bomb on Hiroshima. Many Japanese people remember those things."

Brad couldn't believe it. First Sam Hardy, making no bones of his prejudice of the Japanese people. Now Sumiko with a story of her father's prejudice towards Americans. He wondered why Mr. Tanaka had brought his family to America if he felt that way.

"Sumiko, how do you feel about us white folk? Maybe you'd rather not be seen with me?" Brad was just halfway joking. It dawned on him that he was in Sumiko's world while they walked these streets. Was she being treated as a leper, being with him?

"Oh, Logan-san. I'm not like *Papa-san*. You're my special friend. Kathleen, too. Mostly older Japanese think about wartime. Please, don't be mad at me. You mean much to me. Besides, we have job to do. We need to stop *Yakuza*. *Dai jobu?*"

Brad noticed Sumiko getting very emotional as she looked up into his face. The hint of tears in her eyes tugged at his heart. He wouldn't let anything spoil the rapport between them. It was essential to the success of their job.

He took her hand and gave it a squeeze.

"Don't worry, Sumi, I feel the same way about you. You're very special to me. Now, before we break down in tears, let's get back to the car. It's obvious to me we need a lot of work in this part of town. When you start work at Kurasawa, get to know as many of the people as you can. We need names of the leaders of the community. I must get their trust."

"I understand, Logan-san. I'm happy you want to know my people. It's good we have this talk. Don't let anything spoil our friendship. You know…maybe I move out to this side of town. I feel better here, you think?"

"It's a great idea, Sumi."

He grinned at her as he opened the car door for her. "You know, for a girl, you think pretty good."

In the lobby, Sumiko looked for the man she saw in the lobby the past two days. To Brad's dismay, she couldn't spot him. Brad went to the lobby phone and called the local FBI office.

He was told that, yes, they had a man watching Sumiko and, yes, he would continue until further notice. Brad passed the reassuring word on to her, giving her visible relief.

Before he left her in the lobby, they decided how they would stay in touch without causing too many eyebrows to raise.

"I have to get back to work. Call me tomorrow on my cell phone at two o'clock. You start your job Wednesday, right?"

"Yes, Logan-san. Thank you for everything. *Sayonara.*"

She stretched on tiptoes to give him a peck on the check. Her closeness and the wonderful smell she exuded, made Brad reach for her waist with both hands and pull her close for just a brief moment.

"Promise me you won't take any risks when you get into your new job. I get the impression these *Yakuza* people are heavyweights."

"Heavy waits? What is that?"

"It means they're cruel and they kill people. Just do what I say. *Dai jobee?*

He felt foolish using her own words, but she giggled in appreciation of his efforts.

"You do pretty good for round eye, Logan-san. Thank you for being good friend."

Sumiko waved and walked to the elevator.

Back at his desk, Brad concentrated on the paperwork piled up in front of him. It was very difficult when he had so many other things on his mind.

❧   ❧   ❧

Brad couldn't explain it, but as he pulled into the garage at home, every sense tingled as if an alarm was triggered. Without letting Kathleen notice, he reached inside his coat, making sure his automatic was at home under his arm. Before closing the garage door, he took one look outside, peering up and down the street in both directions. Nothing moved.

Inside the house, he turned on the answer machine to listen to messages. The third one explained his tingling senses. The whispered words brought Kathleen screaming into Brad's arms. The message was sinister:

"Nice try, Junkyard. The answer machine's a nice touch. Foxy Kathleen's on my list of things to do, soon. We're gonna get real cozy. Just me and that gorgeous bod'. I've got just what she needs. Nice talkin' to you."

Brad rushed to turn off the machine. "God, I'm sorry you heard that, Hon. Next time, I'll take the messages when you're not in the room. You all right?"

Brad calmed his wife as he removed the cassette tape from the recorder. He'd take it in for analysis. He was sure the tap on his phone couldn't locate the caller after such a short message.

Walking to the front hallway, he picked up the stack of mail from the floor.

When he tossed it on the counter, a large manila envelop caught his immediate attention because of the sound it made hitting the counter. The dull thud was an instant warning. His voice betrayed his calm exterior facade.

"My God, Kate, don't touch that brown envelope! It may be a bomb!"

CHAPTER 11

❀

*K*athleen sought refuge behind her husband. A muffled scream escaped from her throat as she lay her head on his back. Brad stood with arms spread, a grizzly bear protecting his mate from annihilation. Summoning a brief spurt of courage, she peered around his body.

A moment later, she broke out in unrestrained laughter. She couldn't help herself. With one hand she pointed to the offensive mailer. With her other hand she poked her husband on the arm.

"Brad, honey, that bomb is from my mother. I recognize her writing. I don't think Mom became a mad bomber overnight. She must have sent me the photographs of Dan in his uniform. She promised them months ago. My God, I thought *I* was the one getting paranoid. You're getting just as bad."

Like a reluctant parent, removing his child's soiled diaper, Brad picked up the brown mailer and turned it over several times before he handed it to her. A sheepish grin replaced the look of alarm. "Jesus, I'm turning into a marshmallow. I'm so gun-shy, I see a bogie-man under every rock. Can't believe I'm this paranoid. I need a drink. How 'bout you?"

They both breathed a huge sigh as the tension dwindled. Kathleen patted him on the cheek. "Believe me, I understand. I just wish it would stop. I'm worn out from being afraid. Make that a good stiff drink, will you? I need it."

Brad nodded as he watched her head toward the stairs. He hung his jacket in the closet, then removed the holstered gun from under his arm and locked it in the safe. Since there was nothing important in the mail, he left it on the counter and prepared a shaker martini for Kathleen. After straining the silvery liquid into a glass, he uncapped a bottle of Cordova and pushed a piece of lime into the opening. Several quick swallows helped ease the dryness in his throat. Then a growl slipped through his clenched teeth. "Judd Worley, you slime, I won't let you destroy her. I'm gonna be in your face until I nail you. This horseshit's coming to a screeching halt."

"Who are you talking to, Brad Logan?"

Kathleen came into the kitchen wearing a loose fitting duster. She picked up her drink and looked into Brad's face for an answer. Her first swallow brought a quick pucker to her face. Then her tongue made a trip around her lips, savoring the tartness of Vermouth.

Brad sidestepped her question. "Did I tell you I took Sumiko down to Little Ginza? She introduced me to some of the folks down there. The people must have thought I was the Grim Reaper. The community harbors a great deal of hostility toward cops. It's a cinch we dropped the ball by not making sure the people down there trusted the police. Most of them were afraid of me."

"You are pretty intimidating, you know. What made you go there today? Weren't we gonna take Sumiko there for dinner later? Couldn't wait to see her, huh?"

"Get real, Kate. Something happened this morning when Sam and I went there. Sam told me he hates all Japanese. His dad was killed fighting in the Pacific during World War Two. Sam couldn't even stand being in the same area with Japanese people. It sure shocked me."

Brad looked at his wife. Her face revealed her own surprise.

"Anyway, I went back to the area with Sumiko. She helped me by telling me things about their culture. She even introduced me to some of the business people in the area. But then, she informs me her own father distrusts Americans. I guess Sumi's grandfather died when Truman dropped the A-bomb on Hiroshima. I had no idea so many people—-on both sides—-carry prejudices because of things that happened during the War. Jesus, that was almost fifty years ago."

Brad took his beer to the counter and sat on a stool. Kathleen stood behind him and rubbed his neck with strong fingers. Chills traveled the length of his spine.

"Brad, honey, I bet there are a lot of people from that era who have prejudices. But, you know, Dad served in Japan in the service. It was after the war, in the 50's. He always said he enjoyed being over there. He thought the people were nice. I suppose it depends on your own experiences with people of another culture."

"Yeah, I guess. But I was sure surprised Sam was so outspoken about it. He's always seemed so even-handed with everyone. Never showed any kind of prejudices. Came as a real shock to me."

"So, did you enjoy the time with your little squinty-eyed tramp?"

"You just can't leave it alone can you? Kate, don't even joke like that. Does she make you feel threatened?"

"Are you kidding? What's she got? Gorgeous black hair. Skinny butt. Little bitty boobs. Masters degree. Why would I feel threatened? Just 'cause you make all kinds of excuses to be with her? Just for that, you're getting leftovers for dinner. Take your beer and go watch the news, Lover boy."

Kathleen pecked him on the cheek with a grin and stuck her head in the refrigerator.

🍁   🍁   🍁

It was just after 10:00 the next morning when Sam slammed down his phone and shouted across the room at Brad. "We may have a break, partner. A wino out near Southside Park stopped a patrol car this morning. Told 'em a story about seeing a big, bloody fight in an abandoned store."

The news wasn't that earth-shattering to Brad. "Yeah? So what. That's common down there."

"It happened last Thursday night, pal. You know—-the night Mooch bought it. We can't just blow this off. Put on your dancin' shoes, partner. We're gonna check it out. Don't trust anyone else to do it right."

"You got that right. Sure as hell, we can't take a chance on missing something."

"The uniforms sealed off the building, but haven't gone in yet. I told them to wait for us. I'll call out a Forensics team and we can meet them there."

The two veteran cops wasted no time getting to their car. Within minutes, they were weaving through traffic, with red lights flashing. Twenty minutes later, Sam pulled up in front of the abandoned building.

A black and white patrol car sat in front of the boarded store front, red lights flashing. A yellow band of police tape fluttered from several telephone poles. Brad didn't recognize either of the uniformed officers at the curb.

At one time, the building housed a neighborhood grocery store, one of numerous abandoned buildings in the area. Weather-beaten boards were nailed across windows and doors. Graffiti decorated even the barriers. The store was a forlorn shell of its former self. A beaten fighter with eyes swollen shut—-now shunned by a fickle public.

One entire block of 21st Street was part of the blight-infested southwest commercial district. Merchants had abandoned the area in recent years when faced with another year of red ink. Similar to growing cities all over the country, businesses in this part of Langston were deserted for more lucrative areas of commercial development. Gaunt, derelict buildings pleaded for a new lease on life. Their pleas fell on deaf ears.

Two uniformed policemen talked to a filthy derelict sitting on the curb. He clutched a brown paper sack in his hand. His dirty face was pocked with large patches of red, flaky skin. A stubble of white whiskers covered his chin. Brad's nose told him the man's primary need was a bar of soap.

When Brad and Sam approached, the uniforms acknowledged them with a nod and reported the results of their interrogation.

"Sergeant, this upstanding citizen, who has no name, flagged us down while we were on patrol this morning. Claims he and a couple of his friends had a party in the back room of this building last week. Not quite clear what day it was, but thinks it was last Wednesday or Thursday. They hid when three guys showed up at the door. When a fourth dude arrives, a real donnybrook developed. Musta been one helluva fight among the new arrivals. The winos couldn't describe anybody except three of them were dressed in black and wore ski masks. In the end, the biggest guy hits the ground and there's a gunshot. After that, the dudes in ski masks roll him up in a blanket and carry him out."

"Could they give you any details about the guy who got beat up?" Brad eyed the dirty derelict who sat on the curb.

"No. Just said he was a big dude with a bald head. Said he roared like a lion when he hit the floor. You guys call for a Forensics team?"

Sam looked up from making notes in his spiral bound notebook and nodded. "Yeah, should be here right away. Why'd it take this guy so long to tell you what went down four days ago?"

The leather-jacketed officer answered. "That's kinda weird. He claims he flagged down a patrol car the very next day, but the cops wouldn't take a report. Told him to go sleep it off. What do you make of it, Sergeant?"

Brad shook his head. "Don't know, but I'm sure gonna find out who was in that patrol car. You been inside yet?"

"No, Sergeant. We decided we shouldn't take a chance on disturbing the scene. You wanna go in now, or you gonna wait for the lab guys?"

"We're going in. Keep this guy close by, okay?"

Brad and Sam pushed the sagging front door aside, giving them access to the dark interior. Using his flashlight, Brad scanned the cold, damp darkness. Picking his way with care, he made his way to the location described by the witness. The smell of stale air, mold and putrid flesh almost strangled him. He stopped walking when he came upon a large, dark splotch on the floor. An irregularly shaped area some six to eight feet across was no doubt the target of their search. It was a scene not unlike many others Brad and Sam had witnessed during their years on Homicide.

"This must be it, Sam. God, look at the size of that blood stain. I'll bet those God-awful looking chunks of matter are part of the victim's brain. Looks like some bone fragments there, too. What a mess. We've got footprints all around the area. I'd bet my last buck this is where Mooch got it. Where the hell's the lab wagon?"

Brad flashed his light into the farthest corners of the room. Nothing attracted his attention. From the other side of the stain, Sam Hardy used his flashlight to direct Brad's attention.

"Look over there, Brad. Someone tossed his cookies. Mighta been one of the winos, but let's hope it was one of the perpetrators. We might get lucky. Maybe we can find out what the guy ate for dinner, okay? Maybe one of the bad guys upchucked when he saw Mooch get his head blown apart."

"You may be right." Brad dropped to one knee. "What's this? Hey, got a shell casing here. Looks like 9MM. Wait a minute—what's that over there?" Brad shined his light just beyond their search pattern. A bright, shiny object caught his attention when it reflected the beam of his light.

Sam reached the area first and leaned over to poke the object with his pencil tip. "I don't have the slightest idea what it is, Brad. Looks like some kinda toy. Never saw anything like it before. You recognize it?"

Brad knelt down on the dirty floor and shined his light on the tiny carving. It didn't look familiar. It resembled a grotesque likeness to some species of animal. With his chalk, he drew a circle around it. Nothing could be picked up until photos were taken. At this point, all they could do was take copious notes.

"Looks like Forensics is here."

Brad yelled out toward the front door. "Hey you guys, bring in a portable flood light. We're gonna be here a long time. Did Mark come with you?"

The gray haired man in khaki pants and plaid shirt set down his duffel bag and nodded his head. He busied himself fitting his hands into rubber gloves. "Mark's comin'. He's bringin' the light. God, what a mess. No doubt something or somebody bled all over this place. Hey, where's your gloves? Thought you both were experienced at this stuff. You touch anything?"

Sam laughed. "Gus, how long you known us? We know the drill, you old fart. We haven't touched anything. If we do, we'll get out the gloves, okay? Now get us something worthwhile in this mess. Got plenty of footprints to work with."

Another new arrival caught Brad's attention. " Mark, did you bring a light?"

Brad took an armload of equipment out of the arms of the newest arrival. It was Mark Goddard, a longtime friend. He and Mark had gone to grammar school together. Mark's scientific knowledge made him one of the best lab men in the state. Just having Mark work the case himself was a bonus. His expertise was always in demand.

"Man, I'm glad you're on this one yourself, Mark. We need a break in the worst way and hope this scene will provide it. I'm guessing this is where Mooch Kaiser was killed. Be sure you check out that strange-looking item laying over there." Brad nodded toward the carving. "Maybe you can identify it."

Within minutes, they set up the portable lights. Now they could do away with the cumbersome flashlights. The portrait of the scene was one of violence. The entire area was scuffed with footprints. Some clearly defined, others smeared. Several long, skidding marks indicated someone had lost his footing in the slippery mess.

Brad dug the pair of rubber gloves from his pocket and pulled them on. He hated to wear them. They made his hands hot, but department protocol demanded he use them, to avoid contamination of evidence. Recent well-publicized trials had brought that protocol into national prominence.

As soon as the photographer finished covering the entire scene from several angles, Brad widened his search for anything that might provide another piece to this huge and gruesome puzzle. This was one grisly treasure hunt neither man relished.

Sam Hardy wandered off into other parts of the building, making sure nothing was overlooked. Fifteen minutes later, he returned carrying a small piece of paper. He held it gingerly by one corner and handed it over to Mark Goddard for bagging.

"What's this, Sam?"

"Near's I can tell, it's a trip ticket. Used by cab drivers. You know…it shows where they pick up a fare, their destination, mileage. It's sure out of place at this scene. Handle it with special care, Mark, we need a break. This might be it."

"Where'd you find this, Sam? Kinda wish you hadn't moved it."

"Don't worry, I marked the place with chalk, Mark. It's right next to the wall." Sam pointed. "Looks like it may have blown over there. There's a pile of leaves and other bits of paper trapped up against the wall."

Brad's interest soared. "Hot damn, Sam, this could be our home run. That paper might be significant. Let's see if we can confirm where those winos hid out. Their story needs plenty of verification." Brad waved towards a spot on the floor. "Mark, don't forget we need samples of that vomit over there. It may help identify a suspect later on."

Brad and his partner made their way into the rear of the building. It may have been a storage room when this store was still a viable business. Volumes of sunlight filtered in through large skylights. The remains of wooden crates littered the floor. Piles of rags and newspapers created potential bonfires. Empty wine bottles sparkled like green and white gems. Brad wrinkled his nose as the awful smell of stale wine and human excrement gagged him.

"Hey, old buddy, that can sure spoil an appetite. Jeez, how can these guys hang in a place like this? Makes my skin crawl. Musta been some party going on. Do you think they had a clear view of the action out in the other room?"

Brad and Sam experimented by moving to various locations in the room, testing their field of view. From almost every spot, the party goers could observe the bloody ballet as it played out. Unless they were too drunk, and that was a distinct possibility.

"Listen, Sam, I don't know about you, but I could use some fresh air. This place gives me the creeps. Let's go talk to our concerned citizen. Maybe we can get more out of him now, since we've looked around in here."

It was after 2:00 when they left the crime scene. The lab boys loaded up their treasure trove of specimens, minutia, hard and soft evidence. Brad pulled his friend Mark aside. Without shame, he reminded Mark of their *long* friendship, then piled on the compliments before asking him to put this case on the front burner. In particular, he wanted the trip ticket put through intense scrutiny for anything which could identify the owner.

Mark Goddard nodded his head. "Brad, you know I'll do the best I can for you. I realize this case is important. By the way, you and Kathleen going to our twentieth class reunion?

"I'm sure we'll be going. We haven't missed any yet. Listen, we gotta get outta here. Thanks for your fast service. We need a lot of help."

With Sam at the wheel again, they rode with mixed emotions. They could almost hear the tortured screams of Mooch Kaiser. Something just didn't ring true. Was there too much information at this crime scene?

Brad thought aloud. "You know something, pal? That scene is so accommodating. You know what I mean? It's like everything stood up and waved so we could find it. We'd better move slowly on this. I'd hate to blow it because we were too eager to catch Worley in something. It's possible we're getting suckered."

"Yeah, I know. One thing's sure; we need the names of the officers in that squad car who refused to take the report. That's kinda curious."

"Yeah. That's on my list of things to do. Hey, I just realized I'm hungry. Let's stop at the Frontier Grill. Haven't checked it out since you found those matches under Mooch. Can you handle that?"

Sam just nodded and made a right turn on 25th Street.

Walking into the small cafe, Brad wondered what made it such a popular place to the rank and file cops of Langston P.D. Booths lined two walls and a lunch counter stretched across the centerline. Even though it was after 2:00 in the afternoon, there were plenty of customers. Brad recognized many of the faces in the crowd. Many others were strangers. Langston PD was so large now he no longer knew every cop by his first name.

Scanning the faces, he saw a room full of clones. Did he just imagine it or did every cop have a certain commonality about him? What made them stand out from ordinary citizens? Was it their military bearing or perhaps their detached manner?

A lot of mustaches. Short, military haircuts abounded. Similar aviator type wire frame sunglasses. Muscular bodies. Even the men not in uniform looked familiar. He chuckled to himself when he realized, in all likelihood, he resembled a cookie from the same cutter.

"Tell me, Sam, do you know any of Nichols men by sight? I'm curious why they're still driving by my house every day."

"From I.A.? Not sure I would know them anyway. Can't see anyone here who looks familiar. Why don't you just go ask Nichols?"

Brad shook his head. "Not sure he'd give me a straight answer. Truth is, I don't trust the guy. Just something about him doesn't hold up to the light. Know what I'm sayin'?"

"I haven't had much contact with him. You know, I always keep my nose clean. Not like some people I know." Sam looked at Brad with a slight smirk on his face. He put his ridiculous 'Fish' glasses on the tip of his nose and opened the menu.

Brad already knew what he wanted, so he scanned the room again as they waited for service. "Hey, Sam, look over there at the counter. Do you know those two uniforms?"

Brad nodded toward the end of the counter. Two men in blue occupied the two end stools. Both still wore their hats and sunglasses. What caught Brad's attention was the large bruise on the cheek of one of the officers.

Sam let his glasses hang from the cord on his neck. He took a long look at the two men Brad indicated. The man with the bruise must have felt their stares. His eyes rose from his meal to the mirror behind the counter. For a moment, his gaze locked with Brad's.

"Who's that guy, Sam? Any idea?"

Sam continued his appraisal, then shook his head. "I've seen the guy on the right at one time or another. Got no idea who he is. The other one doesn't look familiar at all. Let's get the number off their car when they leave. We can find out from dispatch who's driving it. Don't get too obvious, or you might spook them. I'm sure they know the 'Junkyard Dog'. After all, you *are* a legend." He ignored the one-fingered salute Brad held in front of his nose.

By the time Brad and Sam ordered, the two uniforms had finished their lunch and went to the cashier. On their way to the door, they detoured and walked right up to Brad's table.

"What's up, Sergeant? You seem interested in us. Any particular reason?"

"Yeah, I've been looking for the guys who've been watching my house this week so I could thank them. Haven't I seen you two out in my neighborhood?"

"Not us, Sergeant. Musta been someone else."

Brad wanted a better look at the man with the bruise. "What the hell happened to your face, man? You wreck your car or something?"

Uniform number two turned and gave Brad a look of bare tolerance. "Caught an elbow during a tough collar. Anything else you need?"

Brad shook his head. "Sorry about your injury. Caught a couple of them myself in the past. That stopped when I got smart and learned to duck. See you guys later."

A slight nod and the uniforms made their way out of the restaurant. Sam pulled out his notebook and jotted down the names. The act of coming to his table gave him the opportunity to see their name badges as they spoke to Brad. "He sure has a nasty shiner. You think you've seen him near your house?"

"No, Sam, I was just fishing. The only cop I've recognized out there is Reed."

"Gorman Reed? You know, he's still out on sick leave. You don't suppose he caught the same elbow as Henderson, do you?"

"That would sure be a coincidence, wouldn't it? You can bet I'll find out more about his injury when we get back to the station. You want some more coffee?"

"Just a bit. I want to review my notes before we go back." Sam signaled the waitress, who brought the coffee pot along with their checks.

"You know what, partner? Those two cops are going on my list of potential White Knights. They fit the profile. Wish I could get a look at their right shoulders. Guess I just can't go ask them to take off their shirts, can I?"

"You could, but it might cause some raised eyebrows. I agree they both fit the pattern. You're convinced we have snakes in the department? God, it looks like we don't know who's backing us up any more. You know? If I ever decide I can't count on back-up support from fellow officers, I'll get out of the business."

"I'm with you, Sam. That's why I plan on checking out all the guys we don't know. There must be a way of profiling the ones who might join."

"You suppose they keep a record of tattoos and scars in personnel files?"

"I bet I'll find out when we get back. Let me check for messages."

Brad pulled out his cell phone and dialed headquarters. The operator gave him their messages. He made several notes before he hung up with a big grin on his face.

"Great luck, Sam. We got our subpoena for Worley's bank account. Let's go get it and see if we can get to the bank before it closes."

They drove back to the station where they decided Sam would go to the bank to pick up Worley's records. In the meantime, Brad headed down the hall to Personnel in hopes of turning up something in personnel records. He knew there must be a clue somewhere that might paint a portrait of a White Knight.

What kind of cop would kill one of his own?

CHAPTER 12

The rest of the afternoon went by in a blur of activity. At 4:00, Brad realized Sumiko hadn't checked in with him yet. His concern became so great he couldn't concentrate on his work.

The Commodore Hotel desk clerk said she had left the hotel before noon and was still not in her room. She had not left a message for him. Now he worried. The local FBI office was no more helpful, claiming they knew nothing.

Brad decided he was over-reacting. Sumiko was a big girl. Besides, with an FBI escort, she should be safe. His attention returned to the information he and his partner had uncovered that day. It was significant. "Sam, look at this. Worley deposited more than a hundred thirty-five thousand dollars in his account in the last eighteen months. That's pretty big bucks. Almost every transaction is more than five thousand dollars. I didn't know driving a hack paid so well. He writes several checks every month for five grand or more. What the hell's he doing with the bucks? Think he's dealing dope? Whatever it is, we know it's gotta be illegal. Wonder if the IRS has a record of all this money? Maybe I should call them."

Sam disagreed. "The IRS? Ixnay on that, partner. Let's get all we can out of this before you cut them in, okay? It's possible there's a legit answer for the dough. You know…like the lottery. Maybe he's pimping from his cab, okay? We jump in too fast and we end up with a face full of egg roll."

Brad threw his hands up when he realized his partner was right in his assessment. "Yeah, I know it, Sam, but, dammit, I just wanna grab the scum by the neck and drag him in. Good thing you keep reminding me I've gotta be patient…appreciate it." Brad picked up a folder from the pile on his desk. "How 'bout Gorman Reed? According to Personnel, he went to the hospital last weekend with broken ribs and a severe bruises of the torso. I couldn't find an arrest report explaining those injuries. Marge says he reported he'd be out for the whole week. You think that's coincidence?"

"Could be, partner. Maybe he was in a wreck or fell off his roof. Don't forget, you saw him last Friday. Let's put our pants on one leg at a time, okay?"

Brad mulled over the facts for a few minutes. Whoever killed Mooch must have sustained some injuries in the fight—serious injuries. Mooch was no pushover. One of the cops he saw in the restaurant today showed signs of being in a fight. Gorman Reed has the kind of injuries you could get in a serious fight. Coincidence? Not bloody likely.

"Sam, how can we get a look at Reed's shoes?"

Sam looked up at Brad over the top of his 'Fish' glasses. "Say what? His shoes? What the hell for?"

"If he was at the scene of the killing, he's got blood all over his shoes. How can we get a look at them without knocking him down?"

Sam shrugged. "You got enough information to get a subpoena for them?"

"I doubt Captain Owens wants to hear any more of my suspicions." Brad slammed his open palm down on his desk. "Dammit, I just know this stuff is all related. Somewhere, there's something that'll substantiate my suspicions. Sure wish Mark would hurry up with the stuff he has. He should have results on the fingerprints by now."

"He would've told you this morning, man. Chill out, Brad. You're like a race horse at the starting gate, you know?"

Brad's phone rang. He looked at his watch. It was 4:35. The voice on the instrument brought him a sense of relief. "Logan-san. Sorry I didn't call at two like you told me. I went to Little Ginza. You wanted some information from there. You mad at me?"

"Yes, Sumiko, I'm mad as hell at you, but relieved you're safe. What do you mean, getting information for me? Did I tell you to do that on your own?"

"You're getting me P.O.'d, Logan-san. You're not the boss of me. I work for FBI, remember? You tell me yesterday you wanted information from people in Ginza. You gonna let me tell you or not?"

Brad couldn't tell if she was putting him on or telling him off. Either way, he found himself admiring her chutzpah. "Hey, little girl, we had a deal, right? You check in with me every day, remember? I worry about you. Now, go ahead and tell me what you did."

"*Dai Jobu.* That's more better. Don't forget, FBI man's watching me. When I go out, I see him. Guess what, Logan-san? I call for cab and ask driver if he can drive me all around Ginza town. Is so funny, the driver tells me he's your *tomodachi*—you know, your friend. This guy has lots of tattoos on his arm, like gang boy. His name is something like Jude…or Jug. You know him?"

Brad almost dropped the phone. He felt the blood rushing to his face The bastard showed up in his life every time he turned around. This was no coincidence. "Sumiko, tell me more about this cab driver."

"He's very nice, Logan-san. Takes me all over Ginza town. He leave meter off so I don't pay a lot. You pissed off again?"

It always seemed so out of place when Sumiko used local slang words. It was bizarre coming from her little girl's mouth.

"Sumiko, the man is *not* my friend. He hates me and will do anything to get me upset. He hurts anyone close to me. That means you, if he decides it will make me mad. Tell me about him."

"He says you're his friend. Even bought me lunch. Said it was a gift to you. Why you don't like him? For sure, you think he might hurt me?"

"Listen to me, Sumiko…he can't be trusted. He's evil in every bone of his body. Yes, he'll hurt you if it pleases him, so you can't have anything to do with him. You hear me?" Brad's voice rose to a fever pitch. He could feel himself losing control. Sam was peering over his glasses across the desk. He did the 'tsk' thing with his mouth.

Sumiko sounded contrite. " Logan-san, sorry to make you angry, but how can I know he's bad? He talks nice to me and I wasn't afraid. Besides, he don't charge me for my ride. Do you want me to tell you what I heard when I talk to Japanese people?"

"Yes, but not right now. I'd rather you told me in person. Besides, I'm still not over warning you about Judd Worley. How in hell did he know you knew who I was?"

"Because he saw us at the airport when we fly in from Seattle. Is that bad?"

Brad thought aloud. "He must've been watching for me to come back. Sumiko, are you back in your hotel room?"

"*Hai.* I just get back and call you. I buy some nice Japanese silk scarf. I bring one to Kathleen next time. I don't understand why you get mad at me. I try to help you."

"Sumiko, I'm not angry at you. It's your new *tomo—tomo—*-whatever, friend I'm angry with. Don't ride in his cab again. If he contacts you, you get hold of me. I promised Kelly Garrett I'd watch out for you. Please don't make my job any more difficult. You understand?"

"When I get my new car I never ride in cab again. Maybe then you can be happy with Sumiko. *Dai jobu?*"

Brad sensed her frustration. Here she was, helping him, then he climbs all over her for something she had no control over. He was properly ashamed. "Tell you what, Sumiko, why don't I pick up

Kathleen and we come by the hotel and take you to dinner. Would that make up for my making you unhappy?"

Sumiko's voice took on the tone of a disciplined child. He could almost see her bottom lip quivering. "No. I don't go out tonight. I'll just have dinner in my room and take a hot bath. Maybe tomorrow I can be happy again. I'll call you at two. I promise."

"I'm sorry. I know I upset you. Believe me, I appreciate your trying to help me, Sumiko. Good night." Brad hung up and looked across the desk at Sam, who was frowning and shaking his head. It triggered something in Brad.

"You got something in your craw, Sam?"

"You're a real piece of work, man. You're lettin' that Jap get to you. She ain't worth it, man. How come you talk to her every day? You got something going? Man, you're crazy as hell. A gorgeous wife like you got and you're foolin' around with a slant-eye. Thought you had more sense."

"Butt out, Sam. It's none of your Goddam business. There's nothing going on and if there was, I wouldn't need your blessing—and I wish you wouldn't call these people Japs. That's as bad as the 'N' word. These people didn't kill your dad. That was fifty years ago. For your information, Sumiko's grandfather was killed by our A-bomb. She doesn't call you 'Whitey', for Christ sake."

Sam started to speak, then thought better of it. He just raised his social finger in salute. In silence, he swept papers from his desk into his top drawer and locked it. Without a word, he walked out of the squad room, shaking his head.

Brad wasn't a happy man as he put his work away. He had never had angry words with his partner before. His temper boiled as he drove from the parking garage on his way to pick up Kathleen.

❧   ❧   ❧

In front of the boutique, Brad couldn't keep his anger from Kathleen. When she reached across the seat for a kiss, his response didn't even qualify as lukewarm. It was a signal to her. 'Don't bug me yet'.

Kathleen made one attempt at small talk. She mentioned how busy the boutique was during the big sale. Brad looked straight ahead, absorbed in his driving and his thoughts. Kathleen took the hint and rode home in silence.

As he unlocked the back door, he said his first words to her. "Kathleen, I'll check the house to be sure it's clear, then I have to run an errand. Do you mind holding dinner up about an hour? Something happened today and it needs my attention. Sorry to be such a jerk, but it just has to be done."

"Well, of course, Hon. Can you tell me about it? You're not going after Judd Worley again, are you?"

"Kate. Don't even ask me. I'm not in the mood. Everything will be all right. Please, just trust me. I'll be back soon. Promise."

Brad verified the house was secure, listened to a message on the phone machine and checked the day's mail. Everything looked normal. He kissed his wife and was gone before she could ask any more questions.

Twenty minutes later he reached Judd Worley's apartment complex. He left his car at the curb and walked to the manager's office. He wasted no time explaining his mission.

"Tyrone, sorry I bothered you at dinner time, but I need another favor. I need a witness at Judd Worley's door. I have a message for him and don't want him lying about what was said. Do you mind? Just stand there and listen. Will you do that?"

"Sergeant Logan. You done me lotsa favors an' I owe you for young Ty, but you're askin' me for somethin' I know's wrong. Please, don't ask me to do it."

"Tyrone, trust me. I'll just talk to Worley. I won't touch him, I promise." Brad's voice rose. "Come on, you owe me, dammit. He won't even see you."

"God help me. I gonna do it, but I know I'm gonna regret it."

Tyrone walked out of his apartment and shut the door. He followed Brad to the door of Judd Worley's unit, then stood off to the side, crowding close to the wall.

Brad pounded on the door. "Worley, open this door. I'm an impatient man. Open up now or I make kindling wood of it."

Just as he pulled his fist back, the door flew open. Judd Worley stood in the doorway. His arm was still in a sling, but that didn't keep him from stepping right into the range of Brad's fists. The defiant look on his face was not the look of a man who feared his opponent.

"Well, if it isn't Sergeant Logan. Hero of the Langston P.D. Why the hell you banging on my door, you *A-hole*?"

"Just shut up and listen, you ignorant piece of crap. You've threatened my wife for the last time. You think you're such a bad ass, I'm telling you this just one time…if you don't leave her alone, I'll break every bone in your body. When I'm through breaking bones, I'll stick my 9MM in your mouth and pull the trigger. I'll see your brains splattered all over the ground just like you splattered Mooch Kaiser." As soon as the words left his mouth, Brad knew it was the wrong thing to say. Now it was too late. He had to run with it.

Judd didn't even flinch. He still stood toe to toe with Brad. His words exploded from his mouth. "You crazy son of a bitch! You're so out of control, you talk garbage! I ain't never harassed your foxy wife, but takin' a bite outta her gorgeous ass would be a pleasure. She thinks she's too good for me, but I never let that stop me. Gonna blow my head off, huh?"

"You heard me right, you turd. I've had it with your threats *and* your insults *and* your lack of courage. I'm telling you to leave her alone—and while I'm at it—don't mess around with Sumiko Tanaka again. Did you think I would let you get away with telling her we're friends? You're even dumber than I thought."

"You mean that little Oriental piece? You tellin' me she belongs to you, too? Does Kathleen know about that? By God, you're even a bigger whore than I thought, Logan. Married to the best looking puss in town and you're sniffing around Sweet Leilani? Listen, I'm tired of talking to you. Just take your sorry ass outta here." Judd stuck his jaw up next to Brad's face and sneered. His breath smelled of stale tobacco and cheap beer. Brad almost gagged.

Without flinching, Brad reached under his arm and pulled out his gun. He moved back a step and stuck the muzzle into Worley's face, pressing hard enough to make him pull back.

Worley looked right into the muzzle and sneered. "Shootin' someone takes balls—an' you ain't got 'em. You been scared of shooting a gun since you killed your pa, you simple pud. You don't scare me. You never scared me. You're nothing. Stick that gun up your ass."

Judd's words cut into Brad's soul like a hot knife blade, exposing long hidden emotions. Fighting against his mind-numbing fury, he made a last effort at saving a portion of the bluff. "Judd, you aren't smart enough to be scared. I've never shot a suspect, but, in your case, I'm willing to make an exception. You killed Mooch and I'll see you burn for it. But, when I arrest you, I hope you run, because it's more fun shooting a runner. Just remember my words, you slimy toad, I'm gonna *nail* you!"

Brad shoved the barrel of his 9MM into Judd's face with gusto. Worley's expression didn't change. With contempt, he turned his head aside and sneered. "Oh shit…just remember them yourself, Logan. I'll do what I want and do it to anyone I choose. Don't matter if it's your wife or your girl friend. Makes no difference to me. I may screw both of them, whatever I decide. Now get your sorry ass out of my face before I call some of your idiot friends to haul you off to the funny farm."

Judd turned his back on Brad, ignored the extended gun and slammed the door.

The whole incident took less than ten minutes and left Brad sucked dry of all emotional energy. He was numb as he replaced his gun in its holster. It was then he remembered his witness. Tyrone stood ten feet away with a look of terror on his face.

"Tyrone, I'm sorry. I had no idea it would get so far out of hand. God, that man is so infuriating. I should've just shot him to get him out of my life."

"Man oh man, Sergeant, I don' even wanna hear that kinda talk. Now you get yo'self out of here now and I'll be pleased if you never come back. I don' feel I owe you no more favors. Someday you gonna kill that man. You just watch what I say. Go on now."

The apartment manager turned on his heel, leaving Brad with a feeling of disbelief. Nothing was accomplished by his action. The edge he always believed he owned over Judd Worley didn't exist. The man could not be intimidated. Brad knew he had lost the face-off.

As he entered his car and started for home, he replayed the scenario in his mind over and over. What did Judd tell him that stopped him cold? 'You killed your pa. You killed your pa'. The words bounced around his mind, refueling huge chunks of his memory. 'You killed your pa'.

Brad yanked on the steering wheel and pulled his car over to the curb, unmindful that he was in the middle of someone's driveway. He covered his eyes with his hands and all the pent-up emotion poured out of him. He pounded on the steering wheel with both hands.

"Oh, my God! Dad, I'm sorry. I'm sorry. I didn't want to hurt you. I'm sorry. I didn't empty my rifle. You kept telling me and telling me. I just forgot. Oh, my God, Dad, I didn't mean it."

Brad pounded on the steering wheel until jolted awake by the sound of a horn blasting with obvious impatience. He looked in the mirror at a car behind him. The driver held a fist in the air and pounded on the horn.

For an instant, Brad fought the urge to pull the man from his car and break his head. Then he realized his car blocked the man's driveway. With a half-hearted wave of apology, he put his car in gear and drove off.

He didn't remember the drive home. His mind was in fragments. The day began with brilliant signs of progress in solving a murder case. Now his thoughts centered on the fierce confrontation with his long time partner; scolding Sumiko when she tried to help him; his shortness with Kathleen, and the final offense—-the brutal way he plunged into a senseless confrontation with a man who lived for a chance to get him rattled.

'Brad Logan, you've had quite a day, I gotta admit. How many times will he humiliate you before you realize you're overmatched? Now, you've let him know he's a suspect. You let him know you care what happens to Sumiko. Man, you just loaded his guns with a full charge. Now you have to wonder when he'll pull the trigger on you. You may as well get ready for another suspension. This could mean your job, you stupid jerk!' His mind churned in desperate agony.

When he turned onto his street, he saw the black and white patrol car inch past his house. That was the final straw. Laying on the horn, he came up behind the car and waved his arm at the driver. He slammed on his brakes to keep from rear-ending the police car as it came to a stop in the middle of the road.

Brad leaped out, leaving his car door open. Racing up to the driver, he reached for the door handle, prepared to rip the door off the hinges. Then he recognized the driver. It was Lieutenant Nichols!

"What the hell do you think you're doing, Sergeant Logan? If I hadn't recognized you, I might have shot you down. That was a stupid move, man. Whatever possessed you to flag me down like that?"

"Jesus, Lieutenant, I'm sorry. It's been one hellacious day and something just snapped back there. I didn't know you were patrolling out here. Isn't it a little out of your usual territory?"

"I don't have a territory, Logan, you should know that. I was curious if our patrol cars were still watching your house every so often. Does my being here bother you for some reason?"

"No, sir. Glad to know the department is concerned about us. Sorry to disturb you. Good night."

If there had been a deep hole nearby, Brad would have crawled into it. When the police car disappeared down the street, he pushed the garage door opener. He fumed as he waited for the door to swing open.

A huge sigh escaped him as he turned off the ignition. His confidence was so shaky at that moment, he didn't have strength to open the car door. Then he saw the door to the kitchen open. Kathleen stood in the doorway. He got his feet under him and made his way into her open arms. She had a quizzical look on her face.

"Brad, I saw you stop that cop outside. Who was it? Why did you run up to him like that? It looked like you would tear his head off. Talk to me, Brad. What's going on?"

"Let's just get inside, Kate. I need a stiff drink. Matter of fact, I need several stiff drinks. I'll tell you as much as I can. God, what a day."

When Kathleen told him he could take as much time as he needed before she put dinner on the table, Brad mixed up an entire pitcher of Martinis. He needed the quick anesthetic effect they produced.

Kathleen kept silent, but her anxiety for him showed all over her face. He gulped down two drinks without taking a breath, then slumped into a chair.

"Katie, there's no way I can explain this bizarre afternoon. It may go down in history as my worst ever. Be patient with me, girl, or I'll explode. I don't want to explode at you. I hope you know that."

He felt her walk up behind him and wrap her arms around him in a bear hug. "Brad, no matter what it is, I'm here for you. Nothing can make me stop loving you. You know you're my whole life—long as you don't tell me you slept with that little tart."

It was an attempt at humor and Brad knew it, but it had just the opposite affect. The glass in his hand went sailing across the room, shattering on the floor with a crash. Kathleen was so startled she plopped down on the floor to get out of the way of his flailing arm.

When he ripped off his jacket and flung it on the floor, he was vaguely aware she was scooting backwards, putting some distance between them. Her face reflected her terror. It didn't faze him.

Kathleen's voice was shrill with fear. "Brad—sweet Jesus—you scare me. I've never seen you like this. Please, honey, I…you haven't put your gun away. Let me do that for you. You're too upset. Please, dear, calm down. I won't ask any more questions."

When Kathleen rose from the floor, she began a cautious approach, with her hand outstretched. Her face was drained of blood, leaving her normally full lips pale and thin. The look in her eyes begged him not to hurt her. Her desperation resembled the fear of a wounded animal.

Her look reached into his heart and buckled his knees. He sat down to regain his equilibrium. He didn't object when Kathleen unbuckled his holster and took the weapon from under his arm. It looked as if she stood in a fog bank. She opened the door to the safe and placed the weapon inside. It wasn't until she spun the dial on the lock that a sense of relief crossed her face. "Honey, can I pour you another drink?"

He just nodded. He could feel the emotion welling up in his throat again and was afraid she would see him fall apart. He emptied the glass in two large gulps and held it out for another refill. Kathleen's eyes glistened as tears flowed down her cheeks.

By the time the third drink disappeared down his throat, Brad's mind softened until he could talk. He looked into Kathleen's face with the look of a beaten spaniel.

"Katie. Do you think I killed Dad?"

CHAPTER 13

※

*B*rad couldn't look into her eyes. He could see the shock on her face. Now that the words were out of his mouth, he wished he could retract them. Kathleen grabbed both his hands and pulled him closer. The look of concern and fright on her face added to his misery.

"My God, Brad, what are you talking about? Why did you ask me such a question? What brought this on?"

Brad didn't answer. He continued shaking his head from side to side. Something hideous from deep inside him screamed for release. His voice trembled as disjointed words poured out. Once they started, he could no longer withhold them. It was a stampede of long suppressed emotion.

"All these years...so long—wouldn't let myself remember. All these years. God, why'd he remind me? Son of a bitch won't be satisfied until he makes me kill him, the dirty, slimy bastard! Katie, how can you stand to be near me? I'm turning into an animal. Only animals kill, and I'm ready to kill Judd Worley. That makes me an animal. I hate this. I hate this. Damn you, Judd Worley!"

Brad looked heavenward. He yanked his hands from Kathleen's grip, almost knocking her down, and picked up the pitcher, pouring another martini into the glass. It disappeared in three swallows. His face became a horrible mask as he shuddered from the effects.

Despite her fear, Kathleen put her hands on his chest. "Brad, I—I don't want to nag you, but you shouldn't drink any more. You know you don't tolerate it well, so just keep talking. What the hell did that bastard do this time?"

"He did nothing, Kate. *Nothing.* I stood there with my gun stuck in his face and he just laughed at me. He didn't bat an eye. Said I didn't have the guts to shoot him. Says I killed Dad and can't shoot a gun anymore. Why'd he say that? Of all the other rotten things he's said to me—to us—why dredge up old wounds? He doesn't know anything about it. He wasn't there. I was there. Me and Dad. Oh, God. Dad told me to unload my rifle. Why didn't I listen? Oh God, Kate, it *was* my fault. I *did* kill Dad. Jesus Christ, I killed him! Oh God, Dad, I didn't mean to."

With no warning, Brad's stomach began heaving. He staggered to the sink just as the martinis exploded out of his mouth and nose. The convulsions lasted for several minutes. Then dry spasms replaced the vomiting. By the time it was over, he hung over the sink, panting for air. Kathleen held a cold washcloth on his face. The tears rolled down her cheeks as she sobbed in silence.

"Oh, Brad, darling, why did you go see him again? I know you're worried about me, but he's just trying to make you crazy. I'm sure he wouldn't hurt me. Come into the den; we need to talk this out. Please, Darling. I never thought you killed your dad. No one else did either. My God, you were just fourteen. Worley's doing his best to drive you up the wall. You fell into his trap, can't you see that? Why did it come to a head today?"

Brad couldn't answer yet, but he didn't object when she led him into the den. He was afraid to lie down, so he sat in his leather chair. She kept the damp cloth on his face until he pushed it away.

Kathleen hovered over him like a mother over a sick child. The look on her face told him she was in a frenzy over his emotional state.

"Please, Brad, talk to me. We can't let this get any worse. Maybe you should go see Doctor Fisher. She handles this kind of anxiety attack all the time. Let me call her, please?"

Brad shook his head, babbling with disjointed words: "Don't wanna talk to a shrink—Fisher's a hack—gonna work it out myself—won't let anyone see this. Don't need another suspension. Just be patient, Katie." Brad slammed both fists down on the arm of his chair.

"Can't let that mother f—sorry—Worley, ruin me. Stick with me, Kate. I need your support. You deserve better than this. I'm sorry. I've been acting like an idiot." Brad patted his lap and opened his arms. "Come sit with me, Katie; I need to feel your strength."

Kathleen needed no encouragement. She fell into his lap and sobbed against his chest as he stroked her hair. Neither spoke for many minutes, but his body twitched each time another convulsion hit him. Moments later, Kathleen pulled her head back and stared into his face. Brad realized he must resemble a whipped spaniel. It embarrassed him. He was *supposed* to be the Junkyard Dog.

Kathleen's face took on the expression of an anxious mother, when she becomes displeased with an unruly child. Brad didn't resist when she placed her hands on his cheeks and pulled his face close to hers. "All right, Brad Logan, you listen! We're going to thrash this out and we'll do it now. You're not making things better by wallowing in your own shit. Talk to me. Don't let the gin talk for you. What brought this on? Why now? Why today?"

"Back off, Katie. I'll do it my own way. This crap didn't just happen, you know that. It's been coming on for some time. It's not just Worley. It's the job. It's Sam. It's my worry for you, and now I even worry about Sumiko. Judd made contact with her and I'm sure it was no coincidence. He was at the airport when we came in from Seattle and saw us with her."

Kathleen pulled her head back and stared at him with wide-eyed wonder. "Are you saying Judd threatened Sumi, too? How could he?

How dare he? I'll kill the son of a bitch myself! What did she do to him?"

"Nothing—neither did you. He thinks he'll destroy me by getting at the people I want to protect. I can't let him destroy us, Kate. He'll die first. I'll beat him at his own game. He doesn't know how much I know about him. I'm gonna see he pays for all this shit. But…why did he say that about me and Dad? Where'd he get that? How'd he know it would do this to me? Worley knew it even before I did. Where'd he get the idea? He's not that smart. Someone's coaching him. Someone's leaking stuff from my personnel files, dammit!"

Brad's fingers dug into Kathleen's arm with such intensity, she grimaced and pried them off. She studied his face as she rubbed the finger marks. A strange expression took command of his face, and he was aware that his muscles were losing their tension. The pulsing tic in his jaw stopped its dance as the legendary Mr. Hyde began emerging from the ugly mask of Dr. Jekyll.

The real Brad Logan, veteran hard-nosed cop—Brad Logan, All American football player—Brad Logan, loving husband—returned to his mortal body. He could feel the metamorphosis taking place, even through the martini-induced fog. The Junkyard Dog persona, as if commanded by its master, heeled to the leash.

Kathleen ran the damp cloth over his face once more. Her face turned hopeful. "Brad, Darling, it's incredible. The look on your face…I'm almost afraid to say anything that might spoil it. It's fantastic—the change coming over you! Can you feel it?"

He didn't say a word. He wrapped his arms around Kathleen and kissed her with great tenderness. It took her breath away, sensing the love he communicated with the kiss. "Kate, something just happened to me. I can't explain it, and I won't question it. I've never experienced anything like it before. It's—it's—like swimming in a black pool with no bottom. Then, just when you think you'll drown, you find something to grab onto." Brad's arms tightened around her. "You were the strength, not me. I'm so embarrassed you saw me like that. I'm ashamed of myself, but realize now, I'm not as indestructible as I always believed. Now, I see how reckless I've been in the past. I must have a guardian angel keeping me safe."

Kathleen's tears of anger and concern became happy tears as she kissed her husband on the lips and struggled to her feet. She dabbed at her tear-streaked face. "We both should thank that angel. Right now, we both can use something in our stomachs. I'll fix some dinner. You sure you're all right, Sweetheart?"

When Brad just nodded, Kathleen stood for a moment, staring into his face as if confirming what she had witnessed. Then she turned and retreated into the kitchen.

Brad stayed in the chair alone. The agony created by his father's death, twenty-five years before, was something he wouldn't confront all these years. Now he could face it head on.

With his new-found sense of moral muscle, he let his mind wander back to that terrifying day. It was in early summer when his dad drove them into the foothills of the eastern Sierras to do some small game hunting. For most of the day, they enjoyed tramping through the scrub oak and manzanita, trying to flush out a rabbit or squirrel. Neither cared whether they found anything to shoot. It was just the pleasure of father and son bonding in a setting of such spectacular proportions. Throughout Brad's childhood, the senior Logan traveled the state as a hardware salesman, so the time they shared together was rare and precious.

Brad's mental montage became more intense as he recalled their return to the pickup they left at the trailhead. With Brad bringing up the rear, the elder Logan followed the meager trail. Brad carried his rifle over his shoulder, military style. They had followed the same routine many times before. They were within sight of their truck when Brad's foot struck an exposed tree root. As he fell to the ground, he used the butt of his rifle to catch his fall. The jolt caused the weapon to fire, putting a bullet into the back of his father's head, killing him instantly.

Another wave of guilt passed over Brad. The bitter taste of remorse overcame him as he recalled the many times his father admonished him never to leave a cartridge in the chamber of his rifle when they hiked. 'Why didn't I listen? Why was I so careless?'

A terrified fourteen-year-old Brad had used his T shirt, but he couldn't stop the flow of blood from his father's wound. With no other options available, he picked his father up, put him in the pickup bed and drove the vehicle down the hill to the nearest hospital, even though he had never driven before. A shudder went through Brad as the memory returned.

"Brad, can you eat something?" Kathleen's voice broke through the curtain of his reverie. He realized he was crying. He looked away so she wouldn't see his tears. Heaven forbid she should ever see him cry. Junkyard Dogs don't cry.

Brad followed Kathleen into the kitchen. The trauma of the past two hours had given him a surprisingly strong appetite. They ate in silence because words weren't necessary. Both were drained of feeling. Both sensed a breakthrough had just taken place.

As they sat enjoying after dinner coffee, the phone rang, activating the answering machine. When the caller identified himself as Mark Goddard, Brad jumped to his feet and grabbed the phone.

"Mark, we're here! What's going on? You got some good news for me?"

"Brad, I'm almost afraid to tell you this."

"Mark, old buddy, after the day I've had, you can tell me anything you want."

"Okay, here goes...You remember that matchbook cover you found at a murder scene? I finally identified the prints on it."

The words provided Brad with instant euphoria. "Jesus, Mark, that's great. Whose is it?"

"Before I tell you, you'd better know...the match book I was testing disappeared some time today."

"Disappeared? How can that happen? God damn it, Mark, that was vital to our case! What kind of lab you running down there?" Brad fought against the sick feeling rising in his throat. No, not again.

"It was locked in my desk drawer and someone broke in and took it—-broke the damn lock. It's just a damn good thing I keep computer records of every bit of data that goes through my lab. I have my own private data bank. I also have several good pictures of it."

"God, now I think I want to kiss you. Always knew you were smarter than the rest of us. You got a name for me?"

"Yeah, Brad, but it doesn't make sense. The prints are of the first two fingers, left hand, of one of our cops…Gorman Reed!"

The breath exploded from Brad's lungs. At last—something concrete to go on. It didn't matter at this point who it was. Much as he wished it was Judd Worley's, at least something good had happened on his side for a change.

"Are you sure of that, Mark? We can't make any mistakes about this. We're talking about the murder of an undercover agent. How did you make the match?"

"He's in our CID computer—like all cops. I just can't figure out what it means. You wanna fill me in?"

"Can't. This is big, Mark. You can't breathe a word to anyone."

"You know it doesn't mean a thing if the evidence is gone. It'll just be hearsay evidence if you try to use it. I can't believe someone came right into my lab and—-"

"Yeah, right. Like I say, it goes right along with everything else that's going on, *but*, we've made some progress. It's like a road map, pointing me in the right direction. Appreciate you calling me tonight. I needed something to go my way for a change. How's Paula?"

"I can't believe you won't tell me what this is about. Don't trust me, huh?"

Brad assured his friend it would come out soon enough. It wasn't a matter of trusting Mark—it was too risky for him to know and lives were at stake. He thanked Mark again and hung up.

Kathleen wasn't in the kitchen. He could hear the stereo playing upstairs. She was already up there. Brad looked at the clock. It was 10:40. The evening was a thing of the past. Where had it gone? He knew one thing—he was exhausted.

Brad made his rounds of doors and windows, made sure the alarm system was triggered, then headed up the stairs. He needed Kathleen's bedtime ritual. It would be a wonderful prescription for healing his bruised psyche.

By this time, she was sitting before her mirror, brushing out her hair. The light from the dressing table lamp highlighted the lustrous mane of copper. It also magnified the shape of her breasts as they rose and fell with each brush stroke. He stood, fascinated, for several minutes until she caught sight of him in the mirror.

Turning on her stool, Kathleen held out her arms to him. He hurried to kneel at her feet, burying his face in the sanctuary of those wonderful pillows of strength, savoring the all-healing scent exuded by her body.

The scene was so familiar he knew it by heart. Wood frame storefronts. Wooden signs swinging in the breeze. Dust swirling in the deserted street. There was a difference this time. What the hell was different? He couldn't decide. He just knew the scene wasn't the same.

When he stepped off the boardwalk and began a slow walk toward the figure in the street, he realized what had changed. The other figure was bareheaded—no hat covered the face.

He still couldn't make out the features of the man who stood with hands hovering over low-slung holsters. Even as the two figures got closer to each other, the features remained dark because the sun glared into his eyes.

Brad stopped walking when he was six feet from the man. His hand streaked toward his holster. This time, a gun miraculously appeared in his hand. He raised it until it pointed at the man's chest. His finger tightened on the trigger. It was then he recognized the face. "My God, Dad, it's you!" The gun fell from his fingers into the dust at his feet as the two men fell into each other's arms.

Brad sat upright in bed, his heart pounding against his rib cage. He struggled to breathe through the anguish he felt.

Kathleen bolted upright next to him. "Brad, darling, what is it? Oh, my God. You had the dream again, didn't you?"

He couldn't answer her as the vision kept repeating in his head. "It was Dad, Kate. The man in the street—it was Dad. I didn't shoot. I woke up. God, it was so real."

Kathleen made no effort to cover her naked body. She pulled him tight against her and stroked his head. His labored breathing returned to near normal.

"But, don't you see what it means, dear? At last, the dream has an ending. You didn't shoot your dad. You didn't kill him in your dream—you didn't kill him for real. Brad, the years of unnecessary torture are over. Now you can grieve for him in peace. It's wonderful."

Brad buried his face between her breasts and, with effort, pushed the scene from his mind. A wave of calmness washed over him. Maybe Kate was right; maybe it was over. Now he could grieve for his dad with no guilt feelings.

"God, Kate, it's been such a long and terrible road. It will be such a relief to know I won't have this guilt torturing me any longer. Thank you for being so strong. Have I told you how much I love you?"

"Yes, very eloquently before you went to sleep. We should get some rest now, Sweetheart, there's just a few hours left 'til sunup."

Kathleen kissed him. They slipped back under the bed clothes and she curled her body, becoming a perfect match with his. Both slept a peaceful and pleasant sleep.

❦   ❦   ❦

Brad was waiting in Captain Owens' office at 8:00 o'clock in the morning. It took him fifteen minutes to explain the evidence against officer Gorman Reed. Reluctantly—claiming it was against his better judgment—the captain called the DA's office and repeated the information to a staff attorney. When Brad left the office, he held a faxed copy of a warrant and subpoena.

Sam Hardy looked up as Brad approached his desk. Brad couldn't read anything into his partner's face because Sam's 'Fish' glasses provided camouflage. Before Sam opened his mouth, Brad took the initiative. "Partner, I hope you aren't still pissed about my blowup yesterday. There's no excuse for my stupidity. I was out of line and I'm sorry. I realize what a jerk I've been over this freakin' Judd Worley case. I'll control myself better now, partner, you can bet the farm on that. S'pose you might still work with me?"

Sam let his glasses dangle from their cord and eyed Brad from head to toe. "Funny, you don't look any different. Same ugly face. Nose looks like someone sat on it. Same Wyatt Earp clothes. Why would I want to work with a miserable Junkyard Dog again?"

The words were harsh. It was the devilish twinkle in Sam's eyes that Brad recognized as a sign he could light up the peace pipe. "Can I take that as a 'yes'?"

Brad felt a great burden lifting from his shoulders. Losing Sam as a partner was not something he relished. "Listen, Sam, I got a call from Mark last night. You know the prints on that matchbook cover? Guess what? They belong to Gorman Reed. How's that grab you?" Brad patted his pocket. "I have a warrant. If you have nothing better to do, let's go pick up Reed and his shoes. Gotta get to him before he knows we're coming. We won't even call for back up until we're almost there."

Brad pulled out the papers and scanned them with practiced efficiency. "He lives on Cherry Street. Hasn't been at work since last week. Must have been some fight he was in, right?"

Sam was already putting on his jacket. Even in the warm days of summer, Sam wouldn't venture out without his jacket. Brad knew his partner believed a cop should always look and act professional.

He watched Sam reach into his top drawer for the .38 Special he always carried. He tucked it into the holster in the small of his back. As he came around his desk, he held his hand out. The firm handshake said more than words. Brad knew their friendship was still viable, but he would no longer take it for granted.

During the twenty minute drive to Cherry Street, they called dispatch for a back-up car. Just as planned, the cars arrived on the block at the same moment and pulled to a stop in front of the Reed house.

The building was a small duplex, painted an ugly yellow. A chain link fence surrounded the front yard, what there was of it. A small, weed infested lawn of Bermuda grass, in desperate need of mowing—or better yet a flame thrower. A huge, but seldom trimmed Mulberry tree provided shade for the entire yard. It's huge roots pushed the sidewalk up, creating a walking hazard. A broken tricycle lay on its side on the front porch.

Brad motioned for the two uniformed officers to cover the back entrance. He tucked the legal papers into his inside pocket and led the way up the stairs, to the weather-blasted front door.

He and Sam stood on opposite sides of the door as he rang the doorbell. There was no sound from the interior. The doorbell didn't work, to no one's surprise. Why should it?

Brad pounded on the door. "Open up, Reed. Police Department. It's Hardy and Logan. We have a warrant for you."

As he stood waiting for something to happen, Brad looked around the area. Several people stood on the front sidewalk, their curiosity aroused by the police car in the street. He motioned for them to move along.

After what seemed an eternity of unanswered knocks, Brad looked at Sam, who just nodded his head. Brad tried the doorknob. To his great surprise, the knob turned. He snatched the door shut again, then signaled to his partner he would count to three and open the door with a rush. Sam crouched behind him with his gun ready.

When Brad pulled his gun from its holster, he couldn't help notice the startled look on Sam Hardy's face. Brad felt very uncomfortable entering with gun drawn, and it must have been obvious to his partner. Brad held up three fingers and counted down.

As the last finger dropped, he shoved the door open and watched as Sam rushed into the building then jumped to the side to get out of the light of the doorway. Sam crouched with gun extended in front of him, sweeping the room. Brad jumped into the living room and darted to the other side of the open door. Each waited until his eyes became accustomed to the dark interior.

An ominous feeling swept over Brad as he detected the odor of death. He held his fingers to his nose and looked at Sam with eyebrows raised. Sam sniffed the air, then nodded his agreement. Neither man doubted their senses. This building contained some element of death. Brad's high expectations took a nosedive into the toilet.

Brad pulled his flashlight from his rear pocket and, holding it together with his 9MM, motioned toward the door in the middle of the back wall. Sam nodded and made his way to the doorway, then, with practiced caution, peered into the blackness. He looked back at Brad and shook his head. They had performed this ritual so often, it came as second nature.

Brad stood erect and walked to the doorway and reached into the interior with the flashlight, flicking the beam from one end of the room to the other. It was a small bedroom. The only furniture inside was an unmade single bed flanked by a small, brown chest of drawers. On the top of the chest was a lamp with no shade and a picture frame containing a photograph of a young man and a dog.

Both men entered the room. Sam went to the window and raised the window shade, allowing sunlight to filter in. Brad turned off his flashlight. When their search of this room resulted in nothing of importance, the partners made their way down the hall to the next door.

Using the same practiced procedure they rehearsed a hundred times, Sam covered the door as Brad turned the knob and opened it. The smell rushing into their faces told them their quest was coming to an unsettling conclusion.

Brad's flashlight beam swept the small bathroom. The shower curtain was closed. Sam held his gun at the ready as Brad eased the curtain aside. The search for Gorman Reed was over.

His body lay in a grotesque position, dumped unceremoniously into the tub with no regard for his dignity. Sightless eyes stared into eternity. His swollen, black tongue protruded from his mouth, creating a hideous death mask.

The left side of his head was no longer attached to his skull.

CHAPTER 14

Sam holstered his weapon and knelt beside the tub. He pressed fingers against the neck of the victim, searching for a pulse. Brad knew it was wasted effort, but it was part of their training—make damn sure the victim is dead before you do anything else.

"Sam, I'll call for the M.E. and get the guys outside to seal the area. Are you satisfied this is Gorman Reed?"

Sam just nodded and continued to search for a pulse. Brad fought his anger. "Damn it, I hoped this would be the break we need. Looks like we've been *had* again. I'm getting sick and tired of coming in second every time. Wouldn't be surprised if the same weapon killed him and Mooch. Here's where the slug ended up."

Brad pointed to the shattered tiles in the bathroom wall. When he realized he was still holding his gun, he jammed it back into the spring holster under his arm. He retraced his steps into the living room and shouted out the door for the two uniformed cops. They emerged from the back of the house. At Brad's orders, they sealed off the crime scene with yellow police tape and bright red traffic cones.

Brad called the station. He reported the crime and requested a team from the office of the Medical Examiner, as well as his own crime scene investigators. He asked them to send Mark Goddard, but knew the chances of getting him were not good. Goddard was a very busy man.

While the uniformed officers began canvassing the neighbors, Brad went back into the house. This newest setback was infuriating, but he forced himself to keep calm. Someone knew his every move—someone with access to the same information. That someone, so far, stayed a step ahead of him.

Brad shed his jacket because of the heat in the house. He removed the rubber gloves from his pocket and squeezed his hands into them. He never believed the sign on the package saying 'One size fits all'. His oversized hands protested when he went through the routine.

"See anything in there, Sam?" He stuck his head into the bathroom where his partner was on hands and knees, glasses perched on the end of his nose. He kept poking his fingers into the flesh of the dead man, noting how the indentations stayed on the skin.

"I'd guess it's been less than twelve hours. That'd make it sometime after midnight last night, okay? Blood's still sticky in spots. Just starting to stink. Body's still not too rigid. Still has some temperature. You get the jakes canvassing the neighborhood?"

"Yeah, but I sure hope these two guys aren't part of the Knights. We won't get much useful information if they are. You ever see either of them?"

Sam shook his head. "You're gettin' real paranoid about the Knights, aren't you? Finding them under every tree, seems like. Don't you s'pose we still got some good cops left in the department?"

"Hope so. Listen, can you get a look at his left shoulder to see if he has a tattoo? Can you do it without moving the body?"

Exercising great care, Sam pulled up the T-shirt sleeve so he could see the skin underneath. By putting his head very close to the body, he was able to get a partial view of Reed's shoulder. He wrinkled his nose, revealing his displeasure at being so close to the body.

"Can't see it all, but it sure could be that chess piece. Jesus, look at those nasty bruises. Someone popped this guy pretty good. Looks like about a week old. He's wearing a rib cast too. No great surprise to me. You?"

Brad shook his head. "We'll get pictures when he goes to the morgue. Look, Sam, I'm gonna poke around. We need his shoes. If I'm right, blood residue will show up—Mooch's blood. Mark can check it out himself."

He left Sam and made his way back into the bedroom. A small closet opened off the bedroom. A shabby green curtain hung over the doorway, held up with a length of heavy twine. Two nails pounded into each side of the doorframe supported the string.

Brad pulled the curtain aside and peered into the dark interior. Hanging from the rod were three police uniforms and a number of civilian shirts and pants. On the shelf, Brad saw the stiff brimmed blue uniform hat worn by the Langston PD. Hanging from a large hook on the rear wall was the utility belt and holster all local cops wore. There was no weapon in the holster.

"Hmmm. Where's your gun, Gorman? Was it the murder weapon, or did someone just take it for a souvenir? Was it used on Mooch? Sure wish you'd talk to me, you poor dumb bastard."

Brad dropped to his knees for a closer look at the several pairs of shoes tossed in a pile on the floor. Two pair of athletic shoes showed no unusual stains, but he was very interested in the pair of black brogans and the low heeled boots he found. "I need a bag for these things."

He turned his face toward the bathroom and yelled. "Sam, I'm going to the car for some bags. You need anything?"

He heard a grunt from his partner.

Returning from his car, he noticed the two uniform cops talking together on the sidewalk next door. He waved them over. "You guys getting anything?"

The officers could only tell him neighbors heard several muffled bangs in the early morning hours. No one could put an exact time on the noise. Nobody saw anything else. Brad sent them back for a 'door to door' until they covered the entire neighborhood.

As he headed back to the house, he recognized the blue lab truck approaching. He waited for the lab men to exit the vehicle and helped them carry their assorted pieces of equipment into the house. He knew his day's schedule was already dictated for him.

🍁   🍁   🍁

"Do you still think I'm crazy, Sam? We've got bad cops in Langston and we've got to smoke'em out. They killed Gorman Reed because of those matches. His fingerprint on that cover puts him at the scene. Someone found out about it, broke into Mark's desk and stole it. The fact someone iced Reed before we got to him proves someone knows everything we know."

Sam looked up from his desk. He was involved in the tedious task of sorting out every small bit of evidence found at the scene. Poring over interviews with neighbors and following up on lab reports, Sam was a bulldog at this stage of the investigation. Each day, more evidence found its way to their desks. Now they must sift through the material, looking for the one thing which would unlock the confusing maze of information.

"Brad, I guess I have to agree…we've got problems. We got two dead cops in less than two weeks. No question—the cases are linked. We gotta work fast, but also gotta work smart. One slip and it'll come crashing down on us. Why don't you go see Mark and see if he'll put this case on the top of the list, okay? It's for sure; every honest cop in Langston is at risk until we sort this crap out. You feel like twisting his arm a little?"

"Yeah, but knowing Mark, he'll want the real reason for the rush. I've known him a long time, and I'm sure he's trustworthy. Just hate having anyone know about this." Brad picked up his phone and dialed Mark's number. "You gonna be there awhile, Mark? Need to see you right away—better yet, can you get away for coffee? We need a private talk."

"Can you give me a half hour? I can meet you then. Where you want to go?"

Brad met his old friend in the small coffee shop across the street. Despite his reservations about letting anyone else into the circle of knowledge, he decided it was a calculated risk. He needed Mark's help in the lab. "Mark, thanks for meeting me out here. You want something besides coffee?"

"Yeah. No coffee. I'll have a piece of lemon pie and a glass of milk."

Brad ordered for both of them, then turned his attention to his friend. "Mark, I've known you since grammar school. I trust you, but I'm also putting you in possible danger by what you're gonna hear."

"Jeez, Brad, you have a wonderful way with words. You make me wish I could just get out while I can. I assume you're not giving me any choice about hearing this?"

Mark's frown reminded Brad of his friend's docile manner. Throughout their high school friendship, Brad was Mark's unofficial body guard. If anyone gave his nerdy friend a hard time, Brad made sure it didn't happen again. He always liked Mark and admired his amazing scientific competence. Even though Brad himself was a good student, Mark was better in most classes. The two men were never socially intimate because of altogether different life styles—-Brad the Jock, Mark the Egghead.

"Mark, I'm desperate for answers. No one else can do what you can do. I want you to risk your career—maybe your life—and take a chance with me."

Mark looked up as the waitress brought his pie and milk. He didn't answer until she was out of earshot. He wore the face of a condemned man at his last meal. "Brad, I know you think I'm spineless. You still think I'm your old high school pal, but I've matured…or haven't you noticed? I can handle whatever you want to lay on me. Go ahead."

He slid his pie closer, seldom taking his eyes from Brad's face.

"Okay, pal, I'll start from the top. Stop me if you need clarification." For fifteen minutes, Brad filled his friend in about his trip to Seattle; his dealings with Mooch Kaiser; the chess piece in his locker and now the murder of Gorman Reed. At times, he wondered if Mark was listening, he was so intent on eating his pie. Several times, he asked a question, but for the most part, Mark just listened and wore a worried look on his face.

Brad looked around the near-empty room. "You can see why I'm so concerned about sharing this with you. The point is, every honest cop on the force is in danger until I get to the bottom of this. Sorry for the pressure, but I need answers fast. I need answers only *you* can give me. You see what I'm saying?"

Mark nodded vigorously and leaned forward as he answered. "What can I do, Brad? If I can help, I'm with you."

"Just be sure you're aware it can be dangerous."

"For Crissake, just tell me, Brad. I can handle anything. Spill it, man."

Brad hoped his face didn't reveal the surprise he felt at Mark's bravado.

"Will you do the lab work on these murders yourself? I want them done ahead of anything else—and this is important—don't give the results to anyone but me. No one. Got that?"

Mark's next comment was a bombshell. "Jeez, I think I should sell my personal services to the highest bidder. You're the second person today who asked for priority to these lab tests."

Brad's intuition stood at attention. Alarm bells clanged in his brain. "Someone else? Just today? Who in the hell was it?"

"Brad, this morning, Lieutenant Nichols came to my lab in person. Told me he wanted priority service and he wanted it kept quiet. *Now* what do I do? He outranks you."

"Nichols? What the hell is he doing? This is a murder case, not Internal Affairs. I don't trust him. I can't put my finger on it—he's just too devious for my blood. You ever get that feeling?"

Mark shook his head. "I don't have much contact with him, but I've heard it from others. So, what am I supposed to do?"

"Mark, trust me on this. You can't tell him *anything*. Just stall him when he asks you. My God, man, he may be a turncoat." Brad looked at his friend with what he hoped was a reassuring expression. "I'm telling you...this could cost you your job. I hate that. We've been friends so long, but I need your help. The department needs your help. What do you say?"

"Oh, for Christ sake, Brad, don't get so damn dramatic. Of course I'll help you. Just keep Nichols off my back. What's our first priority?"

Brad's sigh of relief couldn't be disguised. He'd been holding his breath for hours. He reached over and pumped Mark's hand. "Mark, you won't know how important this is until it's over. You have my total respect and admiration for making the right choice. First thing is tying officer Reed to Mooch's killing. If I'm right, you should find Mooch's blood on Reed's shoes. I'm betting the same gun killed both men—compare the slugs. I need analysis of Reed's blood. Was any of it at the scene of Mooch's killing? Have you identified the little gadget we found in the store and is there anything about that trip ticket you can tell me? That's just the beginnings of my shopping list. What do you think?"

"Piece of cake, Brad. Some of the things are already done. The slugs are from the same gun—a 9MM—probably police issue. The little piece of ivory carving you found is called '**netsuke**'. It's from Japan. Can't tell you anything else about it."

"Japan? You sure?"

"Positive. Does that mean something to you?"

"I'm not sure. Anyway, go ahead...what else do you know?"

"The trip ticket's clean. No prints and nothing written on it. I thought there might be an indentation from another ticket on it—you know, like it was in a pad of the things. So far, nothing shows—I'm still trying. The blood samples will take a little longer. Maybe by the end of the week. What am I supposed to tell Nichols?"

"Tell him—let's see—tell him Captain Owens gave you something else to do. I'll talk to Owens and clue him in, but won't tell him everything we know. Not sure I trust him yet either. Mark, be careful, this stuff's dynamite. I know I've put you on the spot, but I'm desperate. What was the name of that Japanese thing again?"

"It's called 'netsuke. Many years ago, Japanese men wore kimonos and carried their valuables in a pouch. They used fancy ivory carvings as fasteners to close the pouch. I don't know if they still use them. Far as I know, they're just collectibles now."

Brad looked at his watch. It was after 5:00. He knew he would arouse suspicion if he and Mark stayed any longer.

"Mark, let's get back. I'm gonna bug you every day. Please do your best for me, man. We all depend on you—especially me. Thanks for being there when I needed you. I won't forget it."

"Believe me, Brad, I'll remind you. By the way, did you ever find the announcement about the class reunion?"

"Tell you the truth, I forgot about it. Kate takes care of that stuff. She tells me when to get ready and how to dress. I'll ask her about it. Promise."

The two men shook hands and headed back to their offices. Brad felt he was at least a step or two closer to some of the answers he craved. But the biggest question still remained: 'What is Nichols up to?'

❦   ❦   ❦

Sam was eager for an update on everything Brad had learned. Above all, he was interested in hearing about Lieutenant Nichols' involvement in the murders. It was very unusual for the head of Internal Affairs to be involved in a murder case.

"Strange that he interfered with the lab. But we can't let him know we're aware of it. You gonna talk to Captain Owens?"

"Yeah, but I'm not sure how much I can tell him. You know, Kelly Garrett in Seattle warned me I would get paranoid about everyone around me. He was sure right. I don't trust anyone. Man, I'm glad we've worked together so long."

Sam let an evil leer take over his face, like the one on the proverbial cat in the fishbowl. "Guess you haven't heard about my new tattoo, have you, pard?"

"Dammit, Sam, don't even joke about that. I'll go see if Owens will talk to me. See you in the morning." Brad walked down the hall to Captain Owens' office. Owens was putting on his coat when Brad tapped on the door. The captain waved him in.

"How can I help you, Sergeant? Anything new on Reed's murder?"

"Yes and no, Cap. That's why I'm here. May I shut the door?"

Captain Owens waved his approval, then sat back down at his desk. Brad took the seat across the desk and let the story take shape as he talked. "I'm having a problem with Lieutenant Nichols. He told Mark Goddard to put everything else on the back burner while *he* works on the Reed case. I know it's important, but it hinders my own investigation. Can't understand why Nichols is sticking his nose in the case anyway. Do you know what he's doing?"

"He doesn't share anything with me. I guess he figures if Reed was involved in a cop's killing, it belongs in Internal Affairs. Not sure I agree, but you keep doing what you're doing…I know you'll get to the bottom of it. If you need backup with Nichols, I'll do what I can. He doesn't often listen to what I say, but I'll try. Do you know anything yet?"

Brad filled his boss in on as much as he felt he could share. He made sure the captain knew about the White Knight tattoo on Reed's shoulder. It was important for Owens to be aware of that. It was crucial that he believe a conspiracy existed. Brad wasn't comfortable releasing any other details so soon; he still wasn't sure Owens was trustworthy.

It was after seven when he picked up Kathleen at her job. They decided it was too late to cook dinner at home, so they stopped at the Commodore for dinner. It was nearby and featured a good selection of entrees. They enjoyed a quiet dinner, then drove home.

When Brad pulled into the garage, he was frustrated when the overhead light did not come on automatically as the door swung open. Kathleen stayed in the car while he fumbled his way forward to the other light. It was then he noticed the back door was not latched. That discovery made every nerve in his body tingle with anticipation.

His gun came out of its holster as he turned towards Kathleen with his fingers to his lips. He ignored her frantic signals and inched the door to the kitchen open. Carefully and methodically, he made his way through the house, opening every door, searching every closet and verifying the integrity of the alarm system. Nothing was out of place.

When he returned to his frightened wife in the garage, he assured her everything was safe and she could go into the house. Before he followed her, he replaced the light in the garage. His senses were in turmoil as he entered the house again.

Was he being too cautious, or had someone been in the house? Wouldn't the alarm have discouraged an intruder? Did the light burn out as a natural occurrence? Did they just forget to latch the door as they left that morning? He couldn't answer any of the questions.

He assured Kathleen that all was well as they prepared for bed. In some ways, she was bearing up better than he. Her safety was his main concern and would continue to be until this disturbing case was over. It clouded his judgment. The only apparent 'up-side' to current events was his newfound ability to curb his temper. He had a right to be proud.

Sleep ignored him as he lay on his back staring at the inside of his eyelids. Every detail of the past few weeks paraded before his mind, and over and over, he filtered each incident until it became a montage of cluttered scenes. He was overlooking something important. Something that would bring it all together.

The blast knocked him onto the floor. He lay there stunned, his ears ringing, until his other senses took over. The room vibrated even after the last echo of sound faded away. He heard the neighborhood come alive with sounds of dogs barking and of muffled shouts. The pungent smell of cordite penetrated the room.

When he was satisfied he wasn't injured, he scrambled to his feet and fumbled for a light switch on the bedside table. He couldn't see if Kathleen was still in the bed.

As light filled the room, he became aware of her moaning from the other side of the bed. He dove over the bed where he found her bundled up in the blankets, rocking from side to side.

"Kate? Honey, are you all right?" He eased the crumpled bedding from around her. Kathleen's face was covered with blood. She struggled to sit up, but Brad pushed her back.

"Don't move, Kate. Let me see where you're hurt."

The floor around the bed was littered with pieces of glass. The drapes blew into the room from the missing window glass. With great care, he lifted his wife back onto the bed and examined her face.

"You were hit by a piece of glass, Hon. You're bleeding some. Hold still. Let me get a washcloth. Looks like just one cut."

"What happened, Brad? Was it an earthquake?"

"I don't think so, Katie. Now don't panic on me, but I'm sure it was a bomb. Just lie there. Be careful about this damn glass. I'll be right back."

On his way to the bathroom, Brad picked up the phone and called 9 1 1. The blast had been reported and fire crews were on the way. He requested an ambulance. He knew he should check the rest of the house, but Kate was his first priority.

Popping his feet into the moccasins in the closet, he picked his way back to her side with the wet cloth. Carefully, he wiped as much blood as possible from her face. It was then he noticed she had two small cuts, and both oozed blood, but didn't appear too deep.

"We'll take you in for stitches, Hon, but it doesn't look too bad. Will you be all right if I go check the rest of the house?"

"Yes, of course, Brad. Hand me a robe, will you? Just be careful. What in the world could have caused this? Don't you think it might have been the gas main?"

"I'll find out. Just wait here. I ordered an ambulance, just in case there were other injuries. Hold this on your forehead until it stops bleeding."

Walking as if on egg shells, he made his way down the stairs. He wasn't prepared for the vision he encountered. It was a war zone. Pieces of glass, plaster and wood covered everything. He picked his way through the rubble to the front door. Someone pounded on the door and shouted to him. It was his neighbor, Ed Swanson.

Brad fumbled with the lock and opened the door.

"My God, Brad, what in the world happened? Are you and Kathleen all right?"

"Yes, Ed, we are. Kathleen's face is cut. Is your house damaged?"

Brad looked out, but a cloud of smoke and dust engulfed the entire area.

"Everyone else is fine, Brad. Your house is the only one. Did you have a gas leak or is someone sending you another message?"

"Ed, I don't smell any gas, so I'll assume it was a message. Will you wait for the fire engines while I go check on Kathleen?"

He could hear the sirens as he made his way through the downstairs disaster area and returned to Kathleen's bedside. She sat on the edge of the bed, the bloodied wash cloth still held to her head. Her shock was gone, replaced by near hysteria. Brad held her close as her body was wracked with convulsions. He used every ounce of fight in his body to overcome the rage boiling up in his throat. His voice was that of a wounded grizzly bear.

"That's it, Katie…you're going back to Omaha until this is over."

CHAPTER 15

*I*t wasn't easy, but Brad finally convinced Kathleen she wasn't safe in Langston. Two days after the bombing, he put her on a flight to Omaha and watched with a sense of relief as her plane took off. It was an emotional farewell. Kathleen made him promise he wouldn't go look for Judd Worley with mayhem on his mind. Brad had no intention of reverting to his 'junkyard dog' days. His plan for Judd was much more cerebral than pure mayhem.

The local glass company replaced every window in the front of the Logan house. A crew from a housekeeping agency spent hours picking through the pieces of plaster and glass. Each night, as he drove up to the empty house, he received a vivid reminder of the blast: A large depression in the ground where once a nice green lawn thrived. Several white sawhorse barricades stood guard over the indentation. A local gardening service would soon replace the front yard.

Although the interior suffered very little damage, the memories of the incident refused to die. Each recollection brought his anger boiling up again. It took every ounce of will power to avoid retaliation against those he felt were responsible.

Sam Hardy offered his spare bedroom to Brad, but Brad's mule-headed stubbornness kept him returning each night to his empty house. He had no intention of being run out of his own house—at least now that Kathleen was no longer in danger.

One positive aspect of the event was the concern his neighbors showed after the experience. Many came by, offering help and condolences. Each said they would keep a closer watch on the goings-on in the neighborhood. Brad wondered how long their new attitude would remain. He was certain most of them wished he would move so they could feel safe again.

When he returned home the second night, he picked up the mail from the floor in the living room. A bright red envelope caught his immediate attention. It was addressed in yellow crayon. There was no stamp. It was addressed to 'Junkyard Dog'. He ripped it open, taking great pains to preserve the wording on the front. Inside was a simple child's valentine, with a chilling message scrawled in crayon:

'Sorry I missed you. I'll do better next time'.

Brad sat on a stool collecting his thoughts. The 'old' Brad would be out the door looking for Judd Worley, but the 'new' Brad stayed in control. It was another severe test of his newfound resolve. With delicate care, he put the valentine back into the envelope and laid it on the counter. He would take it in to Mark tomorrow.

Brad looked at his watch. It was just 7:00 and he didn't feel like cooking anything. On an impulse, he picked up the phone and called Sumiko's hotel. She was not in her room, but the clerk told him she was in the dining room. He asked that she be paged.

"Sumiko, it's Brad Logan. I need some contacts in Little Ginza. Are you too busy to go with me tonight?"

"Logan-san, I just finish dinner. Sure, I can take you to Ginza if you want. I'll go change my shoes and be ready. Meet me in the lobby in twenty minutes."

"See you in about twenty minutes. Thanks."

After he hung up, he wondered if this was such a good idea, but he had made up his mind that Sam would never go to Little Ginza with him again. Sam's attitude about the area was no secret. Brad knew that this part of the investigation was up to him. He would fare better with Sumiko along, because she could interpret for him and soothe some of the injured feelings of the locals. Who knows? She might even have a report about Kurasawa Electronics.

She was in the lobby when he arrived. On their way out, she pointed out the man who kept watch on her. He sat near the elevators, wearing a light blue double- breasted suit. He stuck his face behind a newspaper when he saw Brad looking his way.

Brad walked up to the man and flashed his badge. "Excuse me. You working for agent Manning of the local office?"

The man frowned, then fished in his pocket and brought out the leather case with his FBI identification. Brad explained he was taking Sumiko to the Ginza area. He told the man not to follow them. There was no other conversation between them.

Sumiko took his arm as they walked to his car in the parking lot. As they drove toward their destination, Brad explained the events of the past few days. Sumiko was aware of the bombing, since the story topped the local news the past two days. Brad told her about the valentine he had just received.

She turned in the seat and looked at him, a large question mark in her expression. It was clear she couldn't understand his apparent lack of anger. "Logan-san, how you stay calm? Do you not wish revenge?"

"Of course I want revenge, Sumi, and I'm sure I'll have it. But, first and foremost, I'm a cop and must keep the public safe from the same destructive acts. Now I need your help with my investigation of the **Yakuza**. I've been so wrapped up in other matters, I've done nothing about them in the past few days. Have you heard anything at your new job?"

"Sumiko's busy learning the new job. It's exciting. The people in the office are nice and sometimes helpful, but I think everybody's got their own little group. Not everyone knows what happens in other parts of the plant. I don't go to other parts of factory yet. Is almost a city by itself. Is that the way all big corporations work?"

"Sorry, I can't tell you from experience. Our police department is the same way now. We have so many people in the building, there's no way to know them all. "

Brad reached over and patted her arm. "Sumi, can you start taking the initiative out there? We have to push this investigation. You must find out as much as you can, as soon as you can. We need serious help from inside the Japanese community. I need contact with the leaders as soon as we identify them. You can do that. I'm sure it's easy for you to make friends. Just don't push so hard you make a mistake."

"Maybe so, Logan-san, but I can't go too fast. These people are suspicious of outsiders. Kelly Garrett get super mad if I—how you say it?—blow the cover off."

That *faux pas* evoked serious laughter from Brad, a rare occurrence nowadays. "I think you mean 'blow your cover', Sumiko ."

"Yeah, whatever. I meet some clerks in my department. We eat lunch together. I will ask them who is big honcho down here. They just give me a couple names. I can do better, Logan-san. Here's a parking place." Sumiko waved her hand toward the curb.

Brad swooped into the vacant spot and they began their stroll. As they sauntered past the store fronts, they stopped often to look into a window. He soon noticed the sidelong glances tossed their way by the locals. Several younger men glared at him as if he were violating their territory. Not only by being there, but being there with one of their own. It jolted him awake to the facts of society: Prejudice isn't a sole peculiarity of white, Anglo-Saxon, Protestant men. People everywhere share it.

Brad smiled and acknowledged the glances of all who ventured a look into his eyes. A few returned his smile with a slight bow of the head. Others just looked away as he approached. He refused to get discouraged.

"Sumiko, I know you've eaten already, but I'm getting hungry. Could we find a restaurant so I can put something into my stomach and end its complaining?"

"Sure." She pointed ahead towards the corner.

"There is sign on the corner. It says they have good choices. I will help you read the menu. You like rice with dinner?"

"Yeah, sure. Depends what's with it. I'll trust you to order something without fish heads or dead rodents in it. Here we are."

A blue banner with Japanese writing hung in the doorway. He pushed it aside and followed Sumiko inside. A mixture of strong scents attacked his nose. He couldn't identify anything specific. Frying shrimp was the dominant smell. Maybe ginger—horse radish. The combination almost overwhelmed his senses. His growling stomach told him it would receive anything edible with great joy.

Sumiko spoke to the hostess in her native tongue. The colorful kimono worn by the middle-aged woman dazzled him, with splashes of color resembling bright flowers. Brad noticed that the two women bowed sedately as they spoke. To Brad, that expression of respect appeared natural and genuine—-much more polite than the American handshakes and backslaps.

At the end of the hallway, a door opened into a small private room. The floor was covered with a straw mat. A low table sat in the middle of the room and several pillows lay on the floor, waiting to be occupied. He followed Sumiko's lead and removed his boots before he entered. It was quite a struggle without his bootjack. He'd wear loafers next time.

Sumiko hiked up her skirt and plunked herself onto a pillow and motioned that he should do the same. It was not quite so easy for him. His joints protested with loud creaks as he sat and crossed his legs beneath him. His knees banged against the table when he moved.

"I know why there are no six-foot Japanese people...they could never get their body folded into this position. Is this your revenge for having to look up when you talk to me?"

"Maybe you gonna break in half, Logan-san. Next time, we find place with regular table. You can straighten your legs if I move over on your side."

"That's a good idea, Sumi. I know I can't stay this way long enough to eat. Sure you don't mind?"

"You bet. What you want to drink?" Sumiko scooted around the table beside Brad. He felt great relief when he could straighten his legs. He didn't tell her about his knee which was made, in part, of aluminum and plastic. He chuckled to himself, 'Probably made in Japan'.

"See if they have Cordova beer. If not, any kind of beer is all right. I know I smelled fried shrimp when we came in. I could take some of that when you order. Can you eat anything?"

"No, I already getting fat, but I can drink some tea and eat special rice cake. You will see...I get you good dinner. You can use chop sticks?"

To his surprise, Sumi ordered a drink for herself and a bottle of Kirin beer for him. His first taste of the imported beer made his nose wrinkle, but the more he tasted, the more it compared well to domestic beers.

His dinner arrived, served on a wooden box with several compartments. He was amazed at the artistic way his food was presented. He recognized the fried shrimp in a light colored batter, but nothing else looked familiar. Sumiko patiently showed him the proper way of holding the wooden sticks provided him. It was a lost cause. He kept dropping bites before he got them into his mouth.

In the end, Sumiko fed him until every last crumb was gone. With each bite, she described the item as she lifted it to his lips. "This is all called tempura. Here is yam and eggplant...this one is green bean.

This is ginger and this one's horseradish. Careful, it's hot. Very healthy food, yes?"

Brad liked what she fed him. And there was nothing shabby about being fed by a beautiful woman. She gave the impression she thoroughly enjoyed helping him. She giggled if he made a face when she put a bite of something new in his mouth.

"I gotta tell you, Logan-san, you eat pretty good for a round-eye. Should I order you some more food? Maybe you need more beer?"

Brad placed both hands on his stomach and shook his head. "No more. No more. That was very good. I admit I'm impressed. I know Kathleen will enjoy eating here. She's very brave about trying new things. When she comes home, we'll all come here again—or better still, some place with real chairs."

"I will enjoy bringing her to Ginza. When will she come back?"

Brad looked at Sumiko as he answered. "I have no idea. Not until I'm satisfied she can be safe again. Why?"

Sumiko's face reddened and she looked away. For an instant, Brad sensed a slight feeling of tension pass between them. The feeling didn't linger.

"I miss her. She is my good friend. But I want her to be safe, so I understand why she went to see her parents. Where shall we go now, Logan-san?"

Brad got to his feet and helped her up, politely averting his eyes as her skirt raised to dramatic heights. He couldn't understand why he felt so awkward when he was around this young lady. Wasn't she aware of her own body and its graceful beauty? He couldn't believe she was unaware how she affected him.

He stomped his feet back into his boots and held her arm as she stepped into her sandals. The hostess bowed to them as he paid at the counter. It was then Sumiko spoke at length to the lady. Indicating with gestures, or placing her hand on Brad's arm, it was clear she was telling the lady about him.

Outside on the sidewalk, she didn't say a word until they moved away from the restaurant. Then she pulled herself close to him, squeezing his arm against her body. She spoke in a near whisper. "Something is wrong in there. I don't tell her you are policeman, but she is still afraid. She tell me her husband may close restaurant. It is very sad."

"She didn't give you any idea of the problem?"

Sumiko shook her head and fell silent. Brad could tell the situation was very distressful to her. She cared about these people and wanted to help them.

"Sumi, why don't you find a place down here to live? I'm sure your job at the factory is safe as long as you want it. You will be very happy here and can do more good when you become part of the community. What do you think?"

She turned toward him and looked into his face with great concern. Her brown eyes brimmed with tears. "Yes, Logan-san. I must find a place right away. There is something dangerous in this place. I can feel it and it frightens me, but it's what I came here to do; to help my people. Maybe you can help me find a place?"

"Maybe we can look around Saturday. Now, show me some more stores. I want a store that has something called—let's see—it's netsky. You know that name?"

"**Netsuke**? Yes, I know it. Why you want to know about that?"

"It has to do with one of my crime scenes. We found something there and I was told it was…uh…**net su ky**?"

"Yes. I teach you Japanese someday, Logan-san. Maybe then you learn to eat our raw fish and octopus. Let's go look in that store, okay?" She pointed ahead.

Sure enough, in one of the showcases there was a display of dozens of small, carved figures. Each had its own personality and eccentricities.

"What are they used for, Sumi?"

"**Oji-san**–that means old man—some times still wear kimono. He has no pockets, so he carries his valuables in a little sack—you know, kinda like a fanny pack. They use **netsuke** for a fastener. I have also seen some young boys wear around their neck on a chain. But most of time now, it is for tourists to collect. Will you buy some?"

"Not tonight, but I do want one for Kathleen. I think we should get you back to the hotel. We both have work tomorrow. I appreciate your help coming down here, Sumiko. Maybe if we keep showing up, these folks will get used to me and stop being afraid."

He led her back to the car and twenty minutes later dropped her off at the hotel. She asked if he wanted a cup of coffee, but he knew it was a bad idea.

"I have to get going, Sumi. I'll talk to you tomorrow. Thanks again."

He watched her walk into the lobby and waited until he saw her enter the elevator. When he noticed the FBI man watching him, he sent a halfway salute across the lobby.

Even though it was almost 11:00 when Brad pulled into his garage, he walked around the perimeter of his house with gun in hand. Nothing seemed out of place, but he felt the twinge of anger each time he passed the mini-crater in his front yard. It was a memorial to all the things he found distasteful in today's generation of criminals.

Inside the house, he went straight to the den. A television camera was just activated the previous day by an electronics expert in the department. He installed it in the front window, overlooking the front porch. Brad armed the detection device. It would trigger the camera into action if there was any movement outside.

"Come ahead, you lousy son of a bitch, whoever you may be! I'm gonna burn your ass if you come close again. You may have the upper hand for now, but time's catching up with you. It's time for the good guys to score—-that means *me*."

Satisfied everything was working as it should, he went up to bed. For the first time in his life, his 9MM automatic went upstairs with him and found a resting place on the nightstand. Thanks to Judd Worley's thoughtful attempt at a psychoanalysis, Brad no longer suffered guilt feelings if he relied on his gun for protection.

The telephone jarred him awake at 6:00. His feet were on the floor before the third ring. It was no surprise to hear Kathleen's voice. The sound was so clear she could have been in the next room. "Did I wake you?"

"Are you kidding? The day's half over. How are you, Sweetheart?"

"Lonesome—and you'd better be lonesome too or I'll be suspicious. Are you all right? Is there any news about the bombing?"

"I'm fine. Don't like the empty bed. There's nothing new about the bombing. We know it wasn't meant to kill us. Otherwise, we'd be dead. It's just another warning, but I'm getting tired of this crap. If they want me, I'm available. I want it done with so you can come home."

"Me, too. I miss you holding me when I go to sleep here. But, you listen to me, Brad Logan, don't start getting reckless because I'm not there. I don't want one of those phone calls from the Chief saying you were a big hero."

"Don't worry, I'm being careful. How's the weather back there? It's been hot this week, so far. I suspect it'll be a hot summer. That's another reason I want to get this bomb thing over with, so I can open the house at night. Our night breezes are wasted with the windows shut. Guess what? I went down to Ginza town last night with Sumiko. Ate something called—um—tempura, I think. You ever have that?"

"Yes. Paula and I went to a little place a couple months ago. I like it. 'Specially the veggies. Is that why you sent me out of town—so you could cavort with your Geisha? You don't have an ounce of shame—and <u>her</u> just a child."

He could hear her 'tsk tsk-ing' over the phone. "No. No shame at all. I even let her feed me with those two little sticks of wood. Damn things just wouldn't work for me. Thought I would starve."

"Why, Brad Logan, I had no idea you were so adventuresome. Is there a reason you went down there—other than hangin' with Sumi?"

Brad couldn't decide if Kathleen was serious or joking, so he changed the subject. "Mark Goddard is working his butt off on my lab work. I should have the blood work up today. Sure could use a break. We're pretty sure Reed was involved in Mooch's murder, and the blood work can make it a lock. Next thing we do is find out who he pals with and put the squeeze on them. I have a couple in mind, but there could be others—are you still there?"

The long moment of silence from Kate seemed ominous. Then, "Yes, I'm taking it all in. I'll be so glad when this is over. I hate being out of my house and out of your bed and out of your arms, and I hate thinking where your arms might be. You rat, I think you tell me this stuff so I'll get crazy."

"Katie…you're not jealous, are you? That's silly. I love you and no one else. That's a fact and you should be confident. Now, tell me anything else you want in the next two minutes, 'cause I gotta pee and take a shower."

"That's all. I'm not in the mood any more. I love you and I'll call tomorrow…and if I want to be jealous, I'll be jealous, bye."

Just like that, the line was dead.

Standing under the soothing stream of water, Brad sorted out the events of the past days and planned his schedule for the new day. He would check with Mark Goddard first thing, hoping the latest tests were done, then he would use the computer to research what he found out about **netsuke**. Maybe there were people who used it for something other than a collectible. He also planned a call to Kelly Garrett in Seattle to touch bases. Maybe Kelly knew something new.

As he went downstairs, he stopped in the den and looked at his surveillance camera. The meter showing footage used was still at zero. No one had invaded his territory in the night. The neighbors must have had their best sleep in weeks.

He stopped on the way to the office for a coffee and Danish to go and carried it into his office. It was 7:45. Sam was still not at his desk.

As he sorted through the paperwork on his desk, he finished his pastry and was sipping his coffee when Sam came in. "Glad to see you've finished your breakfast, partner. We've got places to go. I talked to the guys from ATF, fifteen minutes ago, okay? They got a phone tip. The caller said a bunch of explosives are stored in a mini warehouse. We'll meet them there in thirty minutes. Damn it, partner, we deserve a break—let's hope this is gonna be it. My gut tells me this stuff is gonna be the real thing."

"In a mini warehouse? My God, don't these people have any regard for the safety of the public? Christ, that stuff could go up and destroy half the town. Is it the public storage over on the west side?"

"You got it. You ready to ride?"

"Hi Ho Silver."

CHAPTER 16

The west side of Langston featured most of the newest commercial growth in the desert town. The large mall, the factory outlet stores, the ten screen movie house and several large restaurants all had emerged from the desert sands within the past five years. Some of the businesses still struggled for survival; others prospered.

The mini warehouse complex was at the very edge of the new development, flanked on the western and southern edges by desert. On windy days, especially in the Fall, the East wind churned the sand, making it swirl throughout the area. The dusty conditions were not popular, but the locals accepted it.

When Brad and Sam drove up to the gated entrance, they spotted a group of cars and a large truck already congregated at a location near the rear fence of the complex. The group of men, some uniformed, gathered around a man in the uniform of the ATF. He held a clipboard, from which he harvested his remarks.

"Now listen up, all of you. This is a joint operation and I don't want anyone hurt. It may be a piece of cake, or it may turn ugly at any moment. We know this place was rented under a phony name a long time ago. With any kind of luck, a name will turn up in here. All civilians in the area were evacuated and we blocked off the street. That's about the best we can do. Here's the drill: The bomb squad is responsible for cutting the lock. If the place is not booby trapped, the bomb dog will be sent in sniffing for explosives. The next step will depend on whether we're still alive at that time. The smoking lamp is out."

Sam and Brad followed the lead of the others in the group. They donned their bulletproof vests and gathered behind the large bomb disposal truck. Three men wearing suits that resembled the latest fashions from NASA waddled up to the door of the suspected unit.

"Tell you what, Sam, these bomb jockeys gotta have nerves of solid titanium. Don't even see how they can move in those pads. You can have that duty. Sure not my thing."

Sam just grunted and hunkered down on his haunches to wait for the grand opening. They watched as the padded men used bolt cutters to remove the padlock from the door. The bomb specialists inspected every edge of the door, using careful, painstaking movements, seeking hidden trip wires, then, an inch at a time, they raised the door as everyone held his breath. After what seemed like hours, it was open wide enough for one man to crawl in on his belly. Not until he gave the 'all clear' signal, was the door opened completely.

Brad watched the man in the brown uniform bring up the bomb-sniffing dog on a leash. The beautiful shepherd was so eager to work, he strained at the leash, almost dragging his handler. His tail windmilled as he eagerly accepted the command that put his life on the line. Within seconds of entering the storage room, he began going crazy, dragging his human partner from one area to another. There was no question, he had found the target of his training. He ran in circles around the large containers, red tongue hanging from his mouth. On occasion, he rose up on his hind legs and scratched vigorously, as if digging his way into the barrels. His handler's affectionate pats were the dog's reward.

The bomb squad inched forward for closer scrutiny of the barrels and drums stored along one wall of the room. In less than thirty minutes the volatile assortment of lethal chemicals had been identified and inventoried.

"There's enough volatile stuff in here to level the whole town, guys. All it needs is someone to put it together in the right proportions and provide ignition. We have our work cut out. Here's how we'll do it. The ATF guys will take care of loading and safeguarding the chemicals. The FBI boys will check out the rest of the contents of the room. You boys from Langston PD work with them. Everything in the place gets inspected. Every piece of paper, every knick-knack and every box of junk. Let's get cracking."

By noon the chemicals were in the truck. What they found was ammonium nitrate, canisters of thermite, and small containers of black powder. Some of the chemicals were commonly used as fertilizer, but when mixed with fuel oil in the right proportions, became as lethal as any military explosive. All it needed was a means of ignition, such as fire or electricity. Deceptively simple. Terribly deadly.

Also found were several boxes of handout flyers containing hateful, racist themes. In the same box was a book giving specific details on the preparation of various types of bombs. Brad knew such literature existed, but never had seen it before—not in Langston. "I guess I've led a sheltered life, Sam. I can't believe this kinda crap exists in America. Especially in Langston. Have I been asleep for twenty years?"

"Makes you realize there are crazies everywhere—even Langston. This stuff could level most of downtown. Trouble is, we impound it today and they can get more of the stuff any time they want. We can't stop them."

Brad shrugged his shoulders. "Well, maybe we can at least slow the bastards down."

The discovery of the explosives was a very important step forward in the investigation of the bombings. However, Brad and Sam were much more interested in looking through the other boxes found. For the most part, they were personal effects, the kind found in every household in the country: Photographs, old letters, souvenirs, books, family keepsakes. Things one no longer had room for, but couldn't bring himself to toss out.

"Sam, this is just like cleaning out your garage. My God, look at this stuff. I'll bet, if we went through every garage in Langston we'd find the same kinda junk. I know I have some in my own. Somewhere, we'll find the identity of the owners. I'll start through these photographs. There'll be something in there."

When Brad opened a shabby, dilapidated album of pictures, he began a walk into the past. Pictures of unidentified persons clung precariously to the worn-out pages. There were pictures with parts cut off them. Others cut in the shape of hearts. The earliest pages were covered with pictures taken before cameras were much more than a box with a pinhole. Some were even finished in the old time sepia. Some were identified in white ink on black pages. He'd seen the same type of albums in his parents' belongings.

"Jesus, if I owned this old '28 Model T, it would make me a happy fella. Look at this, Sam…did your grandparents have one?"

"Yeah, but Pop was still partial to horses when I was born. Look at this picture here. It must be the kindergarten class at Langston Elementary School, okay? Wonder how many of those people we know today? How many have I put in jail?"

"Look at this one, partner. I swear, I recognize some of those kids. My God, Sam, that's my own class! Look—there's *me* right there. This little guy is Mark Goddard. This stuff belongs to someone I know. It has to."

Brad fanned the pages of the album, looking for later pictures. The lightning bolt struck at about the middle of the book. Brad was so excited, his hands shook. "You know who this is? This is Judd Worley. This must be *his* stuff. I can't believe this. Talk about falling into a bucket of shit. Someone up there is smiling on us today. Man, I need to say my prayers. Look at this."

Brad's adrenaline rush soared. The more he found, the higher his degree of anticipation. To him, it was better than a gold discovery in one's own backyard. They began sifting through the boxes, looking for specific things. Things, which would identify the owner. The results were overwhelming. This locker contained items from Judd Worley's family.

Brad could not contain his elation. To him, it was the Holy Grail—-the Golden Fleece. At last, his chance for some payback for all the insults and threats.

"Hold it, Brad...remember what you told me a couple days ago? No jumping to conclusions about him any more, remember? There's other possibilities. Maybe it's his parents' locker. We gotta move like a turtle...like slow, okay? In the first place, the Feds have jurisdiction over this stuff. You'll play the devil stepping on their case, you know that. Sure wish I had a camera with me."

"Damn you, Sam, you're so Goddam practical." Brad punched Sam on the shoulder. "I was having so much fun beating up on Judd, it was almost orgasmic. Now you pop my balloon. Thanks for nothing."

"My pleasure, pard, spoiling your fun is what makes my day."

The Feds made it clear they were moving everything to their own storage facility. It would be under court order until an indictment was handed down. According to the ATF man, someone name Winston had rented this warehouse space on the day the facility opened. No one could say if the person's address was known.

When Sam told the agent what they had found in the photo albums, there was a great deal of excitement among the gathered officers. It sounded like a major breakthrough. At that point, the Feds made it clear to the local police officers: 'The U.S. Government has total jurisdiction over the evidence'. Sam and Brad had no say in the matter.

A disgusted Brad looked at his watch. It was almost 2:00. They had been there since 9:00, and it was dusty and dirty. Besides, he was hungry. Maybe a good lunch would take some of the sting out of his disappointment.

"Sam, since the Feds just snatched us bald, I don't see much sense in sticking around. They aren't concerned with our puny little murder case. They won't share any of this with us, so let's get the hell out of here and get some lunch. I'll even buy. Where else can you get that kind of deal?"

"Sounds good to me, partner, but first, what do you make of this little box of goodies?"

Sam held a cigar box, which he shoved into Brad's hands.

"Jesus Christ, look at them! Just like the one you found in the storefront. A whole damn box of 'em. What did Mark call them—**netsuke?**"

❧   ❧   ❧

"Captain Owens, you're gonna sit there and tell me we can't touch Judd Worley?"

"You heard me right, Logan. The subject is closed. It's the Feds' case now. You're to keep your ugly butt out of their business. That comes down from The Man. If you screw up their case, you can kiss your career goodbye. End of discussion. Now, shall we talk about something else, or can I assume you're a happy camper?"

It didn't take much imagination. Brad knew he was at the end of his rope. He and Sam had spent two days fashioning their case against Judd Worley—-a case they both felt was strong enough, with information from their crime scenes and from the storage locker. Now, in less than two minutes, Captain Owens just shot them right out of the sky.

"I guess I'm finished, sir. To tell the truth, I wouldn't describe myself as a happy camper, but I can tell, the subject is closed. I'll put this case on hold and go on to other things. I'm still working on the **Yakuza** case and hope to make some headway soon. I just assumed, with all this new information, we might still be interested in Worley. Sorry I bothered you with this crap. Maybe the son of a bitch will kill himself in a wreck and save the state the trouble."

He left the office, as if the playground bully had just taken away his favorite toy. In his years of police work, he had run into bureaucratic nullification before; it was a fact of life and he expected it on occasion. But this time, it was as if someone had stolen his case right out of his back pocket.

On his way back to the office, he stopped off at the Personnel Office. "Margie, I need a great big favor. Can you tell me which cops in the department have military backgrounds? I would appreciate a printout of the names when you get it. Think you can get it today?"

"Sure, Brad. You just stand there and look pretty and I'll have it in five minutes. Looking for anyone in particular?"

"I don't know, Margie. I suppose I'll know if I see it."

Within five minutes, just as she promised, Margie handed him a five page list of names from the Personnel files. It gave the branch of service and what jobs the men were trained in. Brad was looking for explosives experts.

Next stop was Mark Goddard's office in the basement. Brad was glad that Mark was alone in the office, so they could talk in privacy. Mark held his hands up, in a defensive posture, as soon as he saw Brad.

"I know, I know. I promised this to you a couple days ago, Brad, but it's been a hectic week. Everyone wants their stuff done first and expects me to do it. Especially your pal Nichols. He's on my tail from morning to night. I'm a lot closer than I was, but still have a couple other things to do."

"Jeez, Mark, it's not like I ask you for many favors. Can you tell me anything yet?"

"Brad, I told you I was sorry. The blood work is done. Here's what I can tell you. We found traces of Reed's blood at the warehouse. He must've been hurt in the fight. We know there are traces of blood on Reed's shoes, but it's not conclusive if it belongs to Mooch Kaiser or not."

He turned the page on his notebook. "We compared the slugs you found. Kaiser and Reed were both killed by the same gun. A 9MM. We found latents all over the tile in the bathroom, but haven't matched any yet. I can tell you one thing, for certain—-we haven't found Judd Worley's prints on anything at either scene. I know how that breaks your heart, but what can I say?"

"How about on the valentines I brought you?"

"No prints on any of them."

"How about the stomach contents from the store front?"

"We have the analysis, but it shows a great deal of wine and burgers and fries. I'm afraid it was from your wino friend. You're dealing with a very devious person, Brad. He's clever enough not to leave any calling cards for us. Sorry, but so far the guilty person—or persons—is still staying hidden from science. You're not gonna hit me, are you?"

"Hit you? Hell no. Why would I hit you? Tell you the truth, the very lack of clues tells me quite a bit. We know someone's taking great pains to avoid detection. That says the perpetrator makes very careful plans before making a move—like someone who's very familiar with police techniques. Don't you think? He's got to make a mistake soon. When he does, we'll be ready for him…at least, I hope like hell we'll be ready."

"I hope so, too, buddy. I know I'll sure breathe easier when you catch him. How's Kathleen doing at her folks?"

"She's a very unhappy lady, let me tell you. Calls every morning. Making sure I'm sleeping alone. Like I've got time to cat around! Kate's little brother is teaching her how to use a computer. It keeps her from just laying around getting homesick. Hope it won't be much longer. Thanks, Mark. I know you're doing your best. I won't bother you too much. Let me know if Nichols gets on you again. Guess you heard about the storage space the Feds busted into the other day?"

Mark nodded. The frown on his face expressed his concern. "That scares the hell out of me. Any leads yet on whose place it is?"

"It's not my case any more, Mark. Captain pulled me off it. Says the Feds are handling everything now. Just hope Judd blows himself up one of these days. I gotta go. Thanks, old friend. See you later."

Brad was disappointed as he headed back to his office. Every place he turned led to another piece to the puzzle. But never the right one—the key piece. He knew it was there—somewhere. This kind of case demanded total dedication. Everything required close scrutiny. Over and over again. Bit by bit. Page by page.

"How'd you make out, partner?"

"We've been shot down, Sam. Owens says the Feds took over the whole thing and we're to butt out. Can't say I'm surprised."

When the phone on Brad's desk rang, his intuition told him he wouldn't like the call. When he heard the voice, he knew he wouldn't.

"Well, well, how's it feel, asshole? Now you can't harass me anymore, can you?"

Brad couldn't believe Judd Worley knew about the change in the case so soon, but didn't want to act surprised. "Hello, Judd. That's right, I can't harass you anymore. That doesn't mean I've forgotten you. You're still gonna pay. One way or another. So's your spy in the P.D."

"Don't count on it, Logan—or should I call you Junkyard? What's that supposed to mean? You got people convinced you're a bad-ass, don't you? We know better, right?" The sarcasm dripped from Judd's words.

"What do you want, Worley? Just gloating, or do you have something to say?"

"Sure, I'm gloating; why shouldn't I? Got the best of you again, you poor fool. I decided I'm gonna concentrate on your little slant-eyed girl friend. I understand she's a great piece of ass. I'll let you know after I spread those dainty legs. See you in church."

Brad slammed the phone down. He choked back the response bubbling up in his throat like a mouthful of bad whiskey. With his new resolve, he let the anger pass quickly.

"I'm telling you, Sam, if that smart assed bastard isn't nailed pretty soon, I'm going to forget my promise to Kathleen and blow his head off. Just for the satisfaction."

"Worley sure gets the lowdown in a hurry, doesn't he? Makes you kind of wonder where he gets his information, doesn't it?" Sam verbalized Brad's thoughts.

"That's for sure. Listen, Sam, I've got to get out of here and do something to get him off my mind. I imagine you can stand some relief from me for a while, too."

"So, what are you going to work on now?"

" I've got to get busy on this **Yakuza** thing. I'll do it alone because I know how you feel about those people. I'll go work it on the street while you concentrate on the office work. I had Margie run me a list of cops with military background. See who's trained in explosives. That's a place to start. Any objections?"

"Look, Brad. I never said I wouldn't work down there with those folks. I just wanted you to know how I felt. If you need me on the street with you, I can handle it, okay? Just don't be surprised when I don't make a lot of friends. Tell me what you want me to do."

"Sam, I appreciate it, and don't worry…if I need you down there I'll clue you in. This deal with the explosives is just as important right now. Start with the two guys on our bomb detail. We know they can do it. See if they were friends with Gorman Reed. We need to know who his pals were. I nominate those two guys we ran into at the Frontier Grill last week. You think? That should keep you busy. I'm gonna spend the next two or three days making some inroads in Ginza town, if that's all right with you."

"Sounds like a deal, but you be careful down there, okay? Those folks can be mighty sneaky, keeping you from the truth. Call me a couple times, in case something comes up here. You'll carry your cell phone, right?"

"Will do. You have the number?"

As he drove into the main parking lot of Little Ginza, Brad had no formal plan in mind. He just knew he must make some inroads in the Japanese community. It was obvious the Langston Police Department had not improved relations with these citizens, so he was hopeful he could amend that situation. Before leaving his car, he called the police dispatcher and let her know his itinerary.

As he reached the main street, he decided he would walk into each store and introduce himself. Perhaps by striking up a casual conversation, he would gain their confidence. In college, he took several courses dealing with Public and Community Relations. He hoped the professors knew what they were talking about.

By the third store, he realized the task was more daunting than he imagined. To begin with, there was the language barrier. Most of the storekeepers knew just enough English to make a sales pitch, but there was a universal lack of enthusiasm for conversation with Occidentals. They were friendly enough—just uninspired.

The fourth store proved to be an exception. The store reminded Brad of the old five and dime he remembered from his childhood. Aisles of display bins with piles of trinkets, toys, small household goods, all stimulated his curiosity. Atop one counter was a display of various wind-up toys, each one performing its act: spinning, dancing, waving, drumming or barking. Each had some talent to show off.

The words spoken by the clerk startled him by their clarity and precise English pronunciation. "Pretty cute stuff, don't you think?"

At first, Brad thought the woman was sitting down, but she was just short. But then, he realized she was walking as she spoke to him. She couldn't have been more than four feet ten inches. Her black hair was pulled back in a severe bun. Several strands had escaped the confines of the bun and graced the edges of her face. The wide grin she sported revealed a sparkling gold tooth. The smile was genuine, and encouraging.

Brad picked up a small barking dog. "How long do the batteries last?"

"I leave each one going for just a couple hours. Is there something I can show you?"

"I have a Japanese friend I would like to surprise with a little gift. Can you suggest something she might enjoy?"

This woman was very talkative, to Brad's pleasure. She suggested he buy a special puzzle box from a wide selection she carried. The one he chose was made of various panels of different woods. By sliding the different panels in just the right way, you might find the one which revealed a secret compartment. It was attractive, as well as fascinating, so he bought two of them.

The purchase became a 'deal maker' for him. He discovered the lady's name was Judy Misuno. She was a Nisei, born and raised in Los Angeles. Her parents came to America in the '60s from Okinawa. Her husband, a section leader at the Kurasawa Electronics plant, was a native of Japan. Judy seemed eager to indulge in small talk.

Brad felt as if he had hit a home run. He held his hand out for his change for the purchase.

"My friend works at Kurasawa, too. She's in the Marketing Department. You'll meet her some day, I'm sure." Without a pause, Brad changed the conversation to more direct questions. "Do you ever see officers from Langston police department here in Ginza?"

"Not very often. Sometimes they drive by in police car. Unless someone calls for them—like if we have a hold-up or something. Then lots of police come here."

Brad noticed the woman's eyes dart to the front of the store.

Her voice became clipped. "Is there anything else I can show you, sir?"

An invisible wall had materialized between them. She handed him the package, turned her back and walked to the rear of the store. The conversation was over. Brad was shocked at the sudden change of attitude. He turned on his heel and walked outside.

The young man standing just outside the door was dressed in loose fitting brown pants, a gray sweat shirt with no sleeves and rubber thongs. A tattoo of a dragon circled his right bicep. Shoulder length black hair fell in greasy strands around his face. He wore a dirty baseball cap, turned backwards. A gold earring hung from his right ear. He was at least a head shorter than Brad, but what he lacked in height he made up in swagger.

There was no doubt in Brad's mind; this young man was the reason for the abrupt end to his conversation with the store clerk. Was he the local enforcer? His scowl was meant as a tool of intimidation.

As Brad turned to make his way to the next store, the man became a shadow. If Brad stopped to look into a window, so did the shadow. There was no attempt to disguise his intentions. Brad had no intention of forcing a confrontation—not until he was ready.

When he entered the same little restaurant introduced to him by Sumiko, he took a seat at the counter and ordered a beer. When he looked over his shoulder, he could see the man taking up his post at the entrance. Brad decided he'd give the man his money's worth.

"Okay, Junior, when I finish this beer, we'll see if you want a piece of me or not."

CHAPTER 17

*B*y the time Brad finished his beer, his senses tingled. His competitive spirit—the fierce spirit he had controlled so well for the past few weeks—threatened to take over his body. He knew a physical confrontation waited for him, just outside the restaurant. He craved it. The pent-up emotions needed immediate release.

The woman at the register had served them when he was there with Sumiko. A shy smile flashed as she bowed slightly and gave him his change. He did his best imitation of the bow and headed for the entrance. The rumpled young man leaned against the wall, looking with indifference out into the street. He showed no interest in making conversation.

With planned deliberation, Brad turned toward the young man and passed as close as possible to him as he started up the sidewalk. His elbow brushed the man's chest, ever so lightly. It was a glove to the face—a silent acceptance of the challenge.

He could hear the slap-slap-slap of the rubber thongs hitting the man's heels as he took up the pace behind Brad. The sound kept Brad aware of the man's close presence as they approached an alleyway.

Brad stepped off the curb and started across the narrow alleyway. He sensed, rather than saw, the flash of a wild leg thrust aimed at his back. His long years of training prepared him well for dealing with a sneak attack. Every sense was supercharged in anticipation.

By turning his body to one side, the leg blow slid harmlessly by his shoulder. Brad turned toward his assailant, who had quickly recovered from his missed kick. The man performed a series of gyrations made famous by Bruce Lee. His fingers curled and posed before his face—by now a snarling mask of **Ninja** hate. He crouched in the classic pose. A low, savage snarl escaped from the man's lips.

Brad's survival instincts precluded him from resorting to staged posturing. He lowered his head and drove his shoulder into the man's midsection. The force of Brad's charge, carried both men back into the alley where they collapsed in a heap, with Brad on top. He knew martial arts fighters remained on their feet so they could launch their lethal kicks. Since he outweighed his adversary by at least fifty pounds, he would just keep this man on the ground until the fight was over.

Using his superior weight to immobilize the man, Brad's right fist had a clear line to the man's exposed chin. It was just the way he remembered his many schoolyard fights. He unleashed the right hand and felt it land flush on the jaw. His left fist also found its mark. The sharp impact traveled all the way to Brad's shoulder. It was a gratifying feeling. He felt the fight leave his opponent. His right fist was zeroed in when he heard a noise behind him.

As he turned in response to the sound, something almost took his head off. It was such a strong blow, it knocked him off the young man and sent him sprawling onto his side, face down on the pavement. Before he could scramble to his feet, Brad saw a booted foot swinging toward his face. He turned his head aside, but the boot still scraped across his ear, setting off an alarm bell in his head. The sense of immediate danger was overwhelming.

Each time this new attacker swung a foot at him, a loud, guttural sound boiled out of the man's throat. Keeping his eyes on the man's legs, Brad scrambled to his feet, until another kick from the rear sent him sprawling again. By now, Brad had determined there was more than one new attacker and he was at their mercy. Each time he tried getting to his feet, he received another boot in his midsection or in his kidneys. These people knew what they were doing. It took on a methodical rhythm. Grunt, kick, grunt, kick. Brad realized he was helpless to fend off the brutal attack.

When he felt one of his ribs give way under the force of another kick, he decided his best strategy was to stop fighting and just defend his head. His arms took the brunt of the attack as blow after blow found some part of his body. Each blow was preceded by that same guttural snarl. His thoughts turned to Kathleen. How would she get along?

The last thing he heard before the blackness engulfed him, was a new voice screaming like a banshee. He later swore it sounded like Tarzan calling to his friendly apes—except this Tarzan sounded more like Jane.

He was sailing. Sailing with Dad in the little skiff. Just the two of them riding the little boat over huge, snarling, thunderous waves. As they crested each roller, it was as if their little boat was strapped to the back of a raging Brahma bull. Each time the bull leaped forward, Brad felt a grinding pain in his chest and he struggled to catch his breath.

An eternity later, he became aware of someone gently patting his cheeks. A terrible smell attacked his nostrils, forcing him to gulp air and open his eyes. The fuzzy images coming into focus became two men in white jackets, leaning over him. He was aware he was on his back on a hard surface. He didn't have a clue where he was.

"Come on, Sergeant, let's see a little more life in those eyes."

One of the white sleeves held a small light up to his face and shined a beam into first one eye, then the other. When he struggled to sit up, he was forced back by another white sleeve. The effort brought severe pain to his chest.

"Just lie there, Pal. You've got at least one broken rib and you sure don't want to puncture a lung. What's the other guy look like?"

At that moment, a familiar voice reached his consciousness, as a new face came into his line of vision. "Brad-san. It's Sumiko. I was so worried about you. Why you come down here by yourself? You almost get in big trouble. How you feel?"

He tried taking a deep breath so he could answer, but even that effort brought agony to his chest. He knew he shouldn't say anything extravagant. "I'll be fine, Sumiko. Where'd you come from?"

"Never mind that. You gotta go to hospital now. I will follow ambulance. I'll tell you everything when we get there."

He only gave a feeble protest when the medics lifted him onto a gurney and wheeled him to the open back door of the ambulance. The flashing lights reminded him his prowl car was still parked in the local parking lot. He explained to the medic and was told the police were there and would drive his car back to the station.

That's when he caught sight of two uniformed patrol officers standing on the curb, talking to some of the gathered townspeople. He didn't recognize either of them.

The ride to the hospital was uneventful except for the feeling of the mask over his face pumping cool oxygen into his lungs. They told him his other injuries weren't serious, but he was going to be very sore for a few days. His arms felt like someone had spent several hours pounding them with a sledge hammer. Holding his right arm up, he noticed the sleeve of his white shirt was torn from wrist to elbow. A large stain of dried blood decorated the elbow area. It seemed to be the worst injury other than his painful rib cage.

At the hospital, the doctors cleaned several open wounds. They wrapped an elastic retainer bandage around his upper torso and deposited him in a bed in a third floor ward. By the time he was settled in, he was joined in the room by Sumiko and a man in a brown business suit, complete with vest.

"Brad-san. This is Agent Sutro. He is from the FBI office. He's been watching over me this week."

Brad didn't shake the man's hand; raising his arms was too painful. He just nodded toward the agent. It was not the same agent he had hustled in the lobby of Sumi's hotel last week. This man was younger, more muscular and sported a mustache, not unlike Brad's own. With his pale blue eyes, this one resembled the Marlboro man.

"I'll tell you something, Sergeant Logan, this young lady here saved your neck. You might be dead now if she hadn't waded into those Ninja types and held them off until I got there."

"Sumiko? She stopped them?" Brad was startled, to think this tiny slip of a girl could have saved him.

"You bet your ass she did. I was tailing her when all of a sudden, she spotted you in the alley. She ran her car onto the curb, jumped out and waded right into the thick of the battle. I've never seen anything like the way she handled herself. By the time I got my car stopped and ran into the alley, she had them on the run. They passed me like a dog with turpentine on its butt."

Brad looked at Sumiko with new respect for her abilities. "Sumi, you did that? That was very dangerous. Sounds like I owe you my life, young lady."

Sumiko's face reddened and her eyes dropped. Brad sensed she was not comfortable accepting any kind of praise. She was the most unassuming person he'd ever met. Unassuming, sincere and genuine.

"Logan-san. I couldn't let them hurt you. Besides, I told you I could knock you on your butt. Remember? Now you know I can do it. **So desuka?**"

"Can you believe this woman, Sutro? I assume all three of the perps got away?"

"Yeah, to be honest, I was more concerned in protecting her than in chasing them. I couldn't even ID them, it happened so fast. My orders are to not let her out of my sight. She gets hurt and I lose my job."

"Yeah, I know. Listen, man, I appreciate your help. Christ, wait'll they get word of this at the station. I'm s'posed to be the Junkyard Dog down there. I feel more like a Pussy Cat. Not only that—a woman; no, a peanut—comes to my rescue. Jeez, how much will it take to keep this quiet?"

"No sweat, Sergeant, no one will hear it from me. Your reputation is safe with me. But there were a couple of your uniforms making a report. Someone in the neighborhood musta called them. If they know you, I'm sure they'll get word back to your buddies."

The FBI man waved and left the room. He said he'd wait in the lobby until Sumiko was ready to go. After he left the room, Brad took Sumiko's hand and pulled her close to the bedside. "Young lady, you'll never know how much this means to me. You're an amazing person and a true friend. But, what in hell were you thinking to take such a risk?"

"I don't take time to worry about it. I just knew you were in danger and, besides, the FBI man was right behind me. It wasn't such a big deal, Logan-san."

"Well, I think it was a big deal. If I could reach you, I'd give you a big kiss."

To his surprise, Sumiko bent over and suddenly her soft mouth was resting on his. It seemed so natural, he gave no thought to any implications. He just knew that the feel of her lips on his was very tender and stirred strong feelings in him. When she pulled away, he realized his eyes were closed. When he looked into her eyes, she reddened and averted her gaze.

"Sumi, you mean so much to me. You shouldn't risk your life like that. Promise you'll not be so foolish again…promise?"

"You think I am a fool, Logan-san? Why you say something like that?"

Brad realized she hadn't interpreted his words the way he meant them to sound.

"No, no, I don't mean you're foolish. I mean, you *must* be *careful*." Now he was getting flustered again. How could this tiny bit of Oriental fluff affect him so dramatically and turn him into mush? He knew he must be careful with her feelings. There was a pit full of boiling oil waiting for him if he faltered.

Sumiko changed the subject. "Oh, I almost forget why I look for you. I think I find out something very important today. When I call for you at the station, they tell me you were at Ginza, so I looked for you. You want I should tell you now?"

"Yes, of course. What is it?"

"I was messing with the computer in my office and I notice Kurasawa sends many shipments of products to a place in Las Vegas—more stuff than to any other place. I maybe don't understand enough about the business yet, but why do you think so much electronics material goes to a casino?"

Brad's curiosity skyrocketed. "A casino? Are you sure?"

"Yes, positive. It is called Sapporo Casino and Lounge. I wrote the address down. Don't you think that is curious?"

"You bet I do, Sumi. You may have found something very important. As soon as I can get out of this bed, I'll check it out. You know something? I just realized I'm hungry. Haven't eaten all day."

Brad reached for the nurse's call button. A sharp pain jabbed his side, making him gasp for air. Sumiko's concern showed in her face. She reached over and punched the button for the nurse. When an aide showed at the door, Brad asked for something to eat. The lady in pink announced she would bring something right away.

Sumiko waited for the tray, then fed every last bite to Brad. When the last bite was taken and the milk carton sucked dry, she set the tray aside and announced she was leaving so he could get some sleep.

Much as he hated for her leave, he knew he needed some rest so the healing process could begin. Sumiko assured him she'd return the next day.

Before Brad settled down to sleep, he phoned Sam Hardy at his home. Explaining he'd had an accident and was in the hospital with a broken rib. Sam was full of questions and accused his partner of concealing the truth, but Brad eventually convinced him he was all right and would check in tomorrow.

The magnitude of the day's events crashed down on him as he hung up the phone. It was one tired, achy and contrite cowboy who laid his head back and was instantly off into the wild blue yonder.

🍁   🍁   🍁

Brad woke at 6:00 with a body which told him he'd just been in the toughest football game of his life. He was one *big* ache. The rib wrap restricted his movement, and it was obvious, he would be tender for several days.

He knew he must call Kathleen right away or she'd be worried sick when she couldn't reach him. When she got on the phone, he sensed she was very upset.

"Where have you been, Brad? I've been going crazy looking for you. Are you all right?"

"Katie, I'm fine. I got into a little altercation yesterday and broke a rib. I'm in the hospital and a little achy. I'll be just fine. I'll be released later today."

"A *little* altercation? It was Judd Worley. That's right, isn't it? After you promised you'd stop your vendetta. How could you...?"

"Wait a minute, Kate. It wasn't Judd. I haven't been near him. I was down in the Ginza area and some street toughs figured I looked like an easy mark. Turns out I *was* an easy mark. Guess I'm getting old."

After several minutes, he convinced her his worst injury was to his pride. He didn't tell her about being rescued by Sumiko. He was embarrassed about it and had no intention of letting anyone find out, if he could help it. In the end, she calmed down and started crying because she missed him. It was their longest separation since he was in college. Neither of them enjoyed the solitude.

He promised he'd call her again when he got home, then hung up with just a twinge of guilt feelings. He always got those feelings of guilt when he wasn't honest with her, in every way. She was such a strong part of his life. He hated hiding things from her—things like the urges he felt when Sumiko was near.

At ten o'clock, Sam Hardy came in and stood at the doorway, laughing so hard he ended up with tears in his eyes. The sight of Brad's puffy face, bruised arms and black eye was Sam's reward for fifteen years of watching the Junkyard Dog dish out the punishment.

"I've got to tell you, partner, I've waited a long time for this day. There *is* a merciful God up there, after all. He took pity on us poor mortals."

"Oh, you're a real piece of work, Hardy. I get my head knocked off my body and you find it hilarious. You can blow it out your ass!"

"Oh, man, you're a sight. Look at that eye. How many goons did it take?"

"Only three, you son of a bitch! Guess I'm over the hill. Glad it makes you happy. Any news, or you just come to gloat? By the way, if you breathe a word about this to anyone, you're history."

"Too late, partner. Word's already made it through the station. As a matter of fact, a couple of uniforms offered to go down there and bust a few heads open, if you want."

"No kiddin? Wonder if they're the same guys who put the chess piece in my locker?"

"I have no idea. But, there *is* some news for you, okay? Finally got the rest of the bank records from Worley's bank. A very interesting set of documents. Get this—every month, he gets a substantial check from a casino in Vegas. Amount varies, but it's a monthly thing.

Then, guess who he writes a check to every month—and I mean a good size check."

"The same casino?"

"Nope. To his mom. Alma Worley. He's been giving her money every month for a long time, okay? This guy's a dutiful son. Doesn't that make you sorry you're so hard on him?" Sam looked pleased with himself.

"No way, man. That's just too out of character for him, don't you think?"

Sam draped himself over the foot of the bed. "I don't know him like you do, pal. Here's the other bombshell. He also writes a check every three months to that mini-warehouse company, okay? That should make you very happy. Too bad we can't go after him. We have probable cause now. I gave the info to Captain Owens. Don't know what he'll do with it. Guess it's not our problem now."

Brad nodded. "You got that right. You wanna know what I turned up at Ginza town?"

"Hell no, that's *your* problem. Oh yeah, I talked to Mark yesterday. He says he'll have the blood work done today. Oh, and I got through half the list of ex-GIs you pulled up. Nothing significant. At least not yet."

By the time his partner left, just before noon, Brad was ready for another nap before they brought his lunch. Just as he dozed off, the bedside phone rang. It was Sumiko.

"Logan-san. How you feel today?"

"Just fine, thank you, Sumi. A little sore, and I look like a truck ran over me, but I'm gonna live. They tell me I can go home this afternoon. You can give me a ride?"

"Of course, Logan-san. I will leave early from work and pick you up. I will bring you to my house and make sure you get well. You need *a Mama-san* now. *Dai jobu?*"

The simple statement was so direct it didn't register with him. He just assumed he would go to his house to recover. Maybe his sister could come over.

"To your house? Don't be silly, Sumi. I appreciate the offer, but it's out of the question. You have your own life. You don't need to play nursemaid. I'll be just fine."

"Don't give me your sad story, Logan-san; you're coming to my place. Don't give me any arguments. I got two bedrooms and lotsa food. Even got beer. When you're strong enough to get your own dinner, I'll take you home. We can stop by your house on the way and get some clean clothes. *So desuka?*"

"You're something else, lady. Just because you saved my life doesn't mean you're stuck with me the rest of your life."

He couldn't argue with her. He could tell her mind was already set. She told him she would see him after 3:00 and hung up.

Sumiko's new apartment was just on the outskirts of Little Ginza. Brad remembered it was one of the few groups of sparkling new buildings in that part of town. It was so new, the 'Grand Opening' signs still fluttered from flag poles set in the front lawn. The four story apartment building was modern in every way. Private garages, a gated entry and equipped with most of the built in conveniences expected by today's young professionals.

The apartment Sumi rented was on the ground floor and just ten steps from her garage. Brad could shuffle his way into her living room without too much effort. The all-over achy feeling was less now, but the soreness in his rib cage was still very evident each time he moved too fast.

Brad sank into one of the soft leather chairs in the living room as Sumi carried his suitcase into her spare bedroom. She busied herself putting the contents into dresser drawers.

"Hey, you have a nice place here, Sumi. When did you move in?"

"I been here for a week now, Logan-san. Lots of the people who work with me live here. That will make it easier to get to know them. You hungry?"

"No. I don't suppose you have any beer?"

She didn't answer. In seconds, she returned from the kitchen holding a bottle of Cordova beer. Brad just shook his head. This young lady never stopped amazing him. He still felt a great deal of embarrassment at her desire to please him at every turn.

As he savored his brew, he mulled over the events of the past day and a plan of action formed in his head. Sitting still was not an option. Checking out some of the newest information suited him better. "Sumiko, I'm going to Las Vegas tomorrow and check out that casino."

CHAPTER 18

The drive to Las Vegas was just over 110 miles, all on a major free-way from Los Angeles to Vegas. Despite Brad's loud and anguished protest, Sumiko decided he was not well enough to drive, so she relegated him to passenger status for the entire trip. It was the weekend, so she didn't have to take time off from work. After realizing he had very little to say about the decision, he called the FBI office and told Agent Sutro about the trip. Brad wanted no watch dogs who might interfere with his investigation.

When Brad called Vegas to book a room at the Sapporo Hotel, he learned that all the hotel's rooms were reserved by travel agents in Japan, and they had no vacancies. He called four other motels before he found one with an opening—a single room. Brad would have canceled the trip, but Sumiko assured him it was perfect. He could sleep on the couch!

His feelings about the arrangement were mixed. On the one hand, he knew he should check out the Vegas connection with Kurasawa— and Judd Worley, but knew of no other way he could get first hand knowledge. He had to be there.

On the other hand, he and Sumiko would be in a compromising situation if anyone should ask what they were doing together. He knew he would never be able to explain it to Kathleen—and she would know about it. It wasn't something he could keep from her.

In the end, the value of the information available in Vegas outweighed anything else. For some reason, he justified his martyrdom by reasoning there was no other way he could get the job done. Who else would get it for him?

They were on the road by sunup. Brad counted on being in Vegas by 9:00, giving them almost two full days for investigation. By the time they were twenty miles out of Langston, he was glad he let Sumiko talk him into being a passenger. The pain from the broken rib was constant. He knew he wouldn't have been able to drive for two hours.

It was already warm when they pulled into Vegas at 8:45. The weather report predicted it would reach 90-plus degrees by the afternoon. For mid-June, that was normal in Vegas.

Brad directed Sumiko into the parking lot of a large pancake house on the edge of the Strip. It was already crowded, but they found a booth near the back.

"You think I pretty good driver, Logan-san?"

"You're a very good driver, Sumi. I don't remember more than a couple of times I felt my life was in danger." He grinned at her, assuming she realized he was kidding.

"Whatsamatter you? Why you tell me that? Now I never drive again. Maybe we have to stay here until you get all well."

"No, no, no, Sumi…can't you tell when I'm joking? You're a very good driver. Besides, you don't really want to spend a week here, do you?"

"Hell no, if you gonna keep yanking on my legs like that."

"I pull your leg because I like you, Sumi. It's another one of those crazy, impolite things we Americans do to endear ourselves to people of another culture. What do you want for breakfast?"

As they ate, Brad sat in wonderment at what this diminutive young lady could devour at one sitting. He was finished long before Sumiko. It was while he watched her finish off the last two pancakes that he began briefing her about their goals for the weekend. "First thing is to drive around the place for an hour or so. We can see what kind of traffic there is. In particular, I wonder if there are any deliveries on the weekends. How often do the armored cars pick up cash from them? How many cars are in the parking lot? We should make a note of the different license plates displayed on those cars. I should have brought a camera."

"I got one in my over night bag. What you gonna do without me? Even a *rookie* knows to bring a camera." Sumiko looked at him with that look of pure mischief. "Besides, maybe I get to see you in your underwear. Maybe I send a picture to my **Mama-san**. You think that's good idea?"

"Now you're yanking my legs, you little tease."

When they left the parking lot, Brad directed her from the map he had brought along. The club they wanted was in the downtown area, not on the Strip.

They could see the Sapporo from two blocks away. It had sweeping, upturned roof lines with garish blue tile, making it stand out from the crowd of buildings in the area. The design was meant to resemble a pagoda, but somehow lacked the classic beauty of a traditional Japanese pagoda. But, what the hell, it was a casino in Las Vegas, USA.

With Brad acting as navigator, they circled the block over and over, driving slowly so he could become familiar with each entrance and the location of the loading docks. To his great surprise, it appeared there was no major entrance on the front side of the building. They had to turn at the corner and there in the middle of the block was the main entrance. Just a double-wide door with a blue canopy shading it from the afternoon sun, a very unusual feature in a town that prided itself on 'bigger is better'.

At Brad's direction, Sumiko turned into the large parking lot flanking the hotel. Again, Brad's curiosity brought more questions. If this hotel was supposed to be booked up for the weekend, why wasn't the parking lot filled? Did all the guests arrive by bus?

For the next hour, they took their time, cruising around the block, until they were sure they knew where every entrance, every loading dock and every service elevator was located.

Brad took pages of notes. He noted a few of the license plates and states of origin of as many cars as he could. It was after their fourth trip through the parking lot that they attracted the attention of a hotel security patrol.

A pair of burly guards, driving a gray sedan with flashing lights, flagged them down and approached their car with guns drawn. "I'll handle this, Sumiko. Just don't say anything unless they ask you for ID or something."

Brad pulled his wallet with his Langston PD badge affixed. As soon as the first guard motioned for Sumiko to lower the window, Brad shoved his wallet toward the man. He could have been a Sumo wrestler in training. The man had no neck, and large rolls of fat connected his head to the rest of his body. The shirt he wore couldn't contain the huge arms and torso. Great rolls of flesh bulged in every direction.

"Good morning, officer. I'm with the Langston, California, police department, and I'm looking for a stolen car. Hope we didn't get you all concerned about driving through your parking lot."

'NoNeck' held the wallet, turning it first one way and then the other. It was obvious he couldn't read, but knew enough to look at Brad's photo ID. "What kinda car?"

Brad responded as positively as he could on such short notice. He figured if he mentioned a new luxury car it might explain why he came all the way instead of asking the Las Vegas cops for help. When 'Mister Gargantua' handed the wallet back through the window, Brad breathed a little easier, figuring they were over the hump. Not so.

At that point, the guard began a long string of words directed at Sumiko. It must have been Japanese, or perhaps another of the Oriental languages she knew, because her head was bobbing up and down. When the guard stopped to catch a breath, Sumiko shot off her own litany of words in the same tone of voice. That's when Brad realized the two talkers were ignoring him.

To his great relief, they were finally waved on and the guards returned to their car. When 'NoNeck' got behind the wheel Brad could swear he heard the poor automobile let out a scream of pain.

When they were out of shouting distance, Brad asked what had transpired.

"He tell me to get my pretty little ass out of his parking lot and don't come back. He says you are liar and he hope he get a chance to prove it. I shoulda got out and show him my little ass not so pretty when I kick him in his privates. Goddam piece of cow poop."

That remark tickled Brad so much he clutched his sides as the laughter poured out. He sure didn't want his rib separating again. "Sumiko, I swear, you're the most unpredictable person I've met. Do you stay awake at night thinking up these little idioms, or do they just flow out by themselves?"

"What you talkin' about? You make fun of my language again, roundeye?"

Brad thought better of continuing with that line any further. Sumiko parked on the street so he could organize his notes. When he knew what each notation meant, he stuck them into his inside pocket. "Sumi, are you carrying your weapon?"

"Yeah, I keep it on me all the time. Garrett's orders. Why you want to know?"

"Because we'll split up when we go in there. You can be just another Japanese tourist seeing the casino for the first time. I'm gonna sit in the bar and watch the crowds go by. Who knows, maybe I'll see one of the clowns that broke my rib. Let me see your gun."

Sumiko handed him her purse. He opened it, expecting to find a little .25 automatic with a lady-like pearl handle and silver plating. What he found, tucked away in its own separate compartment, was a snub nose .38 police special. He didn't show his surprise, but checked to be sure it was loaded. "Okay, let's hit the casino. When we get inside, I'll head right for the nearest bar while you circulate. You want some money to gamble a little?"

He fished a fifty dollar bill from his wallet and handed it to her. She started to wave him off until he told her he'd put it on his expense account. That satisfied her.

Brad fingered the handle of his own .38, carried in the small of his back under his jacket. He always preferred his shoulder holster, but knew it was too obvious if anyone noticed him.

They made their way through the door and into the casino. Within minutes, Sumiko disappeared into the crowd, leaving Brad to himself. The nearest bar was only fifty paces from the entrance. From his perch atop a bar stool, he could observe most of the floor area of the casino and, in particular, the comings and goings at the front door.

"You saw who?" Brad almost fell off his stool several hours later when Sumiko came up and sat beside him on the next stool. She even ordered a Mai Tai so she would look as if she belonged.

"Logan-san. Your friend Jugg—you know——-the man with tattoos that drive me in cab?"

Brad's senses came alive. What the hell was Judd doing here? Was it just a coincidence, or was it planned? "Where did you see him, Sumi?"

"He was getting on the elevator over there." She pointed toward the back of the casino.

It was then Brad noticed the large bucket she had placed on the bar. It was jammed full of dollar tokens. It figured. The machine probably gave up its riches after she smiled sweetly at it.

"Sumi, let's get out of here. We can't take a chance that he'll see us. Come on, we'll think of something."

He let Sumiko cash in her winnings while he kept an eye out for any sign of Judd. She joined him as she counted her winnings. He hustled her out the front door as she recounted her good fortune in a child's rapid sing-song. "Guess what, Logan-san…I win over two hundred dollars, so I can pay you back and then I will take you to dinner. I have such a good time. We can maybe come back?"

"We'll see, girl. Right now, let's get out of here and go check into the motel. We can use the phone there while I figure out what to do."

The motel was out on the Strip and was not one of the plush inns Vegas is known for. It was just a room to stay in while gambling. Brad was careful carrying the luggage into the room. He sure didn't want his rib cage to begin protesting again. "Oh, oh, this place doesn't have a couch, Sumiko. Just a bed and two chairs. Maybe we should go back tonight instead of staying over."

"No way. We gonna do the job we came for. Don't worry about my honor. I'm a cop just like you, okay? It's gonna be fine. If I don't worry, why should you?"

He couldn't tell her why he worried. She would probably be uneasy if she knew what thoughts were going through his head. While she busied herself putting their few things into a drawer, Brad stretched out on the bed. He hadn't realized how tired he was.

He was disgusted with the way this trip had turned out. Once again it seemed Judd Worley was getting the best of him, even if it was by accident. He wondered how long that loser was going to hold all the best cards? Seconds later, Brad bolted upright on the bed. There was no way he was going home empty-handed!

"Sumiko, will you let me use your car for an hour or so? I'm going to the Las Vegas Police Department. Maybe they can help me get some information."

Sumiko's face reflected her disappointment, but she handed over her keys. "Why you don't let me go with you, Logan-san? You ashamed to have the cops see us together?"

"Sumi, for God's sake, you know better than that. It's just that I want them to know this is a business trip. They might not understand that if I show up with a gorgeous woman. I won't be long and I promise I'll take you somewhere nice for dinner. Deal?"

"Yes, yes, yes."

In her excitement, Sumiko jumped onto the bed and threw her arms around his neck. With her smiling face level with his, he could not resist the temptation of her eager lips. It was a beautiful and honorable kiss between two friends. Very chaste. It just lasted too long. The problem had to do with the other feelings which over-powered his body. He could feel the entire length of her, pressing into him. He forced himself to break away. His mind filled with confusing thoughts of writhing bodies bathed in the heat of tender lovemaking. "Sumiko, I...I'm so sorry. I didn't mean to let that kiss get away from me. I...I'll see you in a couple hours."

Brad bolted from the room with a buzzing in his ears and some extreme heat invading his body parts. It was what he had feared. It was what he was fighting against. It was what he wanted. He refused to allow thoughts of Kathleen come into his head. He knew his guilt would be magnified if he thought of her right now.

At the police station, Brad introduced himself and showed his ID. He asked to speak to the Watch Commander and was introduced to a Captain Henderson. As soon as he explained the reason for his visit, he was led down a long hallway into a small private office. Captain Henderson waved him to a seat. "The Sapporo Casino, huh? What makes you think there's anything going down at that place?"

"Nothing concrete, Captain, but it has surfaced two times involving two different cases I'm working. We're curious why an electronics firm would send so many shipments to a casino. It just seems kinda odd."

"May not be as odd as you think, Sergeant; do you have any idea how these slot machines work? They're almost all run by computers nowadays. It could be as simple as that."

"Yeah, that's right, but why is there just one casino on their shipping lists? If the firm was making that kind of software, you'd think they'd ship them all over this area and to Atlantic City. Wouldn't you?"

"You got a point, Sergeant, what else you interested in?"

"We spotted a suspect in another case in the casino today. We're interested in his connection to the casino. He's been getting big paychecks from them for several years. We don't know if he's dealing drugs or what. It's too much money for a cab driver to be making."

Captain Henderson took notes as he listened. He picked up the phone and dialed. He spoke into the instrument and listened briefly before hanging up. "You're in luck. One of my boys in the Intelligence Division is on duty. He'll be right in".

For the next half hour, Brad got an earful of how the Las Vegas Police dealt with their prime taxpayers. The casinos provided most of the taxes that ran the city government. There was no question in anyone's mind about *who* ran the town. The police didn't say unkind things of any casino and disliked anyone casting doubt on the integrity of their town. They were, however, receptive to gathering some local information for Brad. He was especially interested in how the Sapporo's armored car shipments compared to other casinos of the same size and where the Sapporo did its banking.

"I can tell you that without looking. It's got to be Bank of Yamashita. It handles all the Japanese merchants in town. They have a lock on it. Another thing I can tell you as a fact is that the Sapporo Hotel only does business with Japanese tourists. All their rooms are booked 365 days a year by travel agents in Japan. It's a done deal. Talk about a captive audience."

At Brad's request, the Captain called the Sapporo and spoke to the manager. He asked point blank what connection they had with Judd Worley. He explained there was a request from a California Police Department curious about the large deposits to the man's bank account.

"For what it's worth, Sergeant, here's what they tell me. This Worley guy is, I guess, a teamster who drives a cab for a living. Must be in Langston."

Brad was all ears. He nodded and waited for more answers.

"They say he also runs a weekend charter bus tour. He brings them Japanese folks from California to the casino. They pay him by the head and also give him a bonus from time to time if he reaches certain goals for passengers brought. Sounds pretty legitimate to me. Looks to me like you're on a cold trail, Logan. Sorry we couldn't be more helpful."

Brad thanked the men for their help and left. On the way back to the motel, he drove around the Sapporo site another time, noticing two armored cars parked at the loading dock.

"Business must be super good today. Even with a half full parking lot? Nice trick."

Brad stopped at a liquor store where he found a six pack of cold Cordova beer and two mini bottles of ready made Mai Tais. It was just after 4:00 when he pulled into the motel parking lot.

Sumiko sat in one of the chairs, watching television. She must have showered and washed her hair, as the shiny black tresses flowed freely down her back. She was wearing the tailored rust colored slack suit he first saw her in, and she made a stunning sight.

"I brought you a peace offering."

Brad held up the drinks.

"Why you want to make peace, Logan-san? When did we have war?"

"No, I guess it wasn't a war. I…I thought I was a little out of line and felt guilty."

"Why you feel guilty? Did you smash my new car?" As usual, she disarmed him with her simple outlook on life.

Brad just shook his head. "I'll go get some ice. You look in the yellow pages and decide where you want dinner. But don't pick the Sapporo, I got what information I could from the PD and they'll get a reading on those armored cars for me."

"Hey, you did pretty good for a round-eye. Go get the ice, I'm thirsty."

They had a sumptuous dinner at the MGM Grand and took in a late show. It was after midnight when they returned to the room. Brad felt very relaxed and just a bit light headed. He knew Sumiko must be feeling the drinks because she was even more talkative than usual. Brad turned on the TV to get the late night news and sat in one of the chairs with his last beer.

"Thank you, Logan-san for my most wonderful night in my whole life. I never been to place like that before and I laugh very hard at that Rich Little. Very funny man. One day I saw him on the television. I never thought I could see the real him. Thank you for doing that for me."

"You're welcome, Sumi. It is so much fun to see you enjoying yourself. You go ahead and take the bed. I'll just stay in this chair. I'll be fine."

Sumiko's eyes pleaded with him. Her hands went to her head, lifting her long hair as if to aerate the flowing locks. He could see a tear start a journey down her cheek. "What is it, Sumi? Have I done something to upset you?"

She shook her head vigorously, then placed her hands in her lap and took a deep breath. Whatever was coming, he knew it was serious.

"Logan-san, I…I…I've never been with a man. Once when I was in college, a boy took me to a movie. In his car, he try to take off my clothes. I break his nose. He find out then, I am a pretty tough cupcake."

Brad's emotions ran the scale. He knew she was being serious, but he couldn't stop laughing at her self-description. "Sumi, you shouldn't tell me anything so personal."

"Yes, I want to tell you. You are my very special friend. I think I know you better than anyone. I think I have very strong feelings for you. I think—"

"Don't talk like that, girl. You know we're in a very touchy situation. I won't let you do anything you'll regret later."

She smiled at him through a cascade of tears. He couldn't help thinking how very beautiful she looked—-beautiful, but vulnerable.

"You don't understand, Logan-san. I have decided you will be the first man for me. I don't know about sex. I just know when you touch me I get feelings in my body I never have before. My heart beats faster. Things happen in my...my...you know, down there. I want someone to show me about it and there is no one else I would trust to show me what I need to know. Is that asking too much of my good friend?"

Brad was dumbfounded. How could he have let this situation get to this stage? He should have been smarter and more careful. For certain, he didn't want to insult her or make her feel rejected. He knew he faced a delicate decision. "Sumiko, you're such a sweet girl. I care so much about you and feel you're my good friend, too. You're offering me something I don't deserve. Your first time must be a very special occasion with a very special person. It's a precious moment for a young lady."

"I know that. This is the right time and I know you are the right person. Please, tell me what I must do to get ready. I trust you with my life...why not my first experience?" Sumiko's way of moving right to the core of a subject was unnerving. Was it her culture or simply her own method of reasoning?

Brad's emotions soared without restraint. He reached over to turn off the television, then got up and took a seat on the bed beside her. His hands shook. His vision was blurred. "Sumi, your trust in me is overwhelming. Maybe I can tell you some of the things you want to know without hurting the respect we have for each other." As soon as the words left his mouth, he knew it was a ridiculous thing to say. He knew things were already beyond mere talking.

He put his arms around her and pulled her close, using his hand to brush some of the hair that had fallen across her face. The look she gave him was so full of trust he was afraid he might start crying. He held her chin in his fingers, raised her face and pressed his mouth to hers. There was instant response from her. She yielded to his lips with no reservation.

"You're such a beautiful and delightful young lady. I'm so glad you came into my life and hope nothing can destroy our faith in each other."

"Is this what love feels like, Logan-san?"

"In a way. Can't you call me Brad? You know me well enough I should think."

"That is because I have so much respect for you. Maybe I call you Brad-san when you begin to massage my body. Shall I take off my clothes?"

It was an incredible journey. Savoring each step, he unbuttoned her jacket and lay it on the chair. Then the soft, silk blouse found its way onto the pile. Further action was halted because he encountered a piece of clothing he was unfamiliar with. Kathleen never wore anything resembling Sumiko's undergarment. She helped him push the straps aside and let the silkiness slide down to her waist. Her breasts were firm with nipples standing erect as if shouting for his lips. They rose to greet him as he bent over her.

When, at last, she lay naked on the bed, he struggled, with virginal impatience, to remove his boots. He was so eager, he let his clothing find a pile on the floor. His hands were everywhere as he caressed every inch of her body, making sure he missed nothing. His lips burned her brown skin wherever they touched her. The fragrance of her body sent deep chills washing over him. He tried explaining everything, but his voice wouldn't behave. Although he was the captain on her maiden voyage, she responded superbly with very little direction.

Sumiko's body strained and arched to meet him. "Oh, my God— My God, Brad-san, this feels so *wonderful*! Why did I wait? I want more. Maybe I might explode. Will it last all night?"

"Don't be greedy, little one. We can enjoy each other until the dam breaks."

"What dam? I don't understand all your words."

"Don't ask. You'll know when it happens. Now, let me kiss you in that special spot again. I know it pleased you because you were talking to me in Japanese." Her only answer was a moan of contentment.

His tongue meandered along the length of her body, until she began to writhe and gasp. He felt he must prepare her for what was about to take place.

"Sumi. The next part may frighten you. It may hurt you, but I will be very gentle until we fit together perfectly. Trust me a little longer."

Brad lay between her legs, pulling her closer and softly talking her through the culmination of her first experience. She was an avid student, grasping at him and helping to guide the teacher when he was unsure of himself. At the last moment, he felt her pull away for just a moment, then she made a firm thrust with her hips, performing the coda of their love song.

He wasn't sure if her cries were from pain or from her passion, but he knew she wouldn't let him stop until, with a great burst of final energy, the dam burst and they were both overcome with the purest rush of desire.

"Oh—oh—Brad. I must love you. How else could I feel such things within my body? Oh, please, tell me we can do some more."

Brad was so exhausted he couldn't answer. Instead he just rotated his hips against her to drain the last bit of passion from their bodies. The winding down movement was every bit as thrilling and sensuous as the roller coaster ride.

CHAPTER 19

"*I*s it always like this, Brad-san?"

Sumiko lay with her head on Brad's chest, her bare leg thrown across his. Brad looked at the bedside clock radio. It was 3:20 a.m., and they still had not slept.

"Absolutely not, Sumi. What we enjoyed is *very, very* special. Many people never experience something like that. Not in a lifetime."

"Does this mean we love each other?"

"Yes, I guess it does, in a way. But we can never be like this again. This can never happen again."

"But why?"

Sumiko twisted her head and gazed solemnly into his face. The movement made him wince from the pain in his rib cage. He had earlier removed the elastic bandage from around his chest so it wouldn't scratch her face as they made love.

"Why you look like that? Did I hurt you?"

"Just a little bit. Guess I can handle a little pain so I can enjoy you."

Sumiko's fingers traced a path across his chest and down to his knees. Brad sensed she was using her finger tips as a means of recording every inch of his body into her memory. The light touch on his skin created fresh stirrings in him.

"How come it take you so long to get all swelled up again? You know…down here." Her fingers tightened, just for an instant.

Brad smiled. "If I could answer that, I'd make lots of money. Don't tell me you're getting another urge? You amaze me. With such strong passion I don't see how you could wait so long to be with a man. You're a wonderful lover, Sumi. You've given me pleasures I never experienced before. Do you have a special knowledge of how to please a man? Who taught you that?"

"In our culture, *Papa-san* is big boss of household. He provides woman with good life and protects her. He expects wife will do everything for him and be silent. She believes her husband is like a king. This goes back many centuries. Modern Japanese woman has more freedom, I guess, but still concentrate on pleasing the man we love. I wait all this time to be sure it is what I want to do. Now I know I love—-"

Brad's finger trapped the words in her mouth. "Sumi, please be careful how you use that word. There are many different kinds of love. What you feel now is more of the physical part of a relationship. You'll experience many different kinds of love in your lifetime—-hey, what are you doing to me now? Sumi?"

"Just be still. I want some more lessons. Look—see it is swelling up again. Will it grow faster if I kiss you there? You think?"

Brad assured her it would. He lay back with his eyes closed as Sumiko Tanaka of the FBI turned the page to another lesson in her Primer. Her instructor gave her the highest grades. On this night, the two dedicated law enforcers could care less about the serious crimes going on around them. They lived out the fantasy until dawn.

Brad stood in the shower, letting the steamy water pound at his aching body. He was drained. Drained of all emotion. Drained of all energy. Drained of all self-respect. The recriminations swirled around him with the same persistence as the water. He could hear

Sumiko humming to herself as she brushed her hair. She sounded like a woman fulfilled. His thoughts turned dark. 'How could you do this, you stupid jackass?'

Try as he might, he couldn't stop beating himself up. Sure, there were all kinds of excuses for giving in to that moment. A beautiful and willing woman. The drinks. The excitement of Vegas. They were both vulnerable to their urgent feelings.

'She begged me, didn't she?' He fought to block the image of Kathleen from entering his mind. It couldn't be done. There was her beautiful face staring at him with complete trust. He never doubted her complete commitment to him. Now he'd violated that trust. Things would never be the same between them. His voice roared in the small tiled enclosure: "Dammit, dammit, dammit! You're stupid, Brad Logan!"

"Did you say something? You need me to come wash you?"

Her voice returned his mind to the details of today.

"Too late, Sumi, it's already washed. Not that there's anything left of it."

As he finished his morning rituals, Sumiko made it clear she wanted more time in bed with him. He had unlocked the sexual energy in her. Was the world ready for it? He must get her mind off of last night to avoid another seduction scene. It became a game of cat and mouse. She spent the morning in unabashed nudity, daring him to ignore her. It took a stern warning from Brad before she understood she must stop groping him. She didn't stop pouting until they checked out of the motel.

After breakfast, they drove to the Sapporo Casino again and sat across the street from the parking lot. An hour later, they were rewarded for their patience. A tour bus wallowed, groaning under its load, out of the parking lot. It was driven by Judd Worley.

"Jesus, it's about time. Now we can get back in there and look around. You ready?"

"Yeah sure, Logan-san. Now we can be cops again. *So desuka?*"

Now that their privacy was no longer an issue in their investigation of Sapporo, Brad became more aggressive in his methods. He took one side of the casino and Sumiko took the other side. They visited each table of gamblers and stood to watch the action. At various intervals they played a few hands or would crank up a slot machine. It was important they assume the roles of simple gamblers.

It soon became evident to Brad, there was something ominous about this place. Not only were all the employees Japanese, so were most of the patrons. It was as if he was in a different country. Very few people spoke English. It was an eerie feeling.

Something else stuck in his mind. There was no problem spotting the employees. Each member of the casino staff wore the same uniform. For the men it was black pants and shirt with a white, short-waisted jacket and bow tie. Even the maintenance men. The only difference between various groups was a different colored cummerbund worn, as if to signal the wearer's station in life.

All the women wore a simple blue kimono with a flowered pattern. They wore fancy sandals with a strap between their toes and white socks which were designed for use with the sandals. Each woman wore a lavish hairdo piled high on her head. Brad was impressed with the grace with which the women navigated while wearing such restrictive clothing. The kimono pinched their knees together. It dawned on him that Sumiko had the same graceful, fluid manner when she walked.

Heeding something he remembered from Kelly Garrett's briefing, Brad paid special attention to the lapels of the men's jackets. Within minutes he became satisfied they were all wearing the same type pin in their lapel. He tried not to be too obvious as he looked at them, but determined the pin was engraved with a tiny pagoda. It may have just been a symbol of the establishment, but he had every intention of looking around the Langston population to see if anyone there wore the same pin. Kelly said the *Yakuza* men wore such lapel pins.

He made one other significant discovery. Many of the older men who worked there were missing at least a small portion of a little finger. It was just too much coincidence. There couldn't be that many careless carpenters around.

He rounded up Sumiko at 4:00 and watched as she cashed in another two hundred dollars in winnings. He couldn't believe this girl—and she had so damn much fun all the time. It just wasn't natural.

Her face dropped when he told her it was time for the trip home. He knew she was having a huge letdown as the weekend came to a close. A twinge of guilt choked him again.

It was almost 7:00 when they pulled into Brad's driveway. They stopped by his house so he could get more clean clothes. While he stood in his den, watching the playback of the surveillance video from the living room camera, Brad got the shock of his life.

There in black and white prominence, he watched a furtive shadow mount his front steps and cross the porch to the mail slot. The intruder pushed something into the mail slot. The person wore a police uniform. He couldn't make out the face of the individual. The angle and the lack of light made identification impossible. But there was no mistake, it was one of Langston's 'finest'. The time shown on the film was 3:20 a.m.

Sorting through the stack of mail, Brad located the envelope delivered by his mysterious caller. Inside, was a simple message written in a child's scrawl:

'Your Jap lover is next on the hit list'.

Sumiko gasped when she saw the message. Her hand went to her throat as she read the words again and again.

"Why is cop mad at me, Logan-san? Why he doesn't like Sumiko?"

"This is a bad cop. They aren't all like him, thank God. Most of our guys are human beings. Sorry you saw this. Don't worry. These bastards think they'll keep me from doing my job, but I'll take care of it."

He hoped his words sounded more certain to Sumiko than they did to his own ears.

❧   ❧   ❧

He let Sumiko persuade him he should return to her apartment for a few more days while he recuperated. There were many arguments against the move and just a few supported the decision. Nevertheless, he let his more physical emotions sway his thinking.

In the morning, after Sumiko went to work, he wandered around the apartment in a daze. He called Sam Hardy twice, making sure he wasn't missing anything at the station. Each time, Sam assured him everything was under control.

"We've sent two squads down to Jap town looking for anyone who looked big enough to take you down, but no one fit the description you gave us. They all look alike anyway, you know. Bastards all keep their mouths shut, too."

Brad cringed at his partner's brutal language. Sam didn't hide his prejudice. Brad bit his tongue, avoiding another verbal confrontation with his partner. He knew it would serve no worthy purpose. Instead, he changed the subject and asked Sam to fill him in on the results from Forensics testing.

There had been a report from the ATF regarding the materials they impounded from the storage locker. It was consistent with the fragments of chemicals found at the bombing scenes. When they obtained the payment records from the manager of the facility, they found that each rental check over the last five years was received from Judd Worley. The case against him was building up. In another development, Sam got the names of the officers who refused to take a report from the wino. One of them was the man they'd seen at the Frontier Cafe. The one with the black eye.

"That's good news, partner, so what's next on the agenda?"

"The ATF tried getting an order for a wiretap on Worley's phone. Trouble is, the local FBI office is blocking the order. For some stupid reason, they're keeping a lid on the whole thing."

"That doesn't make any sense—does it? Why are they keeping ATF from solving this case? There's something wrong, partner. This is a murder case. You don't just sit on the evidence. If there's another death, they'll have egg all over their chins."

Brad spoke to Sam for several more minutes before Sam announced he had another phone call. As he hung up the phone, Brad decided he could not put off calling Kathleen any longer. He swallowed the huge wad of remorse in his throat and dialed the number in Omaha.

He almost hung up while he waited for Mrs. Spencer to get Kathleen, but forced himself to keep the phone at his ear. Kathleen's voice was strained when she said 'hello'. It was obvious she knew something was amiss.

"Sorry, I haven't called sooner, Kate. After I got out of the hospital, I decided to drive up to Las Vegas to check out a couple of leads at a casino up there. Just got so busy I forgot."

"Well, I sure as hell hope the leads worked out for you. Damn it, Brad, I've been worried sick about you, not knowing what was going on. Sam said he thought you were in Vegas, but didn't know where you were staying. Otherwise, I'd've called you there."

Brad felt as if he might suffocate. "The leads were very worthwhile, Hon. I'm on to something that may break this thing wide open. Don't get your hopes up too high, but I also have something on Judd Worley. It looks like he's up to his eyeballs in this crap."

"That's good news, Brad…but when can I come home?"

Brad felt the guilt rising up again. The hurt in Kathleen's voice was obvious. She knew he was holding something back. "Katie…I…I—-"

"What's going on, Brad? If you have something to say, just say it, dammit!"

"Katie, I miss you so much. More than anything, I want the whole nasty mess over so you can come back. I feel terrible without you."

It wasn't a lie. He did miss her. She was the most important person in his life. He just couldn't tell her over the phone. He needed to see her face when she found out.

"You son of a bitch, Brad Logan! You slept with her didn't you?"

"Katie, how can you think that? I—-"

"I don't want to talk about this now. Good-bye!"

The phone was dead and so was his hope she wouldn't guess the truth. He knew she was pissed at him and had every reason to be. What could he do now? It was too much to ask that she forgive him. That was something she must decide on her own. All he could do was endure the agony he felt over hurting his life partner. He couldn't bear the thought of losing her, but knew it was a strong possibility.

Brad knew he must put every ounce of his energy into solving these crimes so Kathleen could return to Langston. They couldn't work things out over the long distance phone lines. It was such a high priority, he made a rash decision.

When Kelly Garrett came on the phone from Seattle, the sound of his voice gave Brad a great feeling of relief. It somehow told him things would soon improve. "How are you, Brad?"

"Not so hot, Kelly. Things are in a turmoil here. We've got serious problems. I need your help and support, and I need it now."

For fifteen minutes, Brad filled the phone with events in Langston since he had returned from Seattle. He scolded Garrett for not telling him how deeply entrenched the local FBI was with turncoats.

"These people stop our investigation at every turn. They're even in the way of the ATF people. We have enough evidence on Worley to haul his ass in, but they won't let us interfere. You've got serious problems, Kelly. If I was you, I'd catch the next plane down here and see first-hand."

"You may be right, Brad. As soon as I wind up a couple of serious matters locally, I'll do just that. They may have a good reason for what they're doing. Are you keeping a close watch on Sumiko Tanaka for me?"

The sound of her name brought the guilt feelings rushing back. "Yeah, Kelly. Matter of fact, she's the one who found out about the casino in Vegas. She's a great plant…fits right in. So far, it looks like no one knows what she's doing. Were you aware about this connection between Kurasawa and the Sapporo Casino?"

"Not at all, Brad. That's a major discovery. I'll have our Vegas people set up surveillance right away. I'll alert the Gaming people, too. Sounds like they may be moving a lot of currency. Do you have a good reason to suspect **Yakuza** involvement?"

Brad described the people in the casino, their uniforms and the lapel pins, as well as the missing fingers on some of the dealers.

Kelly sounded impressed. "That's very convincing, Brad, you did your homework. I think you've hit on something mighty big. It just may be the break we need. Look, I'll get my crew up here working on it. You do some more digging in Langston. As soon as I can get away, I'll fly down there to see if we can wrap this up before anyone else gets hurt. In the meantime, don't trust anyone—especially the local FBI."

The two men concluded their conversation leaving Brad with a new feeling of urgency as he sat at the kitchen counter and mulled over the new information, but he wasn't sure he was any closer to wrapping up the case. There were still so many unanswered questions.

"What I do know for sure is, my friend Worley is going down this time. He's dirty as sin and he can't hide it any longer. I also know at least one cop has been leaving nasty letters in my mailbox. Don't know who it is, but I can't rule out anyone except maybe Sam and Mark Goddard. Maybe one of them will recognize the guy in the video."

Brad's thoughts were interrupted by Sumiko's arrival. She came home for lunch so she could check on him. He avoided her warm kiss as she greeted him. He could see the hurt in her eyes when he turned his head.

"Why you don't like to kiss me anymore, Logan-san? Maybe now I am dirty?"

"Sumi, I talked to Kathleen this morning. She knows about us. I've hurt her very much and now I've hurt you, too. I'm not very proud of myself."

"You tell Kathleen we been together? Never happen."

"I didn't tell her, Sumi, she just guessed. Must've heard the guilt in my voice. Don't worry. She won't blame you. She knows I was the cause of it. I'll work it out, somehow. How was your day?"

"Something is going on today. There's been lotsa meetings in big boss's office. He talks to all the department managers all morning. Mrs. Preston was in his office when I arrived there."

"She's Chief Preston's wife, isn't she?"

"Yeah, her name is Chieko-san. Today, I find out she was born in Japan. Her father is big man in export company in Tokyo. His company sends lots of packages to Kurasawa Electronics. Maybe more than anyone else."

"Can you get any idea what kind of things they ship to you?"

"I been trying, but so far can't get a look at any shipping invoices. I'm sure they make some of the chips used in our products...don't you think?"

Brad just shrugged his shoulders. Sumiko busied herself making lunch. Brad ate in silence, sorting out the mixed bag of thoughts racing through his head. Sumiko kept silent, too. Brad could see she was hurting. There was no simple solution. Every option available to him would, no doubt, cause agony to someone.

"Sumi, when you get home tonight, can we take another trip around Ginza town? The guys who jumped me are down there somewhere. Do you think you could recognize the other two guys you faced off with?"

"You better believe it. I got them fixed in my mind, especially the one who called me a name I didn't like. I'm gonna know them. What you gonna do if we find them?"

"I'm not sure yet. Mostly, I'm interested in who they work for. The best thing would be getting their names to run through the computer. Maybe we'll get some luck, for a change. What time you think you'll get home?"

"I guess maybe sometime after 5:30, I don't know for sure. You want to eat down there again?"

Brad told her that was the idea and held her in his arms briefly before she started out the door. This time, she didn't offer her lips to him.

Soon after Sumiko returned that evening, the doorbell rang. What took place in the next few minutes happened so fast neither of them reacted with any degree of intelligence.

As she opened the door, Sumiko was pushed backward into the room and the form of Judd Worley rushed in, slamming the door behind him. Sumiko muffled a scream with her hands. Brad was on his feet in an instant, every fiber in his body prepared for combat.

The words erupting from Worley's mouth were menacing in tone, as well as content. "You hypocritical bastard! I coulda guessed you were screwing this little Jap while Kathleen was home to her mama. Man, you're the biggest whore in the world, Logan!"

Brad's temper soared over the top rung. His right fist found its mark on Worley's chin before another word was uttered. Judd went down in a heap, but before Brad could follow up with more destruction, Sumiko was between them. She crouched with curled fingers extended in front of her. Her whole bearing resembled a rattlesnake coiled to strike.

"Don't do this, Logan-san. I can't let you get in trouble again. Find out what he wants to say. It's maybe not nice, but what can he do to you?"

Brad lowered his arms to his side and stepped back as Judd Worley rose to his feet, holding fingers to his split lip. He shoved Sumiko aside and jammed his face right into Brad's. "I've just got one thing to tell you, you mental pygmy. You can't solve all your problems with your fists. Shows your stupidity. Right now, I've got you right where I want you—by the short hairs. I own you! This is how it'll play, asshole!"

Judd stuck a finger into Brad's face. The smug look on his face said it all. "You drop your investigation of me or I spill my guts to Kathleen. She'll hear how you and Miss Saigon here been shackin' up. You *lose*, old buddy. If you even breathe in my direction again, Kathleen hears all about her big, stupid stud who can't keep his pants zipped. Sure hope this little bitch was worth it."

Sumiko stepped between them again. Her face reflected her distaste for Worley. Her nostrils flared. Her lips were tight across her teeth as she hissed:

"Hey, you dirty mouthed *haku-jin*. Haul your sorry butt out of here or I gonna show you how I turn white man into a white woman. I thought you were okay guy when you drive me around. Now I know why Logan-san hate you so much. What a sorry excuse you are."

Judd flinched as he saw her step toward him.

"Well, listen to the little gook talk like she thinks *she's* something special. You both better listen to what I'm saying…call off the dogs or Kathleen hears from me. That's a promise. And tell your friends at the ATF taking that fertilizer was a stupid move. That's so easy to replace. Tell 'em to put it on their lawn. Works good."

"Just get your ass outta here, Judd. Right now, you're life's hangin' by a thread."

Brad opened the front door and watched as Worley swaggered out, still holding his fingers to the bloody lip. As he walked by Sumiko, he ran the back of his hand across her arm like a snake, until she jerked it beyond his reach. Sumiko's face showed her fury.

Only the slamming of the door kept Brad from letting Sumiko retaliate.

CHAPTER 20

Kathleen Logan fastened her seat belt as she prepared for the landing of United Flight 221 from Omaha. A quick glance at her watch told her the flight was on time. They would touch down in Langston at 11:45. She had ample time for her two o'clock appointment with Dr. Fisher. She had arranged for the appointment with the police department psychiatrist after she talked to Brad two days before.

Kathleen hadn't spoken to her husband since then, not since she accused him of having an affair with Sumiko. Brad didn't admit to the affair, nor did he deny it. She knew Brad couldn't lie to her. That's why he said nothing. Their eighteen year marriage was built on mutual trust and fidelity. Now she felt those building blocks crumbling around her.

When the plane touched down, Kathleen looked out the windows as the airport buildings flashed by her window. She could tell it was already hot outside by the intensity of the shadows and the occasional view of people in shirt sleeves.

As promised, her high school friend, Paula Goddard, waited at the gate as Kathleen walked toward the terminal. Paula didn't ask and Kathleen didn't explain why Brad didn't meet her plane. Even as the women ate a quick lunch at the terminal snack shop, Kathleen's obvious pain wasn't made a topic of conversation. The two friends long ago had learned they couldn't discuss personal problems while eating.

At Paula's insistence, Kathleen borrowed her friend's car for the rest of the afternoon. By the time she dropped Paula off at her house, there was just time to get to Dr. Fisher's office. As usual, just walking into the psychiatrist's office had a calming effect on Kathleen.

"Kathleen, dear, it's so good to see you again. Just sit down and try to relax. How have you been? Your voice sounded so urgent on the phone."

"I've been better, Doctor. Do you mind if we get right to why I'm here?"

"Not at all, Dear. You may talk about anything you wish. Something serious is troubling you, am I right?"

"You might say that. My marriage is finished. Tell me what to do about it. I can't cope with it myself."

Doctor Fisher's expression didn't change. She leaned back in her soft leather chair, looking at Kathleen with a motherly expression, eyebrows raised. "Bad as all that, huh?"

"Yes, it's true, Doctor. I've been staying with my parents for the past month. Brad has a girlfriend. He's cheating on me. I never thought he'd do it to me. I always thought our love was too strong for either of us to stray. What do I do?"

Without warning, the emotions came surging up and there was nothing Kathleen could do to stop them. Sobs racked her body as tears streamed down her checks and formed a waterfall off her chin. She was aware of Dr. Fisher handing her a box of Kleenex. She took the box and extracted a handful of tissues, holding them to her face. The soft, unemotional voice of the doctor soothed her to some degree. "Let go of it, Kathleen. You've held it in too long. Crying is cathartic. When you're ready, we can talk about what you think happened. Then we'll decide what you must do."

"I…I…know what happened, Doctor, I know it." Her voice trembled, but the words came through loud and clear.

"…and how do you know that?"

"B…b…'cause he made sure I was out of town so he could get her into bed."

"You know that, for sure?"

Kathleen nodded her head furiously. More Kleenex dabbed at more tears. "When I accused him of sleeping with his little Geisha girl, he wouldn't deny it, the no-good *bastard*. Damn it, I hate him! God, how I hate him."

Now the anger made its way to the forefront, turning Kathleen's face into a hateful mask. She could even feel her ugliness overwhelming her.

"Did he tell you he was unfaithful?" That soft, steady voice again.

"No, but I know Brad. If it wasn't true, he'd have denied it. He won't lie to me."

Kathleen heard Dr. Fisher's chair creak as she rose to her feet.

"That makes him a very good guy in my book. Would you be happier if he lied to you? You haven't let him explain things, have you?"

"I don't want to hear anything he has to say."

Doctor Fisher frowned and began shaking her head. She pulled her glasses onto her nose, peering at Kathleen with the disapproval brought about by many similar client sessions.

"Haven't you heard? Communication between partners keeps them on the right track? Nothing else is effective. You *must* talk to him. Listen to his side. If it's still as bad as you think it is, then act on it—-*after* you know the facts. There may be nothing to your suspicions. Don't you see? That's all you're dealing with now…suspicions. If they're true, at least you can deal with them better when you know his side. Don't you think?"

The doctor circled the desk and Kathleen felt soft hands stroking her hair and neck. She remembered her mother ministering to her in a similar manner. As always, the soothing hands exorcised the anger from her body, leaving her shaken but more relaxed.

For another half hour, the two women talked, Kathleen pouring out her fears and frustrations while the doctor magically drew potential solutions from Kathleen's own mouth. By the time the session was completed, Kathleen felt calm, her confidence recharged. She repaired her makeup as the doctor capsulated their discussion:

"Kathleen, you and Brad are more in love than any couple I know. You have a wonderful marriage. If you let a misunderstanding ruin that marriage, you're just as guilty as Brad if you break up. Give him the benefit of the doubt. If, in a worse case scenario, your fears prove to be real, then you must decide if you can forgive him. You both must work hard at keeping your love from being choked to death by jealousy. I want you both in for more counseling. Think he'll do that?"

Kathleen shrugged her shoulders. "I'm not sure, Doctor. He's such a macho bastard. Thinks he can do everything himself. Always been that way. I'll know better after we talk."

It was after four o'clock when Kathleen left the lobby of the doctor's office. Her heart didn't ache as it had earlier in the day. She saw things with much more clarity and knew what she must do. She was still convinced of Brad's infidelity, but now felt she could deal with it.

When Paula assured her over the phone she didn't need her car, Kathleen decided she would drive to Sumiko's hotel to talk to her. She planned to reassure Sumiko, letting her know she held no unyielding animosity toward her. Once that was done, Kathleen felt she could confront her husband.

At the desk of the Commodore Hotel, Kathleen discovered Sumiko no longer was a guest. The clerk insisted she could not give out the forwarding address, but Kathleen showed her ID as a member of the Police Auxiliary and, in due time, convinced her she meant no harm to Miss Tanaka.

It was after five as she drove through town and headed East toward Little Ginza. She could see the high rise apartment building several blocks before she drove into the cul-de-sac in front of the building.

As she turned onto the street, a yellow taxi cab came screaming out of the parking area, just missing her car as she yanked the steering wheel toward the curb. The squeal of her brakes and the tug of the seatbelt on her chest explained just how close she had come to a head-on collision. Before she could gather her breath from that close call, a second car whizzed past her with seeming inches to spare.

It wasn't until the moment of panic passed that the realization came to her: 'My God, Judd Worley was driving that cab. What in the hell is he doing here? I'm not even home yet and already he's in my face'.

As she parked the car, Kathleen sat for several minutes, letting her heart slow down and the adrenaline return to its storage place. When she felt normal again, she walked to the office marked 'Manager' and read the tenant's register posted on the outer wall. Sumiko Tanaka was listed in apartment number ten.

To her great surprise, the security gate stood wide open and Kathleen didn't hesitate going through it. As she hurried down the sidewalk to number ten, she rehearsed the lines she intended to use. She knew she must be careful so that Sumiko understood everything she wanted to say. Kathleen was concerned about a possible language and culture barrier between them.

Standing in front of Sumiko's door, Kathleen overwhelmed by sudden remorse.

"My God, what am I doing here? What if I'm wrong about them? It will break her poor heart if I accuse her unfairly."

Brushing aside her apprehension, Kathleen raised her hand to knock.

❧   ❧   ❧

Sergeant Brad Logan was in a squad car driving through Little Ginza when he heard the call from Dispatch. There was an injury call from the Cherryland Apartments on East Fresno Street. An emergency crew was en route. Any police car in the area was ordered to respond.

Grabbing the mike, Brad advised Dispatch he was in the area and was responding. He was concerned about Sumiko. That was her apartment building. His fingers fumbled with the switch to the emergency lights and siren.

Brad arrived at the parking area before the other emergency vehicles. He could see the security gate standing wide open and a crowd gathered on the sidewalk in front of the apartment building.

They were looking through the open door of Sumiko's apartment!

Brad broke into a sprint as he went through the gate. He could hear the sounds of the arriving ambulance and fire trucks as he ran toward the crowd on the sidewalk. Holding his badge aloft, he heaved curious bodies aside and burst into the room.

His shock was mind-numbing. There, in the middle of the living room was Sumiko, with blood all over her, lying with her head in Kathleen's lap. Brad's long years of training to respond to emergency situations with calm detachment deserted him. He fell to his knees beside the two women. "Goddam it, Kate, what have you done to her?"

As soon as the words left his mouth, Brad realized how terrible they sounded. His wife had the same reaction to them. "Brad Logan, you chicken shit bastard! How can you say that? I'm trying to save Sumi's life and you accuse me of killing her! Goddam you, how dare you? Go get more towels and help stop this blood."

Kathleen's angry words cut through Brad's confused mind and made him spring into action. The hall closet yielded a whole stack of towels which he dumped on the floor beside the wounded Sumiko.

"Katie, what can you tell me about this? I know you couldn't do it. Here, put this clean towel on her."

"Judd Worley was here before I got here. He almost ran me into the curb, he was in such a big hurry to get away. You want to blame someone, he'd get my vote."

Brad stopped wiping up Sumiko's blood. "Judd was here? Now he's gone over the edge, the son of a bitch! Damn it, where's that ambulance?"

"They must be right behind you, Brad. How did you find out what happened?"

"I heard the call on my radio. God, Katie, what are *you* doing here? When did you get home? Why didn't you let me know?"

"Just shut up, Brad, and go see where the medics are. I can't stop this blood much longer. I'm afraid she's slipping away."

Brad hurried to the door. He could see the ambulance crew pushing their equipment up the sidewalk, followed by a fire truck crew and two policemen. He motioned for them to hurry and went back inside.

"They're here, Kate. Are you sure you're all right?"

"Nice of you to ask. How the hell do you think I am? Here I am, holding your dying lover in my arms. Her blood's all over me. Angry—-you want to talk about angry, I…"

Brad saw tears forming in Kathleen's eyes again. He turned to face the men coming in the door so he didn't have to see her agony. He couldn't face it yet.

"She's gushing blood, guys. Looks like someone took a knife to her face and then sliced her body up. Come on, Kate, let these guys take over. She'll be in good hands."

Brad watched as the medics gently took Sumiko's head off Kate's lap and began working on the injured girl. Kathleen just sat and watched them. She couldn't mask the anxiety in her face. The front of her clothing was soaked in blood. Her hair hung in tear- soaked strands around her face. Brad's heart ached at the vision. She was hurting.

Brad pulled a patrol officer to one side and told him he was leaving the crime scene in their hands and was going after the person he felt was the perpetrator.

"The redhead's my wife. She found the body and was helping the victim. Hope it's not too late. See that my wife gets to the hospital. She needs to be treated for shock. She'll give you a statement soon, I think."

"Did she do this to the victim?"

"Not a chance, man. My wife couldn't do this to anyone. They were friends. I'm going after the slime who did this."

Brad went to his wife and asked if she was all right. She claimed she understood why he was going after Judd Worley. This was the final showdown with Worley. There was no way Brad could avoid it any longer. There were too many threats. Too much harassment.

Brad wasn't surprised when Kate turned her face away as he tried to kiss her.

By now, the medics had inserted an IV and were doing what they could to stop the flow of blood. As he watched, they lifted Sumiko's tiny body onto the gurney and prepared her for transport to the hospital. They said she was weak, but her blood pressure and heart rate were not life-threatening yet.

Brad was on his phone calling for backup as he walked down the sidewalk to his parked car. With siren wailing and red lights flashing, he whirled out of the parking lot.

* * *

He violated every departmental rule against speeding and running red lights as he wheeled his car through evening traffic. It made no difference to him. Right now, the only important thing was his overwhelming need for revenge. He replayed every insult, every threat, every taunting remark Judd Worley ever made to him.

The first time he tangled with Judd was in grammar school. The memory was still vivid. It was the first day of fifth grade. As Brad talked to a group of his friends, Judd walked up and challenged Brad. Within minutes, Brad sat on Judd's chest, pounding his fists on Judd's face. The playground monitor pulled him off and made him apologize. 'Take the blame for the fight', was the first page in his Book of Hatred for Judd Worley.

In the tenth grade, the two of them tangled several times. The worst fight was after Brad found out Judd tried to put his hand under Kathleen's blouse. That time, Brad waited until after school so the teachers couldn't stop the fight. He gave Judd the worst beating he ever meted out to anyone. It resulted in a broken nose for Judd and Brad being grounded by his dad for a week. Page two.

They were out of touch for a long time after high school. Brad went away to college and Judd ended up serving two years in the Youth Authority for stealing a car. Brad returned to Langston and joined the police department. Their social circles seldom crossed for a long time, but in recent years fate had drawn them together again. The web connecting them grew shorter and shorter. And now, here he was, hurtling through town, like an angry missile, looking for one last confrontation.

His anger burned his throat by the time he screeched to a halt at the curb in front of Judd's apartment complex. With gun drawn, he raced along the sidewalk until he was in front of Worley's door. He didn't even bother knocking.

The door jamb shattered when his snakeskin boot found its mark on the closed door. He was inside before the door hit the wall. It was then he received his second severe shock of the day.

"I been expecting you, jerk. What took you so long?"

Judd Worley sat in the middle of his front room floor holding both hands to his stomach. He was surrounded by a growing pool of blood. It gushed between his fingers.

"You won't need your gun, asshole." Judd's voice was weak, but still defiant. Brad jammed his 9MM back under his arm and knelt beside the man he hated more than anyone in his life. "My God, Judd, who did this to you?"

"I…it was a hired gun…*Ninja* type. N…never saw him before. He killed the Jap girl, too. They knew about her. They knew."

"Who bought the hit? Come on, Judd, give me some answers."

Brad could see the life draining out of the man. His face was painted white as a death mask, his fingers shook and his eyes were vacant glass.

"Dunno…Damn you, Logan. J…just shut your Goddam mouth and listen. Got no time for your sh…shit. I'm dead, man. Ummm…God, it hurts."

"Sorry, Judd. Tell me what you can."

"T…tell Kathleen I'm sorry. Gotta promise me. Go see my mom. Sh…she…Mom's…got my book. Read the book. I…it's all there. Take care of Mom. Pro…mise me…"

Judd's voice trailed off, becoming a whisper. Brad leaned closer so he could hear every word. His heart pounded in his throat. Nothing made any sense.

"…listen, lis…listen close."

Brad leaned over until his ear was next to Judd's mouth. He held his breath.

"D…don't…t…trust Nichols…he…he's a snake…"

Judd's voice stopped. His head dropped until his chin was on his chest. Brad put his arm around the sagging shoulders to keep Judd's body from falling over.

"Judd, Judd, can you hear me? Tell me who did this. Judd…"

A hideous sound gurgled from bloody lips. Brad's heart sank as he allowed the collapsing body to lie back on the floor. Where was the joy he should feel? All he felt was body-numbing grief.

"All right, Logan. Hands over your head. Don't move another muscle."

The harsh voice brought Brad back into real time. He turned with alarm, facing the sound coming from the open front door. Standing in the doorway, with arm outstretched, was Lieutenant Glen Nichols, head of Internal Affairs. The gun in his hand pointed, with ominous intent, at Brad's silver belt buckle. Brad raised his arms over his head, fingers spread to show that he had no weapon.

"Nichols, what the hell are you doing?"

"Shut up, Logan. Now reach in—very carefully—with two fingers and bring your gun out where I can see it. Then you'll toss it, ever so gently, over to me. You got that, Sergeant?"

In a sudden flash, Judd's last words—-the warning about Nichols—-came screaming back into Brad's brain. He shook his head. "Not a chance, Nichols. Use your head, man. This man was stabbed. That's not my style. I'd have killed him with my bare hands."

The only answer Brad heard was the loud *CLICK* as Nichols pulled back the hammer on the silver-plated .38 he pointed at Brad.

CHAPTER 21

*A*s Kathleen sat in the curtained cubicle in the emergency room, she couldn't control the convulsions racking her body. When the doctor finished with his examination, he gave her a tranquilizer and told her a nurse would be in soon. He wasn't sure yet if he would keep her overnight.

Gradually, the tranquilizing effects of the shot spread through her body. The violent shaking and the sobs subsided. For the first time in days, she felt her body relax. The crazy kaleidoscope of mental images faded out, one monster at a time, as the effects of the drug took control of her body. For no good reason, she found herself giggling.

"Sure hope Brad doesn't hurt poor ol' Judd too badly. Jeez if he knew the bastard tried sticking his tongue down my throat when we were in tenth grade, I bet he'd kill 'im."

The giggles continued until a young girl in the pink uniform of the Candy Stripers, came through the curtain. She carried several clean towels and a pan of soapy water .

"Hi, Mrs. Logan, I'm Cindy. The doctor told me to get you cleaned up as best we can. How you feeling?"

"Gettin' better all the time, Cindy. That last cocktail took all my cares away, whoopee!"

The giggles returned as Cindy washed the dried blood from her hands, arms and face. As Kathleen became aware of the amount of blood the young girl had removed, the serious nature of Sumiko's experience surged back again. The giggles left as quickly as they started. "Do you know how my friend Sumiko is doing?"

"Is she the one who came with you in the ambulance?"

"Yes. Have you heard anything?"

"No, Ma'am. They're still working on her. Maybe the nurse can tell you when she comes in. I think that's about the best I can do on cleaning you. I'll bring you a gown so you can get out of those clothes. Gosh, that must have been a terrible thing you went through."

"Hope you never experience it, Honey. I know the memory will stay with me as long as I'm alive. That poor little thing—her life was just pouring out of her body. God, it was awful." The dark thoughts came rushing back, and Kathleen shook her head, again and again, hoping she could exorcise the memory.

At that moment, the curtain was pulled back and a young woman in a police uniform came through the opening. "Mrs. Logan? I'm officer Ann Belding of Langston PD. I need your statement. Do you feel up to it?"

"Glad to meet you, Ann. Has anyone heard from my husband? He went after the person who stabbed Sumiko."

"As I was driving here, there was a lot of chatter on the radio. Several cars headed to that address. Sorry, I can't tell you anything more. I'm sure Sergeant Logan will be all right. He has plenty of backup."

Kathleen didn't think Brad would need any backup, but bit her tongue before the words came out. Before the interview began, the doctor came in and said he wanted to keep her overnight, just for safety's sake. Kathleen didn't resist. All she wanted was sleep. She was sure that rest was the best prescription for what ailed her.

"I'm ready, Officer Belding, what can I tell you?"

"Start at the beginning, Ma'am. Why were you going to see Miss Tanaka?"

Kathleen wondered how the officer would react if she told her she went there to confront the young woman—then forgive her. "I've been out of town for a month—you know—since our house was bombed. Anyway, Sumiko is a new friend to me and my husband. I hadn't seen her new apartment. When I got there, her door was ajar. When I looked in, I saw her lying on the floor. I was terrified. Couldn't think straight. Just knew she was hurt—badly."

"Did you see anyone or anything right before you found her?"

"Well, just as I arrived, I was almost hit head-on by a taxi leaving the scene."

The officer looked up from her notes, a quizzical look on her face. "A taxi? Did you notice the name? What about a color?"

"I can do better than that. It was driven by Judd Worley. I've known him since high school, so there's no mistake. It was Judd, all right."

Officer Belding looked up from her notes. "You saw him that well? Must've happened awful fast, but you think you saw the driver and it was a Judd Worley?"

Kathleen could hear a tinge of skepticism in the officer's voice. It was common knowledge in the Langston PD that the Logans and Judd Worley were feuding.

"He threatened to hurt Miss Tanaka. Did you know that?"

The officer's body jerked to attention. "You heard him threaten her?"

"No, but my husband did."

Officer Belding's demeanor sagged. "I see. I'll make a note of it. Is there anything else you can think of?"

"No, I guess not. Oh—wait—I just remembered something else. There was another car right behind Judd. Like they might be racing. You know what I mean?"

"A second car? What do you remember about it?"

"Nothing. It was such a quick thing. You know...after Judd almost hit me. You know, officer...I'm kind of tired all of a sudden. Can I be excused now?"

"Sure, Mrs. Logan. If we need anything else, we can find you. Thanks for your time. Hope you'll be better after some rest."

Officer Belding parted the curtains and left Kathleen alone with her thoughts.

❧   ❧   ❧

Brad felt the muscles in his stomach tighten in anticipation of the bullet he knew would fly at him in an instant. Black thoughts of death overwhelmed him. He saw Nichols' fingers clenching the gun tighter. He knew he must do something, but his body froze. It was like a terrible nightmare. Everything in slow motion.

At that moment, Brad heard a voice he recognized after the first word. "Hey, Lieutenant, you planning on shooting Ol' Junkyard? Ain't that a little extreme?"

Brad's breath escaped in one loud burst as Sam Hardy's face appeared in the doorway. 'Fish' never looked more beautiful. Brad even detected a halo over Sam's head. He wanted to rush over and kiss his partner's bald head. Instead, he let his body sag, overcome by the tension of the moment.

"Stand down, Sergeant Hardy. This man killed Worley. I want his weapon. Don't interfere," Lieutenant Nichols snarled without glancing at Sam.

"I wouldn't think of getting in your way, Lieutenant. If you shoot the man, it's no skin off my nose. Just remember, you have a witness now."

Sam looked into the room and grinned at Brad.

"Well, Junkyard, what kinda mess you got yourself into now? Did you kill him?" Sam nodded his head toward the late Judd Worley.

"Believe it or not, Sam. I got here too late to kill the son of a bitch. Someone beat me to it. I figure it was about half hour ago. He was gutted by a pro. Told me it was a Japanese hit man."

Lieutenant Nichols smirked, making no effort to hide his disbelief. "That's about the weakest alibi I've ever heard. You'll have to do better than that. A Japanese hit man? Sheeeit…spare me." Nichols lowered his weapon, but held it in his hand, the hammer still cocked.

The move didn't go unnoticed by Sam Hardy. "You make me kinda nervous with that hammer back, Lieutenant. Would you mind putting it away? I can beat old Junkyard to the draw any day of the week. Besides, there's no way he did this. A knife's not his style, okay? He'da ripped Worley's head off with his bare hands. You know…him being the Junkyard Dog and all."

Sam nodded his head toward Brad, then sauntered between Nichols and Brad. A brief smile and a wink of the eye told Brad his partner was in control. The gun went back into the holster at Nichols' waist.

"Don't get too cozy with him, Hardy. This man's still a suspect. The landlord heard him threaten Worley on several occasions. There'll be an inquest, you can count on that." Nichols had taken two steps into the room, but still held a position between Brad and the door.

Brad ignored him and talked directly to his partner. "You'd better call the Coroner and a crime scene team, Sam. If Lieutenant Nichols doesn't object, I promised Judd I'd go tell his mother. Don't know if she'll talk to me, but I have to try. Can you roger that, Lieutenant?"

Brad started out the door without waiting for an answer. Nichols just stepped aside.

It wasn't until he was inside the sanctity of his locked car that Brad took his first real breath and let the tension flow from his body. There was no doubt in his mind: If Sam hadn't arrived when he did, a bullet from Nichols' gun would be in his body—no question. His whole body was overcome with violent shaking.

He called headquarters for Alma Worley's address. She lived in a modest trailer park on the north side. He pulled into her driveway fifteen minutes later. The anxiety choked him. This was Judd's mother. No matter that a son is evil—a mother is still a mother. He wondered: Could he speak when she answered his knock?

The portly woman who answered the door somehow looked familiar. Her snow white hair was braided and twisted into a knot at the nape of her neck. Several loose strands hung from her forehead. Brad fought an urge to brush them back for her. The smile on her face was kind and gentle. She showed no sign of recognition.

"Mrs. Worley. I'm Sergeant Logan of Langston Police. I wonder if I may talk to you?"

Her hands went to her mouth, stifling an outcry. "It's about Judd, isn't it? Is he dead?"

The direct question was unexpected. Brad intended a more roundabout approach. He nodded. "I'm sorry, Ma'am. He's been murdered by someone unknown. I spoke to him briefly before he died. I promised him I'd come tell you."

"Come in, Sergeant. I'll make some tea…or sumpthin' stronger if you'd rather."

She stepped aside as Brad entered the house. Mrs. Worley's home was immaculate. After seeing Judd's version of housekeeping, Brad assumed it ran in the family. Not only was the house clean, the furnishings looked to be of good quality and, in some cases, downright expensive. Brad experienced a twinge of culture shock.

In one corner of the living room was a glassed-in case containing many small statuettes. Brad recognized them as Hummel collector items. He knew they weren't cheap. The other furnishings were equally tasteful.

Alma Worley waved him to a comfortable looking arm chair. He pushed aside the copy of People magazine and settled into the chair. That's when it dawned on him that he was exhausted. The last few hours had taken a toll on him. Finding Kathleen with the injured

Sumiko and then having Judd die in his arms. Not the greatest kind of day.

"Don't be uneasy, Brad, I been expecting this for a long time. Judd warned me over and over his life was in danger—you know—his working for the FBI and all."

Brad couldn't believe his ears. "The FBI? Judd told you he worked for them?"

"Yessir. More'n twenty years, I reckon. I'm so proud'a him. Never let no one else know about it. Only me. I think he—-"

"You sure about this, Ma'am? The FBI?" Brad didn't want to alienate her—she had something he wanted. But Judd Worley with the FBI was just too laughable.

Alma Worley's facial expression became harsh. It was obvious she resented his question. Her words became clipped. "Believe it, Sergeant. That's how come he could support his mama for so long. He paid for all this stuff. A mother couldn't want a better son." She waved her hand around the perimeter of the room.

Brad marveled that Judd had lied to his mother all these years. It made sense that Judd wanted his mother's approval for his lifestyle. "I'm sure you're very proud of him, Mrs. Worley. I guess I've known Judd since our days in grammar school. We didn't always get along, but I sure am impressed with the way he took care of you."

"I know all about you and my Judd. You was always his hero—even after you kept beating him up. He told me he wished he could be like you. Big football star...so many girl friends...scholarships...all that stuff. He thought you was special."

For the second time, Brad's jaw dropped. Was this woman making all this up as a punishment? It sounded like so much nonsense to him. Could it be true? The only other person who might know, was dead. "I'm flattered, Mrs. Worley. I had no idea. Seems like Judd and I were always at each other's throat. Doesn't seem like he could've liked me much."

Alma Worley stared at her guest, as her bobbed from side to side. "You didn't know his dream was being a cop?"

"A cop? Judd? Lord, I thought he hated cops."

"No, sir. My Judd tried joining the force right after school. Them snots wouldn't talk to him 'cause of that little deal about the car. You know, he borrowed that car when he was just a kid. He didn't give up, though. That's when he went and talked to the FBI."

Brad just nodded. It was still too much to digest in one sitting. He needed some quiet time so he could sort out the day's activities. He looked at his watch. It was after 9:00 and he still hadn't eaten or taken off his boots. "Mrs. Worley, Judd told me he left a journal with you and he wanted me to have it. Do you know what he meant?"

"Course I do. He kept his book ever since he got outta school. It's in a safe place. He made me promise long ago that if he got killed or sumpthin' I was to give it to you. Don't know why, but I know it was important to him."

Mrs. Worley rose from her chair and went into her bedroom. He could hear her rummaging around in a drawer, at last returning with a thick leather-bound binder which she dropped into Brad's lap. "I told you I could find it. You ready for some tea now, Brad?"

Brad wasn't all that ready, but knew the woman wanted him to stay and visit for a while. He couldn't believe she was so calm and unemotional after hearing his news. It was almost as if she knew about it before he got here. It didn't seem natural that she wouldn't grieve at least a little. "Tea? Just a little bit, Mrs. Worley. I still gotta get back and fill out my reports. It's been a very long day. Thank you for keeping Judd's book for me. Have you read it?"

She was already on her way to the kitchen sink when she answered. "Lordee no. I never touched nothin' of his. Same with his father. Old Man Worley was a stickler for keeping his stuff private. You know, Judd's father would give me a couple good whacks now and again—beat Judd's butt, too—used a belt lotsa times. You take anything in your tea?"

"No, Ma'am, just tea, thank you. Didn't you and Mister Worley have more kids?"

"Just the one. Old Man Worley told me he'd leave me if I got pregnant again. Can you imagine that?"

"What did he do?"

"Do? I got no idea. Was gone mosta the time. Took Judd fishing a lot. He'd come home sometimes and dump a handful of money on the bed. Never told me where he got it and I knew better'n ask. Kept us in food and clothes. He'd get drunk sometimes. He'd hide my clothes and keep me in bed with him for hours. Wasn't none too gentle, but it was better'n being ignored all the time. Here's your tea."

Her openness about her personal life made Brad self-conscious, but she didn't notice. He got the impression she would talk to anyone who would listen. Her revelations explained a lot about Judd Worley's personality. As a child, no one ever let him believe he was as good as anyone else. He must have been playing out a role. Brad's limited education in Psychology didn't give him a clear picture. He assumed that Judd's childhood molded Judd's adulthood.

At 9:30, Brad was so tired he told Mrs. Worley he was going to the station before he fell asleep. He gave her his card and promised to be available if she needed him. He also hinted that if Judd was on the Federal payroll, he might qualify for a military funeral. That hit a soft spot with her. She even hugged him and kissed his cheek as he said goodnight.

Despite being bone tired, Brad rushed to the hospital after his visit to Mrs. Worley. There had been no time to sort through his feelings, but now he found time to worry about Kathleen and Sumiko. When he parked in front of the hospital, he took time to lock Judd's journal into the trunk of his squad car.

When he checked in with Dispatch, there was a message for him from Lieutenant Nichols. He was to report to him at Headquarters.

At that moment, Brad was more concerned about the welfare of the two women in his life.

The floor nurse was adamant that it was much too late for Brad to see his wife. She assured him Kathleen was sleeping. She was not injured, but her emotional state was of some concern. The RN told Brad he could see his wife during visiting hours in the morning. He was too tired to argue the point.

The nurse told him Sumiko was out of surgery and was in the recovery room. Her wounds required extensive surgery. She had lost a great deal of blood. Prognosis was one of cautious optimism for a full recovery.

"She was a lucky young lady, Sergeant. The fact your wife arrived when she did and slowed the loss of blood saved her life. You should be very proud of Mrs. Logan."

The irony of the situation was not lost on Brad. He wandered back to his car and drove back to the police station. He was so tired he almost forgot to take Judd's book out of the trunk of the car. Once he retrieved it, he wasted no time moving it to the trunk of his own car. He would read it when he got home.

But first, he dictated his report. He learned Lieutenant Nichols was already checked out. That was a relief. He wondered if the Lieutenant's report would read differently than his own. Right now, he didn't give a rat's ass.

Brad drove into his garage at 11:30, hungry and totally beat—in mind as well as in body. He found no surprises in the daily mail delivery and the surveillance video had not been activated. That was the third day in a row no one made a threat against him—not counting the gun in Lieutenant Nichols' hand.

In anticipation of his wife returning to the house the next day, Brad loaded his dirty clothing into the washer and got it started before he went to the refrigerator for a beer. In the freezer, he found leftover burritos. They went into the microwave while he finished off his beer.

When the bell told him dinner was ready, he took the casserole dish to the counter and read the daily mail as he ate. He couldn't even taste his meal, because he was emotionally numb. No one could have been prepared for the events of the past few days. He was sure it was a test to see how much stress a human being was capable of absorbing in a short period of time. If it *was* a test, he figured he must have failed it.

With his complaining stomach now satisfied and his laundry now whirling in the dryer, Brad grabbed Judd's leather bound binder. Upstairs, the bed offered untold rewards.

His boots came off, his 9MM found a spot on the night stand and, with no other preparation, Brad propped himself up on several pillows and opened Judd's journal.

His hopes were not running high as he started reading. Judd's handwriting required a great amount of concentration. Brad figured the entries were Judd's effort to portray himself a hero—-a real piece of fiction. The first entry dated back fifteen years.

It was going to be a long night.

CHAPTER 22

"Sam, cover for me this morning, will you? I'm going by the hospital to see Kathleen. I'll be in by noon."

It was almost eight o'clock and Brad had still not slept. He spent the night reading Judd Worley's journal and the revelations in it were so shocking he couldn't trust the information to anyone else. Not even Sam Hardy. Before he did anything else, Brad wanted a backup copy—-just in case. Once copies were made, the original would go into a safety deposit box. He had no intention of letting the journal out of his possession.

"The hospital…Kathleen's in the hospital? Has she been hurt? Dammit, Brad, I didn't even know she was back in town. What's going on, partner?" Sam Hardy would never accept substitutes for accuracy, so Brad filled his partner in on the previous day's events. Sam's first response was just what Brad expected: "Kathleen was at the scene after the Tanaka girl was stabbed? For God's sake, what in hell was she doing there? Come on, pal, tell me everything, okay? Is this related to Worley's death?"

"Count on it, Sam. Before Worley died, he told me a Japanese hit man had cut him up and, according to him, the same guy stabbed Sumiko. I think Judd walked in on the guy during the assault…looks like he ended up saving Sumiko. That jibes with Kate's story. As she drove up to Sumiko's apartment, she almost got run over by Judd

Worley leaving in his cab. Kate told me Worley stabbed Sumiko. That's why I went after him."

"Are you sure *you* didn't ice him, partner?" Sam's tone was not accusatory, and Brad knew his partner was just probing him for the truth.

"Oh, sure, I stabbed him in his own apartment and swallowed the murder weapon. Then waited for Nichols to catch me. *You can't be serious.* You're not buying that crap Nichols was spouting, are you?"

Brad heard a chuckle from the phone. "Yeah, right. I'll ignore the physical evidence and believe the idiot who had a gun pointed at you! That dude doesn't like you, man, you know that?"

"Yeah, I know. Listen to this. With his last breath, Worley told me I couldn't trust Nichols. Called him a snake. Not sure how Judd knew so much, but it kinda confirms my own feelings about Nichols. He just doesn't come across as being virginal. You watch him, too, Sam. Don't tell him anything you don't have to."

Sam agreed without further comment. Brad's train of thought then switched tracks. "By the way, I had a nice chat with Judd's mother last night. You should see her house. Very nice. Her son took very good care of her. Guess what…Mama Worley thinks Judd worked for the Bureau. How's that grab you?"

"The FBI? Worley? You've gotta be kiddin'. Sure had me fooled. Always thought he was pure slime. FBI huh? But, you know, I kept telling you he wasn't the worthless toad you claimed. You gotta start listenin' to Ol' Sam. Got anything else?"

"I'll tell you more later; I've gotta get moving. Thanks for covering for me. I'll be in by noon. Keep alert, pal. There are lots of bad guys hanging around."

As soon as the line was clear, Brad called the hospital. The nurse said Kathleen could check out after ten that morning. He told the nurse he'd be in after ten, then asked about the condition of Sumiko Tanaka.

Sumiko was still in the ICU, but her condition was improving. More surgery was scheduled for the wounds on her face. She could not have visitors or phone calls for at least another 24 hours. The words were encouraging, but her condition still caused Brad great distress as he hung up the phone. He couldn't shake the pangs of severe guilt.

"Why wasn't I there when she needed me? Where the hell was her FBI bodyguard? This should never have happened. I'm gonna carve Kelly Garrett a new rear-end; I told him it was too dangerous."

He dialed the private number for Garrett in Seattle. He got the answering service, but left no message. Brad blamed Garrett for sending Sumiko into so much danger. He was determined he would deliver the message himself.

Brad looked at the clock. There was plenty of time for making his copies. He busied himself straightening the house so Kathleen wouldn't find it unfit to live in. It was just after nine when he left the house. It pleased him that there were no police cars in the neighborhood. Brad's recent distrust of fellow officers sickened him.

Making copies of the journal took longer than he anticipated. It was after ten when he rode the elevator to the third floor. He struggled with his armful of peace offerings. He carried Kathleen's cosmetics case, her change of clothes and, of course, the large bouquet. He didn't know how she'd react to him, but was prepared for the worst.

She sat on the edge of her bed, brushing her hair. Her smile was less than heart-warming. She accepted a peck on the cheek, but nothing more. Brad gave the flowers to a nurse, who placed them in a vase. Kathleen then set the tone without hesitation. "Brad, don't pretend everything's cool—-it isn't. I feel crappy as hell. Yesterday was the worst day of my life. Maybe I'll never get over it. I still can't deal with my emotions. Do you know how Sumi's doing?"

Kathleen's voice reflected the tension she felt. Brad knew he couldn't comfort her in her present mood. His wife would let him know when she was ready for him to grovel. "I checked this morning. She can't have visitors yet. She'll be in ICU for at least another day. She'll be getting some plastic surgery on her facial wounds. I know it must have been like walking through Hell for you. Did you get some rest?"

The strain between them was thick as melted chocolate. Kathleen didn't respond to his question. Her mind was elsewhere. "I called Paula early this morning. I felt so bad about having her car. She said the cops brought the car back to her when they found out where it was. That was a relief. Can you find out who did it and thank him?"

"Glad to hear we have some good cops down there, after all. I'll take care of it."

"Why don't you go check me out? I'll be ready by the time you get back. I need to get the hell out of here."

A half hour later, they were in the car, heading home. Lengthy conversation was impossible. Neither was ready for a confrontation. The twenty-minute ride seemed like hours.

Brad detected a hint of pleasure in her eyes when she walked into her kitchen and set the flowers down. He was glad he straightened the house for her homecoming. Above all, she needed to see her home as it was when she left. She needed no reminders of the bombing.

"Kate, I told Sam I'd be in around noon. Shall I fix you some lunch before I go?"

"Don't be silly. I'm not helpless, you know. If you're hungry, I'll fix you something before you go in. By the way…you never told me what happened when you went after Judd. Did you find him?"

Brad was withholding that news. He didn't know how she'd take it.

"Honey, I've been putting off telling you. Damn—-there's just no easy way—-Judd Worley's dead."

"Dead? You killed Judd?" The words exploded from her mouth. The shock was obvious. Both hands rushed to her mouth.

Brad dispatched her fears about his role in Judd's death. "No, no, Katie, I didn't do it. When I got to his place, I found him bleeding to death. Feel pretty sure it was the same person who stabbed Sumiko. Judd lived long enough to tell me it was a Japanese hit man. He was positive of that. It wasn't me, believe me."

"Oh, God. I can't handle any more of this. Judd is dead…I…" Kathleen sat on one of the bar stools and rubbed her eyes. Brad stood behind her and gently massaged her shoulders. She didn't shrug his hands off, but he didn't offer any further affection. It was pointless at this time.

"Katie, I promise you it's almost over. I can't tell you anything more, but some things are going on that make me very hopeful. Will you be all right here? I can have Joan come over if you want."

Kathleen shook her head. "No. I'll be all right. Couldn't stand explaining everything to her. You want some lunch?"

"No, no, I'll eat when I get to work. There's stuff in the freezer for you if you get hungry. I'll take you to dinner tonight, if you're sure you're ready. I'd better get outta here."

Before he backed the car out, he locked the photocopies of Judd's journal in a small built-in safe over his workbench. He'd installed it years before as another place to stash a weapon. It was the perfect place to hide his extra copies. The original was already stowed in a box in his bank's vault. He was taking no chances on this bombshell of information. Lives were at stake.

As soon as he arrived at the station, he called for an appointment with Chief Preston at 1:00 that afternoon. It would be his first real face-to-face talk with the Chief. Preston had taken over as chief in the early '80s and, so far, the only time he and Brad had spoken was when Brad received his promotions. Brad found the Chief to be aloof, almost anti-social. All contact with the rank and file was done by his middle managers, men like Captain Owens. There was no question, Chief Preston was not a 'hands on' manager.

Brad planned his strategy during the night. He wanted a safety net as he undertook the job of exposing the dirty cops in Langston PD. Without the chief's protection, he knew his life was on the line as soon as the word got out.

When Sam returned from lunch, the two partners discussed the events of the past 24 hours and compared notes from their own viewpoints. Sam told Brad he should get in touch with Lieutenant Nichols right away.

"The man's been storming around here all morning. Thinks you're avoiding him, for some reason. How's Kathleen? You get her home all right?"

"Yeah. Got her home and broke the news about Worley. Of course she thought I must've killed him. Kinda relieved I could tell her it wasn't me. I still don't feel she's safe at the house, but what can I do? Any idea why Nichols wants me?"

"Who knows? All I can tell you is, be careful what you say, okay? He seems to be in a bitchin' mood—-and his mood has something to do with you. You do have a way of endearing yourself to people…a real charmer, that's my partner."

At Sam's insistence, Brad walked down the hallway to Nichols' office. He could see the Lieutenant through the glass door. He was on the phone. When he saw Brad waiting, he motioned him in and hung up the phone.

"Where the hell you been, you insolent bastard? Why didn't you report to me last night? Have to keep proving your independence, right? Shut the door, Sergeant."

"I looked for you last night, Lieutenant, but you already were gone. This morning, I took my wife home from the hospital. She had a terrible experience. Didn't Sam tell you?"

"Yeah, well, whatever…let's get this out on the table. I don't for a minute believe your story about a Japanese hit man. That's about the lamest story I've—-"

"Excuse me, Lieutenant, can we cut to the chase? I'm still a little foggy about your part in this thing. First place, what were you doing answering a call yesterday? Last I heard, your department doesn't answer a code thirty call. I made the request for backup before I arrived at Worley's. How'd you get there before anyone else? You were gonna shoot me, weren't you?"

"You got that right, Logan. You refused to give up your weapon. I was well within the guidelines. Far as I was concerned, you killed a civilian. I knew your history with Worley. The Inquiry Board would have no problem with my actions."

"You going to carry this any further, Lieutenant? You filing charges or something?"

"It's between you and me right now. When and if I decide you broke the law, I'll bring charges. You'd better spend the day writing up a full report for the Board. Meantime, just keep your nose clean, mister. You've operated on the edge of the rules far too long. It won't break my heart to see you go down."

Brad got to his feet. "If that's all, sir, I have work to do. I turned my report in last night…if you care to check on it. Right now, I'm going after the Oriental hit man as a last favor to my good friend Judd Worley."

"You smartass, get the hell out of here! Go find your invisible hit man."

Brad repressed the urge to shout his response. He just turned and left Nichols' office. The confrontation left him with more troubling questions. Why did Judd warn him about Nichols? Were the two of them connected in some sinister way?

There was one undeniable fact: He couldn't turn his back on Nichols. Not for a second. He was more convinced than ever that the afternoon's appointment with the chief was very crucial to his survival as he carried out his plan.

He just had time for a sandwich and glass of milk.

❧   ❧   ❧

The chief was fifteen minutes late for their appointment. He apologized as he ushered Brad into the office. It was Brad's first view of how the upper echelons of the PD lived. The large office was paneled throughout with rich walnut. The plush carpet was a deep maroon pile that cushioned your steps as you walked. Brad almost felt he should remove his boots before he entered. An American and a California state flag framed the huge desk that Chief Preston occupied. The ambiance was almost Presidential. The sight did nothing to discourage Brad's plans to one day wear the bars of Chief of Police.

"What can I do for you, Sergeant Logan?" Chief Preston possessed the resonant deep voice of a confident leader. He was an inch or two shorter than Brad, but his shoulders were every bit as wide. The hand he extended was strong, but had the feel of soft, pampered skin. Missing were any of the calluses associated with physical work. The chief's tanned face was in stark contrast to the palest blue eyes Brad could remember. They bored into Brad's eyes with confidence.

"Thank you for seeing me, sir. The reason for being here is very serious and may not be easy for you to accept. Please hear me out before you jump to any conclusions."

"This sounds very serious, Logan. Can I assume this has something to do with the homicide yesterday?"

"Yessir, that homicide and several others. It also deals with threats made to my wife and me. Are you aware a bomb was set off in my front yard a month ago?"

Preston nodded and looked at Brad with a level stare. His hands lay atop his desk as he leaned forward in his chair. "If you don't mind my saying so, Sergeant, you should talk to Captain Owens about this.

He can take whatever steps are necessary to protect you and your family, I should think."

"He's well aware of everything, sir, but I can't convince him we have a group of dirty cops in this building. I'm positive fellow officers made the threats. Looks like they think I'm a threat to their organization. Are you aware of the group known as the White Knights?"

"Yes, of course; I know all about them. I know some of our officers are members. But, so far as I know, it's not a major problem. If I get proof they're compromising our department, I'll outlaw the group, no question. Do you have such proof?"

Since the oar was now in the water, Brad rowed ahead. Choosing his words with slow deliberation, he related his theory about Mooch Kaiser's death; his connection with Judd Worley and the threats leading up to Kathleen flying back to Omaha. The chief sat stony-faced, fingers laced and lying quietly across his chest. Brad detected no change of expression as he came to the previous day's assault and murder.

"…and now comes the part that involves you, sir. I have written proof of the involvement of some of our officers. I can't make it public yet—-not until I verify a few things. I want your assurance; if something happens to me, you'll make the evidence public and prosecute the guilty officers." He dropped the bombshell with dramatic flare. It brought the chief to full attention, snapping him upright in his chair.

"What are you talking about, Sergeant? What is this proof and where is it?"

"It's safe for now, Chief. Forgive me, but I can't trust anyone in the department. Hope you can understand…it's a question of my own survival."

"That's all well and good, but if you turn up dead, where will I find this so-called evidence you claim you have?"

"Sir, with all due respect, I'll give that information to FBI agent Kelly Garrett. He's the one who alerted me to this problem. He's in the Seattle office. If I'm burned, you can get the location from Garrett. I'll clue him in about you. Can I have your promise?"

Chief Preston circled his desk and pointed a finger at Brad. "You've gotta lot of guts, I'll give you that. I know all about your reputation as a tough cop, but you're in no position to bargain with me, Sergeant. If you have some proof that my department is corrupt, I want it now and I give no guarantees."

"Chief, we're talking about my safety and my wife's safety. I'll get a guarantee from someone. Either from you or the FBI. I have no choice but to keep the proof hidden until I can make it public. I need authorized wiretaps for confirmation of the accusations before I have a case. I was hopeful you cared enough about this town that you might help me clean up the mess."

Brad was not above using professional blackmail to serve his purpose. He could see a little softening in the chief's body language—a slight sagging. Preston sat on the corner of his desk staring at Brad with a painful expression. It was the look of a fox treed by noisy hounds. "Sergeant, you sure live up to your reputation. Of course I want a clean department. No matter what it takes. Dammit, that's what all of us want. All right, all right, what do you want from me and what kind of guarantee do I get in return?"

Brad hoped the relief he felt wasn't written all over his face. "Sir, right now, I just want a promise you'll protect me when everything hits the fan. There are officers in this department who will kill me if they feel threatened. There's not a doubt in my mind about that. They've had a very lucrative racket going on for quite some time. As soon as I can verify a few things, I'll go public with the evidence. It will make you look good in the process, sir." Stroke, stroke, stroke.

The chief was aware he was being manipulated—no question in Brad's mind. He saw the look of resignation take over the tanned face as Preston surrendered his last bit of resistance. Brad left the office with the verbal promise he wanted. Now it all depended on whether the chief was a man of his word.

On his way back to his desk, Brad detoured to the Forensics Department to see Mark Goddard. The two friends spent a half hour getting caught up on the latest developments. Mark was shocked about Kathleen's traumatic experience. Brad asked Mark to zero in on the two new crime scenes. "There's a good chance both these knife attacks were done by the same person. We're sure a hired assassin, who may have been Japanese, did it. There's very little to go on, but maybe the killer left something behind for us. I know it's not likely, but we can't just give up on it. This is not the same person who killed Mooch Kaiser and Gorman Reed. It's a whole other scenario. Give me anything you can, Mark."

Sam Hardy was on the phone as Brad made it back to his desk. It was almost three o'clock. When Sam hung up, he didn't try to conceal the excitement in his voice. "We may have a big break, partner. A citizen called. Says he watched an Oriental type drive away from Worley's apartment house last night. He says the man tossed something into the trash bin behind the apartments. A black and white crew's on the scene. You wanna go?"

"Does a cat have an ass? Let's ride."

They were both running before they hit the outside door, knowing it takes lucky breaks to solve any crime. This was their case, so they would make their own luck.

A black and white patrol car, with red light flashing, waited for them in the alley behind the Worley murder scene. Two uniformed officers took notes as they spoke to a man sitting astride a bicycle. As was their usual custom, Sam reviewed the cops' notes while Brad went directly to the informant and had him repeat his statement.

The man stated, with no hesitation, that he was riding down the alley the previous evening after 7:30. He lived in the next block, but always took this alley as a shortcut. As he neared the rear entrance to the apartments, a man dressed in black, with a ski mask over his face, burst through the gate, tossed something into the trash bin, then sprinted down the alley to a waiting car. The car screeched out of the alleyway before the man could get a look at the license plate.

Brad wrote quickly as the man completed his story, and then gave a description of the running man as well as the getaway car. The information seemed legitimate. The citizen seemed intelligent. His motives seemed worthy. Brad was elated. Then he heard Sam yell, "Look at this, partner!"

Sam leaned over the edge of the trash bin, pointing at something inside. There, partially hidden under other debris, was a shiny object. It appeared to be covered with blood.

Brad could hardly contain his elation. "Well lookee here, Sam. That appears to be a Samurai sword."

CHAPTER 23

$\mathcal{B}$ rad's lack of sleep caught up with him when they returned to the station with their prize, wrapped carefully in brown paper. By the time they delivered it to Forensics, he was having a hard time focusing on the conversation. With some difficulty, Sam convinced his partner to sign out and go home shortly after four.

When he walked into the house, Kathleen was in the kitchen, talking on the phone. She waved toward him, but continued her conversation. Brad went to the refrigerator and removed an icy bottle of beer. He squeezed a piece of lime into the neck before he took a long swallow. He carried his beer into the den and collapsed into his favorite recliner.

Using his cell phone, he placed another call to Kelly Garrett in Seattle. It was his first opportunity since early morning. Tilting the beer bottle, he let another mouthful of cool liquid trickle down his throat.

"Kelly Garrett." The voice from the other end was brusque.

"Garrett, you'd better have your steel corset on 'cause I mean to do serious damage to your butt!"

"Brad Logan? Wondered what was going on in Langston. Haven't heard from you for a while. You have something to report?"

"Something to report? Jesus, I could fill *volumes*! First of all, Sumiko's in the hospital. She was almost killed. I warned you about—-"

"Sumiko's hurt? Dammit it, Logan, how could you let that happen?"

Brad's temper exploded into the phone. "Why you son of a bitch, don't lay this on me. Sumiko's hurt because your Goddam FBI office fell down on the job. They left her without a bodyguard. Someone slashed her. She's lucky she made it. You've got a lot of explaining to do!"

"Guard? What do you mean? The Bureau wasn't providing a guard for her. They never did. What made you think they would look after her?"

Brad was floored. He thundered into the phone. "You liar! The FBI had a guard on her most of the time—-until the time she needed one. Hell, I even talked to a couple of them. What's going on, Garrett?"

"Hang on, Brad, don't cop an attitude with me. I never once ordered a guard from the local office. I told you I couldn't trust anyone down there. You're telling me someone from FBI watched her all this time?"

Brad couldn't believe it. Was the message garbled? "Dammit, Kelly, somebody's screwed up *big time*, and it ain't me. But forget that for now—her well-being is much more important. What do you suggest I do about her? I'm sure she'll be in the hospital for at least a week…maybe longer."

Kathleen walked in and sat down. It was obvious she planned to hear his phone conversation. Inviting her out of the room was not an option. From her determined look, he knew she was ready for a long confrontational evening. Brad's hope for getting to bed early disappeared.

When Garrett asked for details on the injury to Sumiko, Brad filled him in on as much as he could. Garrett's response added to Brad's confusion. Where was Sumiko's protection supposed to come from? Did he misunderstand Kelly Garrett in Seattle? Why was someone so inexperienced sent on such a dangerous mission?

"Kelly, I'm sure I remember...you told me she'd have someone watching her at all times. I didn't make that up, did I?"

"Brad, I'm sorry for your confusion. I hope I didn't mislead you about it—-it wasn't my intention. Sumiko was well trained. She could handle herself. Someone compromised her cover—-someone in that local office. I'm coming down there to sort this out. In the meantime, will you look after her—-even though you're angry with me?"

"Yes, of course. Now, listen with both ears, Kelly. I can blow the lid off this whole White Knight thing, but I can't trust anyone down here. Can you get a crew of U.S. Marshals down here? I need wire taps and surveillance. I can't arrange it myself."

Brad filled the FBI man in about Judd's death and getting Judd's journal. He watched Kathleen as she realized what the conversation was about. He could see fear returning to her eyes. He held his hand out to her in what he hoped was a reassuring gesture.

In the end, he extracted a promise from Kelly Garrett for a team of Marshals within two days and Garrett himself would fly to Langston by week's end. Garrett was profuse in his apology to Brad about Sumiko's terrible ordeal. He accepted full responsibility and told Brad he wanted the best medical care available for Sumiko's recovery.

"Kelly, I don't mind telling you, my private life's in the toilet. When you come down here, my wife needs an explanation from you. She thinks I'm a no-good bastard for my part in getting Sumiko hurt. See you later."

Brad watched Kathleen's face as he set down the phone. She was in tears.

"I'm sorry, Honey. I wasn't honest with you about what was going on. I had no choice. Too many lives were at stake. I couldn't tell anyone what I was working on. No one could know about Sumi's connection with the FBI. Sam Hardy doesn't even know. Now everything's turned to shit. I have to make it up to you. I promise I will."

"Brad Logan, this is the worst thing you've ever done to me. I've been so scared all this time, and you lied to me about what was going on. Now I find out Sumiko was working for the FBI, and *that's* why she was almost killed? I'll never forgive you for this."

Brad slammed his recliner chair to its upright position. He knew it was time for the confrontation. He felt the house of cards collapsing around him. "Wait a minute, Katie. Don't throw all this guilt crap on me. I couldn't tell you everything. Can't you get that through your head? The FBI and many of the cops in this town are dirty. They're watching this house. We can't breathe a safe breath until we nail these guys. That's why I sent you to Omaha. You've gotta believe me. I wasn't trying to hurt you…just trying to protect you. Can't you understand that?"

"Don't patronize me, you *bastard*. You could've given me some clue about what was going on. All those threats—-they weren't from Judd Worley, were they?"

"Of course they were. He was right in the middle of the White Knights mess. Judd was so rotten he even told his mother he worked for the FBI. That tells you something about the man's moral character."

"Told his mother? How do you know that?"

"I'm the one who told her Judd was dead. She wasn't even surprised. It…it's almost like she already knew about it. Typical mother, she thought Judd could do no wrong. But she gave me something I hope will break this case. I'm sure of it. Maybe then our lives can get back to normal again. It'll be such a relief."

"Normal? I don't even remember what normal was. Was that how we were before you started screwing your little *Geisha*?" Kathleen was losing control. The pent up emotion had gathered momentum—-boiling out as she warmed to the task. Her voice turned shrill and harsh.

Brad hoped she could express all her anger at once. Then maybe he could deal with it once and for all. "Katie, I know you're hurt and

I know I disappointed you. But don't take it out on poor Sumiko. She's paid a terrific price for being involved in this."

"Yeah, that's right, you *bastard*. Stick up for your little sugar plum fairy. It's always Sumiko. What about the price *I'm* paying? Huh? What about *my* pain.? Doesn't that count? You planned the whole thing. I even wonder if you set off the bomb in our front yard. You wanted me out of town so you could get that poor girl out of her pants."

That cut him to the bone, but Brad made up his mind to accept any abuse Kathleen dished out. It wasn't easy, but Kathleen needed to vent her anger and frustration. Besides, she only repeated the same abuse he heaped on himself—-over and over again. He accepted in silence. He had become her Wailing Wall.

"In your eyes I'm guilty of every sin, Kate. I accept your judgment, but hope you understand—-there was no sinister plot to cheat on you. It wasn't done to hurt you. Things just happened…got out of control before I knew it."

Kathleen's snort of contempt was her sole answer. Brad pushed ahead. "I want us to work through this crisis, Katie. I love you—-have always loved you. I can imagine the pain you feel now. If I could unroll the past and roll it back up the way you want it to be, I'd do it. It can't be done. All we can do is work through it, assuming you want to stay together." Brad's tone turned the statement into a question.

Kathleen jumped right on it. "Well, at least you're admitting your guilt. That's a start. Here's what I want, Brad…we need counseling. You think you can work everything out by yourself. That's macho *bullshit*. If this marriage is worth saving, and I'm not sure it is, you'll go with me for professional help. My hurt feelings are just part of the problem."

"I'm willing to do that, Katie, as long as you're serious about working out our problems. I can't imagine not being together. I couldn't deal with it."

Brad realized his lack of sleep had eroded his ability to think straight. He feared he might say something irrational at any moment. "Listen, Kate, is it all right if we go get some dinner? I'm hungry and got no sleep last night I can't think straight. We can continue our talk over dinner, can't we?"

When Kathleen agreed, Brad sensed the reluctance in her voice. He knew his wife hated losing her momentum, along with the upper hand. Kathleen was a bulldog of determination if anyone invaded her private space. Brad knew he and Sumiko had crossed over that line. Now Kathleen wanted back what was taken from her.

As he waited for Kathleen, Brad called the hospital and asked how Sumiko was doing. They reported her condition as being stable and assured him she could have visitors the next day. Brad breathed a silent prayer. When he reported the news to Kathleen, he detected a look of relief on her face.

❦   ❦   ❦

"You're damn right I'm drunk. Don't care who knows it. And don't shush me"

Brad helped his wife out of the car and into the house. During dinner, he watched Kathleen drink much more than her usual limit. By the time dinner was over, he found himself constantly reminding her she was getting loud. Each time he mentioned it to her, she would get a little more belligerent until he saved further embarrassment by asking for the check and hustling her out to the car. He hoped none of their friends were in the dining room while the show took place.

When he took her elbow as they started up the stairs, Kathleen yanked her arm away with such violence she almost fell over. He hovered over her as she started up the stairs. She was so unsteady she bounced from one handrail to the other with every step. She wanted no part of his assistance. "Hey, lemme tell you somethin', El Creepo.

You got nothin' I need. I can handle my booze better'n you ever could. Look at this."

Kathleen unbuttoned her blouse and, with great animation, shrugged it off her shoulders. She let it drop onto the floor. Next, she kicked off her shoes. One sailed clear down the hall, the other bounced off the wall. That brought a burst of giggles from Kathleen. "Look at that, big ass football hero. Two points. Kicked that sucker clean down the hall." She leaned against the wall and yanked at her panty hose until they fell in an exhausted heap at her feet. Those, too, sailed down the hallway.

With amazing concentration, Kathleen unzipped her skirt and let it drop to her feet. Brad grabbed her elbow as she fell to her knees from the effort. Once again, she ripped her arm from his fingers.

"Don't touch me, you pig! Jus' keep your little T——-Twinkie in your pants. You go get a test. Jus' be my luck——-to get——-syph——-syph——-shit——-what's that stuff? V.D."

The statement from his drunken wife shocked Brad. He'd never even given it a thought. He knew Kathleen was right in making that kind of demand of him.

His wife was far from finished. "Don' even want you in my bed-room, you *bastard.* Jus' stan' there like a man and watch me dance off to bed. Get an eyeful of a real woman, you…you S. .S. .O.B!"

She stood before the bedroom door and with great effort, removed every last stitch of clothing. Standing defiantly before him, she began humming a tune of sorts as she offered an amateur bump and grind. A devilish, evil smirk crossed her face as she held her breasts, flaunting their fullness at him. Her hips rotated in her best imitation of an exotic dancer. At semi-regular intervals she would thrust her pelvis in his direction with total abandon. Brad had to admit, it was quite a sensuous sight.

"You'd trade this for her? *Up yours.* Why'd you wander off, you *bastard?* This body not good enough for you? That little twit doesn't have bazooms like these…"

Before Brad could move, Kathleen collapsed in a heap on the floor. Mercifully, the wine did its duty and put her to sleep. He scooped her up and carried her into the bedroom. With great tenderness, he placed her in the bed and pulled the sheet up to her chin. There was a great temptation to crawl in beside her when he saw her lying there, but he knew she would hate that kind of contempt from him. Grabbing a pillow, he went down to the den and collapsed onto the couch. His whole system crashed within minutes.

He left a note for Kathleen as he left the house in the morning. He decided he'd let her sleep, but made a fresh pot of coffee for her before leaving. It was obvious she'd need it. She would feel terrible when she awakened.

On impulse, he detoured to the hospital on his way to work. The receptionist told him visiting hours began at ten. He showed his badge and explained he needed to ask Sumiko a few questions about her attack. After the nurse discussed it with the doctor, Brad received permission to go up to her room.

He wasn't prepared for the way Sumiko looked in her hospital bed, surrounded by tubes, monitors and beeping equipment. She was so childlike. A bandage covered half her face. Her usually lustrous hair was a crumpled black mass on her pillow. The one eye peering around the bandage was dull and expressionless. Her right arm, bandaged from wrist to shoulder, lay atop the covers. Brad choked back tears as he walked to her bedside and took her hand.

"Sumi, I…"

Her face moved toward him as she recognized him. A tear rolled down her check and dropped onto the sheet.

"Brad-san—-I—-I sorry, I screw up."

Her words broke his heart. He couldn't control the emotions invading his body. He stroked her arm—-her face—-crooning words of encouragement. Fighting his own emotional pain, he resisted the urge to clutch her frail body to his chest, to rock the child until her pain went away.

"Sumi. . I'm so sorry. So sorry. I let you down and you were hurt."

"Shhh…hush. Is not your fault. He came after me——it was not an accident. Someone sent him. Probably *Yakuza*. Guess I didn't fool them."

"You ever see him before?"

Brad hesitated asking official questions, but Sumiko seemed alert enough. Her head bobbed up and down. "Same guy attacked you in Ginza. I never forget his face. Looks like a gang boy, you know? Lotsa tattoos on arms."

Brad nodded. "At first, I thought Judd Worley did this to you."

"I know. I worry you were gonna kill him. Couldn't tell you he didn't do it."

Brad decided not to tell her about Worley's death. Not until she was stronger. "You don't need to talk any more, Sumi. We'll have plenty of time to talk later. Save your energy to get better. Don't worry about expenses. Your boss will pay."

"Thank you, Brad-san. You tell Kelly Garrett about me?" Sumiko's hand searched for his. "I still think about Las Vegas. Do you?"

"Of course, Sumi. I'll never forget it. But don't waste time thinking about it. Focus all your energy on getting well. Are you in pain?"

"It's not too bad. Just my chest and stomach, mostly. Did you know they removed my breast? I…"

It was the first time Brad knew of *that* development. Sumiko's brave facade suddenly turned into tears. Brad did his best, but couldn't console her. She needed a female shoulder to lean on. He called a nurse, who responded 'STAT'. When they couldn't calm Sumiko, the nurse medicated her. Brad patted the weeping Sumiko on her shoulder, wishing he could wave a magic wand and make her pain disappear.

"I'll be back later today, Sumi. Try to relax and not worry. Everything'll be fine."

It was a big lie, but he said it anyway. He kissed her unbandaged cheek. They both realized this was the transition point in their relationship. The room turned dark.

In the parking lot, as he stood unlocking his car door, Brad's cell phone rang. The voice was not familiar, but the words were welcome. "Sergeant Logan, this is U.S. Marshal Stan Phillips. Understand you need some help in Langston. Where can we meet? I want to keep a low profile."

"When will you be in town?"

"I'm calling from the I-Hop on the freeway. Take me five minutes to get into town."

"Let's make this easy. On your way in, you'll see a large shopping center on your right as you pass the city limits. There's a donut shop called Dunkers Oasis. I'll get a booth in the back and wait for you. Just look for a big, ugly cowboy, wearing lizard boots, silver buckle and bushy mustache. You?"

"I'm casual. Jeans, tan windbreaker. Shiny bald head. Can't miss it."

"See you in ten. Man, am I glad to hear from you."

The Dunkers Oasis occupied a tiny business space in Langston's most recent shopping mall on the North side. Brad parked in front and found a booth in the rear portion of the shop, out of direct view of the front windows. He wanted privacy for this meeting.

There was no mistaking Stan Phillips when he entered. If you wanted someone to cast a shadow over a small town, this U.S. Marshal looked capable. The jeans he wore struggled to contain the tree trunks attached to his feet. He wore a tan windbreaker over a white starched shirt and blue necktie. Brad guessed the man's neck size was close to 20" and the massive head was a perfect match for the rest of the body. He could have played on any offensive line in the NFL.

Brad got to his feet to let the man know where he was sitting. He extended his hand as Phillips approached.

"Stan? Sure could'a used you on my offensive line in college. May have made it to the pros instead of the hospital. You play some ball?"

"Got me through college...St. Mary's. You?"

"Yeah. QB'd at Midwestern University until I blew out my knee."

"Tough luck. You order some coffee?"

They sat in the booth, their bulk using up every inch of capacity. The waitress brought a carafe of coffee and two cups. Brad ordered a Danish, but Phillips declined.

"Let's have it, Sergeant. I know some of the dirty laundry in the Langston PD and the FBI. You want to fill me in on particulars?"

"Yeah, I'll be glad to unload on you. Gettin' tired of storing it all under my hat. To begin with, I'm not sure how deep—-or high up—-it goes into our PD. I have access to documents that name about fifteen officers. It also names eight FBI agents who belong to the White Knights. They've been involved in strong-arm attacks on local ethnic businesses and I know of at least two homicides they've committed. They've also made threats to my wife and me. It's possible more officers are involved, but I don't have their names."

"I copy that. So where do you want to start?"

"I'll get you the names and the evidence I have available. Also, I have a video taken by the security camera at my house. It shows an unknown officer on my porch at three o'clock in the morning leaving a threatening letter in my mailbox. I think we can enhance the video enough to make an identification."

Brad took a drink of coffee and a bite of pastry before he continued. "Oh yeah, we found explosives in a storage locker tied to a known member of the Knights. They set off several bombs in the area. At first, they just intimidated potential victims with minor bomb blasts. In the end, a bomb killed two people who lived over their family store. I even had a bomb go off in my front yard...another warning. That's when my partner and I were taken off the case. The local Feds are sitting on it. We should get wiretaps on all suspects and I'd like a bug in the local Oddfellows hall. That's where the Knights hold weekly meetings. That's a full menu for you, Stan, but we gotta move fast."

Marshal Phillips twisted in his seat, showing his discomfort in the tight quarters.

"That is a full menu, but I have ten men at my disposal so it's do-able. Where's this list of names you mentioned?"

"It's in a safe in my garage. Where you staying?"

"You tell me a good location. We need secrecy so we can pull this off in the shortest possible time—-and we sure as hell don't want to have any casualties."

Brad spent the next hour briefing him. Marshal Phillips was adept at filling in the gaps as Brad skimmed the highlights of Knight's activities. At ten, he and Phillips agreed to meet in the same place at 7:00 the next morning. Brad would bring the list of names and the video film.

Brad's entire disposition changed for the better after talking to the marshal. Something about the big man gave Brad confidence. Things were looking up in Langston.

On the drive to the office, he called Kathleen. He could tell by her voice, she was not feeling too frisky that morning. He verbally walked on eggshells until he could capture her mood. "Don't say a word about my performance, Brad. I earned that drunk and disorderly conduct. I'm paying the price today, in spades. I won't even apologize."

"No need, Kate. I enjoyed the show. Just checking on you. I'm ready for counseling whenever you say. Make an appointment for next week if you want"

He heard Kathleen's breath catch in her throat. Her elation showed in her voice. "I'm holding you to that, Brad. You find out anything about poor Sumiko?"

Brad crossed his fingers as he told about his visit to the hospital. He wasn't sure how she would take it.

"That poor thing. She must be in terrible pain. I still don't understand how you could let the FBI send such a tiny little thing into a horrible and dangerous job like that. Didn't you try to stop them?"

"As a matter of fact, I did, Kate. But the Feds don't very often listen to us poor local cops. What do *we* know?"

"I want to go see her, Brad. Will you take me over tonight after dinner?"

"Of course. If that's what you want."

He had severe reservations about the three of them in the same room. It would surely test everyone's civility. Then Kathleen offered another bombshell. "Tell you something else, Brad. She's staying with us when she gets released from the hospital. She has no one else and sure can't handle flying home to Seattle for a while. Don't give me any arguments either; I've made up my mind."

Kathleen's pronouncement came out of the blue. Shock didn't adequately cover the range of emotion washing over Brad. Despite her earlier tirades against him and against Sumiko, Kathleen's true character emerged unscathed. Her tremendous capacity to care about people always came to the surface after any emotional setback.

Within three days, the Federal marshals occupied a vacant storefront in the same shopping center housing the Dunkers Oasis. It was in a well-traveled area, with several all night stores nearby. The public would not be curious seeing traffic at all hours of the night. The only equipment in the store was a bank of phones, desks and electronic equipment. The windows were painted over so curious shoppers had no access to ongoing activities.

Brad kept busy keeping up with the demands for more information. He decided he must clue Sam Hardy into the goings on, lest his partner feel deserted. By the end of the third day, there were wiretaps on 23 suspected officers. The marshals also entered the local Oddfellows Hall and implanted several listening devices. Brad hoped they would obtain enough incriminating evidence with this coverage that arrests could be made within weeks.

In the meantime, Brad and Kathleen spent as many hours as possible in the hospital room seeing to Sumiko's needs. As might be expected, she was miserable and, although the pain was less, the anxiety over her future kept the young woman in constant emotional turmoil.

As promised, Kelly Garrett arrived from Seattle over the weekend. Brad took him to meet with the Marshals for an update, then drove him to the hospital to see Sumiko. Garrett was visibly shaken by the injuries to his protégé'. Brad couldn't resist another round of finger pointing at Garrett. "Kelly, I would commiserate with you, but damn it, man, she wasn't ready for this kind of assignment. She was too brave. She didn't know enough to be scared. I think she may have been too aggressive in going after information. Looks like someone spotted her as a plant."

"Yeah, right, Brad…and didn't you tell her to be more aggressive at her new job? There's plenty of guilt to spread around. None of it will undo what happened to her. Our job now is to restore her confidence. That'll take time and a lot of loving attention. In the meantime, what do we do with her during the recuperation period?"

"That's already covered, Kelly. Kathleen insists we put Sumiko up in our spare bedroom until she's ready to go home and there's no sense arguing with my wife, once she has her mind made up. You can rest assured, Sumiko will be cared for."

"Kathleen must be a wonderful wife, Brad. Not many wives would tolerate another woman in their house. You must be proud of her."

"That's an understatement, Kelly. Kathleen's special, no doubt about it."

Brad felt like strutting around with his thumbs stuck in his armpits. To have one of his peers recognize Kathleen's fine qualities brought a surge of pride in him. Pride mixed with the extreme guilt he felt for causing Kathleen's pain. He wondered if events of the next few days would allow him any time for mending fences with Kathleen.

CHAPTER 24

Sam Hardy held the phone away from his mouth and shouted across the desk to Brad: "They found a print on the sword, pal! Computer gave them a match. We *finally* got a break. Mug shot's coming in from CID right now. Keep your fingers crossed, partner." Sam Hardy slammed his phone down. He was as excited as Sam Hardy could get. His fists punched the air over his head as he danced a little jig.

Brad's adrenaline shot up as the good news sank in. He couldn't contain himself as he reached over to slap palms with his partner. "God, it's about time the Good Guys made a score, Sam! Let's hope the slime ball's still in town. I want his ass hanging from the nearest telephone pole."

"Yeah, but don't get your hopes too high, okay? The way everything else's gone so far, I figure he's back in Japan by now. I say good riddance—-one less yellow belly."

Brad bit his tongue to avoid an argument over Sam's choice of words. They had discussed it *ad nauseum*. Right now, there were more important things. He didn't want this killer to get away. The need for revenge festered in his soul. Finding the man who attacked Sumiko and killed Judd zoomed to the top of his priority list.

He couldn't move against the White Knights until the U.S. Marshals finished with their investigation. With so many of his cases on hold right now, he felt as useless as a second fly in a pair of pants.

When the mug shot started printing out, Brad hovered over the fax machine, watching the picture take shape. He recognized the man even before the final lines of the face printed out. It was the man who had lured him into the alley in Little Ginza. Sumiko's ID of him was right on target. Brad rushed back to his desk and showed the picture to Sam.

"We need an APB on Hideko Satori. Subject is a thirty-year-old Japanese National. Has a green card. Several priors, including two ADW's. This scum's not a nice person. Shoulda been deported after his first felony. I'll take this up to Dispatch. You feel like going with me to find the slime?"

"Sure, why not? Maybe we'll box him in and he'll wanna fight. I need to vent my aggression on someone. Might just as well be a Jap."

"Dammit, Sam. You keep talking like that and I'll leave you here. You're supposed to keep *me* from tearing his head off. You don't sound like you'll be much help. I'm serious, man, do you have a problem going down there? If you do, I'll grab a couple of harness bulls."

In answer, Sam Hardy got to his feet, took his service revolver from the desk drawer and jammed it into its holster. Without a word, he walked out of the office and down the hall.

Brad just shook his head. "Was it something I said?"

As usual, Sam took the wheel when they left the police garage. It was common knowledge in the Langston Police Department: Sam Hardy was the best wheelman in the department. When the two partners rode together, Brad always sat in the co-pilot's seat. The practice kept him safe for many years.

The radio crackled as Sam negotiated the morning traffic. Since there was no need for haste, they didn't drive under the red. When they were within ten blocks of the Ginza area, an ominous message blared from the radio.

"We have a Code 30 in the Little Ginza area. Any units in area of Second and Columbus respond Code 3."

Brad flipped on the emergency switch for red light and siren and advised Dispatch that they were responding to the call for 'Officer Needs Assistance'.

Dispatch responded immediately. "Copy…responding, Car 87. Change call to Code 10-53."

"Christ, Sam. We've got a man down. Hope it's not an officer. We're so close. Why didn't he wait for backup? Clear on the right."

Brad checked for traffic on his right as Sam entered the intersection with siren wailing. Halfway down the block they could see an unmarked police vehicle stopped in the middle of the street. The driver's door stood wide open. Rooftop red lights flashed in eerie unison. There was no sign of a policeman, but a small crowd stood on the sidewalk, their attention focused down the alleyway.

Sam whipped the car to a stop and both men were out of the car with guns drawn before the car stopped bouncing. Brad waved his arm and yelled at the crowd. "Everyone back. Get back."

He couldn't tell if the crowd understood the words, but they understood his gestures and the guns in the officers' hands. They cleared a path to the alley.

"My God, it's Chief Preston. What's he doing out here?"

The police chief, dressed in civilian clothes, knelt on the pavement halfway down the alley. The fingers of his right hand propped up the head of the person who was sprawled grotesquely on the pavement. A pool of blood spread like warm molasses under the body.

"Sam, call this in while I check with Preston." Brad then turned his attention down the alleyway. "You all right, Chief?"

"Fine, Sergeant. You guys sure got here in a hurry." The chief nodded toward the body. "This is our 187 suspect. I spotted him when he ducked into the alley. I ordered him to stop, but he decided he'd rather shoot me than surrender. Don't know if he understood my orders to *Freeze*." The chief still held a pistol in his hand. "Never shot a suspect before. Not pleasant."

Brad reached out and took the Chief's weapon and dropped it into his coat pocket.

"I'll keep this for the Inquest, sir. You sure you're all right? What were you doing down here alone?"

"Yes, yes, of course I'm fine. Keep my weapon secured. Do you see the suspect's gun? It must be around here some place."

Chief Preston rose to his feet and began scouring the area. Brad placed his hand under the deceased and ran it as far back as possible, but felt nothing. No gun, no bullet. With great care, he turned the face of the dead man toward him. Brad recognized him right away as the man who had followed him into the alley—-and into the fray which resulted in Brad's butt kicking. He rubbed a hand on his rib cage, recalling the bruises.

"Chief. There's no sign of a gun under the body. You positive you saw one?"

"Of course, Sergeant Logan. I sure as hell wouldn't have shot him if he was unarmed." The chief gave Brad a look of frustration.

It wasn't difficult finding the location of the man's wound. It was in the exact center of the man's chest. Textbook shooting. He couldn't tell if it was an entry or exit wound. He had no intention of turning the body before the shooting team arrived. That was their job.

Brad rose and turned toward the entrance to the alley. He could see Sam talking to the crowd. There were also four uniform cops talking to bystanders. Returning his attention to Chief Preston, Brad saw him rummaging between two cardboard boxes at the back of the alley.

"Here it is." The chief pointed at something on the ground between the boxes.

'It' was a small silver pistol lying on the pavement. Brad cautioned the chief not to touch the weapon. By leaning close, he could see bullets extending from the gun's cylinder. No question about it; the gun was loaded.

"Lucky you found it, Sir. Wonder how it got so far away from the body?"

Chief Preston aimed a withering look in Brad's direction. "How the hell would I know, Sergeant? You making a point?"

"Not at all, Chief; just my innate curiosity."

Brad left the chief wandering about the alley, then joined Sam out on the main sidewalk. Sam took notes as he talked to several bystanders.

"Got anything, Sam?" Brad recognized that his partner was not comfortable talking to the people of the area; there was no question about it. Sam Hardy hated being there at all. Hated being in such close proximity to people he didn't respect. In answer to Brad's question, he merely shook his head.

"Nobody's got anything to say. Pretending they 'No speaka da English'. They're stonewalling me. Why don't you see what you can find out? What's with the chief? What's he doing here alone? Where's his driver?"

"Got no idea. Says the perp pulled a gun on him. Had to shoot. Sure curious how and where he found the gun. Deceased must've thrown it after he caught the chief's bullet. From the looks of the wound, it's my guess he died instantly. Strange how he could've thrown a gun that far. Oh well. That's up to the O.I.S. Board of Inquiry. Glad it wasn't me who did it."

As soon as the Officer Involved Shooting team arrived, Brad turned the chief's gun over to them and filled them in on what he knew. After making several notes in his ever-present notebook, Brad signaled Sam. There was no mistaking the look of relief on Sam's face as he took the wheel for the ride back to the station.

In the car, Brad recited his crime scene observations. It was something the partners always did after a cursory examination of a crime scene. By bouncing theories and observations off each other, it often provided a more accurate picture of the scene.

"You'll find this interesting, Sam. The perp had a *netsuke* carving on a chain around his neck. You know…like the one you found at Kaiser's crime scene. You suppose this dude was in on that? Don't know why he'd be teaming up with rogue cops. 'Course anything's possible."

"You got that right. Nothing would surprise me about this one. Can't imagine a bunch of racist cops teaming up with any ethnic group—not even for a profit. It makes no sense. My hunch is that the Jap wasn't in on Mooch's killing."

Brad rolled that around in his head before answering. "Yeah, I guess you're right. Doesn't seem too logical. Still, you did find that thing at the other murder scene. S'pose it's coincidence?"

"Who the hell knows?"

❧   ❧   ❧

Kathleen sat at Sumiko's bedside, trying her best to brush the patient's black hair. It was a difficult chore, since Sumiko still couldn't sit up for long. The bandage on her face was reduced to one patch on the cheek. Kathleen saw the edges of the healing wound and cringed when she imagined what was under the bandage. The area around the eye socket was still swollen and showed the yellowing remnants of a black eye.

"Sumiko, can you roll over just a little bit so I can reach the other side?"

Like an obedient child, Sumiko grabbed the iron railing at her bedside and moved her body slightly. Her grimace told Kathleen it was still a painful experience, but the nurse said Sumiko should move. She must work through the pain.

"Kathleen, don't bother brushing so much. Maybe I'll cut it all off when I get out of bed. Maybe I can't raise my arms high enough any more. How can I braid my hair?"

"Sumiko, don't let me hear that kind of talk. You're a tough cookie, remember? You can do anything you want and I won't let you become a casualty. You hear me, Sumi? You'll get through this, I promise."

"Why you even care, Kathleen? Two months ago you don't even know me."

"Just hush and turn your head back around for me. I'll braid it for you. Can you stay still long enough?"

Kathleen realized she and Sumiko were tiptoeing around the main issue. But getting Sumiko emotionally and physically healthy was the priority right now. The trauma of losing a breast was the most devastating thing of all. Doctors felt all other injuries would heal with time. The emergency mastectomy was another matter. A huge emotional scar already hovered over Sumiko. Kathleen ached for her young friend.

"The doctor told me this morning you would get out of bed tomorrow. That's a good sign. He must think you're getting better."

"I think it's good idea. Today, they want me to sit up. I tried a little bit already, but it makes my stomach hurt too much. Maybe later on, I'll try again."

When the bedside phone rang, Kathleen reached for it to keep Sumiko from reaching. It was Brad. He called several times a day, as did Kelly Garrett. The two men also kept the room full of fresh flowers and visited as often as possible. Sumiko did not suffer from lack of attention.

"How's she doing, Katie?" There was a sense of urgency in Brad's voice. Kathleen could hear a sense of excitement in Brad's voice.

"She's getting a little stronger each day, Brad. Something's up. What is it?"

"The man who attacked Sumi and killed Judd Worley is dead, Kate."

"Did you do it?"

"No. Matter of fact, Chief Preston caught the guy in Little Ginza and *offed* him when he wouldn't give up. I guess justice was served, but sure wish I could've talked to him first. Someone must've hired him. Don't know if Sumiko should be told about it. I'll leave it up to you whether you think she should know."

"Okay, I'll see how it goes. When will you be home tonight?"

"On time, far as I know. Let's plan on going out again, since you're spending so much time with Sumi. Decide where you wanna go. Is that all right?"

❦   ❦   ❦

When Agent Kelly Garrett called Brad on Wednesday morning, he asked Brad to meet him at the Dunkers Oasis in half hour. He wouldn't give Brad a clue as to the reason for the meeting, just that he should drop everything else he was doing and get there. Brad knew Kelly didn't exaggerate, so did as he was told.

Garrett was in a booth with U.S. Marshal Stan Phillips when Brad entered the coffee shop. Both men briefly acknowledged Brad's arrival, then continued eating their breakfast.

"Is this what was so urgent? Watching you two elephants devour your young?"

"Hey, show a little respect, Logan. Pour yourself a cup."

Brad indulged them by pouring himself a cup from the tabletop carafe. He knew they were enjoying themselves by keeping him in suspense. Both of them looked as if they'd tripped the mousetrap without getting caught in it.

"You should've gone to the basketball game with us last night, Brad."

"Basketball game? What in hell you talking about, Garrett?"

Kelly Garrett pushed his now empty plate aside and pulled his coffee cup in front of him. He filled the cup again before saying anything further. Brad considered tearing the words from the man's throat.

"Yeah, the game at the Y. We watched the local cops playing the local FBI agents. You should go down there sometime. The guys play tough, hard-nosed ball."

"Kelly, if you don't spit it out, I'm gonna reach in and pull out your tongue."

"Oh my, aren't we testy this morning? You think I should tell him, Stan?"

Phillips poured himself another cup of coffee and nodded. "If you think he's man enough to handle it, go ahead."

"Oh, all right. Here's the story. Last night, at the local YMCA, Stan and I and the other marshals from his office watched the Langston cops and FBI boys play their weekly pickup game. After the game, when the guys went into the locker room for their showers, we surprised them by arresting the whole lot of them. You talk about pissed *off...*"

Kelly and Stan grinned as they saw the look of surprise on Brad's face.

"You. . you did what?"

"Arrested eight cops and seven FBI agents. Took the whole lot of them. Naked as jaybirds, they were. Caught them with their pants—- and everything else, including guns—-down. Kinda like a cattle roundup. Not a shot was fired. Not even a punch thrown by either side."

Brad was stunned by the news. "Jesus, you guys took the whole lot of them without a shot? Dammit, I'm impressed. How—-I mean—- what led up to the arrest?"

"Brad, our wiretaps paid off, big time. The wiretaps and Worley's journal. That thing's a gold mine. We had enough evidence to get warrants on the lot of them. There's been a secret indictment by the

Grand Jury. It covers not just the boys we arrested, but also the rest of the ones mentioned in Worley's journal. We'll move a bit slower on this bunch because some of the ringleaders are still out there. They have to be considered very dangerous."

"Aren't they going to be tipped off?"

"I think we have that covered, Brad. We loaded the bunch of them into a bus and transported them to the Federal detention center out at the Naval Weapons Station. They're sequestered there for 72 hours and can't communicate. We hope we'll snatch the others tonight at their meeting at the Oddfellows Hall."

Brad was overwhelmed by the news. To think the nightmare was about over was the best news he'd had in a long time. "How about Nichols? Was he picked up?"

"Nope. We hope he'll be at the meeting tonight. They start at 7:00 and we'll be ready. We're going in with a SWAT configuration because it could become violent and lethal." Stan Phillips eased his body into a more comfortable position.

"I'm going with you. You need Sam or any others?"

"Can't take a chance on anyone, Brad. I'm sure you have a major-ity of clean cops in the department—-we just can't afford to let any-one else in on the action. As it is, we can't expect to be lucky two nights in a row. We're assuming it will be a battle royal. Meantime, listen to this tape recording we picked up this week."

Kelly Garrett produced a small pocket sized recorder and snapped the 'On' switch. The recorded voices were loud and clear as they spoke on the phone. After a brief exchange of patter, Brad recognized the voice of Lieutenant Glen Nichols. The other voice was not famil-iar, but the words spoken were chilling. For several minutes the voices discussed a potential bombing, planned for the very near future. As the plan unfolded, the total brutality became clear. When the conversation was ended, Brad sat in stunned silence.

"Brad, you can see how urgent this action tonight has become. We can't let these people carry out this attack."

"That's got to be number one, Kelly. These Knights are as vicious as a crowd of hungry tigers. I can't believe they'll destroy the Kurasawa Building with a bomb. My God, there's more than two hundred people in the building during peak hours."

"Yes," Stan Phillips added, "two hundred Japanese people. My God, you expect this is the type of ethnic cleansing from terrorists in other countries, but it's a shock to believe Americans would conceive such a plan—-especially cops who are sworn to protect citizens. I have no sympathy for these idiots. Whatever it takes…we'll stop these guys before they hurt anyone else."

Brad agreed without reservation. "It sounds like they already have the van packed full of explosives. Do you suppose they'll complete their plans at the meeting tonight?"

"We'll be listening in, just in case. Oh yeah, for your information, we had your surveillance video enhanced in our lab." Kelly Garrett finished his coffee. "Guess who that cop was on your front porch?"

"My guess would be Nichols himself, right?"

"Bingo. Are you positive you want in on this raid, Brad? You could be in extreme danger. Wouldn't be surprised if some of them want you dead. I'm sure we can handle it without you. By the way…I know you trust Sam Hardy, but don't tell him. We can't take a chance. Can you live with that?"

Stan Phillips finished the last of the coffee and pushed his cup aside as he spoke. Brad knew how the man felt. Security must be maintained at the highest level.

"Whatever you say, Stan, I understand the need for caution. Even though I trust the man with my life."

"Copy that. Just go with me on this, man. Lives are involved."

"No sweat. When will we saddle up?"

"We'll take off from here at seven. Their meeting should be underway by the time we get there. The military's sending down an armored personnel carrier and a chopper today. We aren't taking any chances. Another Federal SWAT team arrives just before we get underway. We don't know what to expect. The Knights will all be armed, I'm sure, so we're expecting the worst. We'll seal the building off, then place a phone call to let them know they're surrounded and ask for a peaceful surrender. Let's hope they act like reasonable people. If not…. " Kelly Garrett shrugged.

"Wouldn't count on it, Kelly. Double that if Nichols is with them. He's a bloodthirsty sucker. There's no doubt he would've shot me last week if Sam hadn't shown up, bless his soul. Do you have a background on Nichols?"

Kelly Garrett nodded. "You bet we do. Served in the Marines for twelve years as a munitions expert. He was cashiered for hitting a superior officer. Surprised your P.D. hired him."

"Well, he's been on the force over ten years. We didn't check people out all that close if they passed the test. Hell, they hired me, didn't they?"

That brought a loud guffaw from Stan Phillips, who then immediately turned deadly serious. "Don't make the mistake of taking these birds lightly, Sergeant. I've heard every one of the tapes we've made of them. They're committed to this so-called crusade they've undertaken to purify the world. Each one is a dangerous element by himself. Together they make a formidable force—-a lethal force. I hope we can take them all down at one time so there's no chance of any further damage to the locals."

"I buy that, Stan. Now tell me, how'd you cover up for the guys who didn't show up for work today? You sure it didn't tip off the others?"

"They're all attending a seminar on Human Relations."

"I beg your pardon?" Brad wasn't sure he heard right.

"Yeah, we called in for each of them and told the watch commander his men were attending a seminar for the day. We made it look official by having a bulletin faxed from the Capital to your police chief and to the local Agent in Charge."

Brad shook his head. "Sounds like you two have all the bases covered."

"God, I hope so, Brad. We can't afford any mistakes."

When Brad left the two lawmen in the coffee shop, he walked to his car with a sense of elation. It was the first time in months he felt something good was about to happen. Now at least there was something encouraging on the horizon.

Kelly Garrett had enhanced the feeling even more when he said he was sure Sumiko's much improved condition was a direct result of Kathleen's tender loving care. He recognized how much time she spent every day at the hospital. He told Brad he sent Kathleen an official letter of appreciation. Brad knew Kathleen would be pleased.

Latest word from the hospital was very encouraging. Sumiko was to be released by the end of the week. Kathleen was busy preparing the spare bedroom to receive their houseguest. Brad knew the two women were still skirting the issue between them. It was not something he looked forward to either!

When Brad walked back into the station house, he was not prepared for the message lying on his desk.

'Sergeant Logan. Report to Chief Preston ASAP. He's expecting you.'

CHAPTER 25

"What was that all about?" Sam looked up from his desk when Brad returned from his meeting with the chief. Brad knew his partner was hoping for some answers. So was everyone else in the building.

Rumors ran rampant throughout the department. Rumors that the Junkyard Dog's job was on the line. There was mass dissension in the ranks. Officers throughout the department were aligning themselves into factions. One thing was certain: Morale was at its lowest level since Brad joined the force. He hoped tonight's raid by the marshals would relieve the tension.

"Sam, you wouldn't believe it. Preston thinks I know why so many cops are out today. He thinks there's something fishy about that seminar story. I told him maybe it was a new version of the 'Blue Flu'. You know anything?"

Brad still couldn't tell Sam what occurred in the chief's office. The State Attorney General had contacted the chief, telling him about the arrested cops and tonight's planned raid. He warned Preston to keep it quiet. Chief Preston insisted Brad tell him everything he knew about the situation. Brad covered his tracks, never admitting he knew anything. He reminded the chief of his promise of protection when things came to a head. Like now.

Sam's not-so-subtle probing continued. "You gotta admit, it sure looks strange. How come no one knew about the seminars yesterday? There's a cover-up, partner."

"Hey, don't ask me. I'll tell you the same as I told him…I'm not responsible for all the crap that's going on in this place. Someone besides me is causing the morale problem. I have my own ideas, but——-"

"You think it's Nichols, right?"

Brad frowned at his partner. "I wouldn't be throwing any names around in public, man. I don't doubt someone's listening."

"Yeah, well I'll be glad when this all comes to a head, okay? I'm sick and tired of getting no cooperation from anyone and the horseshit people throw at each other. I can't remember it ever getting this bad. I've got at least five cases drifting around because nobody wants to cooperate. Can't even get anything from Mark Goddard. I'm about ready to chuck it all." Sam slammed his drawer shut in frustration.

Brad realized his partner was very upset because he didn't know what was going on, but it was too dangerous to clue him in yet. To Brad, the wagons were being circled for the safety of the upcoming operation by the U.S. Marshals. He hoped breaking up the White Knights would end the department's morale problems. For sure, it would take a great deal of pressure off him. Maybe he could even patch things up with Kathleen.

"Sam. I know just how you feel. I've never seen this department so screwed up. All I can say is, something will break very soon. You gotta keep the faith, old buddy."

Sam looked at his partner and shook his head. "You're pathetic, Logan. You think I don't see through you? Trying to make it sound like you know something. You're just as much in the dark as all of us are. Even your friends in the FBI don't tell you anything. This place is going down the tubes in a hurry and there's nothing any of us can do about it. Next thing you know, they'll send in the National Guard to do our job."

Brad grinned at Sam who looked over the top of his glasses with eyebrows raised, trying to draw a reaction. Sam Hardy was one cagey old bastard. Brad knew he wasn't fooling his partner about recent developments, so he changed the subject. "Do you know if the Gaming Commission has looked into that Sapporo operation? How about the bus company—they still running those trips to Vegas every weekend?"

"Man, you're a piece of work. Change the subject in the middle of the road. Far as I know, there's been no word from Vegas or the Gaming Commish. I didn't expect to hear from them, but I talked to the bus company last week, okay? They're still looking for a new driver to replace Judd Worley. I guess one of the supervisors is driving the weekend run, for the time being. You wouldn't think there was that much demand. Bet it's the same bunch who make the trip every week."

"You may be right. I wonder…can we find out who these people are? The bus company probably has a sign-up sheet, don't you think? If it's the same people each week it might mean something. Sure leaves a lot of questions."

Sam's expression became more serious. Brad could almost hear the wheels grinding in the cunning old fox's head. He prodded Sam for input. "Hey, you getting an idea, or are you just constipated?"

"You want theory? How's this for a shot into the barrel? Suppose these people going up every weekend aren't really gamblers? Let's just say they have something else in mind—-you know—-some other vices."

"Like what? You mean, like prostitutes? I doubt it. We saw both men and women on the bus. Gotta be something else. Can't imagine they'd go every week for the shows."

Sam removed his glasses, leaving them dangling from his neck on their red cord. "Hell, Brad. It could be most anything. But try this on for size, okay? Let's say these people are all couriers. That bus is booked solid every weekend, no exceptions. But, no white folks on the tour—-it's always a busload of Orientals, right?"

Brad nodded. "So?" He still couldn't see Sam's line of reasoning.

Sam pressed on. "Jeez, you're dense. I'll draw you a picture. Suppose these fine folks are all couriers. They're delivering something to Vegas—-or maybe bringing something back. Let's say something like a controlled substance. You know, for sure, that law enforcement seldom stops those tour buses for an inspection. That's a fact."

A loud bell went off in Brad's head. Once again, his partner's powers of comprehending the criminal mind amazed him. Brad slapped his palm on his forehead with a loud grunt. "Sam, you're a genius. You should join the criminal division of Mensa. Your mind is just as devious. Everything fits. They could be making deliveries of something...anything...and you can bet it's contraband. Let's talk to someone from the bus company. See if they can give us anything useful. You know, like...is the Sapporo Casino the only place they go? Is it the same folks each week? Do—-"

"Do passengers carry more than just overnight luggage? Who are the people who go on the trips? You want me to follow up at the bus company?"

"It would be a great help. Sam, I think this all ties in with the guy who killed Judd Worley. There's just too much coincidence. The bombings—-Mooch and Gorman Reed getting iced—-the *Kamikaze* killer—-all of it fits together some way. We just need a couple breaks. I'll tell you something else. I think there are people in this station house who have the answers."

Sam looked across the desk and his lips formed the word 'Nichols' as his eyebrows arched in one big question mark. Brad nodded, then shrugged his shoulders.

☘   ☘   ☘

It was after six when Brad pulled into a parking space behind the
store front office now housing the U.S. Marshal's office. He noticed a
large gray Brinks armored truck parked in the near vicinity. Next to
it was a military type personnel carrier.

Inside, he found himself mingling with a roomful of obvious lawmen. Everyone wore a windbreaker with the words 'U.S.Marshal'
emblazoned on the back. Each wore body armor and wore a holstered handgun tied to his thigh. It could have been a staging area
during World War II, or a posse preparing for the OK Corral. Every
face held a look of grim determination. Conversation was held to a
minimum as each member of the group concentrated on his own
thoughts of mortality. The scene was grim—-the tension fierce.

"Okay, guys and gals, listen up." Kelly Garrett took a position near
one of the desks and looked around the crowd. He cleared his throat
as he waited for silence.

"Thanks for your attention. We have a serious job ahead of us. A
job no one could anticipate. In my estimation, it's the worst thing
any of us can be asked to do: Going 'mano-a-mano' with fellow
officers. Unfortunately, it happens, on occasion. For whatever reason, people are sometimes swayed by a cause that seems worthy or
patriotic. Many times, those so-called worthy causes are illegal.
That's the case with the White Knights."

Garrett waited for those words to sink in. "As near as we can tell,
there will be at least twenty persons remaining in this group calling
itself the 'White Knights'. They're holding their weekly meeting at the
Oddfellows Hall, as we speak. Most of the group is made up of officers of Langston Police Department. Also included are a number of
local FBI agents."

For the next twenty minutes, Garrett highlighted the activities of
the Knights for the past year and how their activities came to light.
He introduced Brad Logan as the officer who stuck his neck on the

line getting some concrete information on them. Brad was a little self-conscious as Kelly told of the threats made and the actual bombing at his house. He felt the eyes of the crowd on him. He felt like saying "Aw shucks, t'warnt nothin'."

"All right, now that you have the background, U.S. Marshal Stan Phillips, will brief you on our game plan. Stan is our lead officer and will call the shots at the scene. Stan."

"Thanks, Kelly. Good of you all to come to my party."

A nervous laugh traveled the room. Then everything focused on the words coming from the considerable bulk of Stan Phillips, as he pointed to the diagram on the blackboard.

"Here's the setup of the building. It's single story with an entry foyer; main meeting auditorium; four separate bathrooms…here and here and a kitchen…here. Two external exits on the front side, a fire exit at the rear and two skylights on the roof. We'll have a presence at each location."

Stan looked at the faces staring at him, then continued. "The secret to any successful mission is communications. With each other and with those we are trying to arrest. We have a mobile Comm Center rolling with us. You each have a personal communicator. Use Channel 5. First thing we do is secure the entire block. We get one good break; the Oddfellows Hall is a freestanding building with a vacant lot on either side. There's just four other businesses in the same block and they should all be closed. That makes our job of isolating the building a little easier."

Phillips drew a deep breath before he continued. "When we're all in place, we'll telephone the group inside and instruct them to surrender. If they don't answer the phone, I'll be on the bullhorn giving them their options. I don't want even one casualty tonight. Remember, you're dealing with fellow officers. Granted, they're dirty, but they *are* fellow officers. If they're smart, they'll give up and face the courts. If there are some diehards in the group, we may be faced with a standoff. We'll treat it as if it was a hostage situation. No one goes in and no one comes out. If we have to lay siege for a day, a week, a month…it doesn't matter. We can be patient if it will save lives. Our biggest problem may be keeping the media in line. Kelly Garrett will be PIO. A couple of you will watch out for press people sneaking through our perimeter."

Brad looked at the officers around him. He was sure each one had faced this type of situation in the past. Their faces were stony as they waited for further instructions.

After filling in all the gaps in the game plan, Stan Phillips swore them all in as members of a Federal posse. As Stan pointed out, there was no room for mistakes in this potentially lethal operation. Then he led the group in a brief prayer. Brad was glad this man left nothing up to chance. It was a comforting feeling.

The group left the building and loaded aboard the armored vehicles brought in for the skirmish. The Brinks truck was equipped as the communications truck. The convoy was in place at the Oddfellows Hall in twenty-five minutes.

Ten minutes later, traffic cones and barriers sealed off the entire block. It was an efficient, professional performance. Using hand signals, Stan directed each group of men to strategic locations around the perimeter of the building. The noose was now ready for the final tightening.

Brad's group sealed off the main entrance. They were all armed with riot guns as they crouched behind the armored vehicle parked on the front sidewalk. Since Stan Phillips was now sequestered within the communication truck, Kelly Garrett took a position behind the Brinks truck so he could relay orders as soon as things developed.

Chief Warren Preston took his place in the communications truck. He would have the task of identifying his men if they were arrested or killed during the assault. Other than Brad, the chief was the only other member of the Langston Police Department on the outside of the building. Just before the operation started, the chief ordered all police units out of the area as a precaution. It was feared some of the officers might sympathize with the Knights and come to their defense. The downtown area took on the appearance of an armed camp.

As soon as Stan placed the call to the assembled White Knights, a figure was seen coming to the front entrance. The man took one look at the surrounding ranks of marshals and beat a hasty retreat back into the now darkened interior. Brad was certain someone from inside the building also checked the rear entrances with the same results. The noose was now pulled taut. From this point, it was a waiting game.

In less than half an hour, Stan sent word to the marshals that the Knights were ready to negotiate. It was a good sign. At least now the posse could relax, to some extent.

Crouching low for safety reasons, Kelly Garrett flopped down on the pavement next to Brad. With his hand on Brad's shoulder he spoke in a hushed voice. "Brad, they want to negotiate. You up to going in with me?"

"Hell yes, Kelly…lead the way. Any ideas what they want?"

"Sure. They want us to let them go. That'll never happen. Far as I'm concerned, we're holding the dog's leash, so their position isn't too strong. But let's go see what they say. Leave your guns at the door. Let's hope they're gentlemen."

Brad followed the FBI man as they made their cautious entrance. The interior was dimly lit. Most lights had been extinguished some time before. In the foyer, two of the men had set up a card table with four chairs. Brad and Kelly held up their hands to show the lack of weapons. The two men followed suit.

As Brad approached the table, he recognized one of the men as agent Sutro of the FBI. He was the man at the hospital with Sumiko the night of the attack on Brad. The other man did not look familiar. Names were exchanged, but the four men did not shake hands. That would have been farcical.

Agent Sutro seemed a little cowed by the presence of Kelly Garrett, who's reputation in the Bureau was wide-spread. Garrett wasted no time in setting the tone. "You men must realize there isn't a whole lot we plan to negotiate. Your position is untenable. As lawmen, you know how serious and deadly this situation has become. We want no one hurt. Now, how many of you are inside?"

Sutro averted his eyes from Kelly as he answered. "Eight FBI agents and twenty one police officers."

Brad was shocked at the numbers. With the men arrested the night before, the total was over forty. He had no idea so many officers were involved. "I assume you're all armed?"

"Of course, but believe me, none of us is ready for a fire fight. We all have more sense than to pick the losing side in a shootout. We've all had training with an assault team and know the consequences will be bloody on both sides."

"You got that right. Tell me, Sutro, is Lieutenant Nichols inside?"

Sutro's face took on a look of stubborn resolve. He shook his head, but said nothing.

Brad pressed on. "Is he the leader of this outfit?"

"You know better than to ask that, Junkyard. You haven't even read us our rights yet. Every rookie knows better than that." Kevin Porter, the Langston cop, looked smug as he answered.

Brad growled back. "Listen, you stupid putz, every rookie cop also knows better than to get involved in a ring of rogue cops that break the law every day. You keep your smug answers to yourself or we're going to get nowhere."

Kelly Garrett intervened to keep the conversation from getting off track.

"Let's get back to business at hand. You asked for a negotiation team. We are it. You don't get any others. Tell us what you think you're entitled to and we'll take the message back with us. You've got five minutes to state your case."

"Jesus Christ, Garrett, it was my understanding that negotiating meant a little give and take between adverse parties. You're leaving no room for us to talk."

"You got that right, Sutro. I share Sergeant Logan's contempt for dirty cops, so I admit my mind is pretty well set. You now have three minutes." Kelly Garrett made a sweeping gesture of looking at his watch. Brad was impressed with the man's coolness in a tight situation.

Agent Sutro gave his answer. "Here's the deal, man…we give you a peaceful surrender in exchange for not making us culpable for Lieutenant Nichols' behavior."

Brad and Kelly looked at each other. Neither expected such a request. Kelly asked the obvious. "Nichols? What part of his behavior are you referring to?"

"That's all you get until you give us a concession about Nichols. I guarantee you one damn thing: You'll understand why the rest of us want a divorce from that freak! He's gone off the end of the road. Now, can you give us an answer or do you need to get back to us?"

"Are you talking about blowing the Kurasawa building?"

Sutro and Porter looked at each other with abject surprise on their faces. It was obvious they weren't aware of the bug planted in their clubhouse.

"I think we've said all we can without an attorney present. We each want an attorney present before we'll give up. That demand is not negotiable."

"That might prove logistically impossible. Tell you what I will do. I'll bring someone from the Attorney General's office in. He'll speak to you about your rights, if that'll help. Right now, that's the best I can do."

Kelly Garrett pushed his chair back and stood. Brad followed his lead, showing the others the talks were over. Sutro and Porter looked frustrated by the turn of events. Neither could add anything further to the conversation.

"Well, do you accept my offer or not? Speak up." Kelly bored in, now that he had attained the upper hand. Brad played up his own role, as it appeared to him. He walked away from the table without looking back.

"Wait. Let us go back and talk to the others before you leave."

"No way, Sutro. We're outta here. You can telephone your answer. We don't trust you going back to them. We're unarmed. Let's go, Sergeant Logan."

Before another word was said, Brad and Kelly were out the door and safely behind the armored vehicles. At that point, Brad became aware of his rapid heartbeat and labored breathing. He hadn't been aware of the level of stress until it was all over. He and Kelly slapped palms before Kelly headed for the Brinks truck.

By the time the phone in the communications center began ringing, Brad knew Stan Phillips was up to date on the negotiations.

Ten minutes later, a man carrying a briefcase walked through the picket line of marshals and into the communications center. Brad guessed it was the lawyer from the AG office. If so, it looked as if there might be a peaceful surrender.

Several of the men in the posse raised a clenched fist as a signal of triumph. Brad felt great relief, but knew he should wait until everyone was in custody before he allowed himself to relax. Too many things could still go wrong.

At that moment, the unmistaken 'POP POP' of small arms fire shattered the night air. The line of marshals dove for cover. Kelly Garrett shouted for everyone to hold their fire and to stay under cover. Brad saw the FBI man make a dash for the Brinks truck and disappear inside.

Brad stood behind the armored vehicles, leaning the barrel of his shotgun across the hood, ready to fire if anything moved in his line of vision.

It was then he saw the first of the men from inside standing at the door with hands held high over his head. Kelly Garrett was holding a bullhorn aimed at the front of the building.

"All right, you people inside…come out, one at a time, with hands in plain sight. You all know the drill. As soon as you clear the building you'll spread-eagle on the pavement until a marshal checks you for weapons. You'll be cuffed and taken to a holding area before the next man leaves the building. Be advised these marshals out here are plenty pissed at missing their dinner and would like nothing better than for one of you to challenge them. Let's move it."

It took almost a half hour to process each person. As the Knights left the building, they flopped themselves onto the pavement. Then two marshals descended on them, frisked them with practiced efficiency, and secured their wrists behind them. After that, they were hustled off to a secure area in the middle of the block where each man was allowed to speak with the State Attorney.

Left behind, inside the building, were the three men who decided they would shoot their way out. The other White Knights disarmed them and left them unconscious on the floor, all cuffed together. It could be said, cooler heads had prevailed.

Once they secured the building, the marshals searched it from one end to the other. Using the journal written by Judd Worley, Brad and Kelly compared the names entered in the journal with the actual men in custody. To their great relief, the only person missing was Glen Nichols.

Based on comments made by several of the Knights, the fact Nichols was missing was of great concern to everyone. There was no doubt in anyone's mind Nichols was a dangerous criminal with homicidal tendencies. Their job wasn't done until they stopped him. As the last name was checked off the list, Kelly Garrett turned to Brad with real concern in his voice. It was just after 11:00. "We'd better get out to Kurasawa Electronics. He means to blow it up."

Chief Preston approached them and offered the use of his car. "I'm going with you. We can't let him kill those people."

CHAPTER 26

"Sumiko, you have such beautiful hair. You just can't be thinking of cutting it off."

Kathleen had finished brushing her friend's hair and was fashioning a braid. She marveled at the thickness and healthy shine, despite the fact it received little attention during Sumiko's stay in the hospital.

"If I can take care of it someday, then maybe I keep it. Kathleen, you're so kind to Sumiko. You come every day. How can I ever repay your friendship?"

Kathleen's first thought was, 'Stay out of Brad's bed', but kept it to herself. "Sumi. Friends take care of friends. I know you'd do the same for me. Did you sit in the chair today?"

"Yes. This morning after breakfast. It was just for a couple minutes, but it made me very proud. Sure hope I can get up soon. My butt's getting sore. You know?"

Kathleen giggled. "You don't even have a butt, Sumi. Now me…that's what you call a butt." Kathleen patted her posterior to emphasize her remark.

That brought a polite giggle from Sumiko, who seemed pre-occupied.

Finally, words tumbled unchecked from her lips. "Kathleen-san, it is crazy for us not to talk about this. The words must be spoken. Why you don't yell at me and pull my hair? Why you don't scratch my eyes out? I know you are angry."

The remark came right out of the blue, catching Kathleen off balance. Even though both women knew they must discuss the topic sooner or later, they kept pushing the subject away. Now, here it was raising its repulsive head——demanding attention.

"Sumi. . I…I have no desire to hurt you. Why should I hurt you? That wouldn't make everything better. Haven't you been hurt enough already?"

Hot tears welled up in Kathleen's eyes. She couldn't explain the deep compassion she felt for this young woman——compassion which overwhelmed any feelings of anger she harbored. She wouldn't allow the anger to come out. Not when Sumiko was still coping with her serious injuries.

"Kathleen-san, I know you hate me for being…you know…with Logan-san. I am sorry if I hurt you, but we can't wish it did not happen. The water already went over the dam. Don't you see? I, too, love him, even though I know he can never be mine. For that one night, he gave me something so beautiful I will cherish the memory my whole life. How can something so wonderful turn into something so painful? Do you think you could ever forgive me for hurting you?"

The simple beauty of Sumiko's heartfelt plea broke down the last of Kathleen's emotional armor and her tears came in a torrent. She held Sumiko's hands in both of hers until she calmed down enough to speak. "Sumi, you are the dearest, sweetest young lady I have ever met, and wise beyond your years. How could anyone ever be angry with you? I don't blame you for what happened with Brad. He's to blame because he knew it was the wrong thing to do. You were not at fault. He took advantage of——"

Sumiko was vehement in her denial, shaking her head from side to side. "No, no, no. You don't understand, Kathleen-san…it was all my fault. I choose Logan-san to be my first lover. I ask him to teach me about love. He is such a good teacher. He was very kind and very gentle. I enjoyed much pleasure. You are such a lucky person to have him. Do you know how lucky you are?"

The words fell on Kathleen's disbelieving ears. Either Sumiko was the most naive young lady she'd ever met, or the most conniving vixen on the face of the earth. How could anyone discount such a straightforward and honest statement of belief? It was infuriating. "Well, yes, dammit, of course I know how lucky I am; believe me. But sharing Brad with another woman is not my idea of spreading the wealth. Not even with a good friend like you. At least, I *hope* you're my friend."

Sumiko nodded. "Yes, but you still have Brad. I just have my memories. Even losing a breast will not destroy them. Can you at least let me keep my memories?"

Try as she could, Kathleen could not make herself scream and yell at Sumiko. Just getting the subject out in the open was a relief. Both of them would feel better when they brought everything out front for honest scrutiny. It was just that she got no enjoyment from hearing all the intimate details. At least not in the graphic way Sumiko described them. A light of understanding clicked on in Kathleen's head—-Sumiko had been a virgin. A *virgin*! She almost shouted. "Sumi. You haven't had much experience with men, have you?"

"Why you say that, Kathleen-san? You think I sound like. . like…Bonehead?"

"Of course not, Sumi. I just get the impression you didn't go out with boys very much, am I right?"

"I guess so. *Papasan* and *Mamasan* never let me go out. They say when I get out of school and become old enough, they would find me a nice Japanese boy to marry. That is the way I thought it would be. That is tradition. It's…it's…just that I have these strong feelings when Logan-san gets close. I never have those feelings before. My whole body talks to me."

"Oh God, Sumi, are you telling me you were a virgin? *Brad* was the very first man for you?"

"Why you ask me if I am cherry-girl? You think Logan-san rape me? You can't think he could do that? You don't know Logan-san very well if you think that."

"No, no, not that…but—-but—-my God, dear Sumi, did he have any idea?"

"Yes. I told him I chose him to be my first. He told me it is bad thing for us to be together, but then we went to a nightclub. We have drinks and have good time. When we return to room, I started kissing him and…"

"Stop. Stop! No more. Please. This is such a shock. I can't talk about it anymore." Kathleen covered her ears.

Sumiko burst out in tears. "Oh. I am sorry, Kathleen-san. See, I've hurt you some more. I didn't mean to. I didn't mean to." The two women cried so loud, a nurse came running. She pushed Sumiko back into her bed, pulled the covers higher, then lowered the bed to a level position. She glared at Kathleen and told her she must leave because it was time for Sumiko's medications. It was obvious she was very protective of her patient.

Kathleen told Sumiko she'd return tomorrow and assured her there was nothing to worry about. Then she rode the elevator down to her car. She ignored the strong urge to bang her head against the wall of the elevator.

"God, I've mishandled this whole thing. Sumiko doesn't believe what she did was so wrong. I can tell how much she loves Brad. Oh God, the poor thing."

The drive home was torture. She realized her anger toward Brad just made a bad situation worse. There must be some common ground on which she and Brad could pitch their tent and seek resolution. Kathleen decided it was up to her to find that campground.

By the time she pulled into the driveway, Kathleen's feelings of remorse were replaced by the fear that always overcame her when she pulled into the garage. Because of all the threats, Brad made her leave her car doors locked until the garage door lowered into place. When the garage door banged shut, she got out and made her way to the back door.

Brad was working late, so the empty house was expected. The menacing silence did nothing for her nervous tension. She spoke aloud to break the disturbing silence: "Kathleen, stop being such a goose. Get your butt inside and stop shaking in your boots. You're supposed to be a big girl now. You could take courage lessons from Sumi."

By the time she reached the kitchen, her fears had subsided. Turning on the stereo with the volume as high as she could tolerate was a good way of easing her tension. The sounds of a swinging Artie Shaw CD soon filled the house. The wail of his clarinet quickly uplifted her mood. It always did. The familiar melody soon had her humming to herself and letting her feet move to the rhythm.

She enjoyed her safety until she heard the sound of a car's backfire. An instant later, the window in the living room imploded, sending shards of glass flying everywhere. Her screams brought the neighbors running.

Brad and Kelly carried on a two-way conversation all the way to the site of Kurasawa Electronics. Chief Preston's silence didn't go unnoticed. It was obvious to Brad—his boss had problems sorting out the night's dramatic happenings.

"You know, Kelly, I can't remember in all my years on the force ever feeling so good after an arrest. Gotta admit, Phillips' game plan went off without a hitch. Arresting that many armed men with no injuries is amazing."

"You bet it is. We were very, very lucky. I have a feeling things would have been different if Glen Nichols had been in the building. Interesting that he missed both our parties."

"Yeah, but remember what he said on the recording of their meeting. He said he wanted the Kurasawa plant blown up this week. Since he was the explosives expert in the bunch, I'm sure he volunteered himself for the final extravaganza." Brad turned toward Chief Preston. "Chief, didn't you ever have any suspicions about him?"

Chief Preston ignored the question. He remained silent, concentrating on the road ahead.

Brad sensed some turmoil in his boss's silence, but couldn't guess at the reason. He turned his attention back to Kelly Garrett, sitting in the rear seat. "How do we handle this if we spot the van? If it's loaded with explosives we sure need to tiptoe our way around it, don't we? There's no time to get the bomb squad out."

"Yeah, I know, Brad, but whatever we do, we can't let that thing explode in a populated area. From what I read about these terrorist operations, they wire shut all the doors on the van. It keeps the doors from blowing open. That results in a more contained bomb—much more violent."

Chief Preston came alert as the conversation turned to the potential danger. "You two listen to me. I have a lot of experience with explosives. When we see what we're dealing with, just stand back and let me handle it. Just remember, my wife has worked in that building for a long time. I know many of the employees. It's my job. Don't give me any arguments. You understand?"

Kelly Garrett leaned forward, speaking from the back seat. "Let's not jump to conclusions. First thing we need to do is neutralize Nichols so he can't set the damn thing off. Chief, did you call for any backup?"

"No. I'm afraid if too many cars come screeching out here, Nichols will panic. A lot of people could be injured. It's better with just a few of us."

"You may be right, but let's not lose this guy for lack of manpower. Maybe we should set up roadblocks on every exit road from the plant. At least that would hinder any possibility of him escaping."

"Agreed. As long as they're kept far enough away that they won't be hurt, in case, Heaven forbid, the bomb does go off."

Brad grabbed the mike and as soon as Dispatch answered, he handed it to Chief Preston. The chief gave orders for roadblocks surrounding the plant and no closer than a block away. No lights or sirens. Keep the media far away. He identified the suspect as Lieutenant Nichols. "Consider him armed and extremely dangerous. Approach with caution."

The trio became silent as they approached the parking lot of Kurasawa Electronics. At that point, Chief Preston turned off the headlights and slowed to a crawl.

The parking lot, lit only by the orange glare of mercury vapor streetlights, took on the ambiance of a horror movie. One lone car sat by itself at the far border of the lot, as if deserted by its owner. There was no other sign of life. The setting was eerily sinister.

Kelly Garrett and Brad both drew their side arms and made sure they were ready for action. Preston waved a hand toward the shotgun in its rack on the dashboard. "Sergeant Logan, make sure that shotgun's ready to use. It may be our best bet for stopping Nichols."

Suddenly, Kelly shouted from the back seat and pointed ahead of them. "Hey! There's a van! There. . near the main entrance. No lights on. Can't tell if anyone's inside. Where the hell's security for the building? Chief, stop here. We'll go on foot the rest of the way. We can stay in the shadows next to the building."

Preston stopped the car as close to the building as possible and the three men jumped out with their weapons ready. With Kelly Garrett leading the way, they inched forward, using the shadowed marble exterior of the building as partial cover.

When they were within 50 yards of the van, they could see smoke wafting up from the exhaust pipe. The motor was idling. Nichols must still be inside—-maybe setting the explosive charges.

Kelly signaled the others to stop. Using hand signals he sent the other two on a course that would bring them up to the right rear of the van. From there, they would ad-lib their next course of action. Kelly would proceed straight ahead.

Crouching as low as he could, Brad made his way to the rear of the van, each step boosting his heart rate. He felt Chief Preston hot on his heels. As they reached the van, Brad motioned the chief to remain there. The chief indicated he understood. He took a defensive stance, shotgun at the ready. Brad started toward the front of the van.

Just as Brad took his second step, a harsh voice shattered the stillness of the night.

"Freeze! What the hell are you doing here, Chief?"

Brad took no chances. He froze—not knowing if Nichols could see him. He heard Chief Preston's voice coming from behind him. "Drop your gun, Nichols, it's all over. We just arrested the entire White Knights organization. You're all going to do hard time. Throw it out."

Brad could see nothing from his vantage point behind the van. He couldn't tell where Nichols was located and had no idea where Kelly Garrett was. He strained his ears, hoping some sound would draw him a diagram of their locations.

Nichols' voice became louder and took on a lethal quality. "Drop the shotgun, Chief. You can't even see me, how do you expect to shoot me? Drop it or die where you stand. Do it now."

Brad heard the desperation of a man who knows his time is running short. It was the most dangerous time to confront a violent criminal—-when they imitated the worst qualities of a wild animal treed by a pack of dogs. Their desperation often gave them supernatural abilities.

The chief's voice was steady. "Calm down, Glen...don't panic on me. You're right. I can't see you, but I don't need to see you to hit you with a scattergun. All I need is the general location. I figure you're in front of the van, right?"

Brad knew the chief was sending him a message. With all the caution he could muster, he inched his right foot forward, feeling for the ground beneath him, in order to maintain his balance. Where the hell was Garrett?

"Tell me, Nichols, did you think you could get away with your activities?" The chief's voice remained steady, despite the tension Brad knew he must be under. Brad's left foot inched forward. He kept one hand running along the side of the van, giving him a reference point. One more step and he would be able to see through the side window.

'**Bam, bam, bam**!' Sudden muzzle flashes. Three shots in quick succession. The sickening sound of a steel jacketed bullet striking flesh. Then a man's voice shouting in pain. Brad wasn't sure, but he thought it was Kelly Garrett. He froze and listened, but only stillness rewarded him.

"I don't know who your friend was, Chief, but he made the mistake of letting me see him before he could shoot. I hope it was Ol' Junkyard Dog. I sent a couple rounds through his front window at his house a little while ago, for old time's sake. Now throw down your damn weapon and move out into the light, you bastard! I'm not going to wait any longer. This Goddam van will be flying through the air in pieces within the next ten minutes, and I don't plan on waiting around, now move!"

Now the voice became the menacing snarl of a wounded grizzly bear. Brad sensed there was no more time to waste. Two more steps would take him to the front of the van. He had to chance moving his head forward enough to see through the window. One quick glance was all he needed to spot Glen Nichols crouched near the left front fender, pointing his gun toward the rear. Brad could still smell the smoke from the last gunfire.

One thing was sure: He'd have just one chance to fire before Nichols saw him. He also knew shouting a warning was out of the question. Proper procedures be damned, this was life or death, for a lot of people. It would be shoot, and then shout.

Taking his 9MM in both his hands, he took one deep breath before he leapt forward, leveled his pistol in one motion and squeezed off three rounds in rapid fire. Before the sound died down he was crouching back down beside the van. His breath fought its way from his lungs as he dealt with his choking fear.

The stillness of the night paralyzed him as his mind counted off the possibilities. Was his aim true? Was Nichols down? Was a bullet waiting to find his skull?

"Sergeant Logan. What's going on up there?" It was Chief Preston.

Brad kept quiet, but the chief's voice spurred him to action. With pistol held in front of him, he slowly rose to his feet, halfway expecting to feel a bullet strike him at any instant.

As soon as his head cleared the top of the hood, he could see there was nobody standing where Nichols had been.

"God, maybe I lucked out and hit him with a blind shot."

Brad tiptoed his way to the front of the van and peered around. Slumped against the front bumper was Lieutenant Glen Nichols, still wearing his police uniform, and clutching a gun. In one quick step, Brad was at Nichols' side, kicking the gun away from his clenched fingers. The sound of it clattering on the pavement brought a great sigh of relief.

"It's all clear, Chief. He's down. Do you know where Garrett is?"

"He was next to the building near the front door, last time I saw him. GARRETT! Talk to me. You hit?" The chief's voice roared through the silence.

The strained voice of Kelly Garrett could scarcely be heard. "I'm hit, guys. I'm not ready to get up yet. Don't worry about me. Just get that damn *van* outta here! It's gonna blow soon!"

Brad's jumbled thoughts were jolted back to reality when he felt for a pulse on Glen Nichols' neck. He could only detect a feeble rippling of the skin over the carotid. With very little pomp, he placed his hands under the lieutenant's armpits. With the same homage you offer a sack of manure, he dragged him clear of the van and dumped him on the sidewalk.

"Chief, I'll drive it as far away from here as I can. Then I'll jump clear. With any luck, I can still get it out of range of any occupied buildings. I'll use the old mining road. Take care of agent Garrett."

As he walked toward the driver's side door, he became aware of a person sitting behind the steering wheel, waving him out of the way.

"Sergeant Logan, go take care of Garrett. I know more about these things than you. Besides, you saved my life just now. It's my turn to be a hero. Call in and get some cops out here, right now. Just get the hell out of my way!"

"Chief. Let me do this. Jesus man, this son of a bitch is ready to *blow!*"

"Not a chance, Logan. Stand aside. I owe this to the Langston Police Department. Now listen…if I don't make it, you and Garrett go into my office. Get the video I left for you. It will explain a lot of things."

Preston slammed the vehicle into gear and roared away before Brad could say another word. He gathered his wits about him and ran toward the front of the building, looking for Kelly Garrett. He spotted him ten yards from the front doors, slumped against the wall. "Where you hit, Kelly?"

"Is Nichols dead?"

"He bought it, Kelly. Where you hit?" Brad repeated himself.

"Left shoulder's busted. Took two slugs in my vest. That knocked me off my feet. Man, it's just like getting hit by a train. I don't recommend it as a daily routine."

Brad knelt beside his friend and inched the shirt material aside to reveal a jagged hole in Garrett's upper shoulder. There was very little blood; so at least no arteries were severed. He reached for the radio on his belt.

"Dispatch? This is Sergeant Logan. Send an ambulance and get some uniforms out here at Kurasawa Electronics' parking lot. An officer is down and a 187 suspect was shot. Looks to be DOA. Also, warn any cars in vicinity to steer clear of a black Ford van proceeding north from this location. The van is full of explosives and is about to explode."

"10-4, Sergeant. I have a number of units near your 10-20. Oh, and Sergeant, there was a 10-57 called in from your next-door neighbor an hour ago. Can you respond? Over."

"Shots fired at my house?"

"That's affirmative, Sergeant. We dispatched two cars to the area. No one was injured, but your front window was smashed. Shall I patch you through to your wife?"

"Yes, yes, of course. Jesus, that's what Nichols meant."

Kathleen's anxious voice was on the phone in seconds. "Oh, Brad, I thought all this madness was finished. I can't take any more. Can you come home? I need you, Honey." Her words came pouring out in rapid-fire succession.

Just as Brad opened his mouth to respond, he was knocked off his feet by the force of a terrible explosion. As he hit the ground, the phone flew from his hand.

He could still hear Kathleen's tiny voice coming over the instrument. "Brad? Brad! What's going on? Oh, my God. Someone help me!"

CHAPTER 27

Kathleen stared at the phone in her hand. "Brad Logan, talk to me this instant, you son of a bitch! You're making me crazy. Where are you, Brad? Please…"

Her mind was a whirlwind of competing thoughts. "I'm losing it. Losing it, big time. The edge isn't very far away and I'm about to sail over it. Off into the black pit of—-of—-whatever fills black pits."

One minute Brad was on the phone. Then she heard a terrible explosion and he was gone. She held the phone to her ear and shouted into the mouthpiece. "Brad, if you don't get on this phone right now…"

The occasion called for a threat of immense proportions, but she couldn't think of one. The phone came alive.

"Hello, Mrs. Logan?" It was a voice she didn't recognize at first.

"Yes, who's this?"

"This is Archie Collins, Dispatcher at Langston PD. I patched you through to your husband a few minutes ago. Then his line went dead. There's been a huge explosion on that side of town. We don't have any details yet, but have several cars in the area. I need to break this connection now. Are you all right? Shall I send a patrol car to your home?"

Kathleen couldn't make her brain function in an orderly manner. "An explosion? What do you mean? Where was it? Where was my husband when he called?"

"Mrs. Logan, I'm sorry, I need this line. He was at the Kurasawa Electronics plant with several other officers. We have no more information. I promise I'll get in touch with you as soon as I have more information. Do you need someone to come to your house?"

"No, no, don't bother. Just call me back when you hear something."

The line went dead. Kathleen looked at the clock. It was after midnight. It had been the longest day of her life. The longest and the most traumatic. And she knew quite a little bit about traumatic days——and nights. Yessir——this was the king of them all.

"I find out my husband deflowered that poor innocent child; she turns out to be a spy for the FBI; my front window gets blasted out by some chickenshit who won't even stay around to see what he's done; now my husband pretends he's been blown up just so he can't talk to me on the phone. Remind me not to send him a Christmas card."

Kathleen took the bottle of Chardonnay from the refrigerator, poured herself a water glass full and slumped to the floor, leaning against the front of the dishwasher. The stereo was still belting out Artie Shaw's version of "Frenesi". She set the bottle of wine down on the floor beside her, then held her glass high, saluting anyone who might be listening.

"Here's to all policemen's wives. We stand by our man through all his trials——ha ha, that's a joke——and trib——-trib——-whatever. What do we do, you ask? Massage his body when it's sore. Massage his ego when he's low. Hold his face on our boobs when he needs his mommy. Kiss his twinkie when he's horny. For what? Does anyone notice——-or care?"

The glass of wine disappeared. Another refill led to another toast. "Here's to all cops. The macho, uncaring bastards. They think they're the only ones with emotional needs. Sheeeit! Who needs them? We can get along quite well without them. Right, girls? Thank you very much."

The second glassful went the way of the first. This time, the refill operation took a little more concentration. The glass kept moving out from under the stream.

"Here's to my own special cop. Here's to Sergeant Brat—-yeah, that's it—-*Brat* Logan. We deflowered each other when I was sixteen. We were so clumsy. Sure improved since then. Oh boy, did we! Bless his stamina. Bless his hairy twinkie. Oh God, I love that worthless cheat. I don't care if he did park his twinkie in someone else's garage, as long as it comes back to me in good working condition. Jeez, I *need* him."

The room started spinning as she tilted the wine bottle up for a drink. It didn't matter that she poured faster than she swallowed. A good deal of the Chardonnay found its way onto the front of her dress. When she realized more wine was on her dress than in her mouth, she started giggling.

"Jeez, maybe ol' Brat will just come along and lick that stuff off for me. That'd be a hoot. Oh God, where is he? Please God, let him be safe."

With great dramatic flare, Kathleen set the wine bottle beside her, let her chin drop to her chest and closed her eyes. It had been an exhausting day.

The ringing in Brad's ears created an echo chamber. Every sound reverberated, bringing a loss of equilibrium. He staggered to his feet, fighting the dizziness that demanded he stay on the ground.

"Kelly, you all right?" His mouth was so dry the words barely came out.

"Hey, Brad, that was one hell of a blast. You all in one piece?"

"Yeah, but it gave me one *helluva* hangover! Sure hope Preston ejected from the van before it blew. Christ, it must've broken half the windows in this building." Brad kept yawning—-trying to clear the obstructions in his ears. It was the same feeling he got while driving in the mountains.

"I'm having a little trouble with my ears, man...you?"

Kelly propped himself up to look at Brad. "Yeah. Been through it before. They'll bother you a couple days—-you know, ring like hell. You get any cuts or bruises?"

"Damn, I just remembered, I was talking to Kathleen when the thing went off. Where the hell's my phone? God—-I'll bet she's terrified."

Brad searched the ground, finally locating his phone out in the street. He lifted it to his ear, but heard nothing. He wasn't sure if the phone or his hearing was impaired. "Kelly, are your ears working? See if there's anyone on the phone, will you?"

He handed the phone to the FBI man, who tried, but failed to hear anything. "I think the phone's broken, Brad." Kelly waved his good arm. "Well, look at this. Here come the troops. Now that the hard part's all over. Two bits says the TV people will be here first. "

A line of police cars and ambulances descended on the scene. The din raised by so many sirens made Brad hold both hands over his ears. The parade arrived with such a flourish; it gave him a renewed rush of adrenaline. The first man out of his car was Sam Hardy. Brad ducked from Sam's attempted bear hug.

"Damn you, Sam Hardy, let go of me. *I* decide who hugs me."

He made a big production of peeling Sam's arms from him. He'd never seen so much emotion in his partner. "Yeah, I'm fine, Sam. What's the report on the explosion? Chief Preston was in that van. Anyone been on that scene yet?"

Sam looked at Brad for instructions. "How many wounded at this spot, Brad? The ambulances need directions."

Brad shrugged. "We don't know if anyone was in the building. Kelly Garrett's over there—caught one in the shoulder. You'll find Lieutenant Nichols by the front door. Pretty sure he's DOA. What about the Chief?"

"Units are just getting to the site, partner. You'll hear as soon as I hear. Now sit your ass down and let this nice medic check you over. You look terrible."

Despite his protestations, the medics took Brad's blood pressure and pulse. Both were elevated, to no one's surprise. A small trickle of blood seeped from his right ear, but the medic couldn't tell anything more. He said Brad should go to the hospital for a more thorough examination.

"Yeah, yeah, soon as we get this mess cleared up. Sam, you'll need a shooting team out here. Nichols shot Kelly Garrett. I shot Nichols. You'll find Nichols' gun somewhere over in the hedge where I kicked it. Listen, I've got to get hold of Kathleen. I was on the phone when the bomb went off. I imagine she's scared to death if she knows about the explosion."

"I'll get a patch through to your house. Hold on."

The operator tried, without success, to reach Kathleen. There was no answer at the Logan's house. Five minutes later the result was the same.

"Sam. Something's happened to her. Can you take charge here? Let me have your car and I'll go see what's wrong with Kathleen."

"You sure you can drive safely? Why don't you let me get a uniform to drive you?"

"I'm fine, Sam, I can handle it. A uniform couldn't drive to my house in ten minutes like I plan on doing. I'll check in with you in the morning, but I plan on sleeping in tonight."

Brad walked to the gurney where the injured Kelly Garrett now lay strapped down. He patted Kelly on the shoulder. "Hang in there, Pal. I'm heading for home now. I'll check on you in the morning."

"You got it, Brad. Listen, you did a helluva job out there. I'd go into combat with you any time. You know, we're all pretty lucky. Take it easy."

With siren screaming, Brad made it home in eight minutes. He was sure he broke every traffic rule of the department, but it didn't matter. As he pulled into his driveway, the sheets of plywood nailed to the front of his house reminded him of the last message Lieutenant Nichols had sent him. He wasn't fond of cursing a dead man, but made an exception in this case.

The burglar alarm was not even armed as he unlocked the front door. That by itself gave him reason to worry. As he stepped inside, he could hear the stereo blasting out Artie Shaw's "Summer Ridge Drive". The only light burning was the kitchen ceiling light. That's where he rushed.

"Kate. What the hell are you doing?"

Leaning against the dishwasher, Kathleen sat sprawled out on the floor. Her skirt was hiked up to her thighs and both shoes were kicked into a corner. The wine bottle lay on its side, part of the contents spread in a pool under Kathleen's legs. An empty glass lay on its side near her feet. Her wet blouse clung to her breasts.

Brad dropped to his knees and took her face in his hands.

"Kate, haven't you learned you can't drink wine like you do iced tea?"

He gently patted her cheeks, but got a weak moan in response. She did raise one hand far enough for a half-hearted pat to the back of his hand. Brad picked up the wine bottle and set it on the sink. Grabbing a handful of paper towels, he sopped up the spill on the floor.

On impulse, he lifted the wine bottle and raised it to his lips. The feel of the cool liquid flowing down his throat was so stimulating he raised the bottle a second time for a more substantial swig.

"Come on, Kate. It's your bedtime. I'd like to join you down there, but to be honest, I'm so damn tired, I'd crash before I got comfortable. Poor Baby, you've had a terrible year. Maybe it's all over now."

As he lifted her from the floor, he muttered under his breath. "Dammit, Kate, I sure hope you're not making a habit of passing out like this. You aren't getting any lighter, you know."

Without opening her eyes, Kathleen wrapped her arms around his neck and pulled herself closer to him. "Hush up, you idiot! My husband might hear you."

Kathleen resumed her snoring even before Brad reached the top of the stairs. In the bedroom, he dumped her unceremoniously on the bed, then went back downstairs and turned off the stereo and lights. In the kitchen, he tilted the wine bottle, siphoning the last swallow of Chardonnay before throwing the bottle into the trash.

In the bedroom, Brad covered his wife with a blanket then went into the spare bedroom where he crashed on the single bed——fully clothed. Despite the constant ringing in his ears, he was asleep in less than two winks.

In the semi-darkness, he couldn't identify the figure standing in the middle of the street, legs spread and hands on hips. It looked familiar, but the lighting was very poor. As he watched, dumbstruck, another figure stepped off of the boardwalk and swaggered forward, thumbs locked in his gun belt. Both figures wore slouch-brimmed hats, hiding their faces. Both wore guns in holsters tied down at the hips.

When just a few feet separated them, each man turned his back on the other. Slowly, deliberately, they walked in opposite directions—— away from each other. It seemed as if they walked in quicksand. At last, in ultra slow motion, they turned, and drew their weapons. It was then Brad could make out their faces.

Glen Nichols fired his gun first. His bullet missed its target. He just stood there waiting, as the second man raised his gun and fired. The gunfire created a huge explosion in the street. When the smoke cleared, Nichols' body had disappeared, leaving the other man alone in the street. Brad finally got a good look at the man who was staring at his gun in disbelief.

The second man was Judd Worley!

❦   ❦   ❦

Brad stood in the shower, letting the warm water pelt him with new energy. He did not wake up until after 10:00. Kathleen was already downstairs. He could hear the television playing in the kitchen.

He stood under the shower until his aching body showed signs of rejuvenation. He still experienced some 'tinitis' in his ears as he stepped out of the shower and toweled off. That's when he heard Kathleen enter the bedroom.

"I brought you some coffee, Brad. Sorry about me last night. I'm embarrassed you saw me like that again. My God, you had a full night, didn't you? You okay?"

Brad stuck his head out the door and acknowledged his wife's delivery. "We both had a full night, Katie. I 'd give you the details, but I'm still a bit groggy. Would you settle for a full report over breakfast? Is there anything on the TV news?"

"Lord yes…it's all over the news. Even the networks have crews in Langston."

"Oh, crap. Sure hope they're gone before I get to the station."

"I wouldn't count on it. They're like vultures. I've got breakfast started. Come down soon as you can. I hope you have lots of good news for me. I can sure use it."

Ten minutes later, he joined her at the breakfast table. The shower and shave made him feel almost whole again, but the ringing still persisted in his ears. It was a real bother.

"What do you want to know about first?"

"I already know some of it from television. You know—-about the raid at the Oddfellows Hall and then the shootout and explosion at

Kurasawa. My God, Hon, I had no idea you were so damned involved in all this undercover crap."

"To begin with, Judd Worley is still one of the central players in this. He helped to bring everything to a head. Without the journal his mother gave me, none of this would have come about. I still hate everything he stands for, but I certainly have a different way of looking at him now."

"Did I hear you right? God, Brad, after all this time you see some *good* in Judd? It must be like having an enema…Getting all that hate out of your system."

Brad chuckled. "You always have such a colorful way to paint a picture, Katie. Maybe Judd had some redeeming qualities, after all. Still, I can't forget all the misery he gave us. He was a real pain in the ass most of the time."

Kathleen passed a plate with toast on it. Brad helped himself, then went on. "Because of information in Worley's journal, we got indictments on all the White Knights. Besides the journal, wiretaps gave us even more incriminating evidence. Arrest warrants were issued and the marshals served them. The Gods smiled on us, Katie. Not a shot was fired at either arrest site. I take that back—-a couple of them fired their weapons. The rest of the Knights out-voted them."

"What happened to them?"

"Their own buddies overpowered them and turned them over to us in the surrender."

Brad enjoyed a few more bites of his breakfast. He was anxious to fill Kathleen in on everything. He knew the news would be welcome.

Before he could continue, Kathleen blurted out, "I talked to Sumiko yesterday."

"You've talk to her every day, Katie. Was it something unusual?"

"A little…but finish telling me about the rest of it first."

"Did you call the glass man yet? Lord, he should know the measurements by heart."

Kathleen nodded. "Yes, they'll be out at eleven. Also, the cleaning service to clean up the glass."

"Did the cops find the bullet in the living room wall?"

"Yes, but I don't imagine they'll ever find out who did it. Will they?"

Brad held his cup so Kathleen could refill it again.

"Honey. I found out last night that Lieutenant Nichols was the man who shot out our window."

"Nichols? I don't even know him. Why would he do that?"

"I was getting too close to him. By the way, he's also the one who left the valentines and threatening letters."

"You mean it wasn't Judd?"

"Well, yeah. Judd sent the first one and gave the idea to Nichols. They were in the Knights together. Nichols figured we would blame Judd for it—-like we did. Judd talked about it in his journal. He really did have a thing for you, you know?"

Kathleen shuddered. "God, don't remind me. So Nichols shot at the house?"

"He's the only one of the Knights we didn't arrest in the raid at the Oddfellows. He was busy loading explosives in the van and missed the meeting. Nichols was obsessed with bombing Kurasawa Electronics. He would have done it if we hadn't located him out there. Jeez, it just dawned on me. Did the news say anything about Chief Preston?"

"The chief? Why? Was he there, too?"

"After the shootout, he drove the van away from the building, trying to get it out of the populated area. Have you heard if anyone was hurt in the blast?"

"That's another strange thing. For the first time in four years, the plant was closed yesterday. No one was in it. Isn't that amazing?"

"Yeah, it is. That explains why we found no security guards. I wonder if someone tipped them off about the possibility of a bombing?"

"The news report confused me. They mentioned a shootout at the plant. They said a cop was killed and another wounded. No names were released. Then they talked about the bomb blast. Are those things related?"

"They sure are, Hon, the cop who was killed was Lieutenant Nichols. I shot him." He saw Kathleen's face darken for a fleeting moment, but she said nothing. "He shot the FBI man, Kelly Garrett, and was holding a gun on Chief Preston. He didn't see me and I shot him. It's not such a great feeling. I even dreamed about it last night."

Brad told her about the gunfight in his dreams.

"That's one more thing for you to fret about. Damn. Maybe Doctor Fisher can interpret that for you. We have an appointment to see her tomorrow. Hope that's all right? You want more coffee?"

"Sure. Doctor Fisher tomorrow, huh? I'm glad, Katey, I know that's the best thing for us to do. What did you and Sumiko talk about? How's she doing? Didn't get a chance to talk to her yesterday."

"You knew she was a virgin, didn't you?"

Brad looked into Kathleen's face. He wasn't prepared for the question. He didn't have an answer ready. "*Sumiko told you that?*"

"How could you, Brad? She was just a child."

"That's where you're wrong, Kate. She's a woman. Did she tell you everything?"

"I guess. Lots more than I wanted to hear. Was it just that one time?"

"Would it matter to you? Hell, Kate, let's face it—I screwed up. Big time. I know that. I'm sorry I did it. But it's done. It's over. I can't take it back. The big loser in all of this is Sumiko. She thinks she's in love with me, but *knows* I love you. To top it off, someone almost kills her. Then, she loses her breast. I wouldn't be surprised if she thinks it's her punishment. She may never recover."

"Brad. She'll recover. I promised her she'd recover. I won't let her be a victim. She told me she chose you to be her first lover. If she had picked any other man, I would have said that was sweet. But she picked you—-and you accepted."

They fell silent. For the time being, everything had been said.

It was 11:30 when Brad left the house and drove to the police station. As he went through the front door, his wife turned her face up to him for a kiss. It gave him reason to hope.

🍁   🍁   🍁

"Morning, partner. You sure look a lot better than you did last night. Feelin' all right?" Sam greeted his partner with a wave followed by a two-fingered V for Victory sign. "This place has been a zoo this morning, Brad. Captain Owens is acting Chief. The department is short fifteen full-time cops, okay? Rumors still flyin' around, but, so far it seems like most everyone took the news pretty well."

"Chief Preston is dead?"

"When they sifted through the crater out in the desert, pieces of his clothing were found. He's a hero in the media. They're saying he gave his life to save the town from a terrible catastrophe. You buy into that?"

"Didn't find a body?"

"Brad, there wasn't a piece of that van bigger than a bread box. Found the axle at least 200 yards away, okay? No one thinks he could've made it. Looks like he may have tried to jump just as the thing went off. Gotta admit, he thought it all out as he drove out of there. He went to the only spot within a mile that had no people around it. In my book, that makes him a hero."

Brad was non-committal. "I've got to get into his office. Will you help me?"

"Preston's office? You wanna fill me in? Or you gonna keep this to yourself like you been doing the last six months?"

Brad knew Sam was not happy about being cut out of the information loop. It was a damn good way to lose a partner's trust. "Sam, when I tell you everything, you'll understand. But, for now...will you help me get in there? Chief left something for me and Kelly Garrett to see."

"What is it?"

"You gonna help me or not?"

"Shit, you're impossible. Let's go burgle his office. You wanna know something, Logan? You're a pain in the ass."

To Brad's great relief, everyone in the Administration Division was out to lunch. He and Sam walked right into Preston's office. Five minutes later, they walked out with a large manila envelope addressed to Brad Logan and Kelly Garrett. They found it taped underneath his middle desk drawer. It was fortunate, no one had ventured into the office before Brad could retrieve it.

Sam stared at him. "Now you've got the damn thing, what's in it?"

"Don't have the slightest idea, Sam. It's gotta be important, though. He told us about it just before he took off in that time bomb. He must've figured he might not make it. I have a strange feeling he knew more about this White Knight stuff than he let on. Maybe he figured it was time to go on record. Or not…I'm just guessing."

"When you gonna watch it?"

"I've gotta talk to Garrett at the hospital and see how he's doing. I think he should be a witness to the first viewing. Think you should sit in on it, too. You've been out of the loop too long. I owe you big time for putting up with me."

"Screw you, Junkyard. What makes you think I give a rat's ass about it?"

"Yeah, that's right, Hardy. Cop an attitude on me. I'll send you a ticket for the premier. If you wanna come, I'll even provide the popcorn and beer. Suit yourself."

Brad's phone interrupted the lively conversation. It was Captain Owens. He wanted Brad in his office. Now!

Captain Owen's office was not as plush as the Chief's, but served its occupant well. Brad closed the door on his way in and found himself seated across from a very angry man.

"Sergeant Logan, when you came to me several months ago with your theory about the bad cops in this department, I expected you to keep me informed as things developed. Now, with no warning, I find myself short fifteen cops. To top that off, the chief's dead. It would have been nice if you'd kept me up to date. You sure disappointed me in all this mess. Why wasn't I informed of everything going down?"

"Captain Owens, since I talked to you about my suspicions, my whole life's been turned upside down. People have threatened me; threatened my wife; set off a bomb in my yard. You have to understand—I couldn't trust *anyone*. I'm sorry you're upset. What could I do?"

Captain Owens' brow furrowed as he mulled over Brad's statement.

"Yeah, I admit you and Kathleen have had a couple rough months. But dammit, Sergeant, you guys out there are my eyes and ears! That's the only way we can keep this department afloat. I'll need your promise of better cooperation from now on. Do I have it?"

"Yessir, that's a promise. By the way, are you bidding on the Chief's job?"

"I'm not sure, Sergeant. Haven't had time to think about it. Can't say I ever thought about being chief. Right now my biggest challenge is restoring morale. I've never seen it so bad. That damn Nichols almost destroyed this department. I should have seen it. He did a lot of things to make me suspicious. I just figured it was because he was in Internal Affairs. Those guys are always a little squirrelly."

"Guess we all were fooled, Captain."

"Well, it's over now. We'll start hiring some new cops as soon as possible. I'm going to need everyone's cooperation as these new people come in. Can I count on you?"

"You have my word."

"Glad to hear it, Sergeant. Incidentally, nice job last night. The department owes you a big debt of gratitude. Soon as all the smoke clears, I'm recommending you for the Merit Citation."

CHAPTER 28

Kelly Garrett looked very uncomfortable as Brad walked in. He sat on the edge of his hospital bed. His left arm was bound to his chest in a sling.

"Well, if you aren't a sight. Baby blue is sure your color, Garrett. And the cute little polka dots are you, man. Nice legs, too."

"Yeah, that's right—-get your kicks. Your time will come. I've gotta get out of this place. The food's almost as bad as the boredom. What's up, Brad?"

"Hell, it's only been a couple days. Why don't you just enjoy the rest? Glad to see you're almost on your feet. What's the prognosis?"

"I'm afraid I'll live, dammit. The slug went clear through. No permanent damage, but it'll be sore for a while. Man, I'll tell you one thing, if the guy who invented the flak jacket was here, I'd kiss…no…I'd French kiss that son of a bitch—-right on the mouth. He saved my life. I have bruises to show where the slugs hit my vest." Kelly indicated on his torso where the bullets hit him. One was over his heart.

Brad shook his head. "Hey, Pal, we were both lucky. The chief distracted Nichols just long enough for me to get in position. Another few seconds and it could have gone another way."

"Preston played it pretty smart, letting you know where Nichols was standing. What's the latest on the chief?"

"Not much, and, you know, that still bothers me a little. If he hadn't insisted on driving the van away, I'd be splattered all over the county. But it also leaves more questions unanswered."

A deep frown crossed Kelly's face. "Yeah? Like what?"

"Like, no part of his body was found—-not even a toe nail. Just some tatters of clothing. If a person needed an escape cover, what better way? No way to prove it, either way."

Kelly Garrett stood up with some difficulty and twisted his body from side to side. "Something to think about. You look at the video yet?"

"Just waiting for you. Figured we should see it together. Might need some corroboration, you know, if it contains something incriminating."

"You think the chief's part of the cover-up, don't you, Brad? Haven't you had doubts about him all along?"

Brad shrugged his shoulders. "You're the one who told me I couldn't trust anyone. Got damn near got paranoid about it."

"Your paranoia saved your life, bud. No question in my mind. I'll be outta here tomorrow if you can wait 'till then. Otherwise, maybe you could rent a VCR and bring it up here. You gonna have anyone else watch it?"

"Just Sam Hardy. I want someone else from Langston PD. Sam's still miffed I didn't let him in on what was happening. He's a good cop, Kelly. If the video tells us some serious stuff, we can decide later who else should see it."

"I'll buy that, Brad. That'll be enough for confirmation of the contents. You tell Captain Owens?"

"No way. Not 'till we know the contents. Maybe he's mentioned on it, you know?"

Kelly Garrett nodded in agreement. "I've got no problem with that. You wanna look at it this afternoon?"

"That'll be good. Kate and I will check Sumiko out of here this morning and take her home with us. Then I'll rent a VCR and bring it up here. I'm sure Sam can make arrangements."

Brad saw a look of approval flash across Garrett's face. "How's my little girl doing? Haven't seen her in a couple days."

"You should look in on her before I check her out. She'd like that. Can you walk up to the next floor with me?"

"Hell, yes, I'm looking for an excuse to get out of this bed. Let me get a robe. By the way, Junkyard, how do you feel about your first fatal shooting? Need to talk about it?"

"I'll be honest, Kelly, I haven't even thought about it. I did have a strange dream later that night, but no guilt feelings at all. Hey, it was him or me. That's where our training comes in. Guess things just kinda happen."

"You may get some later repercussions when things quiet down. I've been involved in two, and I still remember them in sharp detail. But you're right—it's what we're trained to do. The shoot team was here yesterday afternoon for my interview. This one's gonna be easy for them."

Both men received a pleasant surprise when they reached Sumiko's room. There was Sumiko dressed in her street clothes, sitting in the bedside chair. She was pale, but much improved from the previous week. A small bandage on her cheek was the only visible reminder of her facial injury. Kathleen stood beside her, brushing that long, black hair.

Kelly crossed the room in three strides and grabbed her hand. "Just look at you. How are you, Darlin'? I'm so glad you're going home."

"Garrett-san…what happened to you? I didn't know you were in hospital." She pulled him down where she could plant a kiss on his cheek. Her face lit up with pleasure, mixed with concern over his injury. She apologized profusely for 'screwing up' on her first assignment. Kelly would have no part of it, absolving her of any blame.

They spent the next fifteen minutes getting caught up on all the gossip. Brad intervened with a frown when Kathleen got on Kelly Garrett's case for sending Sumiko into so much danger. It wasn't the proper time or place.

The reunion broke up when the nurse arrived with a wheelchair. After kissing Sumiko goodbye, Kelly took his leave. The nurse helped Sumiko get into the chair and rolled her to the elevator. The entire third floor staff gathered at the elevator, applauding her recovery.

Thirty minutes later, Brad pulled the car into the Logan's driveway. He explained to Sumiko why there was still a huge hole in the middle of the front yard and pockmarks all across the front of the house. They were nasty scars, giving testimony to the months of terror.

✤   ✤   ✤

It was a touching moment when Brad carried Sumiko into the front bedroom and she caught sight of the freshly redecorated room. Kathleen spent hours shopping for and installing new curtains and bed covers with a Japanese motif. Several large, colorful paper parasols hung from the ceiling, as well as a string of paper lanterns. A bamboo room divider stood at the foot of the bed, separating it from a sitting area. Japanese artwork flourished on the walls.

Sumiko was moved to tears, seeing the extent of Kathleen's handiwork. She hugged Brad's neck as he lowered her onto the bed. She couldn't speak through her excitement, just held her arms out so Kathleen could accept the hugs and kisses of her appreciation. There were tears flowing from all three faces.

"Welcome to your new temporary home, Sumi. We're so happy you're part of our family, at least for a while. Just lie back there. Can I get you anything yet?"

The words escaped Sumiko's mouth between sobs. "I…I don't deserve this, Kathleen. . how can I ever th…Thank you?"

"Just hush now, Sumi. Friends don't expect rewards. You're our guest. We want you to feel at home."

Brad reached over and put his hand on Sumiko's cheek. "There's just one important thing right now, your health, so our house is yours as long as it takes for your recovery. We both love you very much."

He was on the verge of getting even more emotional when Kathleen took over the conversation. She announced that Sumiko needed some rest, then they would have some lunch.

Brad kissed Sumiko's cheek then went to the den, where he scanned the phone book for a TV rental store. He reserved a VCR for that afternoon, then called the hospital and reserved a small conference room. It took him almost an hour to reach Sam Hardy. Sam claimed he was up to his 'ass in alligators', but there was no way he would miss the premier of Preston's film. He'd meet Brad at 3:00.

Brad walked into the kitchen. Kathleen was bent over the sink, so he slipped loving arms around her waist. She didn't pull away, nor did she move closer.

"Kate, you are, without a doubt, the most amazing woman I've ever known. I hope you know how grateful I am that you're helping Sumiko in her recovery. Her mental health is so fragile now. Your love and support is better than any medicine. Thank you. I love you for being who you are."

Kathleen turned her head from her cooking chores to look into his eyes. "Brad, I feel obligated to help her. You were right…she's a victim in all this mess. I feel I owe it to her. We both do, and, despite my disappointment with you, I still love you. Let's just hope our marriage survives."

She moved her head back until their cheeks touched. It was her first show of affection in a long time. Brad felt encouraged, but knew he couldn't jump to conclusions.

❦   ❦   ❦

"Sorry, I couldn't smuggle in the popcorn and beer. Will you settle for Fritos and Diet Coke? You ready for the show?"

Brad looked at his associates for approval before pushing the button on the remote. At first, the picture was out of focus, but soon adjusted itself. From the looks of the furniture surrounding the chief, Brad surmised the video was shot in someone's living room.

There was no mistaking Chief Preston, although he appeared in casual civilian clothes. He wasn't quite so imposing without his uniform, but his most distinguishing feature, those pale eyes, left no doubt who he was.

The camera operator must have given Preston a cue because he nodded just before he spoke. He began by giving the date of recording. It was made four days before.

His introductory comment alluded to the fact he must be dead or incarcerated. If not, he would have destroyed the video before it was seen by anyone. Preston made it very clear he was making the video because he had very high esteem for the men of Langston PD. He felt he owed them an explanation for recent events. Above all, he disclaimed any connection with the White Knights.

Brad and Sam exchanged glances. All three men leaned forward in their chairs, intent on every word coming from the screen. The narration continued.

"You'll soon understand why the Knights came to be very detrimental to my own agenda. In some ways, my conflicts with the Knights probably brought this whole thing crashing down on us."

At this point, Preston took a seat. The camera wobbled as it followed him. "To make sure you can understand everything, you'll need some background."

Chief Preston's story began back in the 1950's. His father was a career military man, stationed in Japan during the allied occupation after World War II. Warren was ten years old when his father was killed, fighting in Korea. Mrs. Preston worked for the Department of the Army in Tokyo, so she remained in Japan. Later, she married a wealthy Japanese merchant. Young Preston's entire education took place in Japan; his stepfather made sure he attended the best schools available.

"When I was in my early twenties, I met and fell in love with Chieko Shimada. She was from a very wealthy family with close business ties with my stepfather. After we were married, I became involved with the family business. That's when I learned that the family business was a large division of the *Yakuza* underground crime network."

The shock of that statement brought everything into sharp focus for the lawmen. It was clear this video had the potential to affect them all in very dramatic ways.

Chief Preston went on with his narration. He explained how he was educated in the various phases of the *Yakuza* culture. It was obvious; he was not ashamed of his accomplishments.

"You must understand one thing: In Japan, the *Yakuza* is accepted by the citizens of Japan as a somewhat benevolent social order. Many of the top *Yakuza* leaders are descendants of the ancient and honorable Samurai warriors who were champions of the masses. The *Yakuza* is involved in a large part of the commercial economy of Japan. It provides many jobs. It provides welfare to the underdog. It is tolerated because it provides some benefits even as it exploits business and industry of the country."

The litany which followed staggered even Kelly Garrett, who had spent five years studying the *Yakuza*. Preston explained a caste system used by the organization for discipline and to establish the pecking order of its members. The lowest ranking members were given the most menial jobs. Their unquestioning loyalty to their superiors was demanded. In return, they were given protection and advice from the *Oyabun*—-almost a father/son relationship.

Preston then explained how the *Yakuza* expanded to Hawaii in the 60's, getting heavily involved in the tourist trade and prostitution, then moved onto the mainland a decade later. In the United States, they concentrated on cities with a large Japanese citizenry.

The next revelation was a stunner. It struck them with the force of a tornado. "In the early 1980's, a deal was struck with the city fathers of Langston. The *Yakuza* would build a large, multi-million dollar manufacturing plant in Langston. To make the plum even sweeter, the city need not put up any capital, nor were any tax concessions made. In exchange, the Kurasawa people could bring in their own Chief of Police. The deal was good for everyone. Langston had its plant and the *Yakuza* had a police chief. That's when I moved to Langston with my wife."

The shock wave took Brad's breath away. He never anticipated the extent of Preston's planned confession. One shocking revelation led to another—-and another.

"The *Yakuza* coveted the Langston location in California because of its proximity to Los Angeles and Las Vegas. Los Angeles with its population of a half million Japanese and Las Vegas because of its gambling. Gambling was one of the *Yakuza's* most profitable enterprises. It's been considered an acceptable vice throughout the world for hundreds of years."

Kelly Garrett burst in with an observation. "Not only that, but what a way to launder money! That's gotta be the connection with the Sapporo Casino. They've been shipping currency to the casino. No one will question a casino with that kind of cash flow. It's common in Nevada."

A bell went off in Brad's head. "Of course. What a sweet deal. Sam, you almost hit a bulls eye when you guessed the people going on the bus trips were couriers. But it wasn't drugs they transported from Kurasawa. It was good old greenbacks. I'll bet a week's paycheck it was money they took in from drug sales. Man, what a setup!

I wouldn't doubt the bank was even part of the laundering operation.

Brad reached over and turned off the video. He was afraid they
would all suffer from information overdose. All three were dumbfounded at the contents of Preston's video.

Sam broke the stunned silence with an observation. "I'll bet that's
exactly what they're doing. The couriers haul a suitcase of dirty
money to Vegas, then make phony bets on special tables and, within
several hours, all the money is in the *Yakuza's* safe. Man, it's genius.
They may be doing that at other locations, too. We'll have to turn
this thing over to the Justice Department."

Garrett held his hands up. "Don't get too excited yet, Sam. Take it
from someone who's studied this kind of crime for many years—-
just knowing crimes are being committed doesn't make it possible to
shut them down. These folks are too smart to leave many loose ends.
Trouble with this kind of close-knit organization is that it's like a
snake, you cut off its tail and it grows another. Soon as we deport one
boss, another replaces him. Not only that, but you can bet there's
plenty of bribery and political corruption going on. I'm sure these
guys own a lot of politicians. You saw how they handled the Langston City Fathers. Hell, they might even be part of the White House
contribution scandal. God, this could be a huge conspiracy. But let's
take a little break, then watch the rest of the video before we decide
what to do about it. Hey, Brad, you got any more corn chips in your
pocket?"

Responding to the need for a break from the tension, Sam took a
stroll to the snack bar. While he was gone, Brad pressed Kelly Garrett
about some matters outside the scope of the video. "Where do we
stand with the Nevada Gaming Commish? Do you know if they've
done anything with the last information we fed them?"

Kelly shook his head. "You have to understand about the Nevada
criminal justice system, Brad. All the money in their budget comes
from the gambling industry. The public pays no taxes in Nevada.

The Commission won't bite the hand that pays their rent. I'm sure they'll just tell us they appreciate our concern, but for us to mind our own business."

Brad wasn't too surprised. "You really think so?"

"I've dealt with them before." Kelly looked up as Sam returned. "Hey, Sam, what's on the tray?"

"All the junk food I could find in a hospital, Kelly. Help yourself. You didn't run that video while I was gone, I hope"

"Nope. We figured you wouldn't believe anything unless you saw the video with us. I doubt anyone would believe this stuff unless they heard it first hand."

Brad pushed the 'Play' button again. Chief Preston explained how he worked for the Japanese State Police for two years, learning enough about police work to make a good impression. He insisted he was proud of his police work and felt a deep affection for the men who worked for him the past ten years in Langston.

Brad couldn't help snorting, "You're so full of crap, Preston."

The chief enumerated a list of the *Yakuza's* illegal activities. Drugs, gambling, smuggling, prostitution, protection, extortion—all aimed primarily at the Japanese population. It was tradition—-the Japanese people seldom complained to the American police.

Preston's job with the police department gave him access to any statewide police information, which might be dangerous to the survival of the *Yakuza.* But, recently, a snag had developed.

"In Langston, the *Yakuza* began getting competition in the early 90's. A group calling itself the White Knights became active in the area. Within a year, it grew to more than a hundred members. They hated all ethnic people and targeted them for violence. Many of the Knights were from law enforcement—-even some from my own department." A painful expression crossed Preston's face.

"They muscled into our territory with impunity because of their connection to the police and FBI. Obviously, the *Yakuza* couldn't complain to law enforcement, and I couldn't step in with police action, for fear of being exposed. It became a turf war. That's when I sought out an unsavory character, a petty criminal, as a way to infiltrate the Knights. For five years, we paid him big money for providing us inside information about the Knights' plans. There wasn't an honest bone in his body. Here he was, one of the most outspoken members of the White Knights, taking big money from the *Yakuza* to rat on his own organization. I hated him."

Brad's anxiety reached a fever pitch, waiting for the name of the turncoat. There was no doubt in his mind who it was, but he wanted the chief's confirmation.

The chief droned on. He took his job as police chief very seriously and felt a certain loyalty to the officers. But there was no doubt where his primary loyalties remained. His wife's father was the number one *Oyabun* in Japan. Mrs. Preston herself was Operations Officer of Kurasawa Electronics, and was responsible for keeping the legitimate business of Kurasawa Electronics separated from the illegal operations. The money laundering and transportation of drugs were a separate division of the company. *That* division operated out of the shipping department, in the building's basement.

"Then, one day, we received a communication from the *Oyabun* in Seattle, Washington. He said there was an FBI spy working in our plant, and gave me her name. He said we should hire a local hit man to kill her. I refused and told him that was too extreme. He left no doubt in my mind where my loyalties should lie, and gave me 24 hours to get the job done. I couldn't refuse his order. His power was far greater than mine."

Brad and Kelly looked at each other with wide-eyed amazement. Neither man dared hope the video would reveal so much information. They felt much like a starving man at a seven-course dinner. So much to eat…so little time.

"My God, Kelly, can you believe it? He's giving us everything. This is major, major big time expose' of a criminal conspiracy. Preston must've figured he was a dead man after this video got out. He committed suicide by driving off in the van." Brad glanced at Sam Hardy. The look on Sam's face was of total disbelief.

Kelly's expression became intense. "Come on, Preston, give us the name of the snitch."

Chief Preston's filmed demeanor changed when he talked about the hit man. For the first time, he gave the impression he felt some remorse. "The first slip-up came when the hit man began his attack on the girl. Before he could complete the assassination, he saw a man at the window. He knew the witness could identify him, so he chased the man and killed him. Turns out the witness was my snitch. Judd Worley!"

Brad jumped to his feet with a shout and switched off the video. "Bingo! By Goddam *BINGO*! Finally, he's given us a name. Hot damn to hell and bless you Chief Preston! You're a sorry-assed bandit, but you did have a little class. I need a break. My teeth are floating, guys. Can I go for anyone else while I'm out?"

Kelly Garrett's head moved from side to side as he muttered under his breath. It was obvious; something on the video affected him personally. "That miserable son of a bitch! Dirty bastard stiffed me. May he rot in hell. All the money I paid him—-the dirty, sneaking low life."

"What are you muttering about, Garrett?"

"He flat out made a fool of me. Took Uncle Sugar's money and then thumbed his nose at us."

"Hell, that's common practice. Who in particular do you mean?"

"That worthless bastard, Judd Worley."

﹡   ﹡   ﹡

The next morning, after Brad left for work, Kathleen tiptoed down the hall and peeked into Sumiko's room. Assuming her guest was still sleeping, she received a shock when she found Sumiko engrossed in some sort of physical gyrations. She was so engrossed in what she was doing, she wasn't aware she had an audience.

Kathleen watched in fascination as Sumiko rotated her body from one position to another in swan-like graceful, flowing motions of hands, arms, legs and feet. Sumiko's eyes remained tightly closed, but she never lost her balance, even though much of the time she stood on just one foot. Kathleen sent up a little prayer of gratitude for Sumiko's seeming recovery.

When Sumiko sensed she wasn't alone, she stopped in mid-stride and opened her eyes. That marvelous smile lit up her face. "Kathleen-san, O *haiyo gozaimasu*. Good morning. It is nice day, no?"

"Good morning, Sumi. What were you doing?"

"It is Chinese meditation called *T'ai Chi Ch'uan*. Most people just say *Tai Chi*. You want to learn?"

"It looks so graceful, but are you sure it's safe for you to do?"

"Oh yes. I ask doctor. He say I can do anything I want unless it hurts me. He say *Tai Chi* is wonderful for making body well. You want to try?"

Kathleen was afraid she might look like a cow doing the hula, but decided, 'What the hell…who cares?' She let Sumiko show her some of the graceful moves, but still felt very awkward. It was as if she were tethered to a sea anchor.

"Sumiko, my body just doesn't like to do anything pretty. My boobs are too big and my butt's too big and I'm just plain clumsy. It's more fun watching you. You want some breakfast?"

"Kathleen, you are not clumsy. You are a beautiful woman with a wonderful heart. I can teach you. Maybe after a while. Yes, I would like something for breakfast. I feel hungry. Maybe that is good sign. You think?"

Sumiko insisted on walking to the kitchen. Kathleen was sure her guest felt better. It was the first time she walked from her room for a meal. They were both ecstatic at the obvious improvement in her mobility and strength.

"Did Logan-san find out anything from the video tape he watched yesterday?" Sumiko was on her third helping of scrambled eggs and buttering another piece of toast. There was no doubt about it. She felt better. Kathleen wondered where she stored it in that tiny body.

"He said he heard so many things his head was swimming when it was over. I guess they'll keep watching it until it makes some sense."

"How can that be…his head swimming? Is that more slang?"

Kathleen smiled as she explained the American cliché. Sumiko accepted the English lesson with a huge smile. Her next question went right to the heart of the matter. "Was it about the *Yakuza*?"

"How did you know that? Did you know Chief Preston?"

Sumiko took another sip from her tea before she answered. "When I work at Kurasawa, one day I see Chief Preston in the plant. He seemed to be friends with most of the big bosses. His wife was in the meeting, too. If she is part of *Yakuza*, Preston would know about it."

Kathleen was out of her element discussing police matters. "Well, I don't know about that. Brad said the video explains a lot about crime in Langston. They'll talk with Captain Owens about it today. Let's keep our fingers crossed that the information will help stop those people."

Sumiko looked pensive as she used her toast to push the last eggs onto her fork. "I don't mean to…to…How you say?—-Pop your bubble gum, but maybe it is too early to celebrate. *Yakuza* is very old society. It is very strong, and, like a jungle animal, it has survived for many years. I don't think you can kill it so easy."

Sumiko's dire prediction threw a somber blanket over Kathleen's joyful mood.

CHAPTER 29

Captain Owens sat in stunned silence as first Brad, then Sam Hardy, divulged various aspects of the Preston video. With each new revelation, his head shook from side to side in disbelief. He was as surprised as the others. Brad was relieved his boss was not a participant in the conspiracy. Owens seemed dumbfounded. "It's not possible. He couldn't have kept everything quiet all these years. I would've known. How could he deceive us all?"

"Don't beat yourself over the head about it, Captain, he was very good." Brad reminded him. "I'm sure he had a lot of training back in Japan, preparing him for the big deception. Hell, even the FBI didn't have a clue what was going on. We should consider ourselves lucky more people weren't killed before the story broke."

Sam jumped into the discussion. "...and to think Judd Worley, himself, opened the floodgates. Bless his rotten, malicious heart. Christ, the guy took money from everyone. The FBI paid him to spy on the White Knights. The *Yakuza* paid him to spy on the White Knights. He ratted on the *Yakuza* to the White Knights. Gotta give him credit for having a creative mind."

Brad took over the narrative. "Kelly Garrett is so mad about the money he paid Judd, he's calling the Attorney General, in case there's a chance they can sue Worley's estate for restitution. We saw the guy's bank account. He's got some serious bucks stashed away."

"Yeah," Sam reminded him, "and don't forget the journal he kept. I'll bet if he hadn't gotten himself killed, he planned on offering it to the highest bidder. With his flair for getting publicity, wouldn't be surprised if he was lining up some tabloid or talk show. He loved the limelight. Tell you the truth; I never gave him enough credit for being that smart. He played the role of loud mouth, stupid red neck to the hilt."

Brad nodded in agreement. He and Sam had already spent hours, playing and replaying the video. They had taken volumes of notes. Extra copies of the video were now locked in an evidence locker. Security on the evidence locker was extra tight. There was a great concern that the media might offer big money for release of the video, and enough money might corrupt even an honest cop.

Captain Owens asked what he could do to expedite the investigation.

Brad was ready with his shopping list. "Captain, right now, I need a subpoena for the telephone records of Preston's home phone as well as his private line here at the station. We need phone numbers of any calls he made or received from Seattle. He talked on at least one occasion to the head mukkity muck of the *Yakuza* in the U.S. The man lives in Seattle. He's the one who ordered the hit on Sumiko Tanaka. That's what led to Judd Worley getting sliced up."

"I'll call right now, Sergeant. Anything else we need from Judge Gilmore?"

Brad was delighted at Captain Owens' attitude. "Yeah, see if he thinks the Grand Jury should get involved. The city council may have acted improperly letting the Kurasawa people name a police chief in 1982. It may not be illegal, but it sure sounds unethical as hell."

Captain Owens picked up the phone and within minutes reached Judge Gilmore. It was obvious his comments created quite a stir in the Judge's chambers. Things moved with unbelievable speed. Within minutes, the paperwork came over the FAX machine. Sam took it off the machine and was on his way to the phone company before the machine stopped whirring.

"Sergeant Logan, I'm sure the Commissioner will be very interested in the job you did in flushing out our turncoats," Owens enthused. "The city owes you a huge debt of gratitude."

"What do you hear from the U.S. Marshal?"

"The good news is, six Knights testified against the others. I think some of them got caught up in the politics of the group before they discovered its criminal side. Their testimony is gonna make our case stronger. Everyone's being charged with Racketeering and Conspiracy. They'll all serve hard time. None will ever work in law enforcement again. It's a damn shame." Owens heaved a huge sigh. "Some of them were good cops."

Brad agreed. "Yeah, but you can't have a police department full of racists or radicals. That's how Hitler got started."

"You got that right. Meantime, everyone in the department, including women, will submit to a tattoo inspection. If we've got any more Knights' supporters on the force, I want them out of here. You have any objections to that action?"

Brad shook his head. Captain Owens' positive response to his newfound responsibilities was a pleasant surprise. Owens was a street cop for most of his career, most of them on foot. Brad considered him a 'cop's cop' because of his time on the street. Having Owens in charge of the Langston PD, even if it was just *pro tem*, was a boon to Brad Logan. His influence over the Captain was considerable.

"This last few months had to be a bitch for you and Kathleen. Sure hope your personal relations at home survived all the stress. Not sure how I would have reacted to it." Owens' voice softened as he probed Brad's personal life.

Brad wasn't sure how to answer that question, so he chose to ignore it and got to his feet. "Captain. I have work to do. Just remember, what the department needs now is a boost in morale and a return to normalcy. Anything I can do to help just call me."

Captain Owens shook Brad's hand with great exuberance. "Sergeant, if I can *ever* do anything for you, call me. I owe you…the entire department owes you."

Brad walked away feeling just a little embarrassed. Even though recent events had put him in the spotlight, he knew that bringing down the Knights resulted from pure dumb luck. Luck and Judd Worley's greed. As to the matter of the *Yakuza*, Brad had no idea if Law Enforcement could control that sinister group. There was no doubt about it: wiping them out would still be a formidable task.

When he arrived at his desk, he was pleased to see Kelly Garrett sitting there. His arm was still in a sling, but he looked none the worse for wear. "Hey, Kelly. When'd they let you go?"

"About half an hour ago. Told the nurses I'd arrest them for kidnapping if they held me any longer. There was no way they could keep me there. Got too much work to do. There are arrests to be made. You just talk to Captain Owens?"

"Yep. We also made a couple copies of the video. One copy will be yours. Sam is out right now getting the phone records on Chief Preston. When we find out who he talked to up in Seattle, we may have the means to arrest the big *kahuna*. Right?"

"Yeah, that's a very promising possibility. But lest you go off half-cocked…that part of this gig is under Federal jurisdiction. You can have a piece of it, but I call the shots. Can you live with that?"

"You arrogant piss ant, Garrett. You don't have an ounce of couth in your miserable body. *I* do all the work; carry the whole thing on my back; and *you* sit there with the gall to tell me *you're* in charge? Well, screw you, Garrett; you can just go to hell. Don't pass 'Go' and don't collect two hundred dollars."

Kelly grinned. "You never heard the expression, 'R-H-I-P'?"

"Rank Has its Privilege? That just means the Feds bullying us poor country boys." Brad returned the grin. After all they'd shared this past few days, he counted Garrett as a good friend. A mutual trust now existed between them, something that was missing before. "What will you do if you get the big honcho's name from the phone records, oh great *Swami?*"

"Don't worry, Brad. I'll nail that son of a bitch! His ass is mine! We'll get a wiretap and 24-hour surveillance on the dude. That should lead to something incriminating. In the meantime, we'll get with Justice and decide about Kurasawa Electronics. That's a pretty ticklish situation. The business is pretty much legit and hires lots of locals. Can't just shut it down. Might just put in a caretaker management team. Too damn bad Preston sent his wife back to Japan before the stuff hit the fan. Would love to talk to her."

"Tell me, Kelly, what's your read on the *Yakuza*? Can we shut it down, or will they just send new bosses in from Japan? Their record of staying in power for hundreds of years makes you wonder if they're untouchable. Money talks, you know."

"Look at it this way, Brad, I won't claim we can shut them down all the way. We can at least cause them some anxious moments and cost them lots of bucks for the next few months. We've already obtained a court order to take a look at the books at the Sapporo Casino in Vegas. Someone at Justice leaned on the Nevada Gaming Commission and an audit is underway. Don't expect much to come from it, though."

Brad tried not to let his discouragement show. "Boy, you sure aren't very encouraging. What's on your schedule now?"

"Couple more days and I'll fly back to Seattle. Hope I can get in on the final push up there. I plan on making the collar on that bastard myself. Sumiko needs to be revenged. When he's in the barn, I plan on getting my sailboat out on the Sound."

Brad nodded in agreement. His very nature screamed for revenge for Sumiko's pain and distress. The mental pictures of her lying in a pool of blood still haunted him. His pangs of guilt had not been appeased by the recent session with Doctor Fisher.

When he and Kathleen had gone into the good doctor's office, she was, as usual, almost sickeningly upbeat. Brad could never stomach Doctor Fisher's Pollyanna-like personality. She never came through as being sincere.

'Brad, you've been through so much trauma the past few months,' the good doctor had begun the conversation. 'I don't see how you've managed to keep your sanity.'

"That's what cops do, Doctor. I'm more concerned with what Kathleen has gone through. I'm sure you're familiar with my recent indiscretion?"

Doctor Fisher had insisted that Brad and Kathleen talk about their feelings and how each of them viewed the affair with Sumiko. Brad accepted all the blame, but the doctor rejected his offer. An affair was something two people did together.

'It's very noble, taking all the blame, Brad, but not very practical. Unless you forced yourself on Sumiko, she was a willing participant. It was her choice. For that reason, there is plenty of blame to go around. What you and Kathleen must focus on now is where you go from here. Wounds can be healed, you know.'

Brad let the doctor's words run through his mind as he stared at the papers on his desk. His reverie was interrupted when Sam Hardy walked to his desk, red-faced and almost out of breath. He carried his coat over his arm. That was not Sam's usual dress code.

"Damn, it's hot out there. Think it's gonna hit 105 today. It's a hell of a lot hotter than usual this year. Think I'll move to Montana. Here's two years of phone records for Preston's home and here. Should be a snap, right?"

Kelly Garrett offered his help. "Let me have some of those sheets, Sam. I may as well make myself useful. I can do that with one good arm. How about a twenty-dollar pool for whoever finds the first number?"

Brad grabbed some billing records from Sam. "You're on, Kelly. I could use some of the FBI's dollars. That is, if Judd Worley didn't get it all."

"Ouch, that was brutal, Logan. Tell me something, pal, do you think you could've hung Mooch Kaiser's death on Worley? Was there anything in his journal about it?"

"Oh, hell yes. It was Nichols who warned the Knights about Mooch being my snitch. They killed him and dumped his body in my backyard as a message. Judd was the set-up guy. He told Mooch he knew some guys who knew about the Knights and offered to introduce him. He drove the poor slob out there and dumped him off. Nichols, Gorman Reed and that FBI guy, Sutro, met him. All dressed up in black and wearing ski masks. They lured him into the store, then jumped him. Ol' Mooch musta put up quite a fight in that building. Nichols finally shot him."

Garrett shook his head in disbelief. "Man, that Nichols was one piece of work. Cold blooded as hell."

"You got that right. He's also the one who iced Gorman Reed. According to the journal, Nichols found out we were closing in on Reed. Reed planned on turning himself in after we got the make on his fingerprints. Nichols stole the evidence out of Mark Goddard's desk, then went to Reed's house and blew him away before he could cut a deal with us."

Sam raised a piece of paper aloft in triumph, and shouted, "Get those twenty dollar bills out, you losers! Here are the calls from Seat-tle——same number four times in a day. Shall I find out who it belongs to?"

Kelly was digging in his wallet. "Yeah, you lucky toad, let's see who set Sumiko up."

There was very little conversation as Sam waited for the operator to put a name to the phone number. A name which, with any luck, could bring the downfall of *Yakuza*.

Sam started writing on his note pad. "Say that again, Operator. Fukuoka Trading Partners? How about an address?"

When Sam hung up the phone, Kelly Garrett was shaking his head violently back and forth. His face was ashen. "No, no! I can't believe it. There's some mistake. There's *got* to be some explanation."

"What are you babbling about, Garrett? You know that company?"

"Hell *yes*, I know that company. It's been in Seattle for many years. I've even met the owner. His name is Tanaka."

Brad's whole body turned cold. Like a slap in the face with a cold towel, he understood the reason for Kelly's shock.

"Wait a minute. Tanaka? Tanaka? As in Sumiko Tanaka?"

"Yes. It's her father's company."

      ❦   ❦   ❦

During the next few days, activity around the Langston Police Department reached a fever pitch. All officers worked twelve-hour shifts, due to the shortage of manpower. The County Sheriff loaned several deputies for patrol duty until permanent replacements could be found. Brad sensed that a new spirit of purpose now permeated the Langston PD, and that pleased him. He spent his time putting the final touches on the case against the White Knights.

Working out of Brad's office, Kelly Garrett kept in constant contact with his Seattle office, coordinating the full time stakeout of Fukuoka Trading Partners. On Thursday, he reported a high level meeting was underway in the offices of the C.E.O. of the company. For several hours, there was a steady stream of sleek limos with blacked out windows arriving at the front door. Agents had their hands full taking videos of all arrivals. Each time agents identified the person, they notified Kelly Garrett. By noon, he had a list of almost thirty. Some of the names he knew; many others were not on his roster of the *Yakuza* leadership.

When the meeting broke up, the same long line of limos filed away from the office, most of them making a beeline for the Seattle airport.

At 4:00 p.m., Kelly hung up the phone and turned to Brad.

"My God, Brad, just when we thought nothing else bizarre could happen…ten minutes ago, an ambulance pulled up in front of Fukuoka. When the medics went into the office, they found the body of Hideki Tanaka in his private office. He had used a ceremonial sword to commit *Hari Kari*."

"*Hari Kari?* Are you saying Sumiko's dad committed suicide?"

"Yes. He drove that blade into his stomach and bled to death. In his culture that's what you do when you dishonor your family. Don't have any other details yet. Lord, what are we going to tell Sumiko?"

"Kelly, we can't tell her about this. She can't take another disaster in her life. Think fast, man, how can we protect her from this?"

"Let me think, Brad. God help me, one thing's for sure…I'm flying back to Seattle right away. Things are breaking too fast up there. Do you think Sumiko's strong enough to fly home? She should be with her mother."

Brad knew Garrett was right; Sumiko should be with her mother. This newest trauma for Sumiko might be enough to break her spirit. He knew she was a very strong young lady. She had amazed everyone during the past week as she made her body stronger by her dedication to physical therapy and her daily sessions of *Tai Chi*. Her body became stronger because she willed it to be so. She was a tyrant, driving her body to be whole again. But could she handle this latest setback?

"Kelly, if you asked me that the first of the week, I'd have said it was impossible. Right now, I have no doubt she's strong enough. I'm more amazed every day at her total commitment to regaining her strength. If the doctor approves, I guess there's no reason she couldn't go. I just don't know how we can tell her about her dad dying. Are you up to it?"

"I have to be, Brad. She'd never forgive us if we kept it from her. I won't tell her about her *Papasan's* role in the *Yakuza*. That's up to her own family to tell her. For sure, I won't tell her about her dad ordering the hit on her. That would kill her. You agree?"

"Yes, of course. I won't even tell Kathleen about that. She would be very disturbed to find out about Sumiko's father. Let's get it over with. It won't get any easier if we wait."

Garrett nodded. "That's right. God how I hate this."

❦   ❦   ❦

"You gonna tell me why you wouldn't share any of this with your partner?" Sam took a bite of his sandwich as he aimed a withering look at Brad. The partners were taking a lunch break. Both had shed their outer jackets in response to a sudden heat wave.

"Sam, you'll never let me forget that, will you? I've already told you it's because you have a big mouth."

"Yeah, right. You keep giving me that same line, but it don't wash, partner."

"What do you want from me? Look, Sam. For a while there, I didn't trust anyone. Shit, we were getting threats every day. That bomb damn near knocked our house down. Nichols was on my butt. Worley was grinding me."

Brad dumped a packet of sugar into his ice tea and paused to stir it.

"...And don't forget your rotten attitude about Japanese people, and Sumiko in particular. I figured for a while you were part of the White Knights, you know?"

Sam peered over his glasses as he took the last bite of sandwich. "Me? You should know by now I don't socialize with other cops. To be honest, they're lousy company. Besides, I never want to get too familiar—you know—in case they get their head blown off. I know you're pissed about the way I talk about Japs. You'll never convince me to change my mind, but I'll try to keep it quiet from now on, okay?"

"That's a deal, Sam. I don't share your views, but won't bug you about it. I talked to Captain Owens and convinced him we need a special detail of officers down in Little Ginza area on a permanent basis. We need a bigger presence there."

Sam agreed. "Long as I'm not part of it. Did Mark tell you he got the blood work on Gorman Reed's shoes back? The boots were covered with Mooch's blood. Too bad it took so long. We may have saved his life if we could have arrested him sooner."

"They call it Kismet, Sam. Gorman sealed his fate when he teamed up with that snake, Nichols. Damn, I sure wish we'd get the final word back from Seattle. Garrett must have shut down that place by now, don't you think?"

Sam shrugged and reached for his wallet. He scooped up both meal tickets as he brushed crumbs from the front of his shirt. "Why don't you call him when we get back? Maybe they have some word from the Justice Department about shutting down Kurasawa Electronics, too."

"Maybe so, Sam, but I sure hope they find a way of keeping the plant open. That place means a lot to this community."

"You'll forgive me if I don't agree with you?"

CHAPTER 30

"A vacation? You mean a *real* vacation? Away from Langston? You're teasing me, aren't you?"

"I was sure you could handle that. I've got a month of vacation time coming and we both need to get out of town. None of my cases are pressing. It's the best time for us to go somewhere and relax. What do you say?"

"Can you give me ten minutes to get packed?" Kathleen threw her arms around Brad's neck and pulled him tight.

"You know, Katey, my promotion to Lieutenant comes through next month. That'll give us a couple hundred more a month. Let's just go someplace and worry about paying for it later."

"You won't get an argument out of me, Brad Logan. Getting out of town for a few weeks is just what the doctor ordered. How soon can we go?" Kathleen was a little girl again, pleading for the circus.

Two months earlier, they had driven Sumiko Tanaka and Kelly Garrett to the airport, where there was a tearful farewell. As the plane soared into blue skies, Kathleen clung to Brad with tears streaming down her face. In the span of three months, she and Sumiko had shared the kind of friendship seldom experienced in anyone's lifetime, despite all the obstacles they had to overcome.

In the rush of days following that sad farewell, the Logans' life shook itself back into the daily routine of Langston. They went to Dr.

Fisher for counseling once a week and were dealing with the pain and emotional upheaval created by the Knights, the *Yakuza*, and their own insecurities. Just a month ago, workmen put the final touches on repairs to their house and front yard, so they had shared a bottle of champagne with their neighbors in honor of the occasion.

They attended their high school reunion with Mark and Paula Goddard. Their classmates spent the entire evening discussing events surrounding Judd Worley's death. It was strange how, almost to a person, they all said they knew Judd was rotten to the core and were not surprised at his violent demise. Brad swallowed the urge to compliment his classmates on the amazing accuracy of their hindsight.

On the first day of August, word spread like a Santa Ana wind around town that the Kurasawa Electronics plant would remain open, but with a caretaker management team. The whole town breathed a sigh of relief that their major employer would continue in operation. Everyone except Sam Hardy, whose inborn hatred for Orientals showed no signs of fading away.

Brad and Kathleen added a new weekly activity to their lives. Every Friday night, they went to Little Ginza for dinner. They even convinced Mark and Paula to accompany them on several occasions. Kathleen, with her outgoing personality, made a whole new set of friends in the local shops. Brad's acceptance by the people was much more reserved. The citizens thought of him only as a cop. They remembered his connection to the arrests of several of the local citizens after the tour bus scandal became public knowledge.

Brad convinced Captain Owens that a new permanent patrol of the area should become an urgent priority. There were mixed reactions from the Japanese citizens, but the majority acted as if they approved. The captain pledged he would hire some new officers from the area—people who knew the local customs. He even invited a group of the more influential members of the Ginza community to an open house at the police station.

Despite all the hustle and bustle in their lives, the Logans could not get thoughts of Sumiko Tanaka very far from their minds. Her indelible impression still hovered over them—a lonely butterfly kissing each flower with tireless energy.

One day, a large package arrived. When Kathleen opened it, there were two beautiful kimonos, along with thonged sandals. Inside was a note from Sumiko:

'My Dearest *Tomodachi*. I promised these to you when first we met. I hope they fit. *Mama-san* made them to honor everything you mean to me. It was good for her to have something to keep her busy. Poor *Mama-san* still suffers from her loss, as do I. My body is healing and I look forward to the future. I shall never forget the two most wonderful people in my life. I love you both and keep you in my prayers. God will always shine his light on you. Love, Sumiko.'

Kathleen cried for another day after reading the note. Since there was no return address on the package, she called information in Seattle. There was no phone listing. In frustration, she insisted that Brad call Kelly Garrett and find out what was happening. Brad called Kelly Garrett in Seattle to get a phone number for Sumiko. To his great shock, Kelly told him that Sumiko and her mother had returned to Japan—-permanently.

"Sumiko told me she planned to find a nice young Japanese boy who liked spaghetti and meat balls. Seems like she's recovering pretty well from her wounds, but I suspect her emotional scars will last a lifetime. I never told her about her father and the *Yakuza*. Perhaps her mother will tell her. It just seems like too much agony has been piled on her tiny shoulders. God, I feel as if I've lost an only daughter. Oh, and Brad…I wasn't supposed to tell you, but Sumiko is expecting a baby sometime next spring. God, I don't know how much more that poor little gal can handle. Can you imagine some scumbag getting her that way, then dumping her?"

0-595-21098-8

Printed in the United States
97495LV00007B/142/A